...Barron and

Jan... ...Scargrave Manor

— *The New York Times Book Review*

"A light-hearted mystery . . . The most fun is that 'Jane Austen' is in the middle of it, witty and logical, a foil to some of the ladies who primp, faint and swoon."
— *The Denver Post*

"Fans of the much darker Anne Perry . . . should relish this somewhat lighter look at the society of fifty years earlier. . . . A thoroughly enjoyable tale."
—*Mostly Murder*

"Jane is unmistakably here with us through the work of Stephanie Barron—sleuthing, entertaining, and making us want to devour the next Austen adventure as soon as possible!"
— Diane Mott Davidson

"A fascinating ride through the England of the hackney carriage . . . A definite occasion for pride rather than prejudice!"
— Edward Marston

"Well-conceived, stylishly written, plotted with a nice twist . . . and brought off with a voice that works both for its time and our own."
—*Booknews* from The Poisoned Pen

"Very good faux-Austen writing combined with a delicious puzzle and excellent historical research. Thoroughly entertaining."
—*Mystery Lovers Bookshop News*

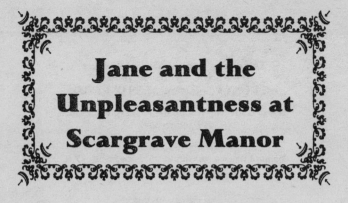

Jane and the Unpleasantness at Scargrave Manor

~Being the First Jane Austen Mystery~

by Stephanie Barron

BANTAM BOOKS

NEW YORK · TORONTO · LONDON · SYDNEY · AUCKLAND

Jane and the Unpleasantness at Scargrave Manor
A Bantam Book

PUBLISHING HISTORY
Bantam hardcover edition published May 1996
Bantam trade paperback edition / January 1997

ISBN 0-553-57593-7

Published simultaneously in the United States and Canada

Bantam Books are published by Bantam Books, a division of Random
House, Inc. Its trademark, consisting of the words "Bantam Books"
and the portrayal of a rooster, is Registered in U.S. Patent and
Trademark Office and in other countries. Marca Registrada. Random
House, Inc., New York, New York.

PRINTED IN THE UNITED STATES OF AMERICA

OPM   20   19

*This book is dedicated with love
to the memory of Cass Sibre,
in whose library, at the age of twelve,
I first discovered Jane Austen.*

Editor's Foreword

IN THE SPRING OF 1995, I VISITED MY GOOD FRIENDS PAUL and Lucy Westmoreland. The Westmorelands are of old Baltimore stock, tracing their lineage to a founder of the state of Maryland, and their home, Dunready Manor, dates to the Georgian period. The Westmorelands had recently completed the renovation of an outbuilding on the estate, the former overseer's house, an extensive project of rebuilding and restoration.

Rescuing the solid stone foundation proved a formidable task. Used for decades—perhaps even more than a century—as a coal cellar, the enormous rock-lined room had to be emptied of its inky contents before being painstakingly sandblasted and lined with concrete. New support pillars were installed, new doors and stairways, and gradually the aged stone of the house's base assumed its former beauty and charm. But more important was the discovery made in the initial stages of the cellar's renovation. Beneath the hills of coal dust, rats' bones, discarded timbers, and unidentifiable rags were several boxes of old family records. The Westmorelands placed them in a storage shed on the property and promptly forgot about them in the flurry of installing the house's new kitchen. But when I visited them that spring, we spent a rainy afternoon in the storage shed, carefully leafing through the fragile yellowed papers, and came to the conclusion that a professional curator was the only solution.

For what we found that day was no less than an entire series of manuscripts we believed had been written by Jane Austen, a distant relative of the Westmoreland line. A daughter of Austen's brother James had married a man whose sister married a British Westmoreland—and by this circuitous route the manuscripts had made their way into the Westmoreland family and, eventually, to the branch of that family in the United States. There they were placed for safekeeping in the cellar, where later generations covered them with coal.

The Westmorelands delivered the manuscripts for restoration to a local rare-books curator of their acquaintance and debated donating them to the Johns Hopkins University Library. Other claims—Austen collections at Paul's alma mater, Williams College, and elsewhere in the country, not to mention Oxford's Bodleian Library—competed for the gift. In the meanwhile, however, as the manuscripts were restored, they turned them over to me.

The Westmorelands are possessed of an imaginative spirit and enjoyment of life that extends to the reading of detective fiction. And what so struck them about these manuscripts, apparently written by Austen herself, is that they recount experiences heretofore unknown to Austen scholars. Narratives in the form of journal entries and letters to her sister, Cassandra, and intended for her nieces—which perhaps explains their eventual appearance in the Westmoreland family line, united as it is to the family of James Austen's daughter—these manuscripts were never meant to be published. They are personal records of mysteries Jane Austen encountered and solved in the course of her short life.

I suggested that the best editor for such works would

be an Austen scholar. The Westmorelands demurred. Knowing of my own interest in detective fiction and feeling that the manuscripts' discovery was in part my own, they asked that I undertake the task of editing the notebooks for publication.

FOR A WOMAN WHOSE WORK HAS ENDURED NEARLY TWO centuries, Jane Austen remains in large part a mystery herself. What is known of her life comes principally from her surviving letters and the memoirs of family members written after her death, from which several scholars have drawn admirable biographies.[1] Since many of her letters were written to her sister, Cassandra, who destroyed them after Jane's death,[2] whole passages of Austen's life remain dark. The discovery of letters sent to Cassandra, along with the journal accounts I have edited here, must be considered a new window on the author's experience.

Jane Austen was born on December 16, 1775, half a year after the outbreak of hostilities in the British colonies of America and at the height of the reign of His Majesty George III. The daughter of an Oxford-educated clergyman of modest means, she grew up surrounded by her six brothers and one sister in the small parsonage at Steventon, in Hampshire. Through the course of her forty-two years, France would be convulsed by revolution; Napoleon would rise to power; George III would go slowly mad, and his rule give way to the Regency of his son, George IV. It was a turbulent time in British history, in which the Tory (conservative and royalist) Austens would play no small part. Jane Austen's

1. For further knowledge of Austen's life, I would recommend Park Honan's *Jane Austen: Her Life* (St. Martin's Press, 1987).
2. Austen died in Winchester on July 18, 1817; the cause is the subject of much scholarly debate, but is believed to be due to adrenal failure, the result of Addison's disease, which may in turn have been caused by tuberculosis or cancer (Honan, *Jane Austen: Her Life*).

brother Frank, a seaman from his early adolescence, served under Horatio Nelson at the Battle of Trafalgar and rose to become First Lord of the Admiralty at the age of eighty-nine; her younger brother, Charles, had a similarly distinguished, though less lofty, naval career. That Jane was aware of and compelled by questions of politics is evident in her letters to her family, and indeed in much of her more famous writing; for example, she addressed the moral turpitude of naval officers in *Mansfield Park*, the work she considered her most ambitious, where the themes of ecclesiastical reform and slaveholding in the Indies are also subjected to her caustic wit. That her fiction was drawn from events in her own life, or from her understanding of the experiences of others within her social set, is apparent from her reaction to events recounted in this memoir.

The bulk of her fiction was written in its initial form when Jane was in her late teens and early twenties; she refined and finally published it during the Regency, which officially began in 1810, nearly eight years following the action of this manuscript. The Regency in England had as its counterpart the height of the Napoleonic Empire in France, and despite the ongoing state of war between the two nations, French fashions and political thought traveled across the Channel to powerfully influence English habits. Wealth and personal display were considered fashionable, and the social freedoms accorded women were somewhat greater than those they would enjoy during Victoria's reign later in the century. Dress was less modest, contact between the sexes less constrained, and the notion of a lady writing novels—or engaging in detection—was permissible according to the mores of Austen's time.

Austen was recognized by those in her circle as a highly intelligent woman. That she often felt frustrated by the limited experience and opportunity accorded women is evident in this manuscript and elsewhere. Her father had attempted to ignore her sex in one important aspect when he sent Cassandra and Jane, then seven, to Oxford for private instruction; but Austen professed herself to be only half-educated, because she was denied the knowledge of Greek and Latin offered her brothers.

I expect many to be shocked by the notion of Austen as detective; but it should not be surprising that a woman of her intellectual powers and perception of human nature would enjoy grappling with the puzzle presented by a criminal mind whenever it appeared in her way. Her genius for understanding the motives of others, her eye for detail, and her ear for self-expression—most of all her imaginative ability to see what *might* have been as well as what *was*—were her essential tools in exposing crime. Spending the bulk of her days in the country, where order was kept by a justice of the peace and more informally by the authority inherent in the local gentry, Austen would look first to her powerful acquaintances for assistance in securing punishment for the guilty and justice for the innocent. As a single woman of modest means, she was forced to rely at times on the men in her circle, whose access to the worlds of commerce, law, and politics afforded them greater power in the cause of justice than she could attain. That they availed themselves of her intellectual ability is a testament to their good judgment.

What follows is, as best we can judge, the first of Austen's detective adventures. It begins in December 1802, immediately following Jane's acceptance and rejection (within twenty-four hours) of Harris Bigg-Wither's proposal of marriage. She turned twenty-seven during the course of her narrative and, with her rejection of Bigg-Wither, must have faced the prospect of spinsterhood full in the face. Isobel Payne's invitation, coming at the height of what must surely have been a difficult period, provided Jane with a welcome avenue of escape. It would prove a painful time of self-reflection as well as diversion; but the narrative is remarkable for its blending of the criminal and the personal, the love of the chase and internal exploration of her own motives and dreams.

TO EDIT AUSTEN IS DAUNTING. I DO NOT PRETEND TO HER skill. I only hope that the essential spirit of the original manuscripts blazes forth from these new pages, with all the power of that remarkable mind.

STEPHANIE BARRON
EVERGREEN, COLORADO
JUNE 1995

Jane and the
Unpleasantness at
Scargrave Manor

Jane's Introduction

17 March 1803
No. 4 Sydney Place, Bath
~

WHEN A YOUNG LADY OF MORE FASHION THAN MEANS HAS the good sense to win the affection of an older gentleman, a widower of high estate and easy circumstances, it is generally observed that the match is an intelligent one on both sides. The lady attains that position in life for which her friends may envy and congratulate her, while the gentleman wins for his advancing years all that youth, high spirits, and beauty can offer. He is declared the best, and most generous, of men; she is generally acknowledged to be an angel fully deserving of her good fortune. His maturity and worldly experience may steady her lighter impulses; her wit and gentle charms should ease the cares attendant upon his station. With patience, good humour, and delicacy on both sides, a tolerable level of happiness may be achieved.

When, however, the older gentleman dies suddenly of a gastric complaint, leaving to his mistress of three months a considerable estate, divided between herself and his heir; and when the heir in question offends propriety with his attentions to the widow—!

The tone of social commentary may swiftly turn spiteful.

The deceased man's fortunes, once proclaimed as rivaling the gods', are now all struck down. He is become to all men a figure of melancholy, a poor benighted dotard, seduced by youth and flattery where probity and good sense should better have prevailed. The lady is turned an object of suspicion rather than general pity; her mourning weeds are reviled as a mockery of propriety; her presence is not desired at the select assemblies; the solicitors burdened with the management of her affairs are much to be pitied; and scurrilous rumour circulates among the *habitués* of the opera box and card room.

Her star is fallen, indeed.

Such has been the fate of my poor Isobel. That a lady gently bred, possessed of intelligence and a discerning nature, should be so embroiled in scandal, must sober us all. None can assume that the winds of fortune shall always blow fair; indeed, the better part of our lives is spent seeking some shelter from their caprice. Women, possessed of a frailty in their virtues not accorded the stronger sex, are more surely victims of the random blast. In considering all that occurred during the fading of the year, I might be moved to rail against my Maker for suffering those least capable of bearing misfortune, to have found it so liberally bestowed. But that would be ungenerous in a clergyman's daughter, and too bitter for my spirit. I have determined instead to turn to the comforts of journal and pen, in the hope of understanding these events that marked the turning of my twenty-seventh year.

I NEVER FEEL THAT I HAVE COMPREHENDED AN EMOTION, or fully lived even the smallest of events, until I have reflected upon it in my journal; my pen is my truest confidant, holding in check the passions and disappointments that I dare not share even with my beloved sister Cassandra. Here, then, in my little book, I may parse my way to understanding all that I have survived in recent weeks.

Indeed, I have gone so far as to walk into town for the express purpose of obtaining this fresh binding of paper, in the hopes that by setting the events apart—by giving them the narrative force and order of a novel, in fact—I might bring some order to the unwonted discomposure of my mind. This story will never be offered for the public reader, even were I to transform the names and disguise the places; for to so expose to the common traffic of drawing-room and milliner's stall what must be most painful in my dear friend Isobel's life, would be rank betrayal. Better to retrieve from Cassandra the letters[1] concerning these events that I sent to her from Scargrave, and insert them between the pages of this journal. It shall live in my clothespress, and be opened only for the edification of my dear nieces, that some knowledge of the forces which so disastrously shaped Isobel's fortune, may prove a moral guide for the conduct of their own.

What follows then, as my journal and letters so record it, is the history of the unpleasantness at Scargrave Manor. May that unhappy abode witness more congenial hours in the coming year than those I spent during the last.

1. Jane Austen's older sister, Cassandra, was the person she loved best and trusted most in the world. Austen scholars have long been frustrated by gaps in their surviving correspondence, and have imputed the missing letters to Cassandra's propensity to destroy those that were most personal. Many of what may be the missing letters have now been found in the Westmoreland manuscript holdings. —Editor's note.

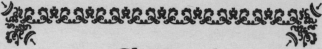

Chapter 1

The Passing Bell

Journal entry, 11 December 1802,
written in the small hours
~

"WHAT DO YOU MAKE OF IT, JANE?" THE COUNTESS OF
Scargrave asked. Her fingers gripped my elbow painfully.

I gazed at the recumbent form of her husband with
dismay. Frederick, Lord Scargrave,[1] was decidedly unwell—so unwell that I had been called to his bedside an
hour before dawn, an indiscretion the Earl would never

1. A brief explanation of English titles and modes of address
may be helpful to American readers, who lack Jane's easy familiarity with both. Isobel Collins married Frederick Payne,
the Earl of Scargrave, and as such became the Countess of
Scargrave. She would be addressed as Lady Scargrave, but because she is a commoner by birth, she would never be addressed
as Lady Isobel; that would be a courtesy title conferred on
the daughter of a peer. The Earl is usually addressed as Lord
Scargrave, taking his name from his title, rather than as Lord
Payne, his family name, which in this account denotes his heir
Fitzroy, Viscount Payne. —*Editor's note.*

have allowed while possessed of his senses. I pulled the collar of my dressing gown closer about my neck and placed my free hand over the Countess's.

"I believe that your husband is dying, Isobel," I told her.

Her fingers moved convulsively under my own, and then were still. "*Dying*. Were I to hear it so declared a thousand times, I still should not believe it possible."

I surveyed my friend with silent pity, uncertain how to answer such distress. The transformation wrought upon her husband's agonised countenance was indeed extraordinary—and had required but a few hours to effect. That very evening, the Earl had led his Countess down the dance in Scargrave's ballroom, revelling in the midst of a company come to toast the fortunes of them both. Despite his eight-and-forty years, he shone as a man blessed with second youth, elegant and lively, the very charm of his race crying out from every limb. And tho' he had complained of dyspepsia before, this illness came upon him of a sudden—and with a violence one may hardly credit to an overfondness for claret and pudding.

"Had he taken aught to eat or drink in the past few hours?" I asked.

My friend shook her head. "Only a milk toddy and some sweetmeats the maid brought to him upon retiring. But I do not believe he had long consumed them before the sickness laid him prostrate."

The stench of the Earl's illness rose from the fouled sheets the maids would not change for fear of paining him further. His breath was caught thick within his throat, and his strength worn down by dizzyness and a violence of puking such as one usually sees under the influence of a purgative. His eyes were rolled back in drowsy oblivion, his skin was pallid, and his features were bloated. It was a trial merely to observe such suffering; to endure it must have been fearsome.

As I watched with Isobel by his bedside, awaiting the doctor summoned in haste from London, the Earl gave forth a great moan, rose up shuddering from his sheets, and clutched his wife's hand. "Blackguards!" his shattered voice cried. "They would take me from within!" Then he fell back insensible upon his bed, and spoke no more.

Isobel was all efficiency; a compress she had in a moment, and ministered to her troubled lord, and the violence of feeling that had animated his poor body but an instant before, troubled him not again.

I am no stranger to death—I have sat watch over too many unlovely ends by the side of my clergyman father, who believes the company of a woman necessary to sustain him in the most mortal hours of his ministry—but this was a sort of dying I had never witnessed.

A chill draught wafted through the chamber door from the great hall below. I turned my head swiftly, in hope of the doctor, and saw only Marguerite, Isobel's maid.

"Milady," the Creole girl whispered, her eyes stealing from her mistress's face to the more dreadful one of the Earl, "the doctor is come." Her countenance was pale and frightened, and as I watched, she made the Papist sign of the cross hurriedly at her brow, and ducked back through the doorway.

I cannot find it in me to scold the maid for such foolishness. She is a simple girl from Isobel's native Barbadoes, who accompanied her mistress upon Isobel's removal to England two years ago. Marguerite has sorely missed her sleep tonight—it was she who fetched me hastily before dawn to the Countess's side. But even I, a child of cold-blooded England less susceptible to horrified fancy, must confess to sleeplessness these several hours past. For the Earl has uttered such moans and cries that none may shut out his agony, and all within Scargrave's walls are robbed of peace this night.

"Lady Scargrave," the physician said, breaking into my thoughts. He clicked his heels together and bowed in Isobel's direction. A young man, with all his urgency upon his face.

"Dr. Pettigrew," the Countess replied faintly, her hand going to her throat, "thank God you are come."

How Isobel could bear it! Married but three months, and to lose a husband one has but lately acquired would seem the cruellest blow of Fate. Yet still she stood, composed and upright, and waited with the terrible fortitude of women for the result of so much misery.

Dr. Pettigrew glanced at me and nodded, brushing the snow from his greatcoat and handing it to Marguerite, who bobbed a frightened curtsey and ducked out of the chamber. As the physician hastened to the Earl's bedside, I strove to read his thoughts; but his eyes were hidden behind spectacles, and his mouth held firmly in a line, and I could divine nothing from his youthful countenance. He reached for the Earl's wrist, and poor Lord Scargrave moaned and tossed upon his pillow.

"Leave us now, my dear Jane," Isobel said, her hand cool upon my cheek; "I will come to you when I may."

AND SO I MUST WAIT AS WELL, SHUT UP IN MY HIGH-ceilinged chamber with the massive mahogany bed, the walls hung with tapestries in the fashion of the last century. I draw my knees to my chest and pull my dressing gown tight to my toes, staring for the thousandth time at the face of some Scargrave ancestress, forever young and coquettish and consumptively pale, who peers at me from her place above the mantel. It is a solemn room, a room to terrify a child and sober a maid; a room well-suited to my present mood. The fire is burned low and glowing red; my candle casts but a dim light, flickering in the still air as though swept by sightless wings—the Angel of Death, perhaps, hovering over the great house. At my arrival, Isobel told me of the Scargrave legend: When any of the family is doomed to die, the shade of the First Earl walks the gallery beyond my door in evening dress and sombre carriage. The family spectre might well be pacing the boards tonight, however little I would believe in him.

And through the snowy dawn, a faint echo of pealing bells; they toll nine times as I listen, straining for the count—the passing bell from the church in Scargrave Close, calling out that the Earl is in his final hours. Nine peals for the dying of a man, and then a pause; the toll resumes, a total of forty-eight times, for every year of the Earl's life. I shiver of a sudden and reach for my paper and pen, the pot of ink I carry always among my things. Much has happened in the two days since my arrival here at Scargrave; much is surely to come. It may help to pass the small hours of morning if I record some memory of them here.

I AM COME TO SCARGRAVE MANOR IN THE LAST MONTH of the dying year at the invitation of its mistress, Isobel Payne, Countess of Scargrave, with whom I have been intimate these eighteen months. When I recall our first meeting—an introduction between ladies still unwed, in the Bath Pump Room—I cannot help but wonder at the present reversal of events. Isobel, with her gay humour and careless aspect, so early blessed by fortune in the form of the Earl, now to be made a creature of misery and loss! She, who is all goodness, all generosity! It is not to be borne. Though I have known her but a little while, I would do all in my power tonight to succour her in despair—so lovely, and so wounded, is she. I owe the Countess my gratitude as well as esteem. I know too well how little attention she need pay me in her present high estate. A watering place such as Bath encourages ready acquaintance—acquaintance as readily dropt, once the sojourn is done. But Isobel would have it that I am a *singular personality,* and that once understood, I am not easily put aside. However that may be, she has spurned the ready affections of her husband's fashionable friends, and proved faithful to her own, more modest ones; many a letter have I written and received, and confidences shared, in the short time we two have called each other by our Christian names.[2]

The Countess is returned from her wedding trip but a fortnight, having married Frederick, Lord Scargrave, three months past and departed immediately for the Continent. Her husband, the Earl, being determined to give a ball in her honour, Isobel begged me to make another of the party—and that I had powerful reasons for finding comfort in her goodness I will not deny. A visit to Scargrave promised some welcome diversions—an agreeable partner or two, and in the frivolity of the dance, some measure of forgetfulness for the appalling social errors I had knowingly committed among friends not a fortnight before. Never mind that the Earl's Manor would be the third home I had visited in as many weeks; there are times when to be in the bosom of one's family is a burden too great to bear, and relative strangers may prove as balm.

Thus I went into Hertfordshire fleeing, in short, a broken engagement and the awkward pity of those dearest to me in the world. I hoped only to find a woman's light dissipation: to talk of millinery and the neighbours with equal parts savagery and indifference, to take my full measure of wintry walks, to see in the New Year in the company of a dear friend lately married. I had no hopes of brilliant conversation, or of being surrounded by those who might challenge my wits; I looked, in fact, for the reverse of what has always been strongest in my nature.

My journey from Bath in the Scargrave carriage was marked by no intimation of pending tragedy; no dark shadows menaced as the horses laboured through the

2. In Austen's day, it was a sign of great friendship and mutual esteem to address an acquaintance by his or her first name. This was a privilege usually reserved for the family circle; between unrelated men and women, for example, it generally occurred only after an engagement was formed.—*Editor's note.*

snowy Park, pulling up with steaming breath before the Manor's massive oak doors. Only warmth and welcome shone from the many windows set in the house's broad stone façade—a cheerful aspect on a winter's twilight, offering rest and sustenance to all who came within its walls. I may fairly say that I descended from the carriage without the slightest flutter of misgiving.

Nor did I feel a presentiment of doom this evening as I readied myself for the Earl's celebratory ball. I had from Isobel the loan of her maid, Marguerite, who having seen to her mistress's toilette, would now attempt to do some good to mine. The disparity in form and finery between Isobel and myself is material, I assure you; and so, while Marguerite fussed and lamented over the creases in my gown, an inevitable result of travel, I took up my pen and wrote to my dear sister Cassandra. It is a letter I fear that I must discard without posting—for soon I shall be required to convey other news, against which last evening's note may only be declared frivolous.

My dear Cassandra—

I am safely arrived in Hertfordshire and more than ready to enjoy the ball the Earl of Scargrave gives in his lady's honour. I must regard it as fortuitous that Isobel's invitation arrived so soon upon the heels of my own trouble. Pray forgive me my sudden flight; I could not stay with brother James—you know how little I enjoy the tedium of a *tête-à-tête* with Mary—in my present confused and downcast state. I will not say that our brother reproached me for refusing Mr. Bigg-Wither; but I did endure a grim half-hour on the fate of impoverished spinsters. I was made to understand that I owe my continued sustenance and respectability (on twenty pounds per annum!) to the good health of our father, and that without a husband, I shall be cast upon my brothers' slim resources once that worthy is dead. Having heard James out, I am more than ever determined to pursue the publication of my little book, for I must earn some independence; better to commerce in literature than in matrimony, for to marry from mercenary motives is to me of all things the most despicable.[3]

But let us leave brother James where he belongs, in the company of his unfortunate wife—I find I must break off, as the maid is come to dress my hair for the ball; though what can be done to improve it at nearly seven-and-twenty, that was not attempted at eighteen, I cannot think. You will be shocked to learn that I have traded my comfortable cap for the allurements of a feather, to be tucked into a beaded band drawn across the forehead; two bunches of curls hang like grapes before my ears, *à la* the huntress Diana. I appear quite ridiculous, I dare say, but the change is a welcome one for all that. And now, my dearest sister, I must bid you good-night and *adieu*. I remain,

> Yours very affectionately,
> J. A.

I wore my yellow patterned silk, the finest thing I own, though admittedly of a vanished season, and kept my head high as I entered the ballroom in Isobel's wake. The great room was ablaze with candles, grouped in their gilt holders against the pier glasses that line the walls, so that we seemed to move among tall trees and branches of leafy flame; and it was peopled with a glittering assemblage of gentlemen and ladies, some hundred at least, come from surrounding Hertfordshire and as far distant as London. It must be impossible for one of my means to rival the grandeur of Scargrave, much less of the Earl's circle of acquaintance; but I fortified myself with the knowledge

3. The novel to which Jane refers was initially called *Susan*. Finished and sold to a publisher for ten pounds in 1803, it had still not been published in 1816 when Jane bought it back from the purchaser. Later retitled *Northanger Abbey,* it was published posthumously in 1818.—*Editor's note.*

of Isobel's kindness and thus braved the stares of my companions.

The Countess of Scargrave was magnificent in deep green silk, a gown she had recently acquired in Paris. That she has always possessed a certain style is indisputable; but now she also may claim the means to obtain it—and the Earl's great fortune could hardly be better spent. Isobel is a tall, well-formed woman, with a figure light and pleasing; it is generally agreed that her hair is her most extraordinary feature, it being thick and of a deep, lustrous red that cannot fail to command attention. For my own part, I must declare it is her eyes that appear to greatest advantage—being of the colour of sherry, and heavily fringed. The charms of her person would be as nothing, however, did she lack the sweet grace that customarily animates her countenance. Tonight, in the midst of her bridal ball, she was truly lovely, her head thrown back in laughter as she turned about the room.

That others were equally admiring of Isobel's beauty and great charm, I readily discerned, and briefly felt myself a pale shadow in her train. To lose one's cares in the gaiety of a ball, one must, perforce, be able to *dance;* and this requires a partner. At the advanced age of nearly seven-and-twenty, I had begun to know the fear of younger women. I had been suffered to sit during several dances at the last Bath assembly, while chits of fifteen turned and twirled their hearts upon the floor, and an unaccustomed envy had poisoned my happiness. I quailed to think that my fate tonight at Scargrave might be the same; but Isobel was as good as I had come to expect, and made me immediately acquainted with several gentlemen in her circle.

First among them was Fitzroy, Viscount Payne, her husband's nephew. Lord Payne is the only son of the Earl's younger brother, these many years deceased; and if the Earl and Isobel are unblessed by sons of their own, Lord Payne will succeed to the title at the Earl's death. As a single man in possession of a good fortune, he must be in want of a wife; and so the eyes of many within Scargrave that night were turned to him in hope and calculation.

From what little I have seen of Fitzroy Payne thus far, however, I should judge him as likely to honour *me* with his attentions and his hand as any lady in the room. Indeed, his heart is not likely to be easily touched—and I suspect it already is given to another. Lord Payne is a grave gentleman of six-and-twenty, and though decidedly handsome, is possessed of such reserve that his notice was hardly calculated to improve my spirits. As Isobel pronounced my name, he kept his eyes a clear six inches above my head, clicked his heels smartly, and made a deep bow—offering not a word of salutation the while.

Next I was suffered to meet the eldest son of the Earl's deceased sister. Mr. George Hearst is a quiet gentleman of seven-and-twenty, charged with all the management of the home farm, which I understand from Isobel is not at all to that gentleman's liking. He wishes rather to take Holy Orders, with the view to obtaining one of the three livings[4] at the Earl's disposal when it should next come vacant. Pale and gaunt, his eyes shadowed with a care that must be ecclesiastical, he bears the stamp of a man long in converse with his God. His melancholy aspect and glowering looks, in the midst of so much rejoicing, cast a pall over the immediate party that even I, a relative stranger to them all, must feel acutely. Mr. George Hearst gave me an indifferent nod, and then returned to his contempla-

---

4. The term *living* applied to a clergyman's post—his salary and usually his home—which passed from one man to another, often as the gift of a patron who "owned" the living, or, if the clergyman himself had purchased the living, through the sale of the position before the incumbent's death. Sale of a living *after* the incumbent's death was considered trafficking in Church property—a violation of the laws of simony.—*Editor's note.*

tion of the grave—or so I assumed, from his stony aspect.

Isobel hastened then to make me known to Lieutenant Thomas Hearst, the ecclesiastic's younger brother; and as different from him as two men formed of the same union may be.

Tom Hearst possesses a life commission in an excellent cavalry regiment, a face creased from laughing, unruly curls that bob when he bows low over a hand, and a charm that has undoubtedly reduced many a fashionable miss to tears and sighing. That the Lieutenant cuts a dashing figure in his dark blue uniform, and dances with more enthusiasm than skill, I may readily attest. When Isobel presented him, he bobbed in the aforesaid manner and immediately asked for my next dance; and so I instantly recovered from my fit of nerves and set out to determine something of the Lieutenant's character.

I did not have far to seek. At the glimpse of a blond head hovering over my shoulder and the scent of violets assailing my nose, I turned and surveyed Miss Fanny Delahoussaye, resplendent in a peacock-blue gown that displayed to excellent effect her ample bosom. Miss Delahoussaye laughed a little breathlessly—the result, no doubt, of too much activity and too little corset string—and reached a plump hand to her coiffure.

"And so you have met that rascal Tom Hearst," she said, and actually winked in my direction. Miss Fanny is Isobel's cousin from the Barbadoes, a well-grown girl of youthful and boisterous appearance, but sadly lacking in sense. "He has snatched you up for a dance or two, I warrant, and now I shall have to go begging for a partner. I am sure Tom should have monopolised my card," she added, displaying that elegant slip attached to her fan, already overwritten with eager suitors, "but for his delicacy in appearing too forward."

"Is Lieutenant Hearst a man of delicacy, then?" I enquired, with more interest in Miss Delahoussaye than I had heretofore felt.

"Oh, Lord, no!" she cried. "As rash a scapegrace as

ever lived! But Tom is that afraid of Mamma"—at this, she tossed her blond curls in Madame Delahoussaye's general direction—"as to be overcareful. I am sure that *I* should not fear her half so much. It is not as though I have a brother, you know, to fight with him and send him off."

"Why should any fight with the Lieutenant?" I said, somewhat bewildered.

"Why, because he is in love with me, of course," Fanny declared, rapping my shoulder with her fan; "and his fortune is hardly equal to my own. And if I *did* have a brother to fight him, it should be the worse for us; for you know Tom is come to Scargrave having killed a man in an affair of honour."[5]

My distress at this intelligence being written upon my countenance, Miss Delahoussaye laughed aloud. "I wonder you had not heard of it. Lord, it is the talk of the entire room! He has left his regiment at St. James for a little until the scandal dies down; though I am sure he should not have engaged in such an affair had he not been cruelly insulted." With this, Miss Delahoussaye attempted to look grave, but her blue eyes danced with approbation for the terrible Lieutenant.

"Undoubtedly," I replied, "though we cannot know what it is about."

"I mean to find out," Miss Fanny said stoutly, "for the affairs of officers are to me the most romantic in the world! Do not you agree, Miss Austen? Is not an officer to be preferred above any man?"

5. To kill one's opponent in a duel was considered murder in England, and as the nineteenth century wore on, the successful combatant was often forced to flee the country if he did not wish to face the law. Around the turn of the eighteenth century, however, the authorities still occasionally winked at dueling—particularly among military men, for whom the concept of personal honor was as vital as wealth or high birth. As Lieutenant Hearst is a cavalry officer, it would be left to his commanding officers to decide his fate.—*Editor's note.*

"I had not thought them blessed with any *particular* merit—" I began, but was cut off in mid-sentence.

"Then you cannot appreciate Tom as I do, and I shall not fear your charms any longer. He is wild about me, Miss Austen; do you remember it when you are dancing with him." And with a flounce of her peacock-hued gown, Fanny Delahoussaye left me to await the return of her heart's delight.

It was but nine o'clock, and light refreshment was laid in a parlour at some remove from the great room; a crush of gentlemen and ladies circulated about the long table, seeking ices and champagne, cold goose and sweetmeats, sent forth from Scargrave's kitchens with a breathtaking disregard for expense. I considered the swarm of the unknown, some of whom were very fine, indeed, and for an instant wished myself returned to the hearth in my room, with a good book for company; but Isobel had taken my arm, and I was not to be so easily released.

"This is what it means to be a married woman, Jane," my friend said, with an arch smile; "one is forever expected to forego refreshment so that others may dance. *You* may eat to your heart's content, but *I* must allow my husband to lead me to the floor, or suffer the contempt of my guests." Isobel then swept off on the arm of the Earl, and proceeded to the head of the room; others equally eager to join in the revels formed up in pairs alongside them, as the musicians laid bow to string.

I felt the absence of Tom Hearst, and knew not whether to wish for the return of such a man or no. But my confusion was to be of short duration. A parting of the crowd, a sight of a curly head, and a jaunty bow in my direction; and I found myself facing the Lieutenant not four couples removed from the Earl and his lady, in all the flushed excitement of a first dance.

The knowledge of Lieutenant Hearst's having killed a man put flight to every other thought in my head, but since it is impossible to move through the figures without *some* attempt at conversation, I cast about in desperation for the slightest word. I fear I blushed, and turned my eyes to the ground, and appeared in every way as *missish* as possible, giving the Lieutenant as inaccurate a picture of myself as perhaps Miss Delahoussaye had drawn of him. My wordless confusion made him hesitate to utter a syllable; and thus we laboured in profound stupidity, for fully half the dance's span. But of all things detestable, I most detest a silent partner—and thrusting aside my horror of pistols at dawn, I took refuge in a lady's light banter.

"I have profited from your absence, Lieutenant, to enquire of your character," I began.

A merry look, from under a lifted eyebrow. "And am I fit to touch your glove, Miss Austen?"

"I learned that you are everywhere regarded as a man of charm and intelligence; that you are an officer renowned for bravery and quick temper; that you are observed to spend a good deal of time on horseback in the Park; and that you prefer saddle of mutton to roast beef, in which you have been disappointed this evening."

"Nay!" he cried, his head thrown back in laughter, "and shall we have the size of my boot and my preference in tailors as well?"

"It was an intelligence I could not, with delicacy, gather," I replied, "but if you disappear with such alacrity again, I shall be certain to find it out."

With great good humour the Lieutenant then began to converse quite freely, enquiring of my life in Bath and the circumstances of my family with a becoming interest. For my part, I quickly learned that he is the son of Lord Scargrave's sister, Julia, dead these many years, and that his father was a dissolute rogue. Having reduced the Lady Julia to penury (for so I interpreted the Lieutenant's more generous words), the elder Mr. Hearst had the good sense to abandon his sons to her brother and depart for the Continent, where he subsequently died in the arms of his mistress. Lord Scargrave has had the rearing of the Hearst boys these twenty years; and it would not be remarkable if they looked to him as a father.

The Lieutenant added that he had tired of schooling while still at Eton, and spurned Oxford for the more brilliant ranks of the military; that he is at present a member of the Royal Horse Guards, resident in St. James, and is at Scargrave on leave through the Christmas holidays; though he failed to intimate that it was an *enforced* leave, due to his having recently killed a man.

Indeed, having spent some time in Lieutenant Hearst's company, I must wonder whether Miss Delahoussaye's romantic notions have not run away with what little sense she commands. For the Lieutenant seems as unlikely to kill a man as my dear brother Henry.

Fond of jokes, liberal in his smiles, incapable of giving offence to anybody, Tom Hearst is a ray of sun; but like the sun, can scorch when least expected. We had been half an hour along in the dance, and were nearing its close, when he turned the subject to Isobel, with some impertinence of manner.

"I may rejoice that my uncle has married," he said, taking my hand as I exchanged places with my neighbour, "when my aunt's acquaintance proves so delightful."

"Did you not rejoice, then, before I came to Scargrave?"

An anxious look, as having betrayed too much, was my reward, and an affectation of laughter. "For my own part," the Lieutenant replied, "I take my uncle's happiness as the sole consideration. But others may feel a nearer interest."

"I do not pretend to understand you." I turned my back upon him in the dance and caught Isobel's eye as she made her way along the line.

"You must be aware, Miss Austen," said Tom Hearst, "that an elderly man without children of his own may disappoint his family when he goes in pursuit of heirs."

"With a father past seventy, I should not call eight-and-forty *elderly*," I replied, turning again to face him.

"Oh! To be sure! I spoke but as a matter of form. I do not doubt, however, that my cousin the Viscount"—this, with a glance at Lord Payne, who stood opposite Fanny

Delahoussaye in the next couple but one—"may feel such a mixture of emotions more acutely than I. Though Lord Fitzroy Payne appears to rank the Countess as chief among his acquaintance, *even he* must acknowledge the blow to his fortunes. If my uncle gets an heir, Lord Payne's prospects are decidedly the worse."

"Your solicitude for your cousin's purse may disarm reproof," I told him, "but your uncle's happiness must be said to outweigh more material concerns." That I wondered at his imparting so much of a personal nature to a complete stranger I need not emphasise; but it hardly dissuaded me from pursuing the conversation further.

"Oh! Uncle's happiness," said the Lieutenant, turning his gaze upon Lord Scargrave, who even then was engaged in a bout of laughter as he moved his elegant wife through the figures. "His happiness cannot be doubted. We should all be as fortunate at eight-and-forty. But as we are blessed with only half his years, Miss Austen, let us throw off sober talk and take up other things. Have you been much in Hertfordshire?"

Recovering his senses, as it seemed, the Lieutenant conversed with great charm until the music ended, and then he bowed low over my gloved hand. After earnestly entreating me to favour him with another dance, and hearing me plead the necessities of fatigue, he took himself off in search of wine punch.

I gazed after him for an instant, turning over his words in my mind, then shook my head and resolved to think of him no more. Tom Hearst is altogether a scapegrace, a rake, and possibly a dangerous fellow, with his likeable face, his vigourous dancing, and his easy manners; a man who might do with a woman as he liked, having once won her heart.

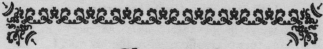

Chapter 2

Enter Lord Harold

11 December 1802, cont.

~

THE MOST CURIOUS OF THE INCIDENTS I WITNESSED LAST night sprang from the arrival of a man—a gentleman and a stranger, but of so malevolent an aspect, that I shiver to find him still beneath our roof as the Earl lies dying. *He* is the chief of what I would understand about life at Scargrave Manor; and I must look to my friend Isobel for explanation, since it was in pursuit of her that he came.

I was engaged in observing Lieutenant Hearst's progress towards the wine punch, when Isobel appeared at my side. Her face was becomingly flushed, and her brown eyes alight.

"My dear Jane! Is not this an excellent ball? Is not it an elegant assembly? And yet I have bade my husband be off, that I may steal a few moments in your company," she declared, taking my hand. "Come into this corner and tell me all that has happened, for since your arrival I have not had a moment to spare for your cares."

She led me to a settee placed conveniently within the

alcove of a window, the better to view the progress of her ball while conversing unmolested. I confessed to some little fatigue after the rigours of Lieutenant Hearst's conversation and enthusiasm, and sank into the seat with relief.

"I had hoped to be able to wish you joy, my dear Jane," Isobel began, "but you are determined to deny me the pleasure. Now, do not run away," she added, as I looked conscious, "in the fear that I am going to scold you—on the contrary, I admire you. Yes," she insisted, when I would protest, "I admire your courage. It is rare to find a woman who places her personal happiness above her fears for the future. You refused Mr. Bigg-Wither, refused his offer of a home, a family, and the comfortable means they assured, to retain your independence, despite the counsel of all who wished you well and threw their weight behind the match. What strength!"

"Did you know Mr. Bigg-Wither, you would think me less noble," I said. "There cannot be *two* men so likely to meet with refusal in the entire country. What is remarkable is that I accepted him at all, if only for an evening. The thought of an eternal fireside *tête-à-tête* with Mr. Bigg-Wither; the endless presiding over the Bigg-Wither teapot; the possibility of little Bigg-Withers, all equally as dull as their father—such nightmares were enough to chasten me by morning."

"But at least your nightmares were of short duration, Jane." Isobel smoothed the elegant folds of her green silk gown, her aspect turned sombre in an instant. "There are too many ladies, I fear, who must suffer them the length of an unhappy marriage. Better to reject a suitor, than to lie forever wakeful in contemplation of one's mistake."

"Indeed. Had I joined my life to Mr. Bigg-Wither's, the alliance must be brief; for I would certainly have died of insomnia before the week's end."

My design was to provoke laughter, but in truth, my decision to reject Mr. Harris Bigg-Wither of Manydown

Park a mere four-and-twenty hours after accepting him—to the joy of my dear friends, his sisters—has caused me great pain and mortification. He is heir to extensive estates in Hampshire, and his position and fortune would be thought a conquest for any lady, particularly one such as myself, whose means are so unequal to his, and whose first bloom of youth is gone. Despite these claims against my person, Mr. Bigg-Wither had fixed upon me as the companion of his future life almost from the moment I entered Manydown House a few weeks ago. In short, his proposal was quite gratifying, coming as it did without even the pretence of courtship. In a fit of gratitude—nay, I must and shall be honest—in a fit of *vanity*, I accepted him.

But he is six years my junior, an awkward, gloomy fellow burdened with a pronounced stutter; and all his consequence could not make of him a different man. As I would assuredly attempt to reform what nature had disposed Harris Bigg-Wither to *be*, I could only do him harm by accepting him. My instinct for self-preservation, my belief that marriage without love is the worst form of hypocrisy, gave me strength after a sleepless night to inform him of my error in encouraging his attentions, and to assure him that I was the woman least likely to bring him felicity in the married state. I departed Manydown not an hour later, in great despondency, certain that I had lost not only a suitor, but some part of my dearest acquaintance.

"And now you are come to Scargrave to forget your cares in a whirlwind of frivolity," Isobel said, casting off her pensive air and reaching again for my hand. "We shall make certain that you do. I shall find some young man to dance attendance upon you, to flatter you and turn your head, and send Harris Bigg-Wither and his stutter to the nether reaches of your conscience."

"Nay, Isobel," I protested, "do not cause yourself the trouble to search further. I believe Lieutenant Hearst will amply serve my purpose. He has good looks and charm without the slightest suggestion of better feeling, and he possesses not a penny he may call his own. He shall do very well for a portionless clergyman's daughter. We may expect him to ruin me and then depart for a noble death before Buonaparte's cannon, at which point I shall throw myself in the millpond and be renowned in wine and song. Has Scargrave a millpond, Isobel?"

"Take care, Jane," my friend said, struggling to be serious; "Tom Hearst is a pleasant enough rogue, but capable of great harm for all that. I would wish him less thrown in the way of my cousin Fanny, for he has so far made her forget herself as to appear a perfect wanton, on occasion—and nothing, as you know, is further from her character."

"Assuredly," I said, with less than perfect confidence in Fanny's character; "but enough of my cares, Isobel." I surveyed my friend, who looked every inch the countess, from the ropes of pearls entwined in her dark red hair to the fashionable slimness of her gown's bodice. I had seen just such a cut to a neckline only once before—in an illustration of Buonaparte's consort, Josephine, from a London journal. Isobel appeared born to wear it. But as I studied her countenance, I was grieved to see marks of strain about her lovely eyes—as though she, the least likely of all my acquaintance, had slept poorly of late. Perhaps the adoption of her husband's station in life had proved too great a burden.

"What of you, Isobel," I asked gently, "these three months married?"

"I? What may I possibly say of myself?" She spoke with more effort at gaiety than I should have thought necessary. "I am as you see me: an old married woman, whose adventures must be things of the past."

"You appear very well."

"I am glad to hear it," she said, as a shadow came over her features, "for I exert myself to that end. I would not have my husband think other than that I am happy; and so my energies are directed."

"Isobel—" I was seized with a sudden apprehension.

"Whatever can be the matter? You possess the *essence* of happiness as well as its outward form, assuredly?"

But she appeared insensible of my words, absorbed as she was in some activity on the nether side of the ball-room. "Jane!" she whispered, clutching at my arm, her features whitening and her brown eyes grown suddenly large. "*He* is here. He has had the insolence to appear in my home, in the first days of my return, and without my invitation. Unless it be that Frederick—" She turned in search of her husband, who had vanished from sight. Swift as a bird, her countenance regained its composure and her eyes fixed once more on her first object. "Good God, will I never be free of him?"

I followed the direction of her gaze and saw with fore-boding the face that had inspired such fear. He was a tall man of indeterminate age, and thin, in the manner of one who is much out-of-doors in pursuit of frequent exercise. His face was tanned, his appearance elegant, and his carriage easy as he paced the margin of the room, hands clasped behind his back and eyes roving through the crowd. I knew with certainty that it was Isobel he sought, and my immediate instinct was to shelter her from his sight. There was something in the gentleman's aspect—the hooded eyes under a sharp brow, the sweep of silver hair, the long scar that bisected one tanned cheek—that inspired fear. This was a man too much in command of himself; and such an one must always strive to command all the world.

"But who is he?" I asked my friend in a whisper, as though his ears might penetrate even our sheltered alcove.

"He is Lord Harold Trowbridge," Isobel replied, her fingers pinching my arm painfully, "the Duke of Wilborough's brother. He is intent upon purchasing Crosswinds, my father's estate in the Barbadoes, which has suffered sad reversals in recent years. He gives me no peace, by day or by night."

"I believe he has seen us," I said, my heart quickening, as the restless dark eyes came to rest on Isobel. A slow smile curled at the corners of Lord Harold's thin mouth, and with the most gracious ease he made his way across the room to where we sat. There could be no flight; the wall was to our backs, and he was before us.

"Countess." He bowed low over Isobel's hand. "It gives me such pleasure to welcome you to your new home."

"I fear the duty must be reversed, Lord Harold," Isobel said, with an effort at a smile; "and that *I* must welcome *you*. I have also the honour of presenting you to my dear friend, Miss Austen, of Bath."

"The honour is mine," Lord Harold said, with a penetrating look and a bow in my direction.

"And have you found everything to your comfort?" Isobel enquired.

"Indeed," he assured her, "I arrived but an hour ago from London, at Lord Scargrave's invitation, and have been settled comfortably by Mrs. Hodges."

At my friend's expression of surprise, I judged she had not anticipated that the man would be taking up residence; but his insolence was equal even to this.

"I confess, I should not have missed such an occasion for the world," Lord Harold continued. "To see a lady so happily and advantageously married must be a joy to those who rank her security among their dearest concerns." His voice, though low and refined, bore a note of mockery that was lost neither on Isobel nor myself.

"I rejoice to hear it," Isobel told him, rising as if to depart, "for it is some time since I believed my security to be the very *last* of your concerns." The words were abrupt and forced, a shock to my ears; but Trowbridge appeared unmoved. His tall form, fixed before us as steadily as a tree, prevented Isobel from passing in a most ungentlemanly manner.

"Countess," he said, his voice as tight and cutting as a bowstring, "I would speak with you in private."

Isobel's mouth had hardened, and her words, when they came, fell with the heaviness of stone. "You can have nothing to say to me tonight, Lord Harold, that cannot better wait until morning. A ball is hardly the hour for business."

"And tomorrow, no doubt, will be no better once it dawns," he replied evenly, and smiled. "I will not wait forever, *my lady.*"

"You will wait as long as I please." Isobel's eyes never left his face. "Remember, *my lord,* that you wait upon my pleasure." Two bright spots burned in her cheeks, but her pallor was extreme, and I feared she might faint in another moment.

It was Lord Payne, the Earl's nephew, who put a stop to the high pitch of nerves, by appearing like a shadow at Trowbridge's shoulder. The two are equal in height, though Lord Payne has the better of Trowbridge in gravity; his courtesy was perhaps the more offensive for being exquisite.

"Lord Harold," Lord Payne said, bowing low, "we are fortunate indeed in your company this evening. But I fear I must tear you from the gentler influence of the ladies at the behest of my uncle. He requests that you join him in his study; and in this, as in all things, I do his bidding."

A few sentences only, but conveyed in such a tone that it served the moment. Lord Harold gave Lord Payne a single look, bowed low to Isobel and me, and was gone as silently as he had appeared.

"Impertinent devil!" Isobel cried, clutching at Lord Payne's hand, "he will hound me to the ends of the earth!"

"I would that I could rid you of his presence entirely," said Lord Payne, "rather than for so brief a space as he is likely to grant us." He retained the Countess's hand an instant, gazing at her with an expression of care and worry, and then recovered himself. "I fear you are unwell, Isobel. I shall inform my uncle that you are briefly indisposed, and have sought your rooms."

More than the surprising adoption of her Christian name, his tender look, when it rested upon his uncle's wife, brought me to my senses. That he was mastered by a feeling unwonted even in so near a relation, I could not doubt; and I recollected Tom Hearst's banter earlier that evening. He had declared Isobel to be chief among Fitzroy Payne's acquaintance; and what the Lieutenant would intimate I now understood all too well—the Earl's silent nephew, so inscrutable in his reserve, was better revealed by strong feeling; Lord Payne knew what it was to love.

"Pray speak to Frederick on my behalf, Fitzroy," Isobel said faintly, turning away from us both, "but say that I retire only for a little. I would not have Trowbridge believe he has me in his grasp." As if remembering my presence for the first time since Lord Harold had withdrawn, she looked at me then, and managed a smile; and so she left us.

I must set down something of my sense of Fitzroy, Viscount Payne, for I find him the very type to serve as a character in one of my novels.[1] He is a tall, well-made fellow, strikingly handsome, with slate-coloured eyes set above sharply-moulded cheekbones. It is his hair that astonishes in one but twenty-six, for it is gone completely grey in a fashion not unbecoming to his grave countenance. All the charm of his person must be weighed, however, against his manner—for Fitzroy Payne is possessed of that reserve that some might mistake for aloofness and pride. That he has a right to be proud, possessed as he is of his father's considerable estates, and being as well the man likely to succeed the Earl in his title and riches, was

1. It is possible that Austen eventually turned Fitzroy, Viscount Payne into her most famous male character, Fitzwilliam Darcy, although strong evidence is lacking. *First Impressions*, in which Darcy is the main male character, was written in 1796, and rejected for publication in 1797. Later retitled *Pride and Prejudice*, it was revised substantially in late 1802 or early 1803, following Austen's visit to Scargrave, and again before publication in 1812.—*Editor's note.*

everywhere acknowledged among the intimates of the Scargrave ballroom; but Lord Payne's haughty silences were no more admired for having a just complacency as their cause. Though many wished to *win* him, I found myself hard-pressed to find any among the assemblage who truly *liked* him; and so enjoyed my time in his company all the more. To be marked out by the singular is a caprice of mine; I would rather spend an hour among the notorious than two minutes with the dull.

"I must thank you, sir," I said, "for relieving me in a desperate moment. I confess I was unequal to Lord Harold in Isobel's defence, lacking full knowledge of the particulars at issue."

"You suffer no dishonour by being unequal to Lord Harold," Fitzroy Payne said. His eyes swept over my head, searching, I fancied, for dark red hair above a daring green gown; but Isobel had quitted the ballroom.

After a pause, and some observation of the dance, which had just then commenced, I assayed another attempt.

"I suppose Lord Scargrave wished Lord Harold present, the better to converse with him in his library—for certainly Isobel was much surprised at the gentleman's arrival."

"Did she have full knowledge of Trowbridge's descent upon this house hours before he effected it, she should still be made as ill," Lord Payne said, with some bitterness.

"You share the Countess's dislike," I observed.

To this sally I received no answer but a knitting of the brows and a heightened gravity.

"Perhaps we shall summon Lieutenant Hearst and have him challenge Lord Harold to a duel," I suggested, in an effort at lightness. "The Lieutenant shall exercise his honour, and be of service to a lady—two pursuits in which I understand he excels."

A chill smile, but again no word.

"I detect a similarity in the turn of our minds, Viscount Payne," I persisted, in some exasperation. "We are both of a taciturn, ungenerous nature, and would rather be silent until we may say what is certain to astonish all the world."

For this I won the barest moment of liveliness in his grey eyes, and the gift of an answer.

"From a better acquaintance with my own foolishness, Miss Austen, I must be silent; but of you I can readily believe a delight in astonishing."

"There!" I cried. "My opinion is proved. You cannot even *insult* without phrasing it well."

"I meant rather to praise than insult, and so my words could hardly fall ill." He turned his dark eyes upon me with a penetrating look. "The desire to astonish may be considered a vice only when it lacks the wit to achieve its aim—but with wit, Miss Austen, you are clearly most blessed. And now, I fear, I must desert you for the office with which I am charged—that of informing my uncle of my aunt's indisposition."

He bowed; I nodded; and a gentleman assailing me for a dance at that moment, I left Fitzroy Payne to find his way amidst the boisterous throng. But during the course of the evening I was made more sensible of Lord Payne's attractions. My subsequent partners were to prove less able in conversation, and less provocative even in their silences, than the Viscount had proved with a single sentence.

IT WAS AFTER A PARTICULARLY TEDIOUS EXCHANGE WITH such an one, that I bethought me of refreshment, and parting with my dubious suitor in some relief, betook myself along the gallery that led from the ballroom to the smallish parlour, where the supper was arrayed. The last of the dances being just then struck up, I found myself blessedly alone in my progress towards the wine punch. I had barely passed the first of the closed doorways lining the hall, when I was halted in my steps by the fierce eruption of argument near at hand. I turned and espied the entrance to the Earl's library, whence Lord Harold had disappeared but an hour before. From behind its closed door emanated the voices of two men, raised in strenuous argument. Lord Scargrave and Trowbridge? It could not be otherwise. I may perhaps be forgiven a woman's curiosity when I admit that, finding myself quite alone for the moment, I lingered along my way.

The words soon became intelligible.

"You are not to mention the name of Rosie Ketch," one gentleman cried. "You have debauched her in speech often enough."

"That is laughable, sir, coming from you."

"You shall not support me in this?"

"Never, sir."

"Then, my lord, I cannot be responsible for the consequences. You have driven me to my utmost extremity, and God forgive me! I know how it is that I must act."

The voices were grown louder, as though one or both of the parties had approached the door; I looked about me for a place of safety, and could find none but the heavy draperies cloaking the tall windows. I had only tucked myself behind them, doing violence to my hair and gown, when the door was thrust open and a gentleman burst from the room, the fury of his words propelling him with like energy from the Earl's presence.

I stole a look around the curtain edge, certain to see Lord Harold—and found myself confronted, to my astonishment, with George Hearst, the Lieutenant's older brother. What could it mean? The gloomy ecclesiastic, revealed as a man of hot temper?

Mr. Hearst was not a moment gone when the Earl himself appeared in the hall, his face reddened as with apoplexy. I remembered then Isobel's care for her husband's health, and smiled. It was not an excess of claret that plagued the Earl, but a surfeit of family; and of this, no one was likely to cure him.

The Earl made for the ballroom, and after an instant's pause to right my feather and settle the clumps of curls about my cheeks, I followed my host. I was in time to see him raise a glass before the assembly to his newly-won bride, drink it to the dregs, and double over in a fit of acute dyspepsia. Protesting and declaring himself to be very well, our host was borne from the room on the broad backs of two footmen, an anxious Isobel in his wake; and so the revels ended.

I WAS JUST NOW RETURNED TO THE PRESENT BY ISOBEL'S appearance at my door.

"Jane," she said, with great steadiness, "the crisis is passed."

"God be thanked!" I cried, and threw down my pen.

"Is He, indeed?" She gave me a strange look. "You mistake my meaning. The crisis is passed, my dear friend, and the Earl is dead."

I went to her in an instant, my countenance conveying all my sorrow, and bent her head upon my breast. But Isobel had no tears; her beautiful sherry-coloured eyes were blank and unseeing, her form as rigid as the Earl lying cold within her marriage bed. I released her without a word, feeling as though my heart should break, and watched her tortured progress down the corridor.

At my window now, I pull back the heavy draperies smelling of must, and gaze out upon a desolate dawn. No sun shall rise today for human eyes to see; the world entire is wrapped round in whirling white, an impenetrable cloud of cold and ice that chills the heart as it freezes the ground. Scargrave's vast parkland is adrift, its black trees etched like wraiths against the grey sky of morning. I think of Frederick, Earl of Scargrave—of his soul gone forth too soon from earthly happiness, and on such a frigid day—and I am consumed with sorrow for all of mortal men. What are last night's revels, its frivolities and petty triumphs, against the magnitude of the grave? I let fall the draperies, blocking out the snow, and shiver in my nightdress.

I came into Hertfordshire seeking diversion; and what I have found is Death, in more vivid and horrible a form than I had yet been taught to expect. I may take it as my reward for cowardice—for so such a flight from one's worst nature is always revealed—to witness the agonising end of the Earl of Scargrave, and be utterly powerless to reverse it.

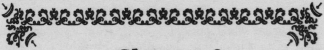

Chapter 3

The Poisoned Pen

14 December 1802
~

THE LIVING EVER FEEL UNEASE, WHEN THE DEAD ARE IN
residence.

I had determined to leave for Bath the morning after
the Earl's death, believing such a passing to be a family
burden; but Isobel would have me stay, and so here at
Scargrave I remain, tip-toeing along its labyrinth of corridors and hoping to draw as little notice as possible.
Upon further acquaintance, the Manor is revealed as an
incongenial house, its furnishings of a vanished generation and its air one of quiet decrepitude. I have trod
the floors of endless rooms, unmarked by their master's
happy spirits or decided taste; it is an abode in which
Lord Scargrave can have spent but little time, and now
departs forever.

The Earl is to be buried tomorrow. These two days
past, he has lain in state in the hall, a vast and draughty
place peopled by his ancestors, as though all the dead
of Scargrave have assembled for this dreary wake. Dark
faces in oil look down upon Frederick's bier with the
smiles of Charles's time, or the dour scowls of

Cromwell's; while suits of armour from an epoch still more distant huddle in the corners, awaiting their moment to joust with Death. The hall lies in the very centre of the great house, and all the principal corridors debouch or spring from it, making any attempt to navigate the lower floor a necessarily melancholy event. Masses of wax candles in branching silver holders surround the Earl's still form, and gold sovereigns are laid upon his eyes; no tallow tapers or pennies for a peer.

In the flickering glow, Lord Scargrave's face appears as ravaged as it did in the dim light of his death chamber; *not* the manner in which such a man would wish to be remembered. Were it not for the superstitions of the local folk, who come to pay their respects in a silent, shuffling file, Isobel should have ordered the casket closed; but the Earl of Scargrave must be seen to be truly dead by all the surrounding country before his heir may take up his title. And so convention is served, and delicacy sacrificed upon its altar.

I confess to a shiver or two myself in passing through the hall; I would forget this anguished look, still stamped in death upon the tortured face, as soon as ever I may. Perhaps then the thoughts that spring to my mind too vividly will be banished as well. The assurances of Dr. Philip Pettigrew, the London physician, have done little to quiet them. The good doctor claims to have seen a like disturbance in the bowels before, and found in its violence no sign of a malevolent hand; he imputes it to the quantity of wine the Earl had consumed that evening, along with a quantity of beef, a recipe I should rather think conducive to apoplexy than dyspepsia.[1]

I cannot forget that Lord Scargrave's fatal sickness, as I have written before, bore the signs of an extreme purgative, as though the vomiting were induced by some force

1. For twentieth-century readers, some explanation may prove useful. Apoplexy was the common nineteenth-century term for stroke, while dyspepsia signified indigestion.—*Editor's note.*

stronger than claret. But Isobel appears satisfied, if such a word may describe her quiet dejection; and the men of the Scargrave household are united without question in their mourning. And so my country knowledge must give way to London's greater experience.

Isobel keeps to her room, as is natural; Fitzroy Payne to the library, where he is engaged with his London solicitors in reviewing a quantity of papers pertaining to the late Earl's estate. Lord Harold Trowbridge, whom propriety should have instructed to depart, divides his time between Lord Scargrave[2] and the billiard room. The Hearst brothers, though dining at the Manor each afternoon, have chosen to mourn in private at their cottage in the Park; I observed George Hearst pacing a snowy lane, hands behind his back and features lost in contemplation of his personal abyss, while the Lieutenant appears to devote his hours to schooling a particularly troublesome hunter over the same series of hedges.

And so Isobel's aunt, Madame Delahoussaye, and her daughter Fanny, prove my sole society. I doubt that such a felicitous term, so laden with the promise of good conversation, mutual warmth, and general elegance, has ever been so wantonly applied. Three women confined by weather, over needlework and books in which they can have little interest, with a dead earl lying in state beyond the sitting-room door! It is not to be borne for many hours together.

Madame Hortense Delahoussaye is the sister of Isobel's mother, these many years deceased, and a native like her of the Indies. Madame has made her life business the social launching of her two girls, as she calls them—meaning her daughter Fanny and her orphaned niece Isobel. She talks enough for a household; we may

2. At the death of Frederick, Earl of Scargrave, Fitzroy Payne became the eighth Earl in his stead. As such, Austen now addresses him as Lord Scargrave, rather than Lord Payne, as he was when merely a viscount.—*Editor's note.*

perhaps impute her husband's demise these two years past to a surfeit of his lady's conversation. I should listen to it with better grace if her manners were equal to her niece's; but Madame Delahoussaye's pride in her station has been too strongly felt. When I appeared at Isobel's side at the commencement of the ball, the aunt swiftly took the measure of my gown; learned that my father is a clergyman; and thereafter reserved her brilliance for others more obviously favoured by fortune.

Far from feeling too great an oppression at her niece's tragic loss, Madame Delahoussaye has busied herself since the Earl's death in sending orders to her favourite London warehouses, in preparation for the household's adoption of mourning; she is wearing even now the gown that graced her late husband's twelvemonth,[3] but is rather put out at its decided lack of fashion. She frequently delivers her opinions—that the Earl should have kept to the lemon-water she prescribed for his health; that the fees to the London physician had better have been saved; and that Isobel should quit Scargrave for Town as soon as the funeral is done—the better to bring Fanny her Season of enjoyment, for the poor child is not growing any younger.

From Fanny's marriage prospects, Madame inevitably turns to the latest style of mourning in France—a nation which, I feel compelled to point out, has had ample scope for study in the art under Buonaparte. Any observation of an historic or political nature must be lost on Madame Delahoussaye and her daughter, however; their heads are formed neither for penetrating discourse nor serious debate. Miss Fanny attends to her mother's recommendations with the greatest care, and is forever engaged in the drawing up of lists, which must be designed

3. It was customary for ladies to adopt dark mourning clothes for varying periods of time at the death of family members—at least a year upon the death of a husband or child, and as little as six weeks for more distant relations.—*Editor's note.*

to keep a multitude of milliners in goose-and-pudding for the coming year. Lacking their funds and their instinct for elegance in the midst of sorrow, I must content myself for the nonce with whatever grey muslin be in my possession; and for my part, there all attempt at mourning shall end.

I should do Fanny Delahoussaye an injustice if I did not set down that she styles herself very fine, indeed. Having spent hours poring over the pages of *Le Beau Monde*,[4] she is never seen in anything less than the most breathlessly current of gowns. Though given to riotous colour in her evening dress, she prefers a young lady's natural choice for day—white muslin or lawn—in the knowledge that it renders her pink-and-gold perfection even more angelic. And since pictures of perfection make me sick and wicked, I have resolved to thrust my *own* white lawn to the side for the duration of my Scargrave stay. Such an invitation to comparison between myself and Miss Delahoussaye *must* be invidious.

Born like Isobel in the Indies, though schooled in London, Fanny's chief business at nineteen appears to be the getting of a husband. She and her mother must needs be at cross purposes in this: Madame Delahoussaye favours the newly-titled Earl, Fitzroy Payne, as any mother should do, while Fanny displays a clearer preference for the penniless scapegrace Tom Hearst. Whether she is likely or able to captivate *either* gentleman is never laid open to question; it is assumed that her loveliness will conquer. I cannot be so sanguine. Fanny's pretty gowns and her fortune aside, she looks very much like any other young woman with a quantity of yellow hair, vacant eyes, and an expanse of exposed bosom. She inclines her head with exquisite grace, but fails to utter a sensible

4. *Le Beau Monde* was simply one of the fashionable journals avidly read by members of select Georgian society; its fashion plates presented the latest in ladies' and gentlemen's clothing.—*Editor's note.*

word; such an excess of elegance can only be imputed to the most fashionable of finishing schools. No doubt she speaks Italian and is highly accomplished—in the art of painting screens, making fringe, and standing before the mantua-maker[5].

I dare say that my words are peevish and cross—and I recognise my demon, jealousy. To have Fanny Delahoussaye's fortune and looks, and none of my own sense and wit, would be an unbearable exchange; but when I see her ready assumption of marriage, her effortless reaching towards that estate, I must own that I should like to stand in her place for a few hours together. I cannot know what it is to be beautiful and possessed of easy means; my conquests have ever been made against the better instincts of the men in my acquaintance, a tribute to my lively mind and good humour. But what woman is willing to accept such a victory as this, unmarried as I remain, in the face of good looks and fortune?

Later that day

~

I HAD NOT BEEN IN THE SITTING-ROOM AN HOUR WHEN a footman appeared with a summons from Isobel. I hastened to her side.

"Dear Jane!" my friend cried, reaching a white hand to me from her chaise longue; "I begged you to remain at Scargrave, only to desert you for the comfort of solitude. I fear I have made a sad hostess."

I glanced around Isobel's bedchamber in some surprise; in this room, at least, Scargrave's musty ghosts were banished. In anticipation of his bride, the Earl had

---

5. Mantua-maker is a Georgian term for dressmaker, after the mantua, a type of gown worn in the eighteenth century. It gradually fell out of use, to be replaced by the French *modiste*, and eventually by dressmaker.—*Editor's note.*

refurbished the apartment with elegance and taste; its furniture was light and pleasing, fresh paper graced the walls, a fire burned brightly in the grate, and the image of Frederick, Lord Scargrave, gazed down upon his wife from a gilt frame above the mantel. A book and a saucer of tea stood companionably on a table at Isobel's side; all was quiet and order. I understood, now, her unwillingness to appear in the chilly rooms below. But the comfort of her boudoir had done little to raise her spirits; indeed, an unaccustomed languor spoke from every limb, and by her ravaged looks, I knew sleep had escaped her these few nights past.

"Never could I reproach you in such an hour," I said, dropping to the floor at her side. "Do not trouble yourself about *me*. Your nearest relations have been at pains to ensure my comfort. But tell me, Isobel, how may I be of service to you? May anyone hope to relieve such melancholy as this?"

"Jane, do not tempt me to thrust aside my sorrow," the Countess replied bitterly. "It is the last honour his wife may offer poor unfortunate Frederick." She turned her eyes upon the hearth, her red hair undone and hanging in a curtain about her face, and suffered in silence a moment. Then she sought my hand with her own and gripped it fiercely. "But to melancholy, dearest Jane, I fear I must add a greater burden. And in this, I fondly hope, you may indeed be of service."

My aspect was all curiosity.

Isobel handed me a slip of paper. "This misbegotten note arrived by the morning post. I hardly know what it is about; and I would have your opinion."

The letter bore Isobel's direction, was sealed with such cheap wax as the taverns provide, and written remarkably ill.

It may plese you to think that you are free of the soupçon, milady, you and the tall lord who is so silent and who looks thru me; but the hanging, it is too good for you. I must keep myself by the side of my Saviour, and no one is safe in your company; and so I have gone this morning and you shall not find me out ware. The next leter, it will go to the good Sir William; and then we will see what becomes of those who kill.

"There is no signature," I said.

"That is not the least of its oddities."

"Putting aside, for the moment, the accusations it contains," I said, glancing at Isobel over the paper's edge, "we must endeavour to learn what the note itself may tell us. It is clearly written by a person of the serving class, on common paper with cheap ink; a person of little application in the art of writing, to judge by the formation of the letters, and for whom English is not the native tongue. From the tenor of the message, we may conclude that the author is of French origin; the word *soupçon*, inserted for *suspicion*, being the strongest indicator. From the reference to the Saviour, I must infer that the writer is female, and probably of the Church of Rome—for a man is hardly likely to be so pious when accusing his mistress of murder."

"Jane!" Isobel exclaimed, sitting straighter on her chaise, "you have managed marvellously! I might almost think you wrote this letter yourself."

"Indeed, I did not. But I may venture to guess who did."

"By all means, share your apprehension." My friend's voice trembled with eagerness.

"Your maid Marguerite," I said soberly. "Have you seen her since this letter arrived?"

The Countess's face was suffused with scarlet, then overlaid with a deathly pallor. "I have not," she answered unsteadily. "Marguerite attended me this morning and has been absent ever since. I assumed she felt all the burden of this unhappy house's misery, and would leave me to endure it in solitude."

"I fear she had worse in train." I glanced at the travelling clock on Isobel's mantel; it was close to the dinner hour of five in the afternoon, and the December dark had already fallen. "We shall not find her in the neighbourhood by this time."

"But, Jane, what can have caused Marguerite to charge me with such cruel deceit?" Isobel's warm brown eyes filled with tears. "I, the murderess of my husband! It is impossible!"

"She does not lay the blame upon you alone, my dear," I said slowly. "There is another to whom she refers."

"The tall lord," Isobel said, faltering. "It must be Trowbridge she speaks of."

"To what purpose?"

"To what purpose is any of it?"

"She cannot have been thrown very much in his way," I said reasonably.

"Indeed, she has not."

"Then, my dear, we must consider her as indicating another." My tone was brisk, but I awaited the effect of my impertinence with some trepidation.

There was an instant's silence as Isobel sought my meaning. Then she raised her eyes to mine with perfect composure. "Fitzroy Payne?" she said.

"I think it very likely. He is more of the household, and thus more likely to have encountered the maid."

"You may have the right of it." The Countess's fingers worked at the fine lace of her dressing gown, as though by sorting its threads she might untangle this puzzle. "It is like Marguerite to add the small aside of Fitzroy having 'looked through her.' I more than once observed her make the gesture against the evil eye when his gaze chanced to fall upon her; she mistrusted grey hair in one as yet young, and avowed that it was the Devil's mark."

"Was the maid so susceptible to fancy then, Isobel?"

"Marguerite was ever a superstitious, foolish child, the result of her island upbringing." My friend's eyes met mine, and her gaze was troubled. "I suppose the violence of my husband's last illness has given her some misapprehension, which, with time, has become a terrible conviction of evil."

"Undoubtedly the case," I said gently, "but the result may be no less injurious to your reputation and well-being, Isobel. The maid threatens to inform one Sir William. And who is he, pray?"

"Sir William Reynolds," Isobel said. "The magistrate."[6]

"Not Sir William Reynolds, formerly of the King's Bench?"

Isobel shrugged and looked bewildered. "I cannot undertake to say, Jane. The man is a stranger to me. Have you known such a gentleman?"

"Indeed, and all my life," I declared with eagerness. "The barrister I would mention is a dear friend of my father's—the acquaintance having been formed while both were yet unmarried, and but novices in their respective professions. Though the name is so very common, *my* Sir William and *yours* may be strangers to one another. Has he been resident very long in the neighbourhood?"

Isobel frowned in thought. "I do not believe that he has. His current office, indeed, is of only recent conference. Frederick—my late husband—was Lord Lieutenant of the County,[7] and appointed Sir William to the post a twelve-month ago. But, Jane, if the justice is so very well known to you, is it possible that he might be moved to consideration on my behalf?"

6. The Countess's use of the term *magistrate* may confuse some readers, who are aware that magistrates were generally salaried individuals appointed to keep order in large cities. The correct term for Sir William Reynolds's office is *justice of the peace*—an unsalaried position usually accorded a member of the country gentry. In rural areas, however, the two titles were often used interchangeably, since the unpaid justice of the peace performed the essential duties of a magistrate. —*Editor's note.*

7. The Lord Lieutenant of the County was an office usually accorded a high-ranking peer; his chief duties were to commission the various local justices of the peace, or magistrates, and to call out the militia in time of invasion.—*Editor's note.*

"Were I an utter unknown to Sir William, I should still look to him for consolation in time of trouble," I replied without hesitation, "for any who seek justice may be sure to find it at his hands."

"What would you have me do, Jane?" the Countess asked simply.

"We cannot stop the maid from sending a note as poisonous as this to the magistrate, and so I would advise that we anticipate her actions, and call Sir William to us without delay. It is within his province to halt such evil rumour before it may do further harm—or to investigate the case for just cause, if any there might be."

"Jane! Can you think it?"

"Of you, my dear, never." I folded the maid's note and offered it to her. "But of others? Anything may be possible in this world, where the fortunes of men are at stake; and the Earl's fortune, you will own, was considerable."

"But only Fitzroy Payne may benefit by it," she argued, crumpling the betraying letter in her hand; "and for Fitzroy to act with violence is unthinkable."

"Isobel," I said gently, "I fear you have not told me *all* where that gentleman is concerned."

Silence and an averted look were my reward, but a flush had begun to overtake the paleness of my friend's complexion.

"If you fall in with my plan of apprising Sir William of the nature of this letter, he will undoubtedly enquire as to the maid's meaning," I observed.

Isobel reached for my hand, her face stricken. "Jane, Jane—you must protect me! It is too much. The pain of Frederick's death—this horrible letter—and now, to expose Fitzroy so dreadfully—I cannot bear it!"

"If I am to help you, my dear," I said, kneeling at her feet, "I must know where I am. You must tell me what you can, Isobel, for everything may be of the greatest importance."

"You fear for me, Jane?"

"I fear for us all."

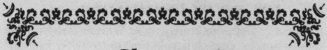
The Widow's Lament

14 December 1802, cont.

~

"YOU WILL HAVE OBSERVED HIS REGARD FOR ME."

Isobel had abandoned her chaise and was standing before the grate, her hand on the mantel and her lovely eyes fixed upon my face. In the fine dressing gown of Valenciennes lace, her dark red hair burnished by the light of the fire, she was magnificent. How could Fitzroy Payne help but adore her?

"There is a measure of warmth in Fitzroy Payne's manner beyond what a man might accord his aunt by marriage," I replied carefully.

"Even an aunt four years his junior?" Her laugh was bitter. "Can ever a family have been so discordantly arranged!"

"You understood the Earl's age when you married him, Isobel. A man twenty-six years your senior must be allowed to have acquired a nephew or two along the way."

"But such a nephew as Fitzroy? The paragon of men?" She began to turn back and forth before the fire, her arms wrapped protectively across her breast, her aspect tortured. "The man I might have encountered sooner, Jane—and having met, married as I should have married, for love and not simply the security of means?"

"I had not known you accepted the Earl from mercenary motives, Isobel." I confess I was shocked; but our conversation regarding the married state, in the little alcove the night of the ball, returned forcibly to my mind.

"But then you cannot have understood the state of my father's affairs at his death," the Countess said, wheeling to face me. "You will recall that he passed from this life but a year before my arrival in England. In truth, his fortunes were sadly reduced. The plantations at Crosswinds—my childhood home—have suffered numerous reverses, due in part to the poor price of coffee, in part to disease among the bushes, and not least owing to unrest among the slaves who work the estate. Lord Harold Trowbridge's shadow has been thrust upon this house because our holdings are at their final extremity."

"You have recent intelligence of the plantation's affairs?"

"I have it from Trowbridge himself. He is returned but six months from a survey of his West Indies investments, of which he hopes to make Crosswinds a part. He had not been in England a week when he obtruded painfully on my notice."

"But what can be his power over you, Isobel, that he chose not to exert over your father?"

"Lord Harold is my principal creditor, Jane. He has bought up all my father's debts, at a considerable discount, and has chosen *now* to call in loans of some thirty years' duration—at an exorbitant rate of interest," my friend said, wringing her hands in despair. "I have no recourse, so Trowbridge tells me, but to hand him the land in exchange for a discharge of my father's debt."

"I had no notion that your affairs were in such a state."

"How could you?" Isobel said, with some distress. "It is a fact I would not have broadly known. But the fear of losing Crosswinds has directed my endeavours since my father's death. My determination to remove to England two years ago was formed with the primary purpose of finding a suitable husband—a man of solidity and fortune who could revive my faltering affairs. I believed I had found him in dear Frederick." Isobel gazed up at her late husband's portrait, her face suffused with tenderness.

"That he knew of my troubles when he married me, Jane, I may freely own," she continued, with a look for me. "I would not join my poor fortune to one such as his without revealing all. Lord Scargrave bore me such great love"—at this, she suffered an emotion that impeded her speech for an instant—"that he was willing to undertake my cause without a second thought. All that it was in his power to do, he would do; even to the extent of entertaining Trowbridge the very night of our bridal ball."

"And you, Isobel? Did you bear him equal love?"

"I thought that what I felt might be called by that name," my friend replied faintly, her hand going to her throat. "Perhaps I deluded myself from a wish to obtain that security he so nobly offered. Oh, how to explain the man that was my husband, Jane?" She sank once more to her chaise, her attitude all despondency.

"He seemed a respectable gentleman," I observed.

"Jane! Jane! Such coldness for poor Frederick!" Isobel's eyes filled with tears. "Lord Scargrave was not young, as you saw, except in his vivacity of spirit and the energy he brought to each of his dearest projects. He was a man of great warmth and good humour, yet could betray the iron of his ancestors when pressed. I admired Frederick, I respected him, I felt towards him a depth of gratitude I could not help but express—I *esteemed* him, Jane, as a daughter might esteem a father. Indeed, I wonder ofttimes if it was not a second father I sought when I threw myself upon the marriage market."

"But love, Isobel?" I persisted.

She was silent, reflecting, her eyes upon the flames. Of a sudden she shivered, and I hastened to draw her lap robe over her. "You must not get a chill, my dear, for we have had too much of violent illness."

The Countess smiled sadly and shook her head. "It is not the cold that would carry me off, dear Jane, but an enormity of regret."

"For your husband?"

"And myself," she replied softly, her eyes finding mine. "I had not known love as a girl. Silly flirtations I had by the score, of course—one could not help it. But the day I married the Earl I knew what it was to feel a deeper emotion, and God help me, it was not for the man I married."

All speech was impossible at so painful a revelation. There can be no proper answer to such anguish—and anguish Isobel clearly felt, had felt during the brief tenure of her marriage, and could not silence even at her husband's untimely end. I could well imagine that the Earl's death had increased, rather than absolved, her sorrow, by heightening her sense of having done him a terrible wrong—a wrong now past all repair.

"The Earl had no notion?" I settled myself on a chair opposite her chaise and took comfort in the heat of the flames. The parkland beyond the Countess's windows was now utterly dark, and the sharp December cold pressed against the house.

Isobel shook her head. "I pray God he did not. Such a betrayal of his best impulses he could not have borne. For his sake, I adopted the strictest propriety; and Fitzroy did the same. No dishonour should come to the man he revered almost as a father while his actions could prevent it.

"That we may have betrayed our sensibility in countless small ways, I do not doubt, when I read that despicable letter," she continued, gesturing towards Marguerite's note. "Not least among the emotions it causes is fear for my husband's sake. If *she* saw, who is but a servant, what may *he* not have seen, and kept to himself in silence?"

I hastened to reassure my friend. "A lady's maid may be even more in her mistress's company than her husband, Isobel. You know it to be true. Marguerite may conjecture only, and her stab in the dark has gone home. From your husband's easy good humour two nights past, I must believe he thought himself the happy man who had won all of your affection."

"You speak with conviction, Jane." Isobel's accent was eager. "Did you yourself believe it?"

"I did, until the very moment when Lord Payne dismissed the devil Trowbridge. The Viscount then betrayed a concern for your welfare beyond what is usual in a nephew towards a newly-met aunt. Oh, Isobel, how could two such people as yourselves, possessed of probity and good sense, forget what is due to propriety?"

A log burst of a sudden upon the hearth, scattering glowing embers at our feet, and Isobel started, her eyes on her husband's portrait. I bent for the poker and busied myself at the grate.

My friend touched a trembling hand to her lips. "It does seem mad, I will own," she replied, "as only such love can be." She drew breath, and with it perhaps, courage to go on.

"Fitzroy is the true companion of my soul, Jane; we think as with one thought, and when deprived of the chance to speak, may find converse in a look enough to sustain us."

Her words had a particular power to strike at my heart, being virtually the same as those I had uttered once to myself, about another young man forever out of reach.[1] Clumsily, I dropped the poker, and covered my confusion in retrieving it.

Isobel perceived my dismay, and misinterpreted its cause. Her next words were accordingly sharp. "But I cannot possibly make *you* know this with all the force of sensibility I feel; not for our practical Jane an indulgence

---

1. It is unclear from the text of which former suitor Jane is thinking. Because these manuscripts were intended as private journals, occasional passages exist where Jane is clearly "talking to herself."—*Editor's note.*

in emotion. It will be enough to make you understand how it came about."

I was wounded, I will own, for there was a time when such feeling was all I lived for; but that time is past. I resolved not to reproach Isobel for words spoken in the midst of trouble, and endeavoured to put aside self-interest. "Indeed, my dear, I would hear it," I told her, retrieving my chair, "if it be that you wish to speak."

Isobel had the grace to look abashed at my kindness, and turned without further preamble to her unfortunate history.

"I first met Fitzroy during the height of the London season, when my engagement to the Earl was already fixed, and my aunt and cousin Fanny had joined me at rooms in Town," she began.

"I recall your letters of that period. They betrayed no unhappiness, but rather excited expectation of the months ahead."

"How could they do otherwise?" my friend cried. "We were to embark upon that most frivolous and light-hearted of ladies' enterprises—the purchase of my wedding clothes. My aunt is well-acquainted with the best warehouses, as you may imagine from having heard her discourse on mourning; and she was invaluable to me in the acquisition of a Countess's wardrobe. I should not have denied her the pleasure in any case; such a venture was to be but the rehearsal for her daughter's wedding, her dearest concern."

"I may be thankful my own mother's inclinations are in a less material direction," I said dryly, "for I should assuredly be the ruin of her hopes."

Having met with my mother frequently while in Bath, Isobel could not repress a smile; but her sad tale reclaimed her attention. "Lord Payne was newly resident in his uncle's Town home, having left his estate in Derbyshire for the season. Fitzroy immediately became the object of my aunt Delahoussaye's excited speculation; for where one union is effected in a family, and the respective members thrown much together, another may well be formed; and to see her daughter as heir apparent to the title I was to assume, by marrying my *husband's* heir, became my aunt's primary object."

"It reigns unabated among her schemes," I could not refrain from saying; "I was nearly pulled from the dance the other evening in Madame Delahoussaye's eagerness to secure Lord Payne as her daughter's partner."

"And that, after I had already asked Fitzroy to lead Fanny in the first dance, behind his uncle and myself. He detests nothing so much as dancing, however he excels at it; and he regards standing up with Fanny as a punishment. He should rather have partnered you, my dear Jane—he told me so himself."

"I am flattered. But we digress."

"In London, my husband-to-be was frequently attended by his men of business, and prevented from escorting me to the season's gaieties as often as he might like. Frederick found it no difficulty, however, to send Fitzroy in his place, and my aunt was ready enough to have Fanny make a third." Isobel stopped short, overcome by memory.

"How many hours the three of us strolled Bond Street, Jane, a lady on Fitzroy's either side; or took the air of the Park in our carriage, Fitzroy seated opposite with Fanny at his right hand. It gradually became a torment; his mind and mine were too much alike not to leap at the chance to converse; we found much in common that thrilled and moved; and yet behind the growing felicity in one another's company, there was a burgeoning despair. The inevitability of my fate approached—and to dishonour the man who had done so much for each of us was impossible. That we thought severally in this vein, without speaking of it to the other—that we had never spoken of the feeling that overcame us in one another's presence—I need not assure you. Such a speech could not but harm." She fell silent, lost in despondency.

"Until?" I prompted.

The Countess hesitated, as if unwilling to repeat in speech the indiscretions of the past. "Until the day Fanny suffered a slight indisposition, due to her greediness for cold stuffing at dinner the previous evening."

"It prevented her from accompanying you the next day?"

"It did. We had formed the design of a visit to Hampton Court, by barge up the Thames, and visit we did—though the party was formed of but two." My dear friend's face was suddenly transformed. "The delight in those few hours, Jane! The carefree happiness of our day! What laughter, what meaning in silence, what trembling in my hand as I took his arm to promenade! We moved through stately rooms and terraced gardens as though they were ours and we had come into our kingdom. A marvelous charade. For a time, we might play at what we never could be."

A little of Isobel's emotion affected my senses, and I strove for calm. "And you spoke, then, of the future?"

"How could we not?" Her glad aspect dimmed. "But it was a discourse saved for the waning of the day, when the long shadows proclaimed our liberty at an end, our paradise lost. In contemplating the necessity of a return, the duplicity it meant, Fitzroy found that he could not bear it; and in the shadow of a great tree in the Court gardens, he seized me in his arms and . . . kissed me, Jane."

I was silent with pity and horror.

"The memory of it burns upon my lips still," Isobel said, reaching a finger to her mouth. "It was to burn in my heart all that night, as I dined with poor Frederick; and dined with Fitzroy, who sat opposite as though turned to stone."

My friend's hand found mine and grasped it tightly. "Have you ever felt, Jane, a crushing sadness while at the same time experiencing a heady euphoria?"

I could only shake my head, unwilling to share my own poor fortune.

"Then you have never been in love," Isobel said decidedly, "and you did right not to accept Mr. Bigg-Wither."

"But what was the outcome, my dear?" I persisted. "Did you never consider a full disclosure to Lord Scargrave?"

"No, Jane. That could not be. We declared our love, canvassed our mutual honour and the esteem we owed the Earl, and came to a tortured resignation. I could not destroy Fitzroy by dishonouring his uncle—as destroy him I should. To do so would bring misery upon all in the Earl's household, and burden the purer emotions we felt with regret and recrimination."

"But how could you go forward?" I cried, all amazement.

Isobel looked her confusion. "I know that *you* should not have done so, dear Jane. With *your* strength and sense, you should have broken off the engagement and retired from the scene." She hesitated, as though her next words caused her pain. "But I had Crosswinds to consider, and all that Lord Scargrave had vouched he would do. For the sake of my father's memory, I determined that I could not choose otherwise than to marry the Earl."

"And Lord Payne? What of him?"

"We deemed it best to part company until the fateful day was achieved. Fitzroy offered the Earl some excuse, and fled to the country. I was married not two weeks later, toured the Continent for some three months, and returned to Scargrave for the Christmas holiday."

"I wonder how you bore it," I said.

"Did not you see the change?" Isobel burst out. "You, who are my dearest friend in the world—did not you discern that I was in the throes of some great trouble?"

"I did not, Isobel," I replied, wondering at my own stupidity. "I thought you only a trifle wearied by the duties of your new station. And that is for the best, my dear—for if I did not discern it, you may be assured your husband was equally in the dark."

"How terrible," the Countess murmured, "that one should find the ignorance of a husband to be a blessing."

"And so you had not met again, the Viscount and yourself, until the night of the ball?" I resumed.

She shook her head. "It was for this I begged your presence on the occasion, my dear Jane. I dearly needed the strength of a friend beside me at such an hour. That Fitzroy came at all was necessary to the duty he owed his uncle; to have stayed away would have seemed strange. But he did not meet me with composure. And I believe his feelings are as unabated by the passage of a few months, as I know my own to be."

"Isobel," I began, and rose to stand before the fire with the maid's crumpled letter in my hand, "we must consider what we are to do. Marguerite claims she will go to the magistrate; we have determined to lay the business before him ourselves, and so prevent her the element of surprise. To contain the affair, this would seem the only course. But what then? Do you disclose what you must to Sir William regarding your feeling for Fitzroy?"

Isobel started from her chaise, cheeks scarlet and eyes ablaze with indignation. "It is impossible! In every respect, impossible!"

"You will dissimulate, then?"

"I shall regard the suggestion as of a piece with the rest of the maid's nonsense—no more to be believed than her accusation of murder," she retorted, with spirit.

"To what, then, do we ascribe her motive? That must be our question." I stopped beneath the Earl's portrait and regarded it thoughtfully. "We must tell Sir William we believe Marguerite capable of blackmail; that she wishes to frighten you into paying for her silence. A paltry art from a paltry maid. He must see the sense of it."

Isobel moved swiftly to her desk in search of pen and paper. "Of course, Jane. It has merit. I shall ring for the footman directly; he may take my note to Sir William. I think it best we meet after the funeral tomorrow, do not you agree?"

"Propriety would argue the same."

"So it shall be."

"Isobel—" I began, and then hesitated. Why disturb further what was already disturbed beyond imagining?

"Jane?"

"You *are* certain in your mind that your husband died of natural causes?"

"Why should I not be?"

"Why, indeed?"

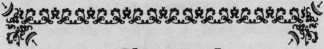

Chapter 5

Lest Old Acquaintance Be Forgot

15 December 1802
~

MY DEAREST CASSANDRA—

You asked that I write you once Lord Scargrave was in the ground, and tell you of the particulars.

The day dawned stormy and soon commenced to snow quite hard, so that we were bundled into closed chariots for the journey to the Reverend Samuels's service in the little church of Scargrave Close. The Reverend is an elderly man, of pinched and nearsighted appearance; he looks to be consumptive and not a little wandering in his wits, as he more than once addressed the deceased by his father's name, and on one occasion by his brother's, both of whom have preceded the Earl from this life. The poor health of the celebrant and his vague demeanour explain why his society is not sought at Scargrave; they bode well for the rapidity with which George Hearst may succeed to the living, if matters are disposed in the Earl's will as Mr. Hearst has reason to hope.

There was, as can be imagined, little remarkable in the good Reverend's eulogy. It was a solemn recitation of the Earl's worldly passage that might have been taken from the account of a London journal, rather than any intimate knowledge of Lord Scargrave's character. I find that there is nothing sadder than such a ceremony, when it is marked by indifference and ignorance of its subject. Better to be celebrated by those whom one has known and loved, than dispatched by a relative stranger, of incongenial habits and temperament, with whom one has passed no more than the trivialities of social necessity. But such was the Earl of Scargrave's fate.

As is the custom, however, only the gentlemen of the family walked behind the carriage bearing his body to the great Scargrave tomb, where his first Countess already lies slumbering; and given the heavy fall of snow, I profess for once having been pleased with the lot accorded my sex. The women repaired to the Manor, there to indulge in that excess of grief considered necessary in any lady of delicacy and breeding; knowing my delicacy, and still more my breeding, you need not be told that few tears fell from my eye. I confess to a period of contemplative silence, however, during which I reflected upon the suddenness of the Earl's passage from this life, and the upcoming interview with Sir William Reynolds—yes, Sir William Reynolds, our dear friend of old, who has traded London for Hertfordshire upon his retirement, and is now turned the local magistrate.

You have from me the particulars of the maid Marguerite's letter in my last,[1] though if I refrained from conveying with perfect frankness all that Isobel discussed that day, you must forgive me. What I heard, I heard in confidence, and there the matter ends. Suffice it to say that we look forward this afternoon to presenting a blackmailer's mark to a man of the law,

1. This letter, presumably the one in which Jane imparted the news of the Earl's death to her sister, is no longer contained in the journal.—*Editor's note.*

and have hopes that our actions may stem unfortunate rumour.

I fear that Christmas at Scargrave will be a grim affair, and could wish myself returned to Bath and my beloved sister, were it not for the comfort Isobel seems to draw from my presence.

I send you my love, and ask that you convey it as well to my father and mother.

Yours very affectionately,
J. A.

Journal entry, later that day

~

WE WERE ASSEMBLED FOR TEA IN THE GREAT SCARGRAVE drawing-room when Cobblestone, the stooped and aged Scargrave butler, announced Sir William. Despite Isobel's anxious looks, I was relieved to observe that his visit was taken as nothing out of the ordinary way by the other members of the family.

"He is come, I suppose, to offer condolence," said Fitzroy Payne.

"And to secure his position with the new Earl, no doubt," threw in Tom Hearst, as Cobblestone withdrew. The Lieutenant stabbed viciously with a poker at a log burning too slowly for his taste, and sent up a shower of sparks. "These petty local justices are all of a piece. Keep firm hold on their sinecures, eat heartily of mutton and ale at the local *fêtes,* and concern themselves little with matters beyond their purses."

"A failing they hold in common with the petty local gentry," came a sepulchral voice in reply.

All eyes turned to Mr. George Hearst, sunk in his armchair in the farthest corner of the room, a volume of *Fordyce's Sermons* open upon his knee. "We cannot expect the men we appoint to govern us, to be better than ourselves. Did Sir William not curry favour at the Manor, it should be a miracle; for assuredly, brother, you and I have been attempting it all our lives."

"I think you mistake, cousin," cried the new Earl, with becoming energy. "Sir William is late of the King's Bench,[2] a barrister known for his perspicacity; and though Scargrave Close may offer little to challenge his wits after London's broad humanity, he is no less careful of his office, for all that." Fitzroy Payne turned to Lord Harold Trowbridge, who sat apart in a high-backed wing chair, watching all that occurred with the lidded eyes of a hawk. "I believe you have reason to fear Sir William's wits, Lord Harold. You encountered him more than once when he was in the Exchequer, did you not?"

A slow smile spread across the narrow, dark face. "He has had his moments of good fortune. At my expense. And I have had mine, at his."

"A barrister in retirement! But this is capital!" the Lieutenant exclaimed. "My fellows at the Cock and Bull had best look to their pints, and find another place to carouse, now a prop of the law is come to Scargrave!"

"If Sir William serves to moderate even *your* dissipation, Tom, we may count his presence a blessing," George Hearst rejoined. A painful pause threatened to silence us all; but I dare say Mr. Spinoza entertained the notion of Fanny Delahoussaye when he declared that nature abhors a vacuum. She rose to the defence of her favourite with more haste than discretion.

"The Bar, of all professions, must be declared the most vulgar," she avowed, with a look for Tom Hearst in his blue coat. "In physick we may detect a nobler calling, despite its trappings of trade, in the saving of lives; the Church is redeemed by the sanctity of its purpose; and the military life, of course, is to be preferred above all others for its bravery and fortitude."

Miss Fanny's pretty speech was interrupted here by a

2. Three London courts heard common-law cases—King's Bench, the Exchequer, and Common Pleas. A King's Bench barrister would try criminal cases; an Exchequer barrister, disputes over money (customs duties, taxes, fines) owed the Crown, and a Common Pleas barrister, small claims.—*Editor's note.*

contemptuous snort from her mother, who cast a venomous look at Tom Hearst. The Lieutenant merely grinned at Madame, and bowed in her daughter's direction.

"But how are we to praise the Bar?" Miss Delahoussaye continued, undaunted. "A nasty meddling in the concerns of debtors, cutthroats, and swindlers, the lowest form of society, for a fee one must pretend not to take by sending the bill through one's solicitors![3] I should not marry a barrister for anything in the world!"

"And he, my dear," Lord Harold said from his corner, "would certainly be ill-advised to marry *you*."

Sir William Reynolds was shown in upon the heels of this curt remark. The new Earl he greeted first, as befit the highest peer in the room; then he turned to the Countess with a bow. Lord Harold Trowbridge he offered but a nod, tho' if he recalled the moments the duke's son had won at his expense, Sir William's face gave no sign. When he had made his courtesies to the Delahoussayes and the Hearsts, I rose to greet him with my hand extended, and said with real pleasure, "Sir William! What good fortune that we should meet again, after so many years!"

"Miss Austen, to be sure!" The smile that suffused his merry old face was like a ray of sun in that mordant atmosphere. "A pleasure for which I could not have hoped! And how is your dear father?"

"Very well, sir, when last we met. I shall be pleased to send him equally good news of yourself."

"You are acquainted with Sir William, Miss Austen?" the Earl broke in, with wonder.

"Indeed, my lord, since I was a child."

3. Because solicitors brought cases to barristers for trial, and collected the fee as a "gratuity" in thanks for the barristers' efforts, solicitors were considered tradesmen while barristers preserved their status as gentlemen. The same distinction prevailed between physicians—educated professionals who could be received at Court—and surgeons, village doctors who could not.—*Editor's note.*

"I was at Oxford with her father," the good man said, his face beaming, "and stood godparent to one of her brothers. How is the rascal?"

"Charles is faring well in his naval career, though Frank, his elder, continues to outstrip him."

"As he should! As he should!" Sir William exclaimed, and smiled all around until, recollecting the reason for his presence in a house of mourning, he assumed a more becoming gravity.

Sir William Reynolds is that mixture of quick parts and good humour, unabashed affection and deceptive shrewdness, that makes for a candid and invigorating acquaintance. He had left his practice at the Bar and his clerks at the King's Bench some five months past, upon receiving his knighthood, and had settled in Scargrave Close to enjoy his remaining years, much as my father had chosen the retreat of Bath. The honour of his elevation had done little to impair his easy manners; Sir William was not the sort to adopt a false pride, but rather a heightened civility, a useful quality in his current duties as justice of the peace. That his good sense might make short work of Isobel's trouble, I was completely assured.

"My very deepest and most sincere condolences, my lady," Sir William said, with a bow to my friend.

"Thank you, Sir William." Isobel's hand went to her throat, a gesture that has become familiar. I feared for a moment that she might faint, and would have moved to her aid; but Fitzroy Payne was before me. In an instant he placed a chair at her disposal, with a tender look that betrayed all his concern. For, indeed, Isobel is a changed woman entirely.

The Countess bears the marks of extreme fatigue upon her countenance, the result not merely of this morning's melancholy duties but of broken repose. In Marguerite's absence, she will suffer no one to do up her hair, and so the pretty ringlets that once graced her brow are now severely drawn back. Her mourning dress proclaims itself as last worn in respect of her late father, it being some three years out of fashion; she has neither time nor inclination to consult a mantua-maker for anything new. With her fixed pallor and eyes reddened from weeping, my friend is far from lovely; except that there might be a sort of loveliness in her pitiable desolation.

"You are very good, Sir William, to venture out in the snow on the late Earl's behalf," Fitzroy Payne said, in an effort, I thought, to fill an awkward pause. I felt all my apprehension at his remark, knowing that Sir William was present by Isobel's invitation, and undoubtedly wondering at its cause.

"Do you find Scargrave Close a congenial place, Sir William?" I broke in, somewhat desperately.

A hint of amusement suffused the old barrister's face as he inclined his head in my direction. "Most congenial, Miss Austen, most congenial. The late Earl was a man of probity and discipline, and the surrounding country reveals his hand. You face a difficult task, Lord Scargrave, in assuming your uncle's duties."

"Well do I know it, sir," Fitzroy Payne replied feelingly, his dark gaze turned inward, "and I had thought to enjoy long years of study before assuming the role. Not the least of my regrets at my uncle's death is the knowledge that all chance for learning is past, however imperfect my present abilities."

"Man is ever overtaken by Death like a child by sleep—too soon, and with much lamenting," George Hearst broke in. His spectral voice, emanating from a chair by the fire, fell upon my ears with all the heaviness of the grave. "We are formed from regret, and with regret we ever leave this earthly life."

Fanny Delahoussaye rolled her eyes, for Tom Hearst's benefit, and at that gentleman's answering grin, she abruptly put aside her needlework and abandoned her chair. "I feel a trifle indisposed, Mamma," she announced, with the most angelic of smiles and a curtsey for Isobel; "I believe I shall go to my room."

"Fanny," Madame Delahoussaye said, with a touch of warning in her tone, "Sir William has only just arrived. You forget yourself, my dear."

"Indeed, I do not. Did I forget myself, I might remain in Sir William's company for hours, Mamma," Fanny said plaintively. "It is because I *cannot* forget myself that I must bid Sir William *adieu.*"

"I should think a walk in the Park might improve your spirits," Lieutenant Hearst observed.

"I am certain that it should." Fanny turned without further ado and hastened from the drawing-room.

"Fanny—" Madame set down her needlework, her eyes on Tom Hearst, who had thrust himself away from the hearth.

"Do not disturb yourself, dear Madame," the Lieutenant said, bending gallantly over her hand. "I shall make certain your daughter comes to no harm."

"But it snows!" Madame Delahoussaye cried, Sir William forgotten. She snatched her hand from Tom Hearst's with a baleful look and hastened after Fanny.

The Lieutenant threw back his head and laughed aloud, much to Fitzroy Payne's dismay and, to judge by his countenance, Lord Harold Trowbridge's amusement. *That* gentleman had set aside his London journal, the better to observe Tom Hearst's tricks. But he rose now in Madame Delahoussaye's wake, and clapped the Lieutenant on the shoulder.

"You had much better play at cards with me, my good fellow," Trowbridge told him. "Leave the chit to her mamma."

"I must offer my apologies, Sir William," Fitzroy Payne said, with a heightened gravity, as Trowbridge and the Lieutenant bowed and turned towards the hall. "I fear our household is in some disarray. The Earl's passing has made us all unlike ourselves."

"Or perhaps," George Hearst observed from his corner, "more truly *like* ourselves?" He closed his book and rose, of a mind to follow his brother. "I fear, Sir William, that Death has forced us all to reckon with mortality. And so you find us as we shall probably face our graves—with determined frivolity, indifferent tempers, and general regret."

"I am sorry to hear it," Sir William replied. "I had always aspired to meet my Maker armed with a comfortably full stomach and a good night's rest."

My old friend's good humour was lost upon Mr. Hearst.

"Then you would indeed be fortunate," he gravely observed, "and in a measure but rarely accorded your fellows. I am sure my uncle wished for the same—with the added thought that Death, however inevitable, was better met on a more distant day. You see how little his hopes availed him. Not all the power and wealth the Earl of Scargrave might summon, could command him another hour of life."

"Assuredly," Sir William said, with an uneasy glance for the Countess. Isobel's brown eyes looked overly-large in her white face, and they were fixed dreadfully upon Mr. Hearst. "You have undoubtedly profited by your uncle's example."

"The Earl loved to instruct, Sir William, however little his pupils warranted the lesson." This last was spoken with an edge of bitterness, and George Hearst's mouth set into a hard line. I thought, as I gazed at him, how little he resembled his brother; where the Lieutenant's eyes were wont to dance, Mr. Hearst's were hollow; and the excellent moulding of the cavalryman's features was turned harsh and angular in the ecclesiastic's. An expression of abstraction swept over his face as I studied it, and with the briefest of nods for us all, Mr. Hearst left the drawing-room. Sir William expelled a heavy sigh, as though shifting a burdensome weight, and turned to Lord Scargrave with a smile.

"Well, my lord, if the spectre of Death has shown us *your* truest self, we may rest easy in the stewardship of the earldom. For in your own case, Lord Payne—or should I say, Lord Scargrave—only an increase in your usual sense, estimable self-restraint, and good breeding is evident. Rarely has a gentleman conducted himself with such dignity, in the midst of so much—distraction."

Fitzroy Payne merely inclined his head, but I silently

applauded my old friend; he had perfectly described the newly-titled Earl. The more I observe of Isobel's lover, the more I must commend him. Fitzroy Payne chose to suffer in silence rather than dishonour his uncle; and the strength of character required cannot fail to move me. I set aside all questions as to the *propriety* of his caring for Isobel in the first place; it is enough to know that he mastered the feeling when it proved most necessary, to the preservation of her honour as well as his own.

With the Earl departed this life, however, and Isobel free—but all such thoughts must await Sir William's better understanding. A blackmailer is still at large, and the faintest air of scandal can blight a thousand tender hopes.

"Ah, a pot of tea," Sir William said, as the footman, Fetters, appeared, bearing a tray before him; "exactly what an old man requires to throw off the chill." He bent himself to his saucer, and all conversation ceased.

"Lord—Scargrave," Fetters said to Fitzroy Payne, "I am asked by Mr. Cobblestone to tell you as the solicitors are come."

"Again? And on the very day of my uncle's service? It is not to be borne."

"I have put them in the libr'y, milord."

"Very well, Fetters. I shall attend them presently." Fitzroy Payne looked to Isobel for comfort, but my friend's eyes were on the fire, and if she had registered aught of the previous conversation, I should judge it a miracle.

The new Earl bowed to Sir William and silently withdrew; and at the closing of the door, Isobel started and looked about her.

"I fear I have presumed upon your attention, my lady," Sir William said, and rose from his chair. "It is unjust to tax the patience of so much sorrow. Please accept my apologies and my *adieux*."

"Indeed, Sir William, you do not presume. It is I who must be faulted for calling you here so precipitately, and then lacking the courage to speak."

"Is there some trouble in train, my lady?"

Isobel's beautiful eyes fixed upon the magistrate's shrewd ones, and she studied his countenance thoughtfully. Then she turned to me without a word in reply. "Jane," she said, "I would speak with you."

I followed her into the hall, where lately her husband's body had lain; the scent of dying flowers and beeswax hung heavy in the air.

"Since you are so well acquainted with the magistrate," Isobel began, in a nervous accent, "could not *you* impart to him some sense of what has occurred? I should feel easier in my mind if one who knew his character were to speak with him; for I confess he is a stranger to me, Jane."

"But of course, Isobel," I said, reaching for her hand. I was shocked to find it remarkably chill. "I shall make a show of returning with him to Scargrave Close in his carriage, the better to pay my respects to Lady Reynolds."

"Oh, Jane!" Isobel cried, her eyes filling with tears, "and in such weather!" She cast her gaze upon the window's bleak prospect of snow. "You are very good to me."

"How is it possible to be otherwise?" I replied, and squeezed her cold fingers affectionately. "Do not trouble about a little wind and wet, Isobel. You may consider the matter as settled."

EVENTS FELL OUT AS I HAD DESIGNED, AND WE WERE NOT three minutes under way in Sir William's comfortable chariot, the snow still falling softly about the lanterns that had been lit against the gathering dark, when he cleared his throat and embarked upon a subject of pressing concern to us both.

"Now, my Jane, perhaps you may tell me why the Countess summoned an old man out in such weather, and then escaped to her room with barely a word? I should almost believe her note of yesterday a subterfuge of your own, for renewing old acquaintance!"

"Indeed, sir, there was a darker purpose, and though

I intend no dishonour to Lady Reynolds in avowing it, I should not be calling at your home this evening were I not charged with revealing it."

"Ah! The matter gains in interest," the magistrate said, his satisfaction in his voice. "Speak!"

I handed him the maid Marguerite's piece of foolscap, and let the ill-written words speak in my stead.

Sir William rummaged among the pockets of his greatcoat for some spectacles, and took a moment to settle them on his nose. In the darkness of the chariot's interior, his eyes strained to make sense of the handwriting. "Very curious," he said, after several moments' silent perusal. "When was this received?"

"Yesterday."

"Have you an idea of the author?"

"We believe it to be Isobel's maid, a Creole girl by the name of Marguerite. She has decamped, and cannot be found, though Isobel sent some trusty fellows in pursuit when her absence was discovered last night."

"And so the Countess is become afraid," Sir William said slowly, "that the evil tongue of rumour is unleashed upon the land. A nasty business for one so shortly married."

"Or so recently widowed. She feels it most acutely," I said, "and would have a stop to such vicious talk."

"There are two accusations contained herein," Sir William said bemusedly, "that she has taken a lover among the peerage, and that she has done away with her husband, with or without her lover's help. One would think there could hardly have been time for all that—she's not many days returned from her wedding trip, I believe?"

"But a fortnight."

"And so the gentleman must have been in her acquaintance before the wedding, and thrown in her way once again upon her return. There cannot be many such fellows in Scargrave, beyond the family itself." And with this last, Sir William appeared to have heard the sense of his words for the first time, and was lost in painful speculation. There was but one lord among the Scargrave family now that the Seventh Earl was dead, and so the magistrate took Marguerite's meaning.

"Dear, dear," Sir William said, turning his gaze once more upon the note, "this *does* put a rather nasty complexion upon it."

"Marguerite would have us look to a lord, but does not tell us which," I said. "She might as well intend Lord Harold as Lord Payne."

"Lord Scargrave, you mean; for so we must call him, from this day forward. But tell me of Trowbridge—is he a near acquaintance of the late Earl?"

"A very recent acquaintance, I believe."

"And yet he remains in the household, when all but those with a special claim on the affections of the family, such as yourself, should long since have left. It is like a man of his cheek."

"It is very singular," I said, with feeling; I could see no reason for Trowbridge's continued presence at Scargrave, and found him a burden on the entire household.

"Indeed," said Sir William. "But Trowbridge is a singular fellow. More than once he has pulled the wool over the Crown's eyes in the matter of some sugar duties on his West Indies imports. When last I heard, he was backing opium runners trading for tea in the South China Sea. I should not have thought to find him in Scargrave, and at such a time; I have long thought death to be the only thing the man fears. And what do you surmise is his motive for such indelicacy?"

"I had understood him to be awaiting the Countess's disposition of some business matters."

"So it is the *Countess* who is acquainted with Lord Harold. And as a business partner, too. That *does* give one pause."

"I believe the term *partner* to be inaccurately applied, Sir William," I said sharply. "Lord Harold merely seeks the Countess's interest, but he is very far from securing it."

Sir William peered at me narrowly, but deigned not to comment. He tapped the poisonous letter and pursed his lips. "If Lord Harold is the man, we must ask what the maid might know of her mistress's business. A great deal, or a very little, depending upon the character of the maid. What think you, Jane?"

"That Marguerite has formed a tissue of lies," I replied, with more stoutness than I felt. A clergyman's daughter may use wit at times, and candour whenever possible, but conscious deceit is more likely to fail her.

"And to what purpose?"

"With the intent of extorting payment for her silence."

"I see no request for sovereigns here," Sir William said.

"I should be very much surprised if that does not appear in the next letter."

"The one I am intended to receive?"

"So we are told."

"Not a very intelligent course, surely? For *I* cannot be expected to pay her."

"She is a very foolish girl," I finished lamely.

"Aha. So you say," the magistrate muttered dubiously, and folded the paper away in his waistcoat. "You were present at the Earl's death, I believe?"

"Not at the moment of his passing, but I observed some part of his illness."

"And what did you conclude?"

I hesitated, and the pause revealed me as less certain of matters than I would wish.

"Come, come, Jane!" Sir William chided. "You are not a blushing girl, given to airs and sighs; you have your wits about you, as I've always approved, and are readier than any I know to form a judgment when the facts stare you in the face. Was it a death you could ascribe to natural causes?"   "In truth, sir, I must own it was not, though the physician would have it otherwise," I told him. "The violence of the Earl's illness was such as I had never witnessed, except under the influence of a deadly purgative."

"Indeed," Sir William said softly. "Indeed. And yet

they called it dyspepsia. I had a few bad moments myself in hearing the news of Frederick's death; I swore off claret for a twelvemonth, though my resolve lasted but two days. The suddenness of his passing shook me. It disturbed you as well?"

"I cannot deny it, though I alone of the Scargrave household felt apprehension."

"That is hardly to be remarked, my dear," Sir William said dryly. "You alone had nothing to inherit."

I STOPPED IN SIR WILLIAM'S HOUSEHOLD LONG ENOUGH TO greet his dear lady, to hear her news of three daughters and four sons long claimed by marriage and profession, exclaim over the domestic arrangements of her new home, and offer what intelligence of my circle in Bath it was in my power to convey. Then Sir William very kindly ordered his carriage to the door once more, against the protests of his wife, who would have had me stop the night rather than venture out again in such weather.

"It takes more than snow to hinder our Jane," Sir William said fondly, as he handed me into the carriage. "I shall communicate with you directly I receive the letter."

The last sight of his bare white head, starred with falling flakes like a Saint Nicholas of old, was to be my comfort the length of that solitary return to Scargrave. It is much, indeed, to have a friend down the lane, when a murderer may be among the household.

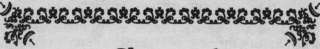

Chapter 6

The Dark Angel

16 December 1802

~

I WAS ENGAGED BY MY JOURNAL WELL INTO THE EVENING
last night, tucked up in my sombre room with the fire
burned low and all the house, as I thought, abed; but
sleep remained elusive, though the great clock in the hall
below would chime eleven, and then the quarter- and the
half-hour. I determined at the last to snuff out my candle
and attempt to find some rest, though the doubts and
fears that have occupied my waking hours *would* fill my
head with a riotous clamour.

I had consigned the room to dark, and placed my head
upon the pillow, when the clock struck midnight; and as
the final toll died away, I heard a rhythmic creaking, as of
a measured pacing, commence along the floorboards of
the gallery beyond my door. The sound—unremarkable
in daylight—caused me now to stiffen with apprehension
and bate my breath. It was the very height of the witching
hour, when dread comes easy to the mind. That the shade
of the First Earl had come to mourn poor Frederick,
his descendant, I might almost have believed; for rather
than cease with entering a room or passing from the

hall, as the footsteps of any mortal inmate of Scargrave should do, the footsteps continued their curious dragging movement.[1]

An age it seemed I lay there, with all thought suspended, until I felt of a sudden that I should sooner die from fright of an apparition, than sweat in my bed from foolish fancies. I threw back the bedcovers, swung a cold foot to the floor, and crept to the door as soundlessly as I knew how. It but remained to turn the knob quietly and slowly, to crack the door an inch or two, and peer around the jamb.

In the dimness of the hall I saw him: a tall, gaunt figure dressed in the outmoded fashion of nearly two centuries past. A gossamer veiling concealed his head, which bore a long wig of cascading dark curls; his shoes were heeled and pitched forward in the fashion of the long-dead Sun King, and from their precarious perch he seemed to plod down the gallery on the tips of his toes. Cobwebs hung from his fingers, and from the hem of his satin coat; he was as dusty as a tailor's dummy fetched from a forgotten attic. The very shade of the First Earl, called from the dead to mourn the late Frederick; and to my thankfulness, the spectre had passed and was departing with turned back. I readied myself to observe him glide through the wall at the gallery's nether end, when he stopped before a closed chamber door, listening in the stillness, never moving a spectral muscle. I felt my skin prickle with consciousness. Would that he did not turn

1. Austen's tone in this passage evokes the breathless morbidity of the Gothic novels that were quite popular in her day. Such authors as Ann Radcliffe and Charlotte Smith penned ghoulish tales intended to titillate and alarm their largely female audience. Though Austen often poked fun at such literature—*Northanger Abbey* is in part a spoof of these novels—she *did* read them, and on this night at least, appears to have been somewhat influenced by their powerful fantasies.—*Editor's note.*

his face and stare with terrible eyes upon my night-clad form! But perhaps he felt the weight of my gaze; there could be no other cause for such suspension of purpose. The door before which he halted led to Fitzroy Payne's apartments; and I prayed for that gentleman to awake, and fright the ghost back into the ether, until I recollected that Lord Scargrave was even still bent over his uncle's papers in the late Earl's library. I drew breath, and disturbed the stillness; and with that, the shade's head began to turn.

I shot back around the doorjamb, my breathing and pulse quickening, waiting for the wrath of the undead to descend upon my room; but all remained silent—no creaking boards, no ghostly wind progressing down the hall. The spectre had not moved. Summoning my courage, I peeked back into the hall and saw with relief that the First Earl had vanished. Movement alone must be adequate to dispel a wraith; but I did not care to test the efficacy of my exorcism. I bolted the oak, fled to my bed, and pulled the covers over my head; and when the boards creaked once more, not long thereafter, I merely burrowed deeper.

AND SO I AM COME TO MY TWENTY-SEVENTH YEAR, WITH the bleary eyes and pale complexion of one robbed of sleep. My birthday has dawned with little of cheer to mark it; the sky is a lowering grey, and a chill wind rattles the leafless trees. I declare that I feel old this morning, despite the gallantries of Lieutenant Tom Hearst (more concerning *that* in time). There was less of the frightening in being five-and-twenty, or even six-and-twenty, than I feel today. There is something so *inevitable* about seven-and-twenty; it is decidedly on the wrong side of the decade for a lady, particularly an unmarried one. But none here at Scargrave is apprised of my birthday, and so I would keep it; too much of a serious nature demands our attention.

Having slept rather heavily in the wake of the ghost's

visit, I was a full half-hour late for breakfast. Tho' the custom at home is to take one's chocolate and rolls at ten o'clock, the sideboard in Scargrave's pretty little morning room is laid an hour earlier, as befits a country household. I thought to find the table deserted, and rejoiced at the prospect of solitude; the peace of bright yellow walls and fresh muslin curtains—a rare note of cheer amidst Scargrave's ponderous decoration—should be my reward for dissipation.

But to my surprise, I found Madame Delahoussaye still lingering over toast and tea.

"My dear Miss Austen!" she exclaimed, studying my pale countenance. "I am sure you slept very unwell."

"I suffered from nightmares, I am afraid," I said.

"It is written on your face, *ma pauvre*. You might almost have seen a ghost."

I peered at her narrowly, fearing myself to be a laughing-stock, but Madame's comfortable features and glittering dark eyes were innocent of intrigue.

"I had understood there to be a ghost at Scargrave," I said, as a footman pulled out my chair, "but I am a clergyman's daughter, Madame, and the perils of the grave must be as nothing to me."

"I rejoice to hear it," my breakfast companion said equably, replenishing her tea, "since your room lies along the First Earl's accustomed walk. Do you endeavour to fall asleep before midnight, my dear, for once you slumber, a wraith cannot hope to disturb you."

My reply was forestalled by the entrance of one of the housemaids, Daisy by name. She is Mrs. Hodges's granddaughter, and only sixteen, a youthfulness she appears to feel painfully in her current elevation—for in Marguerite's absence, Daisy has been placed at Isobel's disposal, and struggles daily to be worthy of her office. I surmised that her mistress had sent her in search of me, and threw down my serviette in haste.

Daisy bobbed in Madame's direction, and then in mine, the ribbons on her cap fluttering prettily. "Please, miss," she told me in a breathless accent, "milady says as she has had a note from Sir William, begging to call at eleven o'clock. Will you join milady then, miss, in the little sitting-room?"

"Of course, Daisy. You may inform your mistress I shall be delighted." I endeavoured to look undismayed, though I confess my thoughts were racing. It must be that Sir William had received a letter from the maid Marguerite—nothing short of urgency would bring him to the Manor so soon upon the heels of his first visit.

"I suppose the magistrate wishes to see as much of you as he may, while you remain at Scargrave, Miss Austen," Madame Delahoussaye said. I turned to survey her face, but it was suffused with only the mildest curiosity. "The discovery of old acquaintance here has assuredly heightened his gallantry. He can have no *other reason*, I suppose, for forcing himself upon a house of mourning?"

"Sir William is so respectable, and his intentions so amiable, Madame," I replied, with something of coldness in my accent, "that his presence can afford Scargrave nothing but relief. That the Countess does not hesitate to meet him must be enough to recommend him."

At her inclining her head, and the footman serving me with fresh chocolate, I endeavoured to converse of other things, the better to speed the meal to its close. Nearly two hours must be endured before I should hear Sir William's intelligence—time enough to lament Daisy's unfettered tongue, and wish that girls of sixteen might have less of the ingenuous and more of *discretion*.

BY THE TIME COBBLESTONE, THE BUTLER, THREW OPEN THE sitting-room door to announce Sir William, I was moved to greet the magistrate's white-haired head with almost violent relief. For my morning was a trial in forbearance—one I have resolved to offer up to my Maker as expiation for a twelvemonth of sins.

Fitzroy Payne was closeted in his library over some letters of business, the Hearst brothers remained in their

companionable bachelor cottage down the lane, while
Fanny Delahoussaye kept to the upstairs sitting room
with her mother and her sketching book—in horrified
anticipation, one may assume, of the visits of retired barristers. Isobel I did not expect to see until eleven o'clock
should strike. And so, sitting composedly by the hearth,
my hands occupied with needlework and my eyes upon
the clock, I was suffered to endure an hour's *tête-à-tête*
with Lord Harold Trowbridge. From closer observation,
I may declare that I have learned to *despise* the man's
cunning manner.

Most in the Scargrave household suffer his presence
with distant politeness that signals a profound dislike,
and a wish that he should be gone; but it is an atmosphere
to which Lord Harold appears utterly impervious. He
might almost be enjoying a holiday among friends, unmarked by calamitous events, rather than hovering like
a dark raven on the edge of so much that is disturbing
and intimate to the family. I have managed to avoid his
company, and rejoiced in my escape; but this morning he
appeared to have too little to occupy his time, and seemed
almost to profit from my discomfiture at being shut up
with him in the sitting-room.

I was already established a quarter-hour on the settee by the fire when he threw open the door and, after
a quick glance to observe that I was alone, strode purposefully into the room. I acknowledged his presence
with an indifferent nod, and hoped that studied application to my needle, and a dearth of conversation, should
drive him away in but a few moments. I bent, accordingly, to my work, and knew not where he went in the
room, or how he intended to employ his time. My in-
dustry was rather to be reviled than rewarded, however.
Setting down his book upon the sitting-room table with
a bang, Lord Harold threw himself onto the settee at
my side, and affected to scrutinise my effort from under
his hooded eyes—as a fond lover might his dearest darling's. After some seconds, unable to bear so painful a
burlesque, but wishing *anything* rather than to cede such

a man the room, I cast aside my work and stared at him balefully. Any *gentleman* should have recognised his impropriety, and hastened to relieve my distress; but not Lord Harold.

"It is as I thought," he declared, sitting back coolly and throwing his long legs across the hearth rug. "You secretly despise the insipidity of women's work, and abandon it when the first opportunity serves. Shall I shower you with contempt, Miss Austen, for failing in the accomplishment of your sisters, or admire you the more for exposing it as the tedium it truly is?"

"You may do me neither the honour nor the injustice, Lord Harold, of offending my sex and its pursuits," I replied. "Say rather I was incommoded by the proximity of so much silent regard, and the invasion of my privacy, and I will find some means to agree with you."

"You think it so unlikely we should see eye to eye, Miss Austen?"

"I should imagine, Lord Harold, that we two must always be looking in opposite directions—so dissimilar and incongenial are our concerns."

"Your opinion of me is decidedly formed for so short an acquaintance!"

"Then we need not prolong it for the improvement of my views." I gathered up my silks and needle, and exchanged the settee for a chair at some remove from Lord Harold—and thus, unfortunately, from the fire. Scargrave is a draughty place, and the expanse of sitting-room but poorly heated.

"Miss Austen! Did I not know you to be a woman of open and easy temper, I should imagine you wished me to be off." To my dismay, he crossed the room in my wake, and hung over the back of my chair—of a purpose, I suppose, to disturb me further. There was nothing for it—I must either seek my chamber above, or use my purgatory to better purpose. Lord Harold remained at Scargrave for only one reason—to wrest Crosswinds from Isobel's shaken hands—and the rogue deserved no courtesy. A frontal assault, therefore, was in order.

"I do wonder at your being so good as to spend Christmas among the Scargrave family, Lord Harold," I replied. "A man of your position must have so many obligations and competing claims among your acquaintance, that to devote so lengthy a period to *one* must be felt a singular honour."

"That it is regarded as singular, I do not doubt," he said, with a thin-lipped smile. "But in this we are very much of a piece, Miss Austen, for I observe you feel no more compelled to depart for home and family than do I."

"I should have been gone already," I replied, searching among my silks for a bit of red, the better to work a robin's breast, "but for the Countess."

"How charming! And how amusing that I may justly say the same—but for the Countess, I should have been gone days ago. I would that our objectives were equally benign, Miss Austen; but alas, they cannot be. And so we are ranged the one against the other, you and I—you, her light angel, stand firm against all the fury of my dark one." He moved to the fire and stood looking into its depths. The flickering light sharpened the planes of his face and threw his eyes into further shadow, so that his expression became if possible more remote and inscrutable. Gazing upon it, I felt for the first time truly afraid.

"I do not pretend to understand you, my lord," I said with effort, and applied myself to my needlework.

"I imagine you understand me very well, Miss Austen," he rejoined quietly, "and I confess to disappointment at your retreat into convention. It is unworthy of your intelligence and penetration."

"What can you know of either, my lord?"

"A great deal, when opportunity to observe is afforded me. But too often you run away at my approach, and would deny me the felicity of your wit."

"Say rather that I choose better company, Lord Harold, and I shall deign it to be possible."

"Capital, Miss Austen! Parry stroke for stroke. I

would that the Countess Scargrave were so deft in her opposition."

"Lord Harold," I said, summoning my courage, "I cannot profess to know all the particulars of what is toward between yourself and Lady Scargrave. It is right that I should remain in ignorance of affairs so delicate and so disputed. But I would ask you, my lord, why you persist in your efforts, having professed them to be ranged on the side of the Devil? In saying as much, are not you bound by honour, by better feeling, by all that is in your power as a peer and a gentleman, to desist?"

In reply, he threw back his head and laughed, and at that moment Cobblestone entered upon the scene, my venerable deliverer. Behind the butler stood Sir William Reynolds and Isobel.

"Lord Harold," Sir William said, bowing towards the fireplace, "Miss Austen. The Countess and I would speak with you alone, my dear Jane, and so I must ask Lord Harold to leave us."

"I believe I have outworn Miss Austen's patience in any event," Trowbridge said, with a mocking smile, and bowed low in my direction. "I look forward to trying it again, when opportunity serves." And with a nod for Sir William, and a courtesy to Isobel, he achieved the hall, to my mingled relief and chagrin.

"A more teasing man I have never encountered!" I exclaimed, when he had gone. "He finds his sole diversion in tormenting and vexing others, as a cat will toss a bird between its paws before the kill."

"An apt image, my dear Jane," Isobel murmured, looking towards the door through which her enemy had vanished; "I have reason to know well its meaning. But I would that you had been spared his company."

I gathered up my silks and canvas, and patted the seat beside me. "If I served to keep him from your door a little while, Countess, I may count the tedium as nothing."

"Is Trowbridge making a nuisance of himself, my lady?" Sir William enquired, as though our discussion of that gentleman yesterday in the magistrate's chariot had never occurred. Sir William hovered by the door, waiting, as he should, for Isobel to take her seat before seeking one of his own; and his lined face was all innocence.

He wishes to know exactly how far the Countess trusts him, I thought.

Isobel smiled faintly and settled herself by my side. "Lord Harold cannot be other than a nuisance, Sir William, but I fear that *that* is gossip for a different day. Your note suggested some urgency. What can have caused you to quit your pleasant abode on such a wintry morning?"

Something fluttered across Sir William's countenance and departed—a hope for Isobel's confidence, perhaps. He crossed the room slowly, his hand in his pocket and his gait marked by what I judged to be the effects of gout. "I have received an anonymous letter, my lady," he replied, handing a slip of paper to Isobel, "and having no reason to hope that its author would be discovered by *delay,* I hastened to acquaint you with its contents."

For Isobel's perusal, was required but a moment; she then offered the letter to me, and I bent my head to my purpose.

> Greetings to the most Grayshus Sir,
> I am late of the Scargrave house and would tell you of the evil there. I do this not for my own gayne, but for *la justice* for the poor man layde in the ground. Milord he was murdered by poyson and it was the grey-hared lord as did so, at the wish of my Ladie. For the love of God I have said it. I trust in your goodness and hand.

As Sir William had informed us, the missive was unsigned; and it asked for no payment in return for silence—an unfortunate circumstance, given my assertions of the previous evening.

"The grey-haired lord," Isobel murmured, pressing a handkerchief embroidered with her monogram to her lips; against the rusty black of her widow's weeds, her skin was so pale as to appear almost translucent. "She might mean either Fitzroy or Trowbridge."

"So she might." Sir William's manner was grave and the humour I had been wont to see in his kindly face, banished from his features. "I confess, my lady, that I am puzzled. How do we explain the persistence of this girl, who appears to seek no personal gain?"

A swift look passed between Isobel and myself. The Countess swallowed and dropped her eyes. "I had not understood how much she hates me. Some great wrong I must have done her, Sir William, tho' all unwittingly; for nothing less than wounded resentment could move her to such malice."

There was a silence as Sir William considered my friend's wan countenance. I wished, of a sudden, that I had kept my needlework within reach; a lady's canvas may always prove her friend, when anxiety would render idle hands a burden. I clasped my fingers together in my lap in an effort at composure.

"She has been in your service how long, my lady?" the magistrate enquired.

"Marguerite came to me from my aunt Delahoussaye's establishment in the Barbadoes, when I was seventeen and the maid some three years my junior." Isobel made a hurried calculation. "I would put it at some five years."

"And your relations were always cordial?"

"Always—or at the least, always before our arrival in England. That is now eighteen months past."

Sir William began to pace about the room, the better to order his thoughts; but his attitude had the unfortunate aspect of a lawyer before the bar, interrogating a reluctant witness.

"And so Marguerite travelled with you from the Indies?" he prompted.

"Indeed," Isobel replied, her eyes following his passage across the rug. "I would not embark on such a journey, Sir William, without my maid. She was the sole person of my household I permitted myself to take, the rest being discharged—but for the few who remained in my overseer's employ."

"And was the maid grateful to be so retained?"

"I assumed so." Isobel's fingers worried at the fine Swiss lawn of her handkerchief, crumpling it to a wrinkled ball. "How does one know the true feelings of one's servants? I confess her behaviour is so strange to me, I must believe I have never known her." My friend paused, as if in thought, and then turned her eyes unwillingly to Sir William's careful face. "But when I consider her manner these past few months, I would declare that she seemed unhappy. She missed her native climate, perhaps, in the coldness of England; snow she had never seen, for example, any more than I had myself; but where I found wonder, she found a strangeness to disturb. That it shook her, as being the opposite of all that was natural and familiar, I may fairly declare. She became quite superstitious and seemed to suffer from a condition of nervous excitement, starting at a sound and taking fixed dislike to what could do her no harm."

"Such as Lord Scargrave, perhaps?" Sir William all but pounced.

"My husband she showed only deference."

"I meant to indicate the present Lord Scargrave, Viscount Payne that was," the magistrate said silkily.

Isobel coloured and started, her handkerchief dropping to the floor. "You have put your finger on it, Sir William. She did not like my nephew at all—something I ascribe to his hair greying overly-young. Marguerite would see in it the Devil's mark. She did not suffer herself to be alone in the same room with him."

"A curious child," Sir William murmured, and looked at me. I read his intention in his eyes, and willed him not to ask of Isobel the true nature of her relations with Fitzroy Payne.

"Lady Scargrave," he began, and then stopped, as though debating with himself. "Have you any reason to believe your husband's death was other than it seemed?"

"None whatsoever," Isobel said. Her chin came up and her beautiful brown eyes met the magistrate's.

"You say this, recognising I in no way accuse you of having any hand in its achievement?"

"I know you could not believe it possible, sir, any more than I may believe an intimate of this household—servant or relation—capable of such monstrous evil."

Sir William sighed gustily and turned his back upon the Countess, his brow furrowed and his hands clasped behind his back. He paced the full length of the room again before he suffered himself to reply.

"My lady," he said, wheeling to face us in his best barrister's manner, "I cannot for the life of me say what is to be done. The girl is not to be found, and her defamation, it would appear, is but meant for an audience of one—myself. Your reputation remains untarnished in the surrounding country."

"But how long may we presume upon the maid's restraint?" I broke in.

Sir William raised an eyebrow. "She says nothing in that note, my dear Miss Austen, about any more letters. I suggest we do little for the present beyond our efforts to locate the maid, and pray God that her malice withers of itself with time."

"You are very good, Sir William." Isobel rose and extended her hand. "I will trust my welfare completely to your care."

"MY DEAR JANE," SIR WILLIAM SAID BRISKLY, AS I WALKED with him to his carriage, "I would know the name and direction of the London physician. Have you any recollection?"

"He was a Philip Pettigrew," I replied, "and I believe his offices were in Sloane Street. His fees should certainly support such an establishment."

"Excellent! Excellent! You are a jewel among women, my dear." And to my surprise, Sir William bent low to kiss my hand.

And so he was gone, on purposes and with intents he chose to keep to himself, but that I believe I divined nonetheless.

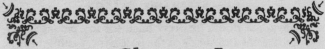

Chapter 7

Methinks He Doth Protest Overmuch

16 December 1802, cont.

~

THE COUNTESS HAVING RETIRED, AND THERE YET remaining several hours before I must dress for dinner, I bethought myself of exercise—prohibited heretofore by the heavy fall of snow—and donned my pelisse. With the aid of my pattens,[1] my boots might escape complete ruination; but, in truth, I do not care a fig for the fate of my boots, when weighed against the claims of sanity. Another hour's confinement among Scargrave's grey walls, with Isobel's poor spirits and the Delahoussayes' poor wits, should render me fit only to play the part of madwoman in one of Fanny Burney's novels.

I nodded to Fetters, the footman, and slipped through

---

1. Pattens were small rings, usually of metal, that were strapped onto the bottom of shoes to raise the feet a few inches above muddy streets or slushy paths. Though still worn in both country and town in Austen's day, they were considered decidedly unfashionable by mid-century.—*Editor's note.*

the heavy oak doors he drew back for my passage, feeling immaterial as a shade in the pale wintry sunlight. The air was fresh and sharp, and smelled bitingly of snow; we should have another fall before dawn, I surmised. I breathed deeply and felt a pressure ease within my chest; my sight cleared, and a pounding at the temples I had suffered for some hours began to recede. The world, however bleak I have found it in the last few weeks, must nonetheless be formed of goodness, if but a few moments in Nature's company may suffice to renew one's health and mental aspect.

The grand flight of steps that spilled before me had been swept clean of snow; and a passage of sorts cleared by carriage wheels along the drive. I hesitated an instant, considering the security afforded by an adjacent shrubbery, but suspecting it to be still enshrouded in drifts, I set off determinedly down the lane. A walk that has served daily to relieve a mind so sunk in melancholy as Mr. George Hearst's, should undoubtedly offer excellent advantage to the happier spirits of Miss Austen. But after a little I stopped short, and turned back to survey the Manor; a gloomy picture in the afternoon light it made, with the Scargrave hatchments[2] mounted above its many windows. Fully forty-five of these I counted off, in three storeys of fifteen, marching across the façade with a glint of glass and leading; but the effect remained merely dismal where it intended to be imposing. Built, so Isobel informs me, in the reign of Elizabeth, Scargrave Manor has been "improved" within an inch of its life on too many past occasions; it is now such a mixture of Tudor and Jacobean, with a bit of Inigo Jones thrown in for good measure, as to be a veritable Tower of architectural Babel.

I put the Manor to my back, and, since an aimless walk cannot hope to please, determined to make

2. Hatchments were family shields, shrouded in black crape and mounted over the windows of a great house to inform the public that the family was in mourning. —*Editor's note.*

Scargrave Cottage my object—though with no intention of disturbing its occupants, the Hearsts; I desired some solitude, the better to consider the import of the maid Marguerite's latest letter. But I had no sooner summoned the Hearsts to my thoughts, than I espied a lonely black figure some distance before me, all but indistinguishable from the darker ranks of trees that lined the drive. The very Mr. Hearst, engaged in his habitual ramble! I faltered, and strained to make out his features; but his head was bent in thought, his countenance obscured. Should I turn back, or attempt to converse with the gentleman? I had little relish for the latter task. But I recalled the gravity of Sir William's parting look, and considered Isobel's unhappiness—two thoughts that could not but hasten me along my way. Did the Earl meet his end by violence, all within the Manor's walls must be suspect; and Mr. Hearst, at least, had quarrelled with his uncle the very night of that gentleman's untimely end. His low spirits were assuredly fled on *that* occasion; for something very like passion had animated Mr. Hearst's bitter gibes.

The incipient curate's strides outstripped my own, and the way being decidedly encumbered by mud and wet snow, I progressed but poorly. And so, thrusting propriety to one side, I drew up my skirts and set off at a brisk trot in pursuit of Mr. Hearst. As I approached the gentleman, the ringing of my clumsy pattens upon a stone alerted him to my presence, and he turned to meet me with some surprise.

"Miss Austen!" cried he. "I did not take you for an ardent walker."

"Indeed, sir, it is my chief enjoyment. As it appears to be your own."

He removed his hat, and bowed, and turned back to accompany me towards the Manor. "It is very healthful, assuredly, for mind as well as body. Particularly in this season, when one is confined so much within doors. I fear that too much sitting plays poorly upon my spirits."

"You do not ride, as your brother does?"

"I find, Miss Austen, that my brother's passions instruct him to perfection in their pursuit. And thus I cede him whatever employment he chooses to master—I do not wish to attempt to emulate him, and suffer by comparison."

A silence then ensued, and I cast about for a means of introducing the subject of Mr. Hearst's quarrel with the Earl. How to attempt it with tact and decorum? Impossible! I should be forced to lower myself in his eyes, by appearing a malicious gossip. But what was the adoption of the meaner arts against the preservation of Isobel's peace of mind? A mere nothing.

"And are you equally passionate, Mr. Hearst, though in pursuit of that which your brother spurns? For on one occasion at least, I have heard you argue with energy."

My words, I fear, were too oblique; and rather than respond to their import, he merely used the opportunity to distinguish himself from the Lieutenant.

"I have so far learned from my brother's example, Miss Austen, as to spurn passion in anything. It is too often the means of unmastering a sober mind. Better to approach all that one can in life, with probity and discretion. *Reason* is my beloved tool, as *ardour* has become my brother's."

"I commend you, sir—though I might consider a judicious mixture of the two, as the best guarantee of happiness."

He merely nodded, his thoughts apparently elsewhere, and left me as desperate for an opening as before. We laboured on in silence a few moments, but at the broad face of Scargrave approaching, I forced myself to the purpose.

"I suppose the Earl's death has only heightened the attractions of the out-of-doors," I observed, "for to sit by the fire in contemplation of his sudden exiting from this life, should do little good to anybody."

"Indeed," Mr. Hearst replied, his eyes upon the muddied path at our feet.

"I suppose you held the Earl in deep affection?" I

persisted. At his expression of surprise, I added lamely, "It is just that I had so little opportunity to study his lordship's character—the Countess having married so recently, and the Earl departing his life almost upon the moment that I entered it."

"And are you a student of character, Miss Austen?" Mr. Hearst enquired, avoiding the necessity of answering my question.

"Oh! But of course!" I exclaimed, with greater enthusiasm for the game than I felt; "is there anything more worth the study?"

"In my opinion, there is little that is *less* worthy of your penetration. The character of a man is formed for disappointment, I believe; the more one knows of one's fellow beings, the less one is inclined to cherish them—or oneself."

"Mr. Hearst! I am all amazement! Are these the sentiments of a man of the Church? You must seek to reform your views, if Holy Orders remain your object."

"But perhaps it is my poor opinion of my fellows that spurs my aspirations heavenwards, Miss Austen."

"I dare say," I rejoined, "your contempt for the human condition leaving you no alternative. But it cannot serve to improve your parishioners' lot. As a clergyman's daughter, I must advise you to choose the solitude of the cloister, Mr. Hearst, rather than the pulpit. Its lofty height cannot preserve you from the disaffection of your flock, if you offer them only scorn."

"You think me ill-suited to the office?" he enquired, with an anxious look.

Rather than crush him entirely, I took refuge in a lady's prevarication. "I should never attempt to judge a gentleman's ambition," I replied circumspectly.

Mr. Hearst appeared to hesitate, as if in debate with himself, and then stopped in the lane, the better to hold my attention. "That is, perhaps, an answer to my question, though not one I should wish to hear—for had you unreservedly believed me fitted for the Church, I believe you should as readily have affirmed it. I fear my uncle was of your opinion, Miss Austen. He told me I should make a sorry clergyman. He would not hear of Holy Orders, and urged me to take instead the part of gentleman farmer."

"His lordship thwarted you deliberately?"

"He did," Mr. Hearst replied. "My uncle believed I lacked what is essential for a man of the cloth."

"That being, in the Earl's opinion?"

"Obedience. Humility. The Earl would have it that I suffer from pride, Miss Austen, out of all proportion to my station in life. Though how I could be expected to do otherwise—" At this, he broke off, and glanced around the expanse of Scargrave Park. I understood him all too well. He was of good birth—his mother the daughter of an earl—but utterly without an income capable of supporting such claims as family imposed. Neither freedom of will, nor freedom from dependence, should be his so long as he remained in Scargrave Cottage; and yet, how go elsewhere, on so little means? Pride, indeed, might be all that remained to such a man.

"And so you were subject to the Earl's whims," I said, as we plodded on. Very little of the lane remained to be travelled, and if I were to learn anything to my advantage, I must press the case.

"To his continued security, I was and am," Mr. Hearst replied heavily. "All that I have in the world, I owe to his goodness. If he wished me to play at overseer for the estate, then overseer I should be, however ill formed for the office."

"How unfortunate was the Earl's lot," I mused. "To have such power over others for happiness or despair. It might justly have made his dearest relations hate him."

Mr. Hearst did not immediately respond to this sally, as though lost in consideration of its merits. Finally, however, with a sidelong glance from his hollow eyes, he said, "Hate may perhaps be too strong an emotion. But in my breast, at least, the Earl assuredly engendered ill feeling."

"Did you quarrel with your uncle, Mr. Hearst?" I enquired boldly, though I hardly expected him to answer.

Had he done the Earl some violence, he should be little likely to admit to the fact; and the very notion of discord would be one he must refute.

"At seven-and-twenty, Miss Austen, I am as you see me," he replied, stopping before the Manor's steps. "Ill-suited to my enforced profession, thwarted in my hopes, resentful of my fellows more graced by fortune. Of course I quarrelled with my uncle. Why else should I feel such a depth of remorse at his passing? It is ever thus. We find the words to speak when all hope of converse is past."

An unwonted frankness, perhaps—but lonely walks in winter's snows will sometimes urge a confidence. At the very least, Mr. Hearst's utter lack of dissembling suggested that the gentleman saw no utility in deceit.

"I am heartily sorry for you, Mr. Hearst," I said slowly. "I, too, have known what it is to wish for an estate that my means would not allow. But perhaps the Earl thought better of his opinion, and provided in his will for your adoption of the clerical life."

"Perhaps," Mr. Hearst said, glancing back down the lane towards his cottage, "but I shall not hope for it. He is more likely to have left Tom an additional sum for the squandering in a gaming-hell. It was ever my uncle's way to reward with as much blindness as he punished."[3]

He bit back whatever bitterness had urged these words, and cast a penetrating glance in my direction, as though only just sensible that his thoughts had been shared with a lady, and a virtual stranger. Then, recollecting himself, as it seemed, Mr. Hearst bade me *adieu,* and trudged back along his way to the cottage.

A curious gentleman, the would-be ecclesiastic. In one respect only does he resemble his brother the Lieutenant: They both of them are wont to say more than discretion would advise—although not enough, in this instance, for my purposes. For though I had learned much about Mr.

3. A gaming-hell was the Georgian term for a gambling den.—*Editor's note.*

Hearst's animus towards his uncle, I still knew nothing at all about one particular argument—the night of the Earl's death, and in his library.

I WAS LOATH TO REENTER THE MANOR'S DARKENING HALLS; and so, snow or no, I betook myself to the shrubbery and made my way through its light drifts a little distance from the rear of the house, in an effort to organise my mind. Scargrave's gardeners had been before me; a footpath of sorts was dredged along the broad avenues and terraces.

The day that had dawned in storm was now graced by a thin sun; the long blue shadows of afternoon advanced before me like cheerful ghosts of last summer's growth, dancing past the withered flower borders and the stiff hedges to fall at the feet of a stone nymph, her cascade of water frozen in her urn. The brilliant winter landscape could not effect a similar elevation in my spirits, however; for I could not shake the apprehension that further trouble lay in wait for the intimates of Scargrave.

I chose a stone bench swept clean of snow, but fearsomely cold against my backside, for all that, and settled into my pelisse to mull over all that had occurred. I turned first to Sir William's interview.

That the maid Marguerite found no opportunity to turn a coin from the whole affair must baffle; for without mercenary motives, I was left with only two—the desire to mortally wound her mistress, and Fitzroy Payne into the bargain; or an honest attempt to bring foul murder to light. Neither made for happy consideration. If the former was Marguerite's motivation, it suggested some great wrong had been done to the creature that Isobel was loath to avow. Or perhaps Isobel was as yet ignorant of it, and Payne was guilty of the evil.

Was the sober young Earl the sort to dally with a lady's maid, and think no more of it than he might a morning's ride to the hounds? Many a woman has attempted to place her foot upon the neck of a man she loved in vain, or hated for just cause, whether that neck be stations above her or no. When I considered Fitzroy Payne, however, I could not imagine him causing such injury. What I have seen of that gentleman's conduct is irreproachable. His temper is always held in check, despite the absurdities of his nearest relations; his words reveal nothing but a fine understanding and the exercise of good sense. In general, Fitzroy Payne is so far removed from what is base in human nature, that I should think him guilty of the grossest duplicity, were I to discover him prey to vice. But I must needs discover it, if vice there be. Marguerite should surely have good cause for revenge against Isobel if she felt herself ill-used by Payne.

And if the maid's motive is nothing less than a desire to expose murder?

Such a powerful aim would seem necessary to drive a girl of the islands from the security of Scargrave in the midst of an English winter. If this be the force that moves her, then it cannot be denied that she *believes* murder to have been done. It is but a moment's leap to say that Marguerite is convinced Frederick was dispatched by his wife's hand, in concert with Payne's—and her anonymous letters are written from the purest of motives.

If the maid's desire is to expose Isobel, rather than blackmail her, then my faith in my friend might be profoundly shaken. But I am not so lightly possessed of friendship. Marguerite must be in error, however firmly she believes herself in the right; and my object *now* must be to put my finger upon the killer.

I raised my head and sniffed the wintry air, revelling in its power to clear my senses. The disposition of Isobel's trouble seemed, in that instant, to be the subject of only a few hours. I drove my hands more deeply into my muff, the better to warm them, and took up the matter once more.

If not Fitzroy Payne, if not Isobel—then whom? The villain must be an intimate of the household, and was hardly likely to be a servant; another member of the family, or Lord Harold, was all that remained to me.

Harold Trowbridge I could readily cast in the role of

murderer. He had the resolve, the ruthless aspect, and the motivation—for the late Earl had stood between him and his acknowledged goal, the acquisition (at a pittance) of Isobel's West Indies estates. Intent that Trowbridge should not secure her birthright, the Countess had implored her husband's protection; and by all appearances, the late Earl had been empowered and inspired to settle all her financial troubles. In favour of Lord Harold's guilt, I noted that Frederick's death occurred the very night of Trowbridge's arrival at Scargrave— the night that gentleman was summoned to the Earl's library for an interview, the conduct of which we knew nothing. Had it provoked Trowbridge to such violence that he poisoned the Earl's wine—drained to the dregs but a few moments before poor Frederick's fatal indisposition?

Yet, I reminded myself, I had no proof that Trowbridge in fact *met* with the Earl the night of the ball—the interview I myself overheard was between the Earl and Mr. George Hearst. Nor could I assert that Trowbridge possessed any poison, nor that he had administered it; and he was certainly not the man to let slip anything to his disadvantage.

In fairness to the scoundrel, however, I should as readily consider the motivations of others. It was but an instant's work to turn from a *purported* interview in the Earl's library to the one I had in fact overheard—an interview marked, by the evidence of my own ears, with intimations of violence. George Hearst had not parted from his uncle on friendly terms. Indeed, it was clear that the embittered nephew had sought Frederick's support for some scheme, had not received it, and had been enraged as a result.

You have driven me to my utmost extremity, and I know how it is that I must act, George Hearst had cried, or words to that effect. Much could be made of such sentiments, did we discover the Earl was murdered. But despite my recent effort at interrogation, I had not an idea what Mr. Hearst's affair was about. Holy Orders, perhaps, or worse yet, money—for we are ever driven to extremes by lack of funds, and pressure of obligation; I have reason to feel the force of *that* argument myself. Yet I distinctly recall Mr. Hearst mentioning a woman that night—Ruby? Rosamund? *Rosie*. Rosie it had been.

I must endeavour to learn more about Rosie, the better to weigh the strength of Mr. Hearst's outrage against his frankness during our walk in the Park.

As I sat engrossed in my thoughts, the sound of feet rapidly coursing through the snow fell upon my ears, and I looked up to see Lieutenant Hearst, his smart blue uniform the most vivid spot in all that grey landscape.

"And so I have found you at last," he cried, approaching my seat with alacrity. "I had feared you returned this morning to Bath. But my heart rises to learn that you have not deserted us quite yet." He peered at me closely, his banter trailing away. "Miss Austen, I declare, you look as though you had seen a ghost."

"Is the entire household arrayed against me?" I muttered crossly, and stood up, dusting off my skirts. "Can not a woman lose sleep of nights, without exciting the concern of her entire acquaintance?"

Tom Hearst's handsome face was instantly contrite. "I beg your pardon," he said hastily. "I meant no harm."

"Oh, Lieutenant—the apology must be mine," I said, recovering myself. "One consequence of broken sleep is assuredly diminished civility."

"So you *did* have a disturbed night."

"It is only the First Earl," I replied, attempting humour. "He treads the boards nightly in my dreams, mourning the late Lord Scargrave."

Rather than laughing as I expected, Tom Hearst looked pensive. "I would that I might believe you to speak in jest," he said gravely, holding my eyes, "but I saw him once myself, while yet a child, before my dear mother died. This is not a household for peaceful dreams, I fear." Then he slapped his thigh and assumed his customary grin. "Come for a short ride on Lady Bess. The air will do you good."

"Indeed, I am no horsewoman," I said with a smile. "My father lacked the resources to furnish us with mounts when we were children, and I must confess to some trepidation at the prospect of assuming the art at my advanced age."

"Nonsense!" The Lieutenant tucked my arm firmly under his own and led me back up the path. "I shall do everything in my power to render the experience so delightful, Miss Austen, and your trust so well-placed, that you shall hesitate to refuse me anything in future."

"And have you been taught to fear the refusal of young ladies, Lieutenant?" I enquired archly.

He *has* a very satiric eye. "Taught so well, Miss Austen, that I have made it a rule never to plead for that which I am not certain of desiring," he replied, "and so it may seem to *some* young ladies"—at this, he glanced upwards at the second-storey window where Fanny Delahoussaye's profile was clearly limned, bent over her work—"that I never *will* ask."

LADY BESS PROVED TO BE A GENTLE MOUNT, AND WHEN taken at a walk, her stride was so little disturbing as to quell even my violent fears of being unseated. Lieutenant Hearst spent some time walking before me, his hand on the bridle, and his own horse blowing contentedly at my side; but after a little, he thought it wise to rest by the hedgerow in conversation, and I was glad enough to dismount while Lady Bess nosed at the snow.

An awkwardness here ensued; my hands being engaged in supporting myself upon the saddle, the Lieutenant gripped my waist and abruptly pulled me to the ground. A furious blush overcame my features at being thus made so closely acquainted with his jacket front; but Tom Hearst was unabashed.

"Come, come, Miss Austen," he said teasingly, his hands still about my waist, "a young lady of your experience and perspicacity cannot be entirely a stranger to a gentleman's embrace."

"An unmarried lady of my station cannot admit to being anything *but*, Lieutenant," I retorted firmly, and moved to thrust the offending hands from my person. To my mortification, he tightened his grip, and added to the embarrassment of his stance, the discomfiture of my own. I was forced to grasp his gloved hands in mine to win my freedom, and the image of how we must appear only increased my blushes.

The Lieutenant laughed heartily and released me, but I failed to see the humour in his affront.

"Is it Fanny Delahoussaye who has taught you such indelicacy, Lieutenant? Or is it thus you school her on your snowy walks?" I turned on my heel and would have left him in my anger, but he caught me up in a moment, the horses on the rein, and apologised most prettily.

"I must declare myself a complete reprobate, Miss Austen," he avowed. "A life too long spent among the soldiers of the garrison has made my conduct rough and ungentlemanly. You, who have brothers in the Navy, must acknowledge we have few opportunities for the study of civility. In your company, perhaps, I shall learn better how to behave than in Miss Fanny's."

"I do not think you shall have another chance at my company, Lieutenant," I said, refusing to meet his eye and increasing my pace.

"Miss Austen!" he cried, halting the horses in the midst of the field, "what cruelty is this? Does my gentle offence truly merit such censure? And are you not in part responsible? I should not have been tempted, did the winter cold not heighten the beauty of your cheeks, bring sparkle to your eyes, and in general make of you such a picture!"

"I fear you give way all too often to temptation, Lieutenant," I replied, thinking of Fanny Delahoussaye. Tom Hearst can have little constancy in his attachments if he plays as idly with her as he has done with me.

"I beg your forgiveness," he said earnestly, dropping to his knees in the snow, "and your heart cannot be so hard as to withhold it. I meant no dishonour to your virtue—if anything, Miss Austen, I meant to honour your charms." He made a pretty enough picture, his curling head raised in supplication, his uniform a darker splash against the horses' chestnut. As I watched, Lady Bess exhaled a steamy breath, and nuzzled Tom Hearst's shoulder; he looked around and fondled the mare affectionately. "Lady Bess would have your forgiveness on my behalf," he continued penitently. "And in return I will pledge to molest you no more."

It is not in my nature to preserve a prudish distance; the Lieutenant's present earnestness called to mind my brother Frank, the darling of my concerns; and so I unbent my stiffened posture and walked to his side.

"Please rise, Lieutenant," I said. "The snow cannot be good for your breeches."

"Nor my knees," he said, jumping to his feet. "My batman will have my head in the morning, when I'm too stiff to get out of bed. But I shouldn't mention such things to a lady. I forget myself. Will you walk back to the house with me, Miss Austen, and teach me the proprieties Miss Fanny cannot?"

"I will consent to accompany you, Lieutenant, on one condition."

"Anything, dear lady."

"That you will instruct me in the art of horsemanship while I remain at the Manor," I said, by way of reward for his penitence. "Lady Bess is a mount to suit my tastes, and I believe I should profit from the exercise."

"Capital!" Tom Hearst cried, slapping his thigh, "and I from your gentle schooling."

"Let us talk no more of that."

"Very well. Though of what else we may converse, I hardly know. All subjects are contraband. Did we talk of our intimates here at Scargrave, we should touch upon death; and I refuse to traffick in melancholy in the company of a lovely woman."

"Lieutenant!"

"What, no compliments may I extend?" He stopped,

as one amazed. "No praise of all that is before me? Miss Austen! Your cruelty is beyond belief! You provoke my enthusiasm, and then chide me for its expression!"

I may, I think, declare myself to be no fool. I have looked at my face and figure in the glass these six-and—no—*seven*-and-twenty years; and neither is of a nature to drive a young man wild. Either Tom Hearst is quite bored with life at Scargrave, and finds in me some amusement; or he hopes to turn my head with flattery for a purpose I have not yet divined.

At his next observation, I felt all the force of my latter conjecture.

"Have you known Sir William Reynolds long?" the Lieutenant enquired, as though to turn the conversation.

I hesitated before replying, wondering what possible interest he could have in the good Justice.

"Since before memory serves," I replied, picking my way through the snow. I had discarded my pattens in order to ride, and my boots should *assuredly* be ruined. "Sir William has always been a fond intimate of my father's house. To me, he is as much like an uncle as a friend."

"He avails himself of your presence to visit Scargrave with greater frequency than in the past."

"It cannot be surprising," I said, studying his face. Did Tom Hearst desire to learn of *some other reason* for the magistrate's attention? "And in winter, one discovers the closeness of one's friends. A call upon an acquaintance may prove more attractive in the tedium of the season, when simpler pursuits are denied us by weather."

"Certainly Sir William finds it so," the Lieutenant commented, "though any man might find attraction enough in your presence, summer or winter."

I could not suppress a smile at his relentless gallantry, and thought it best to seek refuge in a different subject.

"An officer such as yourself must be wedded to his horse," I said. "Have you been a rider since infancy, Lieutenant?"

"I have," he replied, reaching up to stroke his hunter's nose. "My father placed me astride at the tender age of two, thereby predestining his second son for the cavalry. It was perhaps his last fatherly act before departing for the Continent, his mistress, and his death."

"You are very much attached to your profession?"

"I would sooner be an officer in the Blues,"[4] he avowed cheerfully, "than a duke. There is all the style of a position at Court, and the elegance of such a set, aligned with the freedom and adventure of military service; the command of men, and the camaraderie of one's fellows—all things which I find delightful. I owe much to my uncle's goodness, Miss Austen, for it was he who purchased my commission."

"Did he?" I enquired, though it was no more than I had suspected. "Then he served you better than your brother, Lieutenant. Had the Earl treated you both in a similar fashion, he should have made you a clerk, to be shut up indoors in every season—your inclination being so clearly in the opposite direction."

"And so George has availed himself of your kindness, and poured out his grievances," the Lieutenant observed, amused. "He is never done lamenting his thwarted hopes, though he knows my uncle thought better of his choice, and has left him a living. It seems to me that George suffers vastly in parting with regret—though he but exchanges it for his heart's desire. Perhaps he has grown fond of the attitudes of blighted youth."

"Mr. Hearst is to receive a living under the Earl's will?" I exclaimed, in some surprise.

"So I believe, though I have not seen the document," the Lieutenant replied, "my cousin Fitzroy and his solicitors being too bound up in affairs of the estate to give us all a proper reading. But my uncle informed my brother of the fact, upon his return from his wedding trip; marital bliss had made the Earl even more generous. In amending

4. The Royal Horse Guards, one of three cavalry regiments charged with guarding the Royal Household, were nicknamed the Blues due to the color of their uniforms.—*Editor's note.*

the will's terms to provide for the Countess, my uncle attended to George's affairs as well. If there is cause for any rejoicing in the melancholy event of the Earl's demise, my brother may justly claim it."

"Indeed," I said distractedly, my thoughts in some confusion. Had Mr. Hearst ignored this point in conversing with me, out of a natural delicacy? Or from the counsel of a guilty conscience? For he clearly benefited from his uncle's death; and that death had been achieved not long after that gentleman had imparted the news of his inheritance. Given the violence of argument I overheard the night of the Scargrave ball, Mr. Hearst's entire aspect appeared worthy of probing.

I suddenly became sensible of the Lieutenant's narrow gaze, and endeavoured to shift our *tête-à-tête* to lighter matters.

"Your commission in the Blues, now, Lieutenant—it affords you an added advantage in your role as a rival for Miss Delahoussaye's affections, in that she dearly loves the military profession," I said, with an attempt at playfulness. "And being attached to the Royal Household, you are unlikely to serve in garrison towns far from places and people of fashion; this must decidedly recommend you to her mother, who will often make of the two of you a third."

I had meant the remark in jest, of a piece with his own raillery against that lady; but he flushed and regarded me earnestly.

"You have discerned, then, Miss Fanny's partiality for me?" he asked anxiously. "I would that it were less pronounced. But she was never a lady to conceal her affections from the object of them, though propriety would counsel such. I cannot expect her to do so now, even before those less intimate with my family."

"My apologies, sir," I said hastily. "I spoke rashly, when I intended to speak lightly. As a stranger to Scargrave, I should have held my tongue. One cannot be a part of a household without sometimes giving offence, however, and that when one least intends it."

The Lieutenant ran a gloved hand through his hair, his expression remained troubled. "It is just that you have touched upon a point that I have been at pains to avoid. I may have reacted thus too warmly. Madame Delahoussaye's dearest object is to affiance her daughter to my cousin Fitzroy, whose fortune may be said to eclipse Fanny's own; but Lord Scargrave's accustomed aloofness has told against him, and so Miss Fanny searches elsewhere for flattery."

"Which *you* certainly know how to supply," I said reprovingly. "Life at Court has at least taught you *this*. But I am surprised, sir; can even such a gallant as you win her young heart in but a few days?"

"I have been acquainted with Miss Delahoussaye some seven months," he replied, "full as long as she has known my cousin. During the last London Season, I was as much a party to their revels as it was possible to be."

"And it being summer, and she a pretty girl, you thought it no harm to engage in light flirtation. I see how it was."

"Her attentions were marked whenever we met." Tom Hearst laughed shortly. "Her attentions! Can such a word encompass Fanny's absurdity? She has completely thrown herself in my way. No man would scruple to take what Fanny offers, Miss Austen. Certainly not I. Though it pains me to admit it. I must regard myself with contempt, for succumbing to physical charms, where character and sense are so lacking."

Such frankness! The Lieutenant hesitated not in revealing himself as utterly wanting in principle. But his careless derogation of Fanny Delahoussaye was such as another lady could not suffer to pass in silence, even one who esteemed her as little as I.

"And since her fortune is not a small one," I observed, "you should have been a further fool to offer coldness in the face of such warmth. Self-interest has been your sole mover where Miss Delahoussaye is concerned."

"You *are* possessed of decided opinions, Miss Austen! Would that they were formed of less truth," the Lieutenant said, with a doubtful look. "But too late I took the measure of her grasping mother's plans, and hesitated lest I offend Fitzroy, whose perfect command of countenance allows no one to suspect whether he is partial to the lady or no. Were Fitzroy to have formed honourable intentions towards Fanny, I should have done him a serious wrong; but to speak of it with such an one as the Viscount—the *Earl*—is impossible. I determined to put myself in the clear and leave him to his chances."

The Lieutenant pretends, now, to have no notion that Fitzroy Payne's affections were already engaged elsewhere, as he so clearly intimated during our dance at the Scargrave ball. A curious omission, as though Tom Hearst would wipe clean the blot of his former impropriety.

"Whatever Fanny's fortune," I said, recovering myself, "the retention of your cousin's good opinion must be said to have greater value."

"Indeed." He pursed his lips thoughtfully. "But I fear I tarried too long. Miss Delahoussaye's teasing ways have lately brought the wrath of her mother upon my head. Madame has had the temerity to suggest that I have encouraged her daughter in displays that offend propriety!"

"I am all amazement," I said, with deliberate irony.

"You would laugh," Tom Hearst replied, "but Madame went so far as to request it of my uncle before his death that I be barred from Scargrave for the Christmas season."

This was news, indeed. The result of the rumoured duel, perhaps?

"Did she!" I cried. "I had not an idea of it! And what did your uncle reply?"

"I remain here, as you see," the Lieutenant said, smiling, "and feel myself completely free to devote myself to others more worthy of my interest."

And so we turned for home, absorbed in forming a plan for further riding lessons in subsequent days. Lieutenant Hearst appears eager for my company; and though he is an untrustworthy rogue, he is charming enough for all that. He amuses me, and I am in no danger from his attentions; I have too much sense to credit the Lieutenant's flattery, particularly when I feel it to be offered by design.

Thus, we have struck a bargain, of sorts, though the terms remain unspoken. My skill as a horsewoman shall benefit from his attentions; and in turn I shall be much persecuted on the subject of Sir William Reynolds. The *why* of Tom Hearst's interest in the magistrate, however, eludes me.

Chapter 8

She Stoops to Conquer

17 December 1802

~

I AWOKE THIS MORNING RESOLVED TO PAY MORE ATTENTION to the perplexing problem of the Earl's demise, and less to the rakish Lieutenant Hearst. Such a man cannot be taken seriously by one in my position; however charming, and attentive, the Lieutenant is little likely to ally himself with a lady as destitute as I, and can be seen only as a poor fellow marooned in the country—who finds what solace he can in idle flirtation.

With such sensible thoughts in mind, I descended to the little breakfast room with alacrity, my progress hastened by a healthy appetite and a vigorous sense of purpose. I had lain rather late abed—being much fatigued, due to the exertion of the previous day's riding—and thought that I should have the table to myself; but Fitzroy Payne appeared not five minutes after the footman had pulled out my chair, and greeted me with a distracted bow.

"Miss Austen. You look well."

"Thank you, my lord. I feel quite renewed by my excellent rest." I would that I could have returned his compliment, but in truth, he appeared remarkably ill.

"I fear that sleep is an indulgence I must deny myself

for the present—my uncle's affairs demand all my attention." The Earl took a seat and waved away the servant's proffered teapot. "Coffee for me, Fetters, and some fresh rashers."

"Yes, milord."

At the footman's departure, Fitzroy Payne cast a glance over his shoulder and leaned across the table. "I must congratulate myself, Miss Austen, upon finding you quite alone. I would speak with you on a matter of some delicacy."

I set down my toast and touched a serviette to my lips. "I am all attention, Lord Scargrave."

The Earl hesitated at my use of his uncle's title, and then gave me a rare smile. It had the power to utterly transform his face; from being rather a grave gentleman, possessed of sobriety unwonted in one so young, he was turned a convivial and charming fellow. I felt for an instant what it must have been to walk the streets of Mayfair in his company, all those summer months ago, and understood a little of Isobel's trouble.

"I have observed your attentions to the Countess," Fitzroy Payne began. "Though her present misfortunes are heavy, indeed, they must be counted as somewhat relieved by her enjoyment of such friendship."

I inclined my head. "Those who know Isobel's goodness cannot help but love her."

"Would that it were otherwise," he murmured, undoubtedly for his own ears. Then, collecting himself, he gazed at me with the greatest earnestness. "You have noted, I assume, my preoccupation with my late uncle's affairs. It has denied me the opportunity I should otherwise have taken, of pursuing your acquaintance. So good a friend to Isobel should not remain a stranger to myself."

"Perhaps we may better understand one another in an easier time," I said gently. "I should never reproach you for attending to that which *demands* your care and attention, Lord Scargrave. You have been graciousness itself when thrown in my way."

"When *thrown in your way,*" he rejoined, with a gleam of amusement; "how poorly I have behaved to a guest beneath my roof! What would my fellows at White's[1] say of me now, did they observe my manners? But it cannot be helped. I must presume upon short acquaintance, and beg of you your good offices."

"If I may be of service to you in some matter, my lord, I would gladly know it."

"I ask not for myself, but for one who is dear—to us both."

This *was* a sort of frankness; for that he meant Isobel, I could not doubt, and by admitting to me—even in so delicate a manner—the depth of his own feeling for his late uncle's wife, the Earl honoured me with his confidence, indeed.

The sudden return of the footman, Fetters, with coffee-pot and fresh rashers in hand, precluded further speech on the subject; but the Earl's breakfast once served, the man was dismissed. At Fetters's closing the breakfast room door discreetly behind him, I felt myself free to address the Earl's anxiety once more.

"What eager concern for Isobel has robbed you of your sleep, Lord Scargrave?"

His slate-coloured eyes held a surprising humility, and in their depths I read a grudging acknowledgement of my penetration. "You speak the truth, Miss Austen. I would spend less time wakeful at my uncle's affairs, were my sleep undisturbed by anxiety for the Countess."

"And is Lord Harold the author of your demons, Lord Scargrave? For I confess, that where *that* gentleman is concerned, I may offer no assistance. He confounds me utterly."

"To say *utterly* is perhaps an exaggeration. Miss

1. White's was perhaps the most exclusive gentlemen's club in London during Austen's time. It is a sign of Fitzroy Payne's social status and his place among a fashionable set that he is a member there.—*Editor's note.*

Austen of Bath is *never* confounded utterly," Fitzroy Payne said with gentle raillery. "No, Miss Austen—with Lord Harold I feel myself an equal. There is little the man would do to the Countess that I cannot forestall. It is Isobel herself who is the source of my anxiety." The Earl hesitated, as if choosing his words. "I do not know how deeply you are admitted to her confidence—"

"Suffice it to say that I know as much regarding her affection for yourself, as it was possible for her to convey to another person," I said quietly.

A wave of embarrassment overcame his face; but he quickly mastered it, and went on with greater ease. "Then you know that we two have achieved that level of intimacy which can admit of few impediments."

"So I should imagine."

"And yet, not a word beyond the common conventions of the household have I had from the Countess since my uncle's death. She deals with me as with a stranger." The Earl slapped the table with the palm of his hand, and abruptly thrust himself out of his chair, commencing to pace about the room.

"You find this singular, my lord?"

"Singular? It is insupportable!"

"But she is lost to grief!"

"And at such a time, I should be her first comfort! But she appears rather to wish me at the ends of the earth!"

I knew not how to answer his confusion; for to say what I believed—that Isobel's profound grief was mingled with a sense of guilt and shame where Fitzroy Payne was concerned—should only cause him further pain. And it was just possible—Isobel having kept from her beloved all knowledge of the maid Marguerite's blackmailing missives—that the Countess desired to shield Fitzroy from her worry. That Isobel had taken the maid's words to heart, and begun to fear the *grey-hared lord,* I thrust aside as unlikely.

"Perhaps the Countess will be more herself with time," I said lamely.

"But what if she is *not*, Miss Austen? What if my uncle's death has caused in her some reversal of feeling? It is just such a fear as this that robs my nights of sleep."

Such honesty of sentiment, before myself—with whom he is acquainted only imperfectly—could not but win my active benevolence on Fitzroy Payne's behalf.

"Lord Scargrave," I said, "the Countess has borne more than any lady of her tender years and experience should be expected to endure. Consider her disappointed passion for yourself—the strength required to overcome it—the melancholy resignation to a marriage of convenience—and *now* the sudden loss of a husband she revered at least as she might a father. It is not to be wondered that she seeks comfort in solitude. I should rather wonder at her doing anything else."

"That may be true," Fitzroy Payne said, composing himself with better grace. "But I would ask you, Miss Austen, to bend your efforts to improving Isobel's spirits. She *is* too much alone. Persuade her to walk with you, if the weather be fine; talk to her of subjects far from this unhappy house. And if it be possible to plead my cause—to speak warmly on my behalf—"

"Then know that I shall do all that is in my power, Lord Scargrave," I assured him without hesitation.

"Blessed woman!" Fitzroy Payne cried, his gratitude in his looks; and so he left me.

I COULD NOT BE IDLE WHEN SO MUCH ANXIETY WAS ACTIVE on Isobel's part; I hastened to her room, and found her very low.

"My dear," I said, placing a wrap about her shoulders as she sat by the fire, her face pensive and her hair undone, "you are not dressed! And your tea is undrunk! Has Daisy failed to attend you?"

"Oh, Jane," my friend sighed, "Daisy cannot attend to an illness of the spirit! Of what interest is dress to me? I cannot assume a different self, by assuming a different gown. I should rather remain here, in the quiet of my room, and repent of all my sins."

"Come, come," I chided her. "You should better congratulate yourself for having survived so many tests of character, with such grace and fortitude."

"Neither word can apply to me." Isobel thrust off the wrap and rose from her chair. "I have dishonoured a man who would have moved heaven and earth to make me happy."

"Isobel! Such harshness, and so illogically applied! In your sorrow, you are unjust. Let your friend, who knows better your worth, remind you who you are."

"Do not flatter me, Jane," she said brusquely, holding out a hand as if to impede my passage. "I have nothing to offer in return but the shame of a woman who has acted as she should not."

"Of what can you be speaking?" The depth of her guilt was as I had surmised. I must needs exert myself. "Nothing that you have recounted could dishonour Frederick. You esteemed him as your husband, and whatever your feelings for another, your behaviour has been such as no one can reproach."

She put her hands to her face, hiding it from my sight; her voice, when it came, trembled with emotion. "I cannot banish the maid's words from my mind, Jane. Marguerite saw rightly. *We* killed my husband, Fitzroy and I—and our guilt could be no greater if we had poisoned him outright, as the maid claims."

A horror gripped me at her words; and I silently cursed the girl whose vicious pen could wreak such havoc in Isobel's soul.

"My dear," I said firmly, grasping her wrists and drawing her hands from her face, "you can have nothing to regret beyond your husband's untimely death. Mourn for him if you will, but do not take upon yourself the burden of your Maker. The ways of Providence are hidden, but as a clergyman's daughter, I may freely own that they are rarely vindictive."

Isobel struggled free of me and fell languorously upon

her chaise. Her face was hidden by dark red tresses; whether sorrow or anger o'erspread her features, I could not say. Prudence counseled me to desist; but friendship informed me that I had not done.

"You brought your husband great joy, Isobel," I said firmly. "Remember that I saw him happy before his death. You honoured the Earl by consenting to be his wife, and by sacrificing your better feeling to his. Nothing should instruct you otherwise; certainly not the fractured words of a half-wit maid."

"Jane," the Countess said, brushing back her hair and turning her face to mine, "have done. Do not suppose your words are what I wish to hear. You cannot respect me any longer, knowing what you do of my character."

"Say rather that I cannot *endure* you any longer." I was all exasperation. "Isobel, you persist in professing what you should not! Enough of pining, enough of regret. Your task now is to address the future with renewed energy. Scargrave is dead—but Scargrave still lives. And unless I am very much mistaken, you are wronging a man who loves you."

Isobel blushed scarlet, and turned her face aside. "Do not speak to me of Fitzroy. I feel nothing but shame when he is mentioned." Her words were clipped and bitter.

"You should not, my dear."

"How can I not?" she cried. "Oh, Jane, I am utterly miserable!"

"But you care for him still?"

She was silent a time, her fingers clutching and unclutching at the lace of her gown. She looked away from me, towards the portrait of the late Frederick, his jovial face caught in a band of morning sunlight. Then, in a voice so low I must needs struggle to hear it, she said, "How can you ask such a question? My husband is hardly cold in the ground."

I felt all the force of her chastening words, and bit my lip. My vigour in urging Isobel out of a too-heavy sorrow had lacked a certain delicacy. But I felt an active anxiety regarding the guilt of one I held so dear, and so attempted one last injunction.

"You cannot die with Frederick, however much you may believe it is required of your penitence, Isobel."

There was a tense silence, and then the Countess expelled a ragged breath. I hoped for some good effect from my words; but I was not to be so easily rewarded. Isobel bent to retrieve her wrap and settled it once more upon her shoulders, the openness of her expression completely shuttered, her eyes on the flames in the hearth. "Leave me now, Jane," she said.

"I shall." I reached a hand to stroke her wild red waves, but at my touch, she stiffened. I said, "There are many people who love you, my dear. Perhaps more than you love yourself. Remember that, Isobel, when you determine to live."

FEELING SORELY THAT I HAD FAILED BOTH MY FRIEND AND her lover in my awkward attempts at persuasion, I found myself alone with the morning before me. Fanny Delahoussaye was indisposed with a stomach ailment, and Madame had gone off to the apothecary in Scargrave Close; the Hearsts kept still to their cottage in the lane. Fitzroy Payne was closeted in his library, and Lord Harold, thankfully, was not to be seen.

Isobel's melancholy threatened to overtake even *my* energetic spirits, but I reflected that we had at least one cause for rejoicing—the maid Marguerite's vicious tongue, so injurious to the Countess's self-respect, had fallen thankfully silent. Sir William Reynolds remained cheerfully in the company of his dear lady today, having no news of an evil nature to bring to our door. I was not so sanguine, however, as to believe the affair at an end—and judged it wise to pursue what intelligence I might regarding Scargrave's intimates.

I was determined to learn more of the woman named Rosie, who had been cause for such violence of argument between Mr. George Hearst and the late Earl. To that end, I made for the servants' quarters, and after several enquiries, was directed to the housekeeper's apartment.

"Mrs. Hodges," I said, when that good lady appeared at her sitting-room door, neatly arrayed in her habitual black with a snowy cap upon her head, "I would speak with you, if you have a quarter-hour to spare."

"I should be delighted, miss," she replied, stepping back and throwing her door wide.

I was shown to a comfortable chair by the fire and begged to sit. I confess to stealing a glance about me as Mrs. Hodges went in search of her teapot—for the housekeeper's rooms at Scargrave are on such a scale that they might almost be those of the *Austens* in Bath, a comparison that should probably horrify the good Mrs. Hodges, did she know it. But I collected myself as she placed a cup before me, her kindly face eager to be of service.

How to put the question I must ask? I had never been forced to the task of blatant inquisition before, and it rankled. To have done with, then, and suffer through, seemed the advisable course.

"Mrs. Hodges," I began, sipping at my cup, "I wonder if you can tell me whether a young woman by the name of Rosie has ever been a caller at Scargrave Manor?"

A look of bewilderment came into her eyes as she settled herself in the chair opposite. "Rosie?" she said; "I can't recollect as there was a *lady* by that name. There's Rosies enough in the world, to be sure, but I am informed of the Manor's guests by their surnames only, as is proper for one of my place."

Of course this was true; I myself should not have known the lady's Christian name, had she been spoken of in the usual manner; but Mr. Hearst—for it was his voice that had surely pronounced it—had seen fit to drop the "Miss" before her surname. What *had* that been, after all? Catch? Fetch? No—a type of boat. *Ketch.* Rosie Ketch.

"I believe the lady's surname was Ketch," I said.

The transformation of Mrs. Hodges's face was something remarkable—first white, then red, with eyes popping; I thought for an instant that she should fall into a fit of apoplexy. "Mrs. Hodges," I said anxiously, setting my tea aside and reaching towards her with concern, "whatever is the matter? What can I have done?"

"It's nothing, miss," she stammered, recovering herself with effort; "only I've asked as that slattern's name never be pronounced in this house again. She was no example for the younger girls, and a heap o' trouble while she was in service, and I'd forget her as soon as I'm able. I thought it was a *lady* you'd enquired after."

"It was my mistake," I said. "I had no notion she was in service. I merely heard the name, attached to an interesting remark, and wondered when she had last been at Scargrave."

"I'll warrant the remark was interesting," Mrs. Hodges observed shrewdly, and clasped her hands upon her considerable stomach. "Rosie's gone three months now, but if it's news of her you want, you'd best be talking to Jenny Barlow, as is her sister down t'a home farm. Not that Rosie's worth the asking after, mind you; but you have your reasons, I dare say."

That my reasons were unlikely to do me credit, her look and tone clearly implied; and I felt myself blush scarlet.

It remained only to thank her for her hospitality and enquire the direction to Jenny Barlow's home. Then I left Mrs. Hodges by her fire, donned my cloak and boots, and made my way through the kitchen gardens to the lane—which led, in a winding fashion much beset by drifts of snow, some three miles to Scargrave's farm.

THE WEATHER WAS VERY FINE, AND I FELT MY SPIRITS LIFT AS the cold sun touched my cheek. Being anxious to apprise no one of my errand, I could do little but walk; fortunately, I possess such an excellent constitution, and am so accustomed to exercise, that I found the three miles not overly fatiguing. I had been told to expect Jenny Barlow's cottage near the beginning of the fallow wheat fields; and indeed, upon rounding the last bend of the lane, I perceived a tiny hut, its good thatched roof a testament to the late Earl's care for his tenants. A thin thread of smoke was rising from its chimney.

I approached the doorway, and spied a small child blessed with the startled eyes of a doe; at my salutation, she took fright, and dashed within. Her mother soon appeared.

"Jenny Barlow?" I enquired.

"Yes, miss." Her speech was suffused with the softness of Hertfordshire.

I must set down here my first impression of the girl, for girl she undoubtedly is—not much above twenty, I should say, and quite lovely yet, despite the evidence of years of hard work. Jenny Barlow's hair is gold, her eyes are cornflower blue, and her figure full and sturdy, making her seem something of a harvest goddess; but those poor particulars do not convey the truth of it. She is a beauty, her face delicate of line and her features elegant; she is just such an English rose, I judge, as is occasionally still found along its quieter byways.

"Would you like to come in, miss, out o' the cold?"

I assented, and entered the darkened hut, which was filled with smoke; the unglazed windows were covered with oiled cloth, and only heightened the murkiness of the atmosphere. The child I had seen by the door was hiding under the table; another sat in a corner, worrying a lock of its hair; and I perceived Jenny to be yet again in a certain condition. The lot of women is indeed a cruel one—either die an old maid, reviled and unprovided, or die of hard work and childbed, both too liberally bestowed.

"You've come from the big house," she said. "It's not often a lady seeks out the farm."

"I am presently staying at the Manor," I replied, "and though it appears I have been walking for pleasure, in fact I am come to speak with you."

She looked her surprise, and was at a loss; and so provided a chair that I might more comfortably explain myself.

"Mrs. Barlow, I have sought you out of instinct rather than clear purpose," I began, taking the proffered seat, "and I hope that in speaking with you, I may know better how you are to help me. You are, of course, aware of the death of Lord Scargrave?"

"Yes, God be praised," she said quickly, and half under her breath.

"And why should such a death be cause for thankfulness?" I asked.

"He were an awful wicked man, the Earl," Jenny answered, "awful wicked. I have reason to know it."

"That is very strong language, certainly." I paused to survey Jenny Barlow's countenance, but she did not look the sort of girl to strike out blindly, from malice or an envy of her betters. "Has Lord Scargrave had cause to injure you, my dear?" I enquired, feeling a sudden conviction of its truth.

"Hurtin' was as natural to him as breathin'." At that she fell silent, and from the way she glanced furtively around the hut, seemed to regret having said as much; I did not probe her further, but advanced on another tack.

"The night of the Earl's death," I told her, "I had occasion to overhear Mr. George Hearst pronounce the name of Rosie Ketch. I understand that she is your sister. Is Mr. Hearst known to you?"

"That he is, and a truer man never lived."

Such fervour, for the melancholy ecclesiastic! I remembered the vigour of George Hearst's words, when speaking to his uncle about Rosie Ketch; and wondered at such a dour young man in the role of lady's champion. It was a role better played by his gallant brother. Jenny Barlow turned her head at a disturbance by the door. Her eyes widened in alarm.

" 'Ere, what's 'is?" demanded a burly fellow, leaning heavily in the doorway. "Somebody from tha Maner? Well, we wants nothin' of the likes of you, I warrant. Be off with ye!"

"No, Ted!" Jenny Barlow cried, "the lady is but resting along her way. She meant no 'arm."

Ted Barlow, for so I divined him to be, reeled toward his wife, the pungent scent of barley and hops preceding him, and cuffed her a stiff blow to the side of her head. I confess I could not repress a sharp cry at the injustice of it, but the lout paid me no heed, so intent was he upon the poor creature in his power.

"Mixin' wit' the quality, are ye? And look where 'at's got you afore!" He swept a beefy hand toward his children, who cowered away from him. "A passel of brats, and no bread for the table. *That's* for quality," he said, and spat upon the floor.

I deemed it wise at this juncture to depart, but paused at the hut's jamb long enough to seek Jenny Barlow's eye. "If you should need me, Mrs. Barlow," I said, "simply ask the way to Miss Austen."

I RETURNED ALONG THE SNOWY LANE IN SOME PERTURBA-tion, and with the leisure of three miles to give it full compass. That the late Lord Scargrave had marred the young girl's life in some way, and that her husband still harboured a bitter grudge, was evident. I considered it no less likely that her sister Rosie was encompassed in Jenny Barlow's cares. How the harm had been effected remained a mystery; tho' I was just enough apprised of the ways of the world to think it possible the Earl had forced his attentions upon his milkmaid. There are precedents in history for it enough. I must wait, however, for the bestowing of Jenny's confidence; given time and further thought, the girl may resolve to seek me out, and unburden herself willingly.

I was but a few hundred yards from the paddock where I had ridden Lady Bess the previous afternoon; and at a nicker from the fence, I turned and saw her lovely chestnut nose stretched towards me appealingly.

"I have no sugar, Bess," I warned as I approached, "nor yet a piece of apple. But if you like, I shall rub your nose, and promise to visit on the morrow."

The mare bent her nostrils to my gloved hand, and I stood there some moments, scratching the short hairs between her ears and along the bridge of her face, marvelling at the liquid depths of her enormous eyes. It was then that a movement beyond her withers surprised me; I looked up, and caught sight of a bonneted head ducking into a shed to the left of the far paddock gate, on the nether side of the wintry field from where I stood. The lady's pelisse was of a rich cherry, frogged round with black braid, and of a style to be worn by only one person—Fanny Delahoussaye! Perhaps she had come to ride, the better to win the Lieutenant's heart.

Lady Bess blew out a gusty breath, impatient for attention, and at that moment Fanny reappeared, unconscious of my presence, and slipped back through the gate towards the house. Her entire aspect declared her errand a furtive one.

There was no gate in the fence before me—just the one, well around the field. I looked about to see that I was unobserved, swiftly mounted the lower rail, and swung myself, skirts and all, over the fence to stand beside a surprised Lady Bess. Then I set off across the snow-crusted grass, holding my hem above my ankles, the horse trotting alongside in evident enjoyment of the lark.

It was a small outbuilding, no more than a storage shed for hay, really, and possessed of nothing in itself that might appeal to Fanny Delahoussaye. I bent my head to peer inside, and saw immediately what she had left—a small leather pouch tied with a string. I picked it up, and from the weight and jingle knew the purse to contain a quantity of coins.

Fanny, leaving money for an unknown? How very singular. She was not the sort to engage in eccentric philanthropy, of an anonymous kind; more the reverse. Was this a payment for services—of a sort better unpublished in the light of day? There was no note, no sign of the intended recipient; and I did not like to open the pouch itself. I set it back upon the straw in some perplexity. It must remain another mystery, to be resolved another day.

UPON REGAINING THE GREAT HOUSE, I WAS CAUGHT UP in a whirl of maids and footmen to-ing and fro-ing; a strange carriage was at the door, with a coat of arms upon it, and baggage was being stowed behind. I entered the house in haste, fumbling at the strings of my bonnet, and was in time to see Isobel exiting the Earl's study.

I was not, however, allowed to rejoice in her presence, fully dressed in her sombre widow's weeds and becomingly coiffed; for from her expression, the Countess was in great tumult of mind.

"My dear," I cried, all concern for her distress, "whatever can be the matter?"

She halted in the chill hall, the only still figure in the midst of her servants. Then, with neither a word nor a look, she brushed past me for the stairs.

"Isobel—" I began, but she continued silently on her way, never heeding me. I turned towards the library door in consternation. What could Fitzroy Payne have done to so destroy my friend?

But it was not the Earl who was the agent of Isobel's misery. Lord Harold was within, standing by the fire with a cigar and a glass of Port. One look at his face told me he had triumphed finally in his relentless pursuit of Isobel's Barbadoes plantations; Crosswinds was hers no more. I understood, now, the flurry about the coach drawn up to the door. Having gained his object, Harold Trowbridge had no further use for Scargrave.

"Lord Harold," I said, crossing to face him, my fear

of his power banished, "I see that the dark angel has triumphed."

He raised his glass to me in mocking salute and tossed back its contents. "Was there ever a doubt?" he said.

"Lucifer was possessed of just such certainty, my lord, and his prospects in the end were hardly sanguine."

"I would disagree, Miss Austen. Lucifer inherited a kingdom, assuredly, and one of his own design. Many men would wish to claim as much."

I waved a hand dismissively. "You talk but to hear yourself speak, my lord, and I have no time for the cultivation of vanity. I am come to bid you good-bye, but not farewell and hardly *adieu*. I should rather wish you to fare poorly and go straight to the Devil."

Such language, I admit, is shocking in any woman, and particularly in a clergyman's daughter; but the blood was upon me, as my dear brother Henry would say, and I was careless of effect. The one I produced, however, was the last I should have anticipated. Rather than smiling in scorn, or throwing back his head in outright laughter, Harold Trowbridge took his cigar from his lips, and studied me speculatively.

"Your aspect gains something in the liveliness of anger, Miss Austen. Had I anticipated such, I should have provoked you to it sooner, simply for the enjoyment of the effect." His dark eyes actually *danced*, with all the impudence of a man who has never known scruple.

"How can you speak so, my lord, when you have been the ruin of one of the gentlest, the best, and certainly now the most suffering of women?"

"*You* would have it that I find pleasure in my achievements, particularly when they are won at the expense of such."

"You are in every way despicable," I said.

"Perhaps," he rejoined, "but I am nonetheless successful, and the Countess is merely noble and poor."

"How," I began, my voice unpleasantly strident to my own ears, "did you prevail upon her? She was in every way opposed to your purpose. It can only be that the weight of her recent afflictions has enervated her, and that she gave up the struggle rather than contest with one such as you."

"I merely pointed out that she is penniless," Trowbridge said calmly, "and that her creditors have called in their debts. While her husband was alive, I chose to bide my time, and learn what the cost of clearing the estates' encumbrance was worth to him; but with Scargrave gone, there is no point in delaying further."

"Scargrave is gone, but Scargrave is yet with us," I pointed out. "The Earl has an heir, possessed of all the potency of his estates."

"And a healthy debt of his own," the rogue said mildly. "Even if the Countess were to rush in unseemly haste, and marry her lover"—at this demonstration of his knowledge, I gasped, but he took no notice—"Fitzroy Payne must look to his own accounts first. Half of London are his creditors; his own holdings in the Indies are beset with difficulties, and should his uncle not have died, Payne should soon have been hauled into court, or killed in a duel by one of the many men to whom he owes debts of honour."

"Debts of honour?" I was aghast.

"Miss Austen," Lord Harold said with a condescension that made my blood run hot, "I understand you are more accustomed to the ways of the country than of Town. Doubt cannot be in your nature, nor suspicion in your character. But let me assure you that Fitzroy Payne keeps up with a very fast set. Indeed, he forms its chief ornament. The cost of his establishment—his clothes, the maintenance of his Derbyshire estate, the gambling to which he is all too partial—exact a heavy toll on a fortune that is not above three thousand pounds a year. He has wagered heavily on the expectation of his inheritance, and his creditors, recognising his prospects, have been content to give him more line with which to hang himself. But he has reached the end of his rope, and I fear there is no slack for your friend the Countess to grasp."

I was struck by all the power of Trowbridge's words, so

carelessly bestowed, and clearly without a suspicion that the Earl might have died by other than natural causes. That Fitzroy Payne had a motive to murder—and well before the Earl should get himself a son, and thus disinherit his nephew—was patently obvious. The image of Fitzroy Payne's noble face rose in my mind; could such a man be capable of killing? But certainly his appearance gave no hint of the pressure of his circumstances; he had never betrayed the desperation that must haunt his every thought. I understood better, now, why he had not pressed Isobel to break off her engagement to the Earl, and marry him instead; the wrath of his uncle should have blasted his future prospects entirely. Better to win the Countess's heart from her husband—and so guard against the possibility of an heir and the loss of an immense estate.

What had seemed noble, in retrospect was revealed as vilely mercenary. But my thoughts were interrupted by Lord Harold's implacable voice.

". . . and then there is the matter of Mrs. Hammond."

"Mrs. Hammond?"

"A woman he keeps in a flat in Cheapside. It pains me to wound the sensitivities of a lady, but there it is. Her tastes are somewhat extravagant, according to my sources."

A *mistress,* when Payne had professed love for Isobel. By any account, it was too much. "Your information has been complete, indeed, Lord Harold," I said contemptuously. "I would that the gathering of it did you more honour."

"I make it a point to learn all that I can of my adversaries," Trowbridge replied easily. "Finance is war, Miss Austen, and one cannot wage war without knowledge. The force of mine was readily apparent to the Countess."

"You told her of this?" I exclaimed, with horror. "Of Mrs. Hammond as well?"

"It was essential for little Isobel to understand that any hope of succour from the new Earl must be impossible. I could not defer my offer for Crosswinds until such time as she might marry the rogue. I could not depend upon his funds being directed my way."

I comprehended now the utter defeat of my friend's aspect as she sought the stairs; the air of bewildered pain. Where she assumed strength and love to be hers, she was met with treachery and deceit. And *I* had urged her only this morning to put aside regret and turn to the living. *I* had pled Fitzroy Payne's case, when all such pleading must be injury.

"I believe the Countess felt the truth of my arguments," Lord Harold continued, reaching for the decanter of Port to refill his glass. "She agreed to accept a sum—quite generous, under the circumstances—in return for her properties and the discharge of her debt. She shall have something to live on, at least, which she certainly could not say before."

And so he feels himself to have been magnanimous. *Vile* man.

I wheeled for the door, intent upon taking no leave of Harold Trowbridge, but a thought stopped me where I stood. An adventurer like his lordship never wagers without great purpose; and so there must be a value to Crosswinds of which dear Isobel knew nothing.

"What can have been so important, Lord Harold," I said, turning again to face him, "that you should struggle so long against the Countess?"

"Winning alone has made it worthwhile," he answered carelessly, drawing on his cigar and releasing the smoke in a foul-scented cloud. "But then there is the matter of the property itself. The lands run down to a deep-water harbour, perfect for the mooring of heavy ships; it is unique to the Barbadoes in being held in private hands. Such a port is essential."

"Essential for what purpose?"

"One you should hardly understand, my dear. And now," he said, drawing forth a pocket watch, "I fear I must depart. It has been a delightful encounter, Miss Austen. We make a compelling pair. My initiative, and your wits—had you a greater fortune, I should almost think myself in danger. But alas, you are quite portionless; and hardly possessed of enough beauty to make lack of means a trifle."

"That is just as well, Lord Harold," I said clearly, "for your lack of finer feeling, of scruple and honour—of everything, in truth, that turns a man a gentleman—makes you the very *last* person I could ever be prevailed upon to marry."

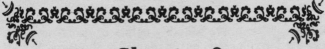

Chapter 9

The Animal Smell of Blood

24 December 1802
~

A CONSTRAINT HAS FALLEN OVER OUR PARTY WITH LORD Harold's departure—an event so fervently desired, and yet in its achievement, offering little in the way of ease or peace. That his disclosures to Isobel have poisoned her feelings for Fitzroy Payne, I do not doubt; she encounters the new Earl with a determined coldness, and spends much of her days alone in her rooms, while he—cast down and grown even more unhappy—keeps to his library, his walks through the Park, and the comfort of his books.

Fitzroy Payne has often during these long hours, by a look or a word, seemed on the verge of requesting my counsel, but is prevented by his strong reserve. I may confess myself relieved at his hesitancy, for it is an interview I would at all costs avoid. He undoubtedly knows of Isobel's decision to turn over her estates to Lord Harold; but it is certain he did nothing to impede that gentleman's departure. And so I must judge him to have failed her when she most required aid.

With the Countess distracted and the new Earl little better, Scargrave Manor's habits of order might be expected to run awry; but Madame Delahoussaye has assumed her niece's role of chatelaine with admirable relish. She now vies with Mrs. Hodges for authority over the principal rooms, and sets about directing the housemaids at their work. When Fitzroy Payne happens to leave his refuge for his customary ramble, Madame descends upon the library and will suffer no one to assist her. Danson, the Earl's man, is banished thin-lipped and grim to the servants' quarters, and a fearsome racket emanates from behind the library's closed doors. When Madame emerges, however, the Earl's papers have been tidied, his cigar ash disposed, and his letters neatly grouped in a pile for Danson to file away. A veritable war has ensued between the Earl's valet and his beloved's aunt; and I must declare Madame to be the winner in the majority of their engagements.

Fanny Delahoussaye continues to suffer from a poor stomach, though most afternoons she rallies enough to play at lottery tickets with Tom Hearst, when he is so inclined—and that is often, for it seems the atmosphere in the cottage down the lane is less than congenial. Mr. George Hearst looks decidedly morose, being lost in a brown study that lifts only when he is repeatedly addressed; hardly the sort of society the boisterous Lieutenant should choose. We are blest in that the moody ecclesiastic rarely darkens the Manor door, and his stupidity often sends his brother in desperation from the cottage.

Isobel's persistent sorrow makes me feel a useless friend, and I have wondered more than once whether I did right by staying on; but when I voiced my intention of returning to Bath in Fitzroy Payne's hearing, he started in dismay, and pressed me so urgently to remain—that *I might endeavour to lift the Countess's spirits*—that I could not in good conscience depart. Whatever Lord Scargrave's faults and vices may be, I can know nothing of them. He remains all that is honourable in my presence.

And since I must await the offer of the Scargrave carriage to convey me home, I am, more to the point, utterly without the means to leave.

With little of a cheering nature to excite my interest, and nothing further from the poisonous pen, I determined to profit by Lieutenant Hearst's knowledge and patience, and had three lessons on horseback during the course of last week. And so, the weather holding fine and steady this morning after several days of snow, I decided to seek some exercise, and betook myself to the stables in search of Lady Bess. I considered awaiting Lieutenant Hearst's company—but as I could not predict his plans with any certainty, and was loath to appear to *seek* his attention by sending to Scargrave Cottage, I settled it that I should make my way to the stables alone. I felt myself impatient to be away; and did a groom prove unable to accompany me, I had no little confidence in assaying to ride unattended.

I crossed the gravel of the stableyard, swept clean of snow, and encountered James, the chief boy.

"Miss Austen!" he exclaimed. "You be wantin' Bess, I warrant?"

"I am," I said, smiling, "unless she is otherwise engaged."

"She's been turned into the near paddock," James said, knitting his brows; "on account of the day being so fine. If you've but a moment, I'll fetch 'er."

And he was about to do so, when Mr. George Hearst appeared, looking as black as the memory of bad weather, and with hardly a nod to me or a word of kindness for the groom.

"Fetch Balthasar as quick as you can, boy," he said, and when James hesitated, gestured emphatically towards the stable door. "Be off with you."

The groom cast me an apologetic look.

"And mind you bring him round to the main entrance," George Hearst added, turning abruptly and walking in the direction of the great house.

What had inspired such haste and truculence, I could

not think, and had half a mind to catch him up and enquire of his trouble. But there was something in Mr. Hearst's aspect that warned me off—a suggestion of an increase in his usual taciturnity, perhaps—and I remained where I stood. Few words enough had passed between us since our conversation in the lane the previous week; I half-surmised that the gentleman regretted of his frankness, and had resolved to avoid my company. So I deemed it best to seek the fields while he retained the Manor. After an instant, I followed James to the interior of the lofty-ceilinged stable, searching out his form in the dim light. The groom stood framed against a stall far down the row, where a great black head reared over the door of its box like a military statue of old. The very Balthasar.

"Do you wait another minute, Miss Austen, and I shall have Bess stamping to bear you," the boy assured me.

"There is no need, James," I said. "If you but give me her bridle and lead, I shall fetch her myself."

"I don't know as it's a job for a lady"—he looked all his doubt—"nor as you'll meet with much success, begging your pardon, miss."

"As I must wait by the paddock, or wait by the stables, I would fain be of use; and it cannot hurt me to try. Do you take Balthasar to Mr. Hearst, James, and follow me to the fields. Then if the horse outwits me, your conscience may be salved by effecting my salvation."

BESS WAS AMONG A SMALL GROUP OF HER FELLOW CREATURES clustered by the paddock's far rail. That the horses were intent upon remaining in their corner, I readily observed; and wondered at so close a converse in so wide a space. Perhaps they missed the comfortable warmth of their boxes, and sought instead to make walls of one another. Whatever their purpose, it caused me to walk the length of the field in my boots, the snow coming up nearly to their tops. Gathering my courage, I clucked to Bess as Tom Hearst had taught me to do. To my delight, she came towards me obediently enough, and thrust her nose into the bridle, a perfect lady; I had but to snap on the halter and lead her to the paddock gate.

It was here that I encountered difficulty, and of so decided a turn that I was completely routed. For Bess would not approach the inoffensive gate, and, indeed, rolled her eyes and whinnied in such a violent fashion, backing onto her hind legs, that I lost my grip on the halter and was forced to watch in despair as she hurried herself back to the field's far corner. It was, by all accounts, inexplicable. That the mare had entered by the gate but a few hours earlier was evident, there being none other in the enclosure; but to approach it now was to her of all things the most distasteful.

There are those who will assert that Providence robbed animals of sense, and thus consigned them to serve at man's pleasure. But it was my lot to have a country childhood, and though I was denied a mount of my own, was often to observe my dear Madam Lefroy[1] in command of hers. That she worked *with* the animal's intelligence, rather than doubting the existence of such, was apparent. And so I determined to discover what had so terrified Lady Bess about the gate.

Upon approaching it, I found nothing amiss—it seemed a gate much like any other. A scrap of fabric, grey against the whiteness of the snow, caught my eye, and I bent to retrieve it; a fine handkerchief of lawn, with Isobel's looping monogram. She left them behind her wherever she went; I had myself observed her drop them countless times, and surmised she must keep a running account with a purveyor in Town. But how had one come to be here? I secured it in my pocket, and turned to study the paddock.

As if for the first time, I saw what had filled my sight

1. Anne Lefroy, "Madam" among her acquaintance, was Jane's dearest friend during her childhood days in Steventon, Hampshire, despite the disparity in their ages. Anne Lefroy was to die in 1804 as the result of a fall from her horse.—*Editor's note.*

unnoticed before: several sets of footprints, crossed and trampled one upon the other, led to the small hay shed at one side of the paddock, and the door was slightly ajar. Fanny Delahoussaye again?

There was no sound from within at my approach, unless it was drowned to silence by the excited nickers that rang out from the horses' end of the field. I touched the wooden door with gloved fingertips, and it slowly swung back on creaking hinges. There could be nothing inside, I determined once my eyes had adjusted to the light, but hay—great mounds of it piled from floor to ceiling, with a slight dusting of snow where cracks in the roof had given way to the weather. The grooms, perhaps, had visited the place upon turning out the horses, and left a sprinkling of fodder fresh upon the snow. I made as if to turn away, when my sharper senses stopped me. The scent of dried summer grass—sweet and musty enough to send one sneezing—had been overlaid with something animal. My heartbeat quickened as I put a name to the odour: it was blood, still warm and wet, and soaked into the hay at my feet.

I bent down and studied the floor, discerning in the dimness a blacker stain. The wetness led to the dark corner of the shed, and though my heart misgave me, I felt that I *must know* what lay there in the fodder. Lifting my skirts and treading carefully, I crept towards the farthest bale.

The fingers of a hand, reaching in endless supplication from a covering shroud of hay, stopped me still; and for an instant, my courage failed me. That it was a woman's hand I readily discerned, and something very like terror held me in its grip for the space of several heartbeats. But I recoiled at the knowledge of my faint head, and determined to go on rather than back. I reached a gloved hand to the hay and pulled it aside.

It was the maid Marguerite, and in no fit state to be seen.

Her throat had been cut from ear to ear, and her head hung at a lugubrious angle from her neck, which was bedaubed with the welter of blood that had poured from her obscene wound. Her sightless eyes were rolled back into her head so that only the whites were apparent, and her mouth was agape in a silent scream. But it was the limpness of her body, thrown like a rag doll's in the mound of hay, that affected me most strongly; the helter-skelter of limbs, nerveless beyond all mastery, were mute testament to departed life. Had she made the sign of the cross, eyes wide with terror, as she died?

I should like to record that I viewed the mangled girl with the equanimity befitting a heroine of Mrs. Radcliffe, or that a black curtain fell before my eyes, and all sensibility failed me, as Charlotte Smith would have it;[2] but, in truth, I lost my head and screamed at the fullest pitch of my lungs, turning and running from the gruesome shed without a backward glance.

Once outside in the air, trembling and frantic, I forced myself to halt and consider the facts. The maid was dead, and hardly by her own hand; that she had been murdered, and brutally so, must be made known to Sir William Reynolds at once. But what of her presence, here in the field? Had she been hiding by day in the shed, the better to post her poisonous letters by night? Or had she been lured here from hiding by the summons of her murderer? If the former, a hasty interview of the grooms should satisfy all doubts; either they would admit to consciousness of her sheltering in the field, or profess it to be impossible.

That she had been murdered in the shed was readily apparent, for had she been dispatched elsewhere and secreted in the hay under cover of darkness, the marks of her blood must surely have been registered on the snow

2. As noted elsewhere, Ann Radcliffe, who wrote *The Mysteries of Udolpho,* and Charlotte Smith, author of *Ethelinde,* were two authors Jane Austen read, although they were also practitioners of the Gothic formulas she sometimes lampooned for their unnatural characters.—*Editor's note.*

that lay everywhere about. It had ceased falling by the previous night's supper; and the blood was too fresh, by my judgment, to have been spilt very long past.

It was then that I became sensible of the import of the footprints that I had first noted leading towards the shed; and bent to study them more closely. That the one foot was Marguerite's own, seemed clear; and that the other represented a man's larger boot, was equally obvious; but beyond this I could tell nothing. Was the man's print that of a poor labourer, or a wealthy gentleman? The bright morning sun had warmed the snow just enough to soften the imprint of both shoes, leaving an outline that revealed nothing of the leather surfaces themselves.

I stood up and craned for some view of the groom, James; he appeared as I did so, a dark speck on the hill above the paddock fence, waving gaily. I raised my hand in return, and with new determination ducked back into the hut.

If the girl had been summoned to her death, she might yet bear the missive somewhere about her person, and so posthumously identify her murderer. That a man bent upon silencing her would also have surmised as much, I acknowledged, but deemed the search no less worthy. When James arrived, Marguerite should become the property of the law, with all the hullabaloo and confusion such a gruesome discovery necessitated; I had best undertake the duty alone, and quickly.

I allowed myself a moment to adjust to the poor light, drew a quick breath against the sickening smell of blood, and determined not to glance at the poor maid's face as I reached for the pockets of her gown. She lay twisted on her back, thrusting one hip upward and guarding the other, and I confess I was forced to wrestle with her corpse the smallest degree to obtain access to the nether side; but it was for nought. Her pockets were empty.

I hesitated an instant and considered the ways of country folk. Where would a simple girl secrete a letter, safe from prying eyes? In her bodice, of course.

Her coarse nankeen gown was a fearful thing, while

the linen of her shift was rucked up and stiffening with blood; I bethought me of my gloves, and removed the right, the better to preserve it from stain. And, God help me, I reached into the upper edge of the dead woman's shift and felt briefly around her corset, closing my eyes as I did.

It was there, the faintest edge of folded paper lodged against the whalebone, and holding my breath, I plucked it out between two fingertips. Just time enough to tuck it into the pocket of my cloak and wipe my hand on some unspoilt hay. Then I drew on my glove once more and ducked through the doorway, my terror on my face, to meet James the groom.

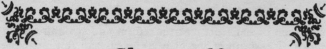

Chapter 10

Nuts in the Gun Case

24 December 1802, cont.

~

SOME HOURS LATER, WHEN SIR WILLIAM REYNOLDS HAD
been summoned and had seen all there was to be seen
in that terrible shed, Marguerite's poor body was borne
away to the Manor by some stout fellows of the home
farm. She was placed upon the oak settle in the butler's
pantry, a sheet covering her still form, and Mrs. Hodges
set about making her body decent—though how the
housekeeper retained the use of her wits, in the midst
of the furore the maid's murder created, I cannot think.
The Scargrave household was in the throes of Christmas
preparation, despite its deep mourning; and a partly-
stuffed goose, its neck hanging at an unfortunate angle,
was Marguerite's companion in death.

I sat before the fire in the drawing-room, quite alone,
for at the news of Marguerite's sad end, Fitzroy Payne
had offered his assistance to Sir William, while Isobel
had hastened to the side of Mrs. Hodges. Their duties
fulfilled, the Earl and the Countess had then retired to
their respective sanctuaries—Payne to the library, and
Isobel to her room. Fanny Delahoussaye, being a fashion-

able miss, had fallen into fits upon hearing of Marguerite's discovery; her mother even now attended her above stairs, with a basin of gruel and pursed lips, while Fanny played the victim. Mr. George Hearst was gone to London, on some errand of a private nature—it was for this he had retained the mighty Balthasar—while Lieutenant Hearst, summoned from the cottage at the body's discovery, had decamped to hit billiard balls in the smoking room.

My thoughts were disturbed by Cobblestone the butler, who flung wide the sitting-room door. The poor man's countenance was ashen; the appearance of a corpse in his pantry had routed his spirits entirely. Behind him stood my good friend Sir William Reynolds, and at the sight of his benign white head, I felt all the force of my late misadventure rush upon me. My eyes filled with tears.

"Miss Austen," Sir William said, hastening to my side, "my poor, dear Jane." He took my hand in his leathery old grasp and patted it gently. "Since it was your unfortunate lot to discover the murdered maid, my dear, I had hoped to speak with you at some length. But you must tell me whether your nerves can bear it."

I managed a smile. "My nerves have benefitted from quiet and contemplation, Sir William. Several hours' distance from events have brought some peace of mind."

"I rejoice to hear it," he said, pulling a chair close to the fire, "for I fear I must return you to your unhappy experiences of the morning. What took you to the paddock in the first place?"

I told him of my apprenticeship in riding, and my determination to bridle the horse alone; of Lady Bess's hesitation at the gate, and the mare's horror of that end of the field.

"And there was no outward sign of anything amiss?"

Without a word, I handed him the scrap of fabric I had found by the paddock gate.

"A handkerchief?" he said quizzically.

"It bears Isobel's initials."

"So I observe. The C is for her maiden name?"

"Collins," I said. "Her father was English, her mother a Creole by the name of Delahoussaye."

"Ah, yes—related, no doubt, to the impertinent miss who would have nothing to do with barristers," he said. "But of what import is the handkerchief?"

"I found it by the paddock gate, before I discovered the maid," I told him. "And though it pains me to avow it, the article cannot have been there long. We must declare it to have fallen once the snow had ceased—well after supper last evening. But it was not frozen, as it might have been had it lain out all night; nor yet was it soaked through, as any fabric lying on melting snow should be. I put its appearance at very little before the murder itself."

"Very well," Sir William said, "the Countess lost her handkerchief by the savaged body of her maid, who had accused her of the murder of her husband. We shall attempt to draw no conclusions from the fact."

"It is possible that another obtained the handkerchief, and placed it where it might be found, with the intent of throwing suspicion upon Isobel."

"It is possible, yes."

"There were but two sets of footprints leading to the body, and one of those was the maid's," I continued. "The other was formed by a man's boot."

"Perhaps the Countess wore her husband's shoes," Sir William said mildly, "the better to counterfeit her appearance."

"It is absurd!" I cried.

"It is as acceptable as the notion that someone dropped her handkerchief by the gate," the magistrate rejoined with equanimity. "You must own it to be at least *possible,* my dear Jane. Now, tell me of the finding of the maid, with your usual sense and power of organisation."

I related all that I could remember of the grim scene in the shed, though the images it recalled were of so vivid a nature as to cause me to pause now and again in my search for composure. I did not except to recount my first exit from that gruesome place, nor my return; and upon closing my recital, I handed to the magistrate the blood-stained slip of paper retrieved from the maid's bodice.

Sir William settled his spectacles on his nose with a frown, and looked at me over their rims. "This is most singular, my dear, most singular. *Two* items of evidence, removed from the scene of the crime? I would advise you in future to leave such corpses as you may encounter, completely untouched."

"But I found the handkerchief before I had reason to wonder at its presence," I said, "and I foresaw that the body should be brought to the house. In preparing Marguerite for burial, the note might have been lost—by accident or design."

"By design? You would have the murderer a member of the household?"

"How can it be otherwise?"

He shook his head. "One might perfectly see how it could be otherwise, my dear Jane. A penniless servant girl, abroad in the depths of winter, may readily fall prey to any number of misfortunes, and none of them at the hands of her employers."

"*You* do not credit such coincidence, Sir William."

He smiled at me in submission. "No, Jane, I do not. It is too much to believe that Marguerite should be found dead upon the very morn that her last missive was received."

"Her last missive—" I began, but was silenced by his raised hand.

"We shall talk of that in good time. For now, I would read this scrap of foolscap."

I knew the words by heart, though the hand was unfamiliar to me; it was a fragment of paper only, with a fragmentary sentence. *let us meet in our accustomed place* was all it said, without salutation or farewell. Its author had not been foolish enough to sign his name, so much was certain.

"It tells us little enough," Sir William said gruffly, "but that the paper is of excellent quality, and so small as to be passed from one hand to another without notice in public. The fragment lacks a watermark, but it is clearly of pure rag, and purchased at some expense." He tucked the note into his waistcoat and stroked his chin, his gaze distracted.

"It is an elegant hand, as well," I observed, "and for my part, I would judge it to be masculine. The diction would suggest a person of higher station than the maid's."

"I am in agreement, my dear."

"And now for the maid's final letter," I reminded him.

Sir William reached into his waistcoat once more and handed me a folded sheet. "This was nailed to the door of the Cock and Bull sometime before dawn," he told me. "Half the town has read it, and the other half has heard the news. I trust you to make as much sense as I of its meaning."

> To the good Sir—
> I have been disapoynted in my hopes of yore justice. And so I must speke out right. Evil is at work at Scargrave Manor. Look among the things of the Lord, and you will find the things of the Devil! Perhaps then you will beleve that Murder has been done, and that it was done by the Countess' hand. God rest the pore Earl's soul.
>
> Marguerite Dumas

I looked up, my question in my eyes.

"It is as bad as it may be," Sir William said, his face sombre. "She accuses the Countess of murder before the whole of Scargrave Close, and deigns to sign the accusation. Odd that she was slain so soon after writing it, do not you think, my dear Jane?"

I wrung my hands in consternation. "Can any be so unfortunate as poor Isobel? What are we to do, Sir William? What are we to do?"

"I am directed to search the personal effects of a lord," the magistrate said. "And since I cannot presume to know exactly of whom the maid writes—whether of an Earl deceased or living—I propose to review both the belongings of Fitzroy Payne, and of the late Lord Scargrave. That should amply serve the purpose, should it not, Jane?"

I SOUGHT ISOBEL IN HER ROOM, AND FOUND HER GONE to the pantry, where all that remained of Marguerite was bathed and freshly clothed preparatory to Christian burial. I requested that the Countess join me in the drawing-room; but words and courage failed me to warn my friend of the outrage she was soon to endure. Isobel read nothing of my dread in my face, and complied with alacrity.

I found the Earl awaiting us in the company of the magistrate. That Fitzroy Payne expected Sir William to address him regarding the maid's foul murder, was obvious by his surprise at that gentleman's hardly referring to it. Sir William lost no time in disclosing the nature of the third letter, to the confounding of the Earl, who had known nothing of the previous notes' existence. His face, upon learning the history of the letters, was a study in composure; never before have I seen the weight of social education brought to bear upon a matter so grievous and intimate. The Earl did not suffer himself to reproach Isobel for her secrecy, nor did he betray the slightest sensibility to the writer's dark words concerning a grey-haired lord. But his anger at the public nature of the accusations was palpable; and when requested to submit his belongings to the magistrate's penetrating eye, Fitzroy Payne's features stiffened.

"Is the very privacy of our home to suffer from the calumnies of this woman?" he burst out.

"This woman, as you call her, has been silenced; and I cannot believe so brutal a consequence to be unconnected to the activities of her pen," Sir William rejoined. "To the public eye, her end does but give credence to her assertions; and as such, we must do our best to answer them, and all rumour into the bargain."

The Earl's hand went to his brow, and he paced rapidly several times before the hearth, a muscle in his jaw working. After a moment, however, and a look for Sir William, he bowed his assent. "My man, Danson, will lay the contents of my apartments at your disposal."

"My late husband's things remain as yet in his rooms," Isobel said, her voice barely a whisper. "I shall escort you to them."

"There is no need to disturb yourself, Countess," Sir William told her. "The butler shall serve as my guide. And you, Lord Scargrave—do you be so good as to remain here as well. It is best that all parties be within reach while the work is toward."

"And barred from meddling with our rooms, if I undertake your meaning correctly," Fitzroy Payne said with a bitter smile; "very well."

WAITING IS ALWAYS A TEDIOUS BUSINESS, BUT NEVER MORE so than when coupled with apprehension. At Isobel's request, I moved to the pianoforte, and attempted to play for her amusement; but my fingers stumbled more often than is their wont, and despite the holiday season, my selection of airs tended almost exclusively towards the melancholy. It was as I was thus employed that Lieutenant Hearst appeared in the sitting-room, having wearied, one supposes, of striking at balls without an adversary to lend the game spice. He stood at my shoulder, his brows knit, and an unaccustomed gravity in possession of his countenance.

"Sir William has been here?" he enquired, with an effort at diffidence.

"And is not yet departed," I replied. "He is about his work above, while we await his pleasure below."

The Lieutenant hesitated, as if debating what to say, and then looked about the room. I ended the minuet of Mr. Mozart's I had struggled to perform, and gave up the piano altogether. As I rose from my place, too restless to seek another seat, Tom Hearst reached a hand as if to stop me.

"The magistrate has found nothing untoward, Miss Austen?"

I stared my amazement. "Un*toward*? Besides a black-mailing maid with a gruesomely ravaged throat, abandoned in a shed? I do not pretend to understand you, Lieutenant. Are such things in the common way, for an officer of the Horse Guards?"

He looked abashed, and cast about for an answer, but I turned swiftly from him and moved to the sitting-room window in an effort to overcome a sudden trembling in the limbs. I confess to feeling more disturbed by the memory of Marguerite's poor face than I should like. I may expect to have nightmares—or another visitation from the ghostly First Earl—by morning.

My companions in tragedy were no less cast down. Fitzroy Payne laboured under the pretence of absorption in his book, but his eyes strayed to Isobel's face as often as they were fixed on the page. I noted the expression, both sad and wistful, that played over his features in gazing upon the Countess; and pitied him for the silence that divided them. Marguerite's death and the revelation of the letters had not unmastered the newly-titled Earl, however; if anything, Fitzroy Payne seemed burdened with a greater dignity, as befit his station, and the uncertainty of events surrounding it.

Dear Isobel's gaze was fixed on emptiness, her hands lying idle in her lap; from the frequent waves of emotion that swept o'er her countenance, I judged her to be reviewing the length of December's sad history, and falling ever more into despair at the terrible reversal in her fortunes. I ached to go to her; but the presence of the others—and the weight of Sir William's impending return—froze me in my place. So in search of calm, I turned my eyes from the room to the snowy view beyond the window, marvelling that a day marked by such terrible events, should still appear so fine.

In the flurry over the maid, all notions of Christmas

Eve dinner had been lost to us, but not to Mrs. Hodges, the dependable Scargrave housekeeper; and it was with a start that I heard the bell summoning us to table. Tom Hearst was first to the door, and held it open for the ladies. Fitzroy Payne closed his book with a slap, his eyes upon Isobel, who rose from her chair as if waking from a dream. I inclined my head to the Earl and followed the Countess down the hall, feeling a trifle sick. But none of the party paused in its progression to the table, however little appetite we might possess; the activity of lifting a fork should at least prove a welcome alternative to restless silence.

Once in the dining parlour, however, I felt my efforts at equanimity completely routed. Mrs. Hodges had endeavoured to impart a seasonal aspect to the meal, by the addition of red bows and holly to the great Scargrave candelabra—and at the sight of such cheerful nonsense, my mind *would* turn to my family circle in Bath. What did my dear Cassandra, my father and mother, say of me tonight? Did my absence cause in their breasts as much loneliness as in my own? But I looked to Isobel, who failed even to notice the table's ornaments, so desolate and bereft was she; and felt my resolve stiffen. The maid's death meant little of a happy nature lay before the Countess; she had need of stalwart friends.

Madame Delahoussaye was already seated, though her countenance bode poorly for the meal's prospects. Her black eyes were sharp and her lips compressed. "Isobel, my dear, your cousin remains indisposed," she said.

"I regret to hear it, Aunt." The Countess sank into the chair the footman held ready, her face as pale as death. "Perhaps you should take dear Fanny to London once the holiday is passed—for certainly Scargrave can offer little to cheer her."

"It is decidedly unhealthy," Madame declared, her eyes upon Tom Hearst, "and I believe we shall depart the day after tomorrow. The society of Town, Isobel, must effect an elevation in poor Fanny's spirits."

"The society of Town being so much superior to Scargrave's, Madame?" the Lieutenant broke in. His distracted air was banished, and he shook out his serviette like a man possessed of good appetite. "I must confess that we are of one mind. In truth, I may congratulate myself that a better understanding has rarely existed between two such people, divided though we are by temperament, years, and experience. I shall seek my regiment in St. James at the first opportunity, the better to escort Miss Fanny to the gaieties of the Season."

"Insolent rogue!" Madame burst out, her face turning white with anger. "You shall do no such thing."

"I fear that I must, dear lady. I received a summons from my regiment this very day."

And what of the affair of the duel? I thought. Did his regiment welcome the Lieutenant with open arms, all his sins forgotten?

Madame clenched the handle of her fork as though she would drive it through the Lieutenant's heart. "There is nothing I desire *less* than that Fanny's prospects should be poisoned by your acquaintance."

"Dear Aunt!" Isobel cried, starting in her chair. "You forget yourself. Lieutenant Hearst is a member of the Scargrave family!"

"He is *all too much* a member of the family. He *presumes* upon his relation, Isobel. He thinks to have Fanny's beauty and her fortune for a song. And what is he? Nothing but an adventurer in a blue coat. The second son of a wastrel." Madame threw down her serviette and thrust back her chair. "I have no appetite for dining in such company. Inform Mrs. Hodges, Isobel, that I shall take a tray in my room."

Lieutenant Hearst raised his glass to the lady. "Your health, Madame," he cried, as she swept by him, her eyes snapping. Then he tipped his wine towards me. "It shall make quite a picture, shall it not, Miss Austen? Miss Fanny and the Lieutenant. So little sense, allied with so much sensibility."

"Good Lord, Tom," Fitzroy Payne chided, "must you

plague Madame so? Her daughter's care is as the world to her. We who know you, know that you delight in provoking; but *she* feels only insult in your raillery."

"Reproaches, Fitzroy?" The Lieutenant affected dismay. "And I had looked for thanks! For by my offices the good woman is returned to her room, and we may take Christmas Eve dinner in peace."

Tom Hearst may have meant his words in jest, but his tone was cutting; and I wondered, as I listened, at the edge of bitterness in his voice. The truth of it all escapes me. Does he admire Fanny? His barbs would suggest the opposite. But he continues to tease Madame unmercifully with his attentions, as though her daughter remains his object. And yet, and yet—when I spend an hour in his company, and feel his warmth, my heart whispers that Fanny hopes in vain.

IT WAS WHILE WE TOYED WITH MRS. HODGES'S EXCELLENT oyster soup that Sir William returned. Not two hours had passed since he had left us, I judged; but from the transformation of his countenance during that time, it might well have been a year.

He stood in the doorway, clearing his throat, his eyes on the Countess's pale face. "I am distressed to disturb you at your dinner, my lady," he said, "but I am forced to ask of those present a few questions."

"But of course, Sir William." Isobel set down her spoon, her features more composed than I could have believed, despite the air of strain that governed the room. "How may we be of service?"

The magistrate glanced at the two footmen ranged against the dining parlour's walls, and then gave the Countess an expressive look. "I should prefer to speak to the family alone. Excepting, that is, Miss Austen."

Isobel lifted her hand in a gesture of dismissal, and the footmen departed. Their removal only heightened the tensions around the table. But Sir William did not prolong the suspense.

"I believe this is yours, my lady," he said, advancing upon Isobel's chair with hand extended.

"Why, so it is!" she exclaimed, taking the proffered handkerchief. "I am forever leaving my linen about like a forgetful schoolgirl. Where did you encounter it?"

"Miss Austen was so good as to retrieve it from the paddock this morning," the magistrate replied.

"The paddock . . ." Isobel's face drained of its last vestiges of colour. "But I have not been to the paddock these several days. Jane—" Her eyes sought mine in confusion.

"It was lying by the gate, Isobel," I told her quietly. "From its appearance in the snow, it was quite recently let fall."

Sir William interposed smoothly. "Have you any recognition of the hand that penned these words, Countess?" He took from his waistcoat the bloody slip of paper I had retrieved from Marguerite's bodice.

Isobel bent to study it with indrawn breath. She looked at me and then at the magistrate. "But what does it mean?" she said.

"The hand, my lady?"

With her eyes fixed upon the Earl's face, she replied slowly, "I should swear it to be Fitzroy's."

Tom Hearst cleared his throat and pushed back his chair. As I watched, he folded his arms across his chest—the better, perhaps, to contain himself. Our eyes met, and his eyebrow lifted—a mute plea for some sense from all this muddle.

Sir William turned to the Earl, and withdrew his hand from his pocket. In his open palm sat a clutch of small brown objects. "My lord," he said, "is it in your power to name these?"

Fitzroy Payne frowned and replied in the negative.

"And you, my lady?"

Isobel peered at the fruit, each one as small as a seed, in the magistrate's hand. "Why, they are the nuts of the Barbadoes tree!" she exclaimed. "The humble folk of my native island swear by them as a physick. But where did you find them?"

"Wrapped in velvet—in the present Lord Scargrave's gun case, my lady," Sir William replied, and his face was very grave. "I had thought it possible, but could not be certain, that they were the very seed you have named." He placed the nuts carefully on a serviette that lay upon the sideboard, and folded it into a neat package.

"And have you journeyed to the Indies unbeknownst to me, Fitzroy?" Isobel looked at the Earl, her brown eyes troubled. She retained admirable command of her voice, but I saw the pulse throbbing at her throat, and knew her heart was racing.

"You know it to be impossible," Fitzroy Payne replied. "Sir William, are the nuts wholesome?"

"The taste is so delightful, that to eat one is to eat them all," Sir William said, "which is what we may judge the late Earl to have done. For the Barbadoes nut is poison, Lord Scargrave; so deadly a purgative, in fact, that illness commences but a quarter-hour after ingestion, and death is achieved in a very few hours."

Tom Hearst leapt to his feet, his hand upon his sabre hilt. "Good God, man, what do you mean to say?"

There was a small sound, almost a whimper, from Isobel, whose face had gone a deadly white. Her hands were clenched on the table edge, as though without its support, she should crumple to the floor.

"Sit down, Tom." Fitzroy Payne's voice was weary. "Sir William intends us to believe the nuts caused my uncle's last illness."

"But, Fitzroy, are you mad? The fellow is suggesting—"

"I know what the Justice is suggesting." At his cousin's look, Tom Hearst stiffened, but regained his seat. Fitzroy Payne inclined his head to Sir William. "Pray continue."

"It is my duty, Lord Scargrave," Sir William said slowly, his eyes upon the floor, "to ask that the body of Frederick, Lord Scargrave, be exhumed from its resting place in the Scargrave vault."

"To what purpose, sir, would you so disturb my uncle's rest?"

"I should like Dr. Philip Pettigrew, of Sloane Street, who attended his lordship at his death, to reexamine the body." Sir William's eyes came up from the floor at that, and the coldness in them startled me.

"And what end may that serve?" The Earl's voice had lost its accustomed courtesy. "Pettigrew has already declared the man to be dead."

Sir William glanced at Isobel, and following his gaze, I saw my friend's hand had gone to her throat. "It is possible, my lord," the magistrate said, "for a physician to divine the contents of the stomach, even days after death; and from those, the cause of a man's demise."

"You would *anatomise*[1] my husband?" Isobel's countenance was sick with shock.

"I fear it is our only course, my lady," Sir William said, not without gentleness. "In the case of poison, even a purgative that induces vomiting, it is the only method for proving the truth or falsity of the murdered maid's claims."

I drew a deep breath, and found I was wadding the brown wool of my gown between my fingers.

"Sir William, I doubt you do this for your own satisfaction," Lord Scargrave said, in a low voice. "There is a public aspect to all of this." His dark eyes revealed nothing of the nature of his thoughts.

"There is, my lord. I should like the summary of Dr. Pettigrew's findings to be presented to a jury summoned by the coroner assigned to Hertfordshire, who shall be charged with finding the cause of the late Earl's de-

1. The medical dissection of corpses was a practice reserved for the bodies of executed criminals, which were often turned over to doctors for scientific study. Anatomization, as it was called, was considered the most degrading fate possible for the body of a loved one, so that even the families of condemned criminals sought to hide their corpses after execution, to prevent such disgrace.—*Editor's note.*

mise. We must in any case summon such a panel for the poor maid Marguerite, and it may as well serve for the presentation of evidence in your uncle's death."

"My dear Countess," Tom Hearst's voice broke in, "I fear you are unwell." Isobel's eyes were closed, and her breathing shallow. The Lieutenant rose as if to go to her, but Isobel stopped him with an upraised palm.

"I feel only what I should, dear Tom," she said, "and for that, there is no remedy. Please—let us hear Sir William out."

The magistrate had the grace to look uncomfortable for having caused a lady so much pain, and turned his gaze from Isobel with relief.

"The two cases can have nothing to do with one another," Fitzroy Payne avowed. "The maid's assertions are calumnies and lies. My uncle suffered a common complaint, and though he died of a sudden and was cheated of his span, such things have happened before."

"Have they, my lord?"

"Fitzroy," Isobel said faintly, and all our eyes turned to meet her own.

"Do as he asks, my love," she said, now past all care for propriety. "We shall never be free of doubt if we resist, and there shall be no living in the country."

"I very much fear, my lady, that you are right." Sir William inclined his head stiffly. "And my duty as a magistrate forces me to insist—for the maid's sake, if not your own."

Tom Hearst coughed, as though he choked, and I raised my eyes to his; but he gazed at something in the middle distance. I observed that his fingers gripped the arms of his chair so fiercely, the knuckles had gone white.

"The maid," Fitzroy Payne said thoughtfully. "That piece of paper, written in my hand, bears the marks of blood."

"You are observant, my lord." Sir William paced about the room and came to rest opposite my chair.

The new Earl appeared to hesitate before asking the

question that burned in his mind, but apprehension is a cruel master. "You found it on her person?" he said.

"It was found there, assuredly, my lord." Sir William cast an uneasy glance my way. I felt my face overcome with blushes, but none of the Scargrave party could spare a moment to study Miss Austen.

"But this is madness!" Fitzroy Payne rose forcefully to his feet, his calm deserting him at the last. "Madness, I tell you!"

We were all of us struck dumb. When a quiet man is moved to passion, it seems the very earth will shake; and at the violence of the Earl's words, Scargrave Manor trembled. Tom Hearst moved to stand tall behind his cousin, and the two faced Sir William with all the strength of their ancestors rising in the blood.

"I swear to you on my honour as a gentleman," the Earl cried, in a fevered accent, "on the reputation of the proud family of which I claim a part, that I have not seen the girl Marguerite since the day after my uncle's death."

"And the nuts found among your possessions, my lord?" Sir William's voice was as mild as the dusk beyond the windows.

"If they *did* cause the Earl's death—"

"*If* they did, assuredly." The magistrate turned and strolled towards the door, as though the Scargrave men suggested no belligerence. "For that, we must await the word of the good doctor."

"—even if it be that those foul seeds struck him a mortal blow, it can have nothing to do with me," Fitzroy Payne asserted. "I have known nothing of their existence until the moment you showed me them."

"Very well, my lord," Sir William said, and bowed to the entire room.

"You must believe me!"

The magistrate's gaze was on the Earl, and I was struck by the grimness of my old friend's countenance. "I greatly fear, Lord Scargrave," Sir William said, "that you plead with the wrong man. It is the coroner you must convince."

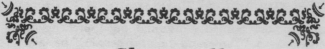

Chapter 11

Eliahu Bott at the Cock and Bull

27 December 1802

~

I MUST CONFESS TO A FEELING OF LASSITUDE AND MELAN-
choly in the three days that have followed my discovery of the maid's body, a mood I may perhaps attribute
to the sleeplessness that has marked my nights. Images
of the murdered girl—her white-rolled eyes and lolling
head, the necklace of gore that encircled her throat—fill
up my sight when I would close my eyes; and so I lie
wakeful in the December dark, intent upon discovering
the hint of footsteps in the gallery. It seems, however,
that the spectral First Earl is possessed of discernment
in his mourning; tonight he does not deign to recognise
the passing of a mere servant with the show that preceded her death. In my present state, however, I cannot find it in me to feel apprehension at his possible
coming; even fear is swallowed up in my general ma-
laise.

It was a poor sort of Christmas, despite my quiet pleasure in a letter and a holiday box I owed to my dear
Cassandra—containing fifteen yards of a lovely pink
muslin for the making up of a new gown. After church

in Scargrave Close, Isobel kept to her room for much of the day, while Lord Scargrave sought the freedom of the out-of-doors, walking Scargrave's surrounding parkland for hours and returning only with the falling dusk. I was left to the company of Tom Hearst, whose every attention was monopolised by the lively Fanny Delahoussaye, and to his brother George—who though returned from London, appeared little recovered from his bad humour of Christmas Eve. The cleric wasted many hours in silent contemplation before the fire, brows drawn down over brooding eyes.

I bent myself to the pianoforte, music being the one solace for my nerves, but was eventually forced to break off by Miss Delahoussaye, who called me to attention long enough to pronounce us all a sad sort of company for Christmastide. She proposed some simple amusement—play-acting in the parlour, perhaps, or the arrangement of *tableaux vivants,* neither of which activity was suited to our mood or situation.

"There is Fanny!" Madame Delahoussaye exclaimed indulgently; "so gay, no trifle can burden her light spirits; so full of good humour, that one forgets all one's cares!"

"I should hardly call murder a trifle," George Hearst remarked in his mordant voice, "though if one is so disposed, all that is serious in life may be ignored by a steady pursuit of frivolity."

"La, George, you *are* a stick," Miss Fanny observed. "I wonder the murderer has not seen fit to send *you* off, out of sheer *ennui.* But never mind. We shall amuse ourselves the better without you."

"As is generally the case," Mr. Hearst replied, "though I count it no dishonour. Since you find amusement in everything, Miss Delahoussaye—even what is serious or tragic—stimulating your ability to laugh must be considered a talent very much in the common way. I confess I pride myself on rarer qualities."

"There must be a store of old clothes about, in such an ancient seat as this," Fanny said, paying him no heed; "I am sure Lieutenant Hearst would delight to see me arrayed as Marie Antoinette, and parade himself as the Sun King."

Madame appeared startled, and surveyed her daughter narrowly. "I should sooner wish you to have the ordering of your history, my dear," she said, "for some several generations separate the two."

Fanny shrugged with elegant disregard. "Pooh, Mamma! When one is play-acting, it makes no odds. I shall call for Mrs. Hodges, and turn the attics topsy-turvy."

"Pray do not, Fanny," Madame said sharply. "We should sooner hear your lovely voice raised in song—and to deprive us of your presence would be a cruel piece of work. I am sure," she said, "that Lieutenant Hearst agrees."

I was surprised to hear her appeal in such a case to a man she despised, and concluded that fancy dress was indeed abhorrent to her. But Miss Fanny was all smiles in an instant, and I must give up my place at the instrument. In truth, I cared little, and soon sought the privacy of my room; for she *would* persist in singing boisterous carols of the season, in an ill-considered display of liveliness.

Yesterday, Sir William presided over the removal of the late Earl's coffin from the great stone sarcophagus in Scargrave Close churchyard, and saw it entrusted to Dr. Pettigrew, the London physician. In this he was attended by Eliahu Bott, the Hertfordshire coroner, a trim little fellow with a perennially dyspeptic look. The inquest is called for this afternoon, and all are to attend. I myself must offer testimony of the finding of Marguerite, and feel no little trepidation at the prospect. And so my life is as suspended as indrawn breath, awaiting that relief of tension that I pray the inquest will bring.

Sir William himself has grown remote in speech and aspect; he has ceased to impart what ever he knows of the case to me, treating me rather with a gentle and solicitous concern that inspires only fear. That he knows some ill of Isobel and Fitzroy Payne—that he believes them, in fact, to be guilty of both murders—I have surmised. Lacking that affection for the Countess born of close acquaintance, or that respect for the character of the new Earl I persist in harbouring, Sir William is unfettered in his judgment; and so I anticipate his harshness with regard to the inquest and fear for its outcome. His duty as magistrate for the district compels him to prove my friends' guilt;[1] and in gathering what may tell against them, he is assiduous as ever in his days at the King's Bench. That he was absent some few days in London, in search of witnesses for the coming panel, I learned from his dear lady upon calling at the house in the Scargrave carriage; and her own gravity of manner, and pitying look, did little to cheer my hopes of a happy outcome.

Though the weather has held fair since Christmas Eve, I have scorned Lady Bess and the pleasures of riding horseback; scorned my journal, my volume of Boswell, even my letter-writing—for how to tell my dear Cassandra of the evil men may do? And, in truth, I hardly know what I should write; for I cannot find the logic in events for myself, much less for the understanding of another. The world is revealed as an uncertain place, where the face of a friend may hide the intent of a murderer; where the stoutest protestations may serve to beguile the trusting into a false complacency. Isobel's handkerchief, found by the paddock gate, and Fitzroy Payne's handwriting on the note found in the maid's bodice—to say nothing of the Barbadoes nuts in his possession—are facts which cannot be denied. Even did no

1. Our notion of a defendant being innocent until proven guilty is relatively recent. Until 1848, a magistrate was not charged with a presumption of innocence on the part of the defendant, or with the objective consideration of evidence, but merely with constructing a case against the accused. Until 1837, a lawyer for the accused was not allowed to query witnesses or cross-examine them, and not until the turn of the century was the accused allowed to testify on his or her own behalf.—*Editor's note.*

word of Isobel's attachment to her nephew emerge at the inquest, the sagacious among the jury might surmise it, from the linkage of evidence and the respective ages and association of the parties. A stranger to either's character might readily assume that the heir poisoned his uncle for the dual purpose of acquiring his fortune and his wife; and that Isobel, needy of money and younger by a generation than her spouse of three months, should happily accede to the plan of her amorous swain. The maid's death is handily disposed of; she had accused the lovers to the magistrate, and won a brutal silence as her reward. And so the prospects for both are most black, indeed.

I say nothing of my own credence in the plot outlined above. To be frank, I know not what to think. An unhappy choice is before me: to find the Countess's and her lover's earnest avowals of innocence to spring from the grossest duplicity, and my own faith in Isobel to be founded upon sand; or to accuse others, equally intimate to the household, of adding to the sin of murder that of entangling the innocent in a deadly web of suspicion. Neither is to be preferred, for both are based upon the worst in human nature; and though I have learned to laugh at such—to look for it among my acquaintance and mock it in my writing—when met with evil in its truest form, I find that even *I* cannot dismiss it with worldly detachment. The maid was too dead, and too anguished in her dying, to permit of it; any more than the ravaged face and painful final hours of the late Earl should counsel mercy to his assassin.

Later that afternoon

~

"MY DEAR COUNTESS," TOM HEARST SAID EARNESTLY TO Isobel, "may I suggest you ride with George and me, and Miss Austen if she will, and leave the Scargrave coach for another day."

"But Percy has brought the horses round, Tom," Isobel protested, with a gesture for the Scargrave coachman.

The Lieutenant appeared to hesitate, and cast a glance at Fitzroy Payne.

"I believe my cousin fears for your safety, Countess," that gentleman said quietly. "The townsfolk's mood is grown ugly since the publication of the maid's letter, and her brutal death."

Isobel's beautiful eyes were shadowed as she studied the Earl's countenance. With a tremor in her voice, she enquired, "You share Tom's fears, Fitzroy?"

"I am afraid, my dear Isobel, that many would relish the chance our public parade affords them. My late uncle was neither so lenient in his management of accounts, nor so indulgent in his stewardship of his tenants, as to win their gratitude and affection. As his heir, I have inherited the malice they bore him."

"There was even talk of stoning the coach," Lieutenant Hearst said apologetically, "the maid having been a favourite among the bloods at the Cock and Bull. Indeed, Sir William advised that any equipage bearing the Scargrave crest should be left in the carriage house today. It is he who apprised me of the danger. Our chariot, as you know, is painted a simple black, and could not hope to draw the attention that Percy and his four matched greys should do."

"Very well," Isobel said, her voice choked. "I shall submit to hiding and deceit, though both are alien to my nature. And I shall leave for London as soon as the inquest is closed, the better to escape this horrid place."

And so we were handed in to the Hearsts' equipage, while the Delahoussayes and the new Earl sought Sir William's chariot; and though a crowd was gathered at the publican's door, we pulled up in the rear of the building, and entered it unscathed.

THE CORONER, MR. BOTT, HAD ASSEMBLED HIS JURY IN THE largest space the Cock and Bull could boast. It was the main tavern-room, redolent of the smoked hams that hung from its rafters and the yeasty aftermath of spilt beer. The floor had been scrubbed for the occasion, and all but one of the tables rolled into an anteroom; behind the last, the twelve men were ranged in an awkward rank upon rank—small holders in their Sunday best, unable to meet Isobel's eyes when she entered on the arm of Lieutenant Hearst; the master of the pub himself, his large wattle tucked into a collar several sizes too small; the local apothecary, Mr. Smollet, red of face and stern of expression; and Squire Fulsome, from Long Farm, resplendent in a red silk waistcoat (a Christmas present from his little Judy), whom Bott had appointed foreman.

Facing this hodge-podge assembly were rows of chairs, posed as for an Evangelical revival,[2] the majority of them firmly held by the good folk of the village. At our appearance a few moments before the appointed hour of one o'clock, only the row designated for the Scargrave family remained at liberty; and I felt myself quail when the mass of heads turned as if with one force, and stared balefully upon our entrance. However, summoning my courage, I followed Isobel to the front of the room, the gentlemen falling in behind, but had not proceeded two paces before a very fat and gap-toothed woman, her large head burdened with an atrocious hat of turquoise and madder rose, thrust herself forward from the assembly with hand extended towards the Countess.

"There she be!" she screeched, her knotty red fingers trembling, "the 'arlot and Jezebel of Scargrave! The woman as has blood stained deep into 'er skin! The murderess and whore the good Earl took in, to 'is peril! Pore

2. Evangelicalism was a reformist movement within the Church of England that arose in the late eighteenth century. Somewhat Calvinistic in its bent, it opposed moral laxity and frivolity of most kinds, particularly among the clergy. Though Jane Austen approved of clergymen taking their duties seriously, she considered Evangelicals excessive in their ardor.—*Editor's note.*

Margie suffered to the death for the telling of it, but 'er life is not in vain! May God's vengeance be swift and 'ard for the cunning woman as has forgot 'is ways!"

Isobel stopped as though turned to stone. Her remarkable eyes were bewildered and one hand went to her throat—her first gesture in moments of anxiety. As the woman's tirade waned, my friend began to sway, and I saw that she should faint. Fitzroy Payne sprang into the crowd with an unaccustomed energy, bent upon seizing the harridan and forcing her from the room; but he was restrained at the last by Tom Hearst.

"Leave Lizzy Scratch to her gin, Fitzroy," the Lieutenant cautioned; "she is a witness Sir William would call, and must remain."

For his part, Sir William spoke severely to the woman, who looked somewhat cowed by his words, and thereafter confined herself to muttering over the steaming drink she held between two fingerless mitts. Supported by the magistrate, Isobel moved on, myself in her wake, and gained the dubious safety of a hard wooden chair.

There was a curious discomfort attached to a position so far forward from the remainder of the assembly; one felt as though the eyes of the entire town were boring into the back of one's head with virulent animosity. But it could not be helped; we had arrived, and must suffer our two hours upon the block.

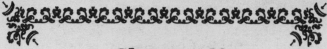

Chapter 12

Convincing the Coroner

27 December 1802, cont.

~

THE EVIDENCE REGARDING THE DEATH OF FREDERICK, LORD
Scargrave, was to be first presented, and the London
physician, Dr. Philip Pettigrew, took his seat by the coroner's side. He looked even younger in the light of day
than he had appeared by the late Earl's bedside; a broad-
shouldered man, of short stature, his eyes cool and grey
behind gold spectacles. Placing his hand upon the Bible,
he was duly sworn, and gazed out upon the assembled
countryfolk with admirable equanimity. To my dismay,
I observed Fanny Delahoussaye smile prettily at him,
when his eyes chanced to fall her way. In a flagrant disregard for mourning, she had insisted upon donning a new
bonnet of peacock blue, with matching feathers.

Mr. Eliahu Bott gave a dry little cough and picked up
his quill. "You are Dr. Philip Pettigrew, of Sloane Street,
London?"

"I am."

Thereafter followed a tedious recitation of the good
man's apprenticeships and learning, surprisingly lengthy
in one who appeared little more than two-and-thirty;

his intimate familiarity with gastric complaints, poisons, and ailments of the bowels; and the history of his relations with the late Earl.

"I was called to attend Lord Scargrave some three years past, in a matter of dyspepsia brought on by the consumption of rich foods, while the Earl was resident for the Season in London. His lordship's complaint being one of frequent recurrence, I became a familiar at his bedside in ensuing months, and was naturally called into Hertfordshire when the ailment took hold more than a fortnight ago."

"Your physick, it would seem, did little to cure your patient." Mr. Bott peered severely at Dr. Pettigrew.

"Even the wisest counsel is useless when it is unheeded," Dr. Pettigrew said, in a tone of reproof. "The Earl was fond of fine food and drink, and little accustomed to having his habits of indulgence checked."

"And how would you describe Lord Scargrave's condition prior to his death on the twelfth of December last?"

"He was severely ill—so severely ill that all help was past by the time I arrived just before dawn. His lordship was bloated and possessed of difficulty in breathing; his vomiting had then occurred some hours without cease; and as is usual in such cases, a dizzyness had come on that prevented him from sitting or standing upright."

"And yet you believed his lordship to be suffering merely another attack of dyspepsia?"

The doctor adjusted his spectacles with great dignity. "I thought that Lord Scargrave had achieved the final result of careless indulgence—acute gastritis brought on by steady abuse of the digestive tract. That he was brought to sickbed following a celebratory ball for his bride, and *that* following a three months' holiday, made it likely that all dietary strictures had been cast off for some time; and so I bled him, and hoped for the best."

Mr. Bott's quill paused in mid-air. "And what was the result?"

"His lordship departed this life a mere half-hour after the bleeding."

There was a murmur at this from the assembled folk, rising behind us like the first hint of thunder on a warm summer's eve.

The coroner's reproachful gaze shifted from his witness to the audience, and he snorted with disapproval. "You may stand down, Dr. Pettigrew."

Next to be called was the Countess herself, deathly pale and faint of voice. Arrayed in outmoded black sarcenet, with her red hair drawn severely behind her ears, Isobel looked the very picture of distressed widowhood; and a hope rose within me that even Mr. Bott might view her with pity, and go gently in his questions. She was sworn, stated her name and place of birth as the Barbadoes, and was questioned as to her familiarity with her husband's dietary habits.

"Had his lordship experienced such an indisposition at any time during your travels?"

"On several occasions in Paris, and again in Vienna," Isobel replied, her voice quavering.

"Harlots and debauch!" someone cried from the gallery.

Mr. Bott glared at the crowd and struck the table with a small mallet provided for this purpose. "Silence!" His head, so like a sparrow's, turned sharply towards the Countess. "And these would have been on what dates, my lady?"

Isobel reflected, her gaze distracted. "In early September and again at mid-November, I should say, sir."

"But this was not an ailment the Earl combated daily." Mr. Bott's hand moved swiftly over his parchment.

"It was not during the period of our marriage, assuredly."

"Did you consider your husband to be in good health when you married him, my lady?"

"The Earl was a vigourous man of excellent aspect." Isobel spoke in so low an accent as to be almost inaudible. "I anticipated a long and fruitful life in his company." Her eyes drifted to where Fitzroy Payne sat, splendidly elegant in dark coat and breeches; I saw him smile encouragement, and hoped that the jury did not observe the exchange.

"Though he was a gentleman some"—at this, Mr. Bott peered narrowly at a paper before his nose—"six-and-twenty years your senior?"

"Married him for his fortune, she did," came another voice from behind me.

Tom Hearst started to his feet and looked about the room, his indignation on his face. To my relief, I saw his brother George reach a restraining hand to his elbow, and with unconcealed reluctance the Lieutenant regained his seat.

"Silence!" Sir William Reynolds bellowed, his aspect furious. The muttering died away, and the coroner returned to Isobel. "Pray reply to the question, my lady."

Isobel drew breath. She looked down at her clasped hands. "My husband's energy was high and his appearance youthful, despite his years. I did not anticipate his passing so soon."

Mr. Bott sniffed, and peered at Isobel with sharp eyes. "Do you recall, my lady," he said slowly, "what the late Earl of Scargrave consumed the evening of his death?"

"He partook of the repast laid for the ball, as did all our guests. It included such victuals as roast beef, a variety of vegetables, roast goose and pudding, pasties and oysters; for drink we had a spiced mulled punch and claret." At this, my friend sought my eyes, her own filled with doubt. "I cannot think what else."

"And how many guests did you entertain that evening, my lady?"

"Some hundred from London and the surrounding country."

Mr. Bott paused before the next question, and looked significantly at the jury. "And you will swear, my lady, that all partook of the same food as the Earl?"

"I must believe it to be probable," Isobel replied. "I myself was handed a dish by my husband; and that he had fetched mine in the same span as fetching his own, I know to be true."

"And did your husband betray any sign of indisposition while the ball held sway?"

The Countess hesitated, and Mr. Bott leaned forward expectantly. "He was in excellent form and spirits for some hours," Isobel told him, "but was overcome after midnight by severe dyspepsia, having drunk down a glass of claret in toasting my health." Her voice faltered, and I keenly felt all her distress. "We bore him to his rooms. I bade our guests farewell."

Fanny Delahoussaye's attention was clearly wandering, like a child's in the midst of the vicar's lengthy sermon; her blond head drifted around the room, seeking an object worthy of her interest, until recalled to dignity by a pinch from her mother.

"And did his lordship then request anything further?" Mr. Bott continued.

"He asked for a milk toddy and sweetmeats, in hopes that it might settle his stomach."

The coroner fairly pounced. "Did you partake of either, my lady?"

"I did not, sir."

"Did any in the household?"

"I do not believe so."

Fitzroy Payne's brows were knit in perturbation. As I gazed at the Earl, Tom Hearst leaned towards him and whispered something in his ear. Beyond them sat Mr. George Hearst, so clearly absorbed in his own thoughts that he must have heard little of what passed before him. He might better have escorted restive Fanny back to the Manor, since neither was engaged by the proceedings.

Mr. Bott's dry voice demanded my attention. "And who, my lady, assembled the plate of sweetmeats?"

"The plate and toddy were brought to my husband by my late maid, Marguerite."

"Were you within the room at this time, my lady?"

"I was, sir, attending to my husband's comfort."

"And was anyone else of the household permitted into your presence?"

"All but the maid had sought their beds."

"Indeed. The maid, your ladyship says." Mr. Bott looked to his jury with a barely perceptible nod. "And did Lord Scargrave consume his sweetmeats and milk, my lady?"

"He did."

"And did his condition improve?"

Isobel hesitated, and looked for me.

"Did it improve his condition, Lady Scargrave?"

"It did not," Isobel said faintly. "Within a very short time, he progressed from pain to vomiting, and his deterioration was swift."

"How short a time?"

"A quarter-hour, perhaps a half-hour; I could not undertake to say."

"And when did you send for Dr. Pettigrew?"

"The village surgeon we assayed first, believing the Earl's illness to be of a common nature; but within an hour the man declared himself unfit for the management of his lordship's case. It was then decided that we should send for Dr. Pettigrew."

The memory of that terrible night overcame me—the Earl's moans banishing sleep from the house, and my own fearful shuddering as I lay alone in the massive mahogany bed, awaiting Isobel's summons.

"What hour of the clock would this have been?"

"I should put it at about half-past one." Isobel swayed slightly in her chair, and then recovered; but that the strain of public exposure told upon her was evident.

"And Dr. Pettigrew has testified that he arrived before dawn."

"I believe it was nearly five o'clock. By that time I had roused my dear friend, Miss Austen, who kindly sat vigil with me by his lordship's bedside."

At this, the coroner's sharp eyes fell upon me, and I blushed—cursing my susceptible cheeks all the while.

"And your husband passed away not long thereafter?"

Isobel dropped her gaze. "He was dead at sunrise."

A shifting among the chairs of the jury; I studied

the twelve men's faces, and read discomfort in their souls. Behind me the assembled townsfolk began to murmur.

Mr. Bott once more took up his mallet, and achieved a disgruntled peace. "I would ask you, Lady Scargrave, whether you recognise the item I am now presenting to you." He held out a fine scrap of lawn.

"I do," Isobel said steadily.

"And could you name it for the jury?"

My friend's eyelids fluttered and she drew a shaky breath. "It is a handkerchief of Swiss lawn, embroidered with my initials, and forming one of a dozen purchased with my wedding clothes in Bond Street last August."

"Thank you, my lady. You may stand down."

I saw all too clearly what the pinch-faced man at the long table intended; he had shown the jury as plain as day that the Earl had eaten nothing that others had not consumed as well but for the sweetmeats; and that these were administered in his wife's presence only—excepting the maid, who was now dead. Further elucidation was hardly necessary.

Next to be called was Sir William himself; and he described for the jury's edification the anonymous letters, not neglecting to advise them that it was Lady Scargrave herself who had summoned him with news of the first—a point, I thought, that should be taken in Isobel's favour; for had she guilt to hide, surely she should have as soon burnt the note as called the magistrate? The townsfolk at my back knew of the letter nailed to the door of the very tavern in which we sat; but the intelligence of *two other* threatening notes, received by the Countess and held in secret, fell upon them with all the suddenness of a spring storm.

Mr. Bott made swift work of their startled ejaculations and flurried conversation. His hammer rose and fell. Then he turned to my friend the magistrate, and sniffed audibly. "The first note, Sir William, instructed her ladyship that the second should be sent to you?"

"It did."

"And when the Countess summoned you to Scargrave the very day of her husband's interment"—how imperious and unfeeling the odious little man made Isobel seem—"she declared herself convinced that the maid was the author of the letters, and entreated your help?"

"She did." Sir William sought my eyes, and must have read my indignation in them, for his own dropped to his lap, abashed.

And so there we had it, courtesy of Mr. Eliahu Bott—the Countess was cunning, indeed. Aware that the second letter with its damning accusations must certainly fall into Sir William's hands, and unable to anticipate its effect, Isobel had cleverly assumed a guise of sincere bewilderment and named the maid as her accuser. I felt my hopes of *any* of my friend's actions being placed in a favourable light, as unlikely of gratification; and suddenly despaired of her future.

For the first time, Fanny Delahoussaye seemed aware of the cruel drama played out before her; her blond curls were bent to Madame's ear, plying her with questions. Her mother's face was grim, and her black eyes snapped. Fitzroy Payne was in an agony of restless dread to judge by his expression; his arms were folded over his chest, his countenance was stormy, and he looked almost as threatening as Beelzebub himself. That he longed to throw the offending coroner the length of the kingdom, I readily discerned, and prayed his better self should master the impulse.

The next witness caused a sensation in the tavern-room, being a stranger to all present, and bearing with him something of the incensed and sacred; he was declared to be Dr. Percival Grant, and once sworn, he turned a benign and cherubic face upon the assembly, as though invited to join a picnic on the lawn.

"Dr. Grant, to what university do you belong?"

"I am a tutor at Cambridge, my good sir, and attached to Christ College."

"And what is your field of scholarly interest?"

"I have made *botany* my life's work, with a particular

interest in the tropic plants of South America and Africa."

A stir of amazement greeted this, and a general puzzlement as to the man's purpose in these proceedings.

Mr. Bott produced a folded piece of linen with all the majesty of a conjurer. "Can you name for us the seeds which I now place before you, Dr. Grant?"

The cheerful gentleman leaned forward eagerly. "They are the nuts of the Barbadoes tree, which is found in the West Indies, in some parts of South America, and in parts of Africa as well."

"And have you seen these nuts before?"

"I assume them to be the same ones presented to me for analysis by Sir William Reynolds."

Another wave of sound as the crowd began to heed the direction of Mr. Bott's questions.

"And after studying them, what did you conclude?" the coroner enquired, his quill at a rakish angle.

"That they were indeed Barbadoes nuts."

"And what is the effect of Barbadoes nuts on the human body, Dr. Grant?"

The scholar cherub smiled all around. "They are a severe toxin, my good sir, and when taken even in small quantities, will produce death in very little time."

The buzz of conjecture behind my chair was so fierce as to make my cheeks burn with consciousness. I heard Isobel sigh beside me, and felt all the depth of her despair. Fitzroy Payne reached a hand to her elbow, but she leaned away from him, and sought support on my shoulder.

Mr. Bott's eyes were on the Countess as he posed his next question. "Is the Barbadoes nut to be found on the island of Barbadoes, Dr. Grant?"

The professor laughed aloud, as though the coroner had posed a very good joke. "From the name which they bear, my dear fellow, could one doubt it?"

After this, he was obliged to sit down, and Sir William was recalled.

"Could you explain to the jury how you came by these Barbadoes nuts?"

Sir William turned to the twelve men, whose faces grew graver by the hour, and inclined his white head. "I found them among the personal belongings of a member of the Scargrave household."

"And how came you to search the belongings of any in that house?"

"I was requested to do so in the third and final note penned by the maid Marguerite, which bore her signature and was nailed to the door of this tavern," Sir William replied soberly. "The note having appeared on the same day as her body was discovered, I thought it wise to explore all possible paths."

Eliahu Bott's small eyes gleamed with anticipation. "And where exactly were the nuts disposed, Sir William?"

"I found them wrapped in a square of velvet in the pistol case belonging to Fitzroy, Lord Scargrave."

Mr. Bott was obliged to exert himself with the gavel, an effort to restore order that for several moments must be declared to have been in vain. Isobel leaned heavily against me, all but overcome. I looked for Tom Hearst, and saw him again on his feet, his mouth open in a cry of protest that went unheard in the general melee. At last the coroner rose from his chair and threw all the strength of his small frame into a demand for silence, his eyes on Fitzroy Payne. The eighth Earl of Scargrave retained a remarkable composure throughout, though from knowing him a little, I could guess at the painful tumult of his thoughts.

Mr. Bott turned avidly to Sir William. "And what did you then, sir?"

"I ordered the body of the late Earl exhumed from its tomb."

This was no news to the jury or the assembled townsfolk; they had seen the grim business in Scargrave Close churchyard but a few days before, and doubtless tossed it among themselves over countless tankards of ale. The coroner dismissed Sir William and recalled Dr. Pettigrew.

"Now, sir," Mr. Bott said, running a pink tongue over

dry lips, "will you describe for us the further examination of the deceased?"

"I removed the stomach and examined the contents," Dr. Pettigrew said, impervious to a feminine shriek sent up by Fanny Delahoussaye.

"And what did they tell you?"

"They retained still the evidence of the Earl's having ingested a large quantity of Barbadoes nuts," the doctor said evenly.

"And would the effects of such nuts be similar to those you observed in the Earl at his death?"

"I should now judge his lordship's entire illness to have been produced by the poisonous seeds themselves."

MR. BOTT PERMITTED US A GRUDGING RESPITE BEFORE THE jury's consideration of the maid's poor case. And so Sir William conducted the Scargrave party to the privacy of a small room at the tavern's rear, where we might take temporary shelter from the townsfolk's spite. His attitude lacked its customary warmth, and I felt all the force of my old friend's suspicion; I must confess to a weariness that was consuming, and a depression of spirits no less profound.

Fanny Delahoussaye declared herself to feel faint, citing the heat of the room, the vulgarity of the crowd pressing about her, the horrid nature of the proceedings—etc., etc. Madame hovered over her anxiously, a phial of smelling salts in hand, and pronounced her daughter unfit to remain in the tavern. That Fanny merely played upon us all, the better to win attention to herself, I little doubted; but her principal object, Lieutenant Hearst, seemed indifferent to her distress, and stood in an attitude of abstracted dejection by the room's sole window. The drama ended only when Sir William called for his carriage, which had conveyed the Delahoussayes hither; and a subdued Fanny was carried home in the company of her watchful mother. That the former had hoped to be escorted by the Lieutenant, and

regretted the folly of her display, I read in her peevish
looks.

Isobel sat with closed eyes and deathly countenance
on a chair in the corner, never speaking and hardly stirring; a silent Fitzroy Payne stood by her chair, his tortured thoughts etched upon his countenance. Mr. George
Hearst bestirred himself, with surprising good will, and
procured a little wine for Isobel, which had a restorative
effect; but the mortifications my dear friend had endured
were hardly at an end, and might be expected to worsen
as the day progressed. I foresaw how it should go; and
in very little time, the wine consumed, we were returned
to our chairs.

TO MY SURPRISE, LIZZY SCRATCH WAS FIRST CALLED AND
sworn.

She was a rough, broad woman in a worn wool dress
that might once have been of a rosy hue, but was faded
now with dirt and age to a dull maroon. Black mitts
partly covered chilblained fingers, and on her feet she
wore the stout boots of a field labourer—her late husband's, perhaps, for that she was a widow we quickly
learned. She reached from time to time to adjust a ridiculous straw hat—which swept up from her frowzy brow
like the masthead of a schooner, arrayed with turnips
and cabbage leaves and what I judged to be a rooster's
wattle. She stood before her fellow townsfolk in all the
glory of notice; she knew the power of having a tale
to tell.

"You are a resident of this village?" Mr. Bott's tone
lacked something of the warmth with which he had
addressed the magistrate.

"That I am, sir, born and bred, wed and bed, as the
saying goes." Lizzy Scratch had profited by the proceed-
ing's several hours to consume a quantity of warm gin,
that much was certain.

"And what is your occupation?"

"It's a laundress as I am, 'aving learned the trade from

168 - STEPHANIE BARRON

my good mother, and taken it up once more when my pore Joe passed from this life."

"And were you acquainted with the maid, Marguerite Dumas?"

"I 'ad 'er ladyship's washing off 'er every 'alf-week," Lizzy Scratch said, staring balefully at Isobel; "and such a lot of shameful finery as the woman wore, I should not like to say. It was enough to turn the stomach of any decent woman, it was."

"That is quite enough, Mrs. Scratch," the coroner said peremptorily. "Please confine yourself to the questions put. Were you on intimate terms with the maid?"

"Well, I knew Margie weren't 'appy, same as everybody else. What with being far from 'er ferrin' parts, and 'ating the cold, and being that shamed by 'er ladyship's goings-on with the Viscount that was—"

A shocked murmur ran through the ranks, and Fitzroy Payne, seated to my right, put his head in his hands.

"Mrs. Scratch, I must insist," Mr. Bott said, with a sharp eye for the Earl. "Confine yourself to the question."

"We was friends good enough," the laundress said sulkily.

"Although the maid was resident in these parts less than a month?"

"Margie 'ad taking ways, and was fond of talk, and I saw no 'arm in 'er."

"And when did you last see Marguerite Dumas?"

"She come to me the day after the old Earl passed on, she did, beggin' for some food and a roof against the cold. Said she couldn't stay in no 'ouse where murder was done, and she'd be off as soon as she'd got 'er story to the Justice."

The outcry in the room now verged on the clamourous, and Lizzy Scratch smiled broadly, bobbing her head to her neighbours and kinsfolk.

"That's the truth, by God, and the pore thing was killed for it," she added.

"Mrs. Scratch," Mr. Bott said menacingly, "if you

cannot control your tongue, I shall dismiss you from this room." He removed his spectacles, wiped them briefly with a pocket linen, and resumed his train of thought. "How long was Marguerite Dumas in your home?"

"Until the day they found 'er pore mangled body in the 'ay-shed at Scargrave," the laundress avowed, and dabbed at her eyes with a fingerless mitt.

"Do you know when she might have left your house that day?"

"A'course I knows. Right after milking 'twas, which I'd given 'er the doing of. Margie come in and took a bit o' bread from the fire and said she was off to see 'er man, and I shouldn't look for 'er before dinner."

"Her *man*, Mrs. Scratch?"

"Some feller as she was sweet on."

"Are you familiar with the identity of this person?"

"That I'm not. Margie could be close-mouthed enough, when she wanted." This Mrs. Scratch said with satisfaction.

"Had this fellow communicated with her in any way that you were aware?"

Lizzy Scratch shrugged. "Met up with 'er 'ere in the Cock and Bull, more'n likely, when I weren't to see. 'E must've done, else 'ow'd she come by those scraps of paper she was forever tucking in 'er bodice? Love letters, I called 'em, right to 'er face, and she'd just smile."

At that, Mrs. Scratch was torn from her moment of glory and forced back among the common folk, but she sailed towards her place like Nelson's flagship, fully conscious of her majesty and the power of her guns. Beside me, Isobel had closed her eyes, and the blue veins on their lids throbbed with a feverish intensity. I placed my gloved hand over her own, and felt some small pressure in return. I looked then for the remainder of the Scargrave party; but the three gentlemen were locked in a stony silence, their features fixed and grim. The time for anger was past; what was required of them now was

fortitude. Fitzroy Payne had ever been possessed of a remarkable command of countenance; but I was touched to
observe that the Hearst brothers—one so commonly hot-
blooded, and the other so commonly cold—were united
in dignity.

It was my duty next to be called and sworn, and I related in as calm a manner as possible the finding of the
handkerchief, the appearance of the footprints, and the
discovery of the body. I stated that the time had been
close to half-past ten in the morning, and that the blood
was quite fresh. I was queried as to my reasons for probing the maid's bodice, which brought a conscious flush
to my cheeks and an edge of severity to the voice of Mr.
Bott; and then I was allowed to go.

Sir William took the chair, and affirmed that the maid
was slain in the shed itself, to judge by appearances; that
she was undoubtedly called there by the note found on
her person; and that the note was determined to have
been written by Fitzroy Payne. I should have thought the
humble audience long since wearied by such revelations;
but they were inflamed anew with every fact let fall, as a
hound will grow increasingly crazed with the letting of a
doomed fox's blood.

At the last, Fitzroy Payne was himself called to the
chair, and asked of his whereabouts on the morning in
question; he could say only that he had been abroad at
eight o'clock for an early ride on his horse, had roamed
throughout the Park, and had met with no one; that
when he returned to the stables, it was eleven o'clock, and
he learned the news of the maid's murder. When asked
whether he had ever communicated by letter with Marguerite, the Earl replied firmly in the negative, and declared that a common forger had grossly imposed upon
us all.

With that, Mr. Bott cleared his throat and turned his
spectacles upon the dozen men who formed the jury. "My
good sirs," the coroner told them, "we have come to the
close of the evidence you must consider. A hard duty is
now before you. If you believe the late Earl to have died

of dyspepsia, you must return a verdict of death by natural causes. If you consider the maid to have been killed somehow, but are uncertain as to whether this was murder, and if so, at whose hand, you must return a verdict of death by misadventure."

Mr. Bott paused, and glared at the assembled villagers with severity. "If, however, you believe the Earl to have been murdered, and feel with certainty and conviction that you may name the hand that has effected his demise, you must return a charge of wilful murder against that person. The same is true in the maid's case. Leave us now, and bring to your deliberations consideration and care. God bless you."

The jury filed away, eyes grim and faces averted from the Scargrave household; and in a matter of moments had returned, with a verdict of death by wilful murder—against Isobel in the case of the late Earl, and against Fitzroy Payne in the case of Marguerite.

AND SO THE GREAT HOUSE IS HUSHED THIS EVENING, IN all the awareness of doom. Several stout fellows stand watch before the Manor's doors, lest the Countess or the Earl conceive the reckless notion to flee. Sir William has allowed them to remain under house arrest this night, until their removal tomorrow for a special session of the Assizes, and then to London, where they will await trial by a jury of their peers. And as Fitzroy and Isobel are members of the peerage—he by birth, and she by marriage—their trial is to be in the House of Lords, a spectacle rare in the annals of England's criminal history.

The household and I are to follow in their train, to take up abode in the Earl's Town house; even if I would be gone now to Bath, my duty as a friend forbids it, for Isobel will not hear of me deserting her in this, her most mortal hour. Indeed, she has charged me with a burden I scarce know how to fulfil.

"Discover the truth, my dear Jane," she pressed me,

her brown eyes dry and her carriage unbent, as she prepared to be shut up in her rooms. "It is beyond my power to do so. As God is my witness, I am innocent of my husband's death. Sir William is unmoved, and the townsfolk easily led; but *your* penetration, your understanding, must be my only hope. Do not fail me, Jane!"

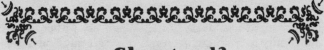
The Calculation
of Miss Fanny

28 December 1802

~

I AWOKE THIS MORNING TO THE RATTLE OF THE UPPER
house maid laying the fire—a comforting sound, sugges-
tive of other winter mornings retrieved from the memory
of childhood, when the certainty of a good breakfast before a blazing hearth awaited one downstairs, and duties no more onerous than the reading of a lesson filled
up the morning. I felt a sharp longing for Cassandra,
and intimate conversation in our dressing gowns—and
for Steventon, the home of my youth abandoned these
eighteen months. Tho' Hampshire is often derided for
its ugly chalk cliffs and quiet farmland, I cannot think
Derbyshire's crags more lovely, nor the gardens of Hertfordshire to have a greater claim on my affections. It
was partly from homesickness that I once entertained
the notion of marriage to Harris Bigg-Wither—for an alliance with his considerable fortune and Hampshire estates would have returned me to the circle I so dearly
loved.

I burrowed deeper in the quilts as the maid lit her
tinder. My person might be in Scargrave this morning,

but my mind was upon home. When my father moved our family to Bath eighteen months ago, my conviction of Steventon's merits was only strengthened.[1] Bath itself I find abhorrent, even as it fascinates—as is ever the case when I am surfeited with a certain kind of society. The sameness of the crowd in the Pump Room, though the faces themselves may change, is such as to weary; the endless parading, the restless nothingness of conversation, the crush of the public assemblies; the *ennui* of one's partners, generally stupid young men with little to recommend them; the insipidity of a crowd that comes for the sole purpose of being amused, and finds it an insult to exert itself towards that end. Not for anything in the world would I have chosen a pleasure place for a permanent home.

And the system of drains in the house at Sydney Place is not to be supported.

I cannot but wonder at my father having chosen such a town for his remaining years, and yearn still for my snug upstairs room in the rectory and the society of Madam Lefroy, my dearest Anne. To consider brother James and his poor Mary now in possession of all that was dear to me is a further source of displeasure; they cannot appreciate its merits as I, nor find the same delight in its simple comforts. *They* exist only to criticise. But I recollect; I myself have been criticising at great length, and must declare it to be a family failing.

I rose up on one elbow and peered around the bed-curtains. "Martha," I said to the maid bent at the grate, "is anyone else yet abroad?"

"I can't rightly say, miss," she declared, sitting back on her heels and brushing away a stray lock of black hair, "seein' as those fellers are posted a'tall the doors. Took

1. In 1801, George Austen, Jane's father, passed his Steventon living (or parish appointment), its rectory, and most of its furnishings to his son James, a clergyman like himself, and moved with his wife and daughters to Bath.—*Editor's note.*

the kindlin' from me and sent me abaht my business, they did, as though I'd 'ave the savin' of the Earl with a bit o' tinder."

"Events have taken a sad turn," I commented.

"That they 'ave, miss, and for nothin' but Lizzy Scratch and her palaverin' ways. That girl Margie was a bad 'un, make no mistake, and she's sure to 'ave met her end from 'er fancy man as anything else. Least, that's what Mr. Cobblestone and Mrs. Hodges be sayin' below stairs."

"Did you know Marguerite very well?" I enquired curiously.

"Didn' 'ave time. She bahn't been 'ere but a week or two 'fore she quit the 'ouse." Martha stood up and dusted off her hands. "There now. That's burnin' smartly. Jest you bide there in bed, miss, until the chill come off the room, and I'll fetch the tea."

When she had gone, I lay back on the pillows and considered all that Lizzy Scratch had recounted the previous day. Marguerite's unknown man may also have been her murderer; certainly Sir William Reynolds believed so, and thought him found in the present Earl. That Fitzroy Payne was hardly likely to have made love to the Countess *and* her maid at one and the same time (particularly when I knew him possessed of a mistress in Town), was not an aspect to trouble Sir William. Perhaps he knew more than I of the habits of gentlemen.

It was equally possible, however, that Marguerite's lover had nothing to do with the events at the Manor, and that fear of the law prevented the man from coming forward. Now that Fitzroy Payne had been charged, perhaps the unknown swain should breathe more easily, and consider acceding to an interview—could one but locate him.

"Martha," I said, as the maid returned with tea-tray held high, "does Mrs. Hodges or Cobblestone know the identity of Marguerite's young man? I wonder that he did not come forward at the inquest."

"That Man," Martha said, implying the coroner Mr.

Bott, "made out as if 'twere the new Earl, Lord Payne as was, 'ad goings-on with Margie. Ha! He'd as like 'ave to do with Mrs. Hodges, and her sixty if she's a day. Lord Payne—Lord Scargrave, I mean—is that proud, he looks through us serving folk. He's called me Kate or Daisy as often as my Christian name."

"Perhaps Marguerite *had* no young man."

"Oh, that she *did*," Martha declared stoutly. "Always goin' on about 'ow flash he were, and 'ow 'e'd bring 'er things that were that costly when she saw 'im again." She set the tray by the fire and poured out a cup.

"So it was an affair of some duration," I mused. "I had supposed her young man only recently encountered—since her coming to Scargrave."

"Oh, Lord, no! She was ever givin' 'erself airs, sayin' as 'ow she weren't likely to be in service no more when 'er ship come in, and 'ow we'd all 'ave to call 'er *Miss* Marguerite." Martha thrust her nose in the air and shrugged her shoulders, affecting Marguerite's haughty disdain. "Showed us a gold locket she'd 'ad off 'im, that she kept real close-like, and wore under 'er shift. Thought 'e'd marry her, she did—or worse."

I threw back the covers and reached for my dressing gown, my eyes on Martha's tray. "Perhaps it was a fellow from her native island, encouraged through steady correspondence?"

Martha looked doubtful. "I don't think as it was a ferriner, miss, but I can't rightly say."

"I suppose she might readily have formed an acquaintance during her months in London."

"Come to think on it, miss, she did say as he'd took 'er strollin' of an evenin' in Covent Garden."

I took a sip of tea and studied the maid over the rim of my cup. "I wonder her mistress the Countess did not know of it. The entire affair is curious, Martha. As curious as Marguerite's friendship with Lizzy Scratch."

"Old Lizzy's 'avin' the time o' 'er life," Martha averred with scorn. "If she were any friend to the girl, I'm yer widowed aunt, I am. You ask anyone, you'll find that woman was chargin' Margie dearly for 'er keep when she took 'er in. She's a warm woman, is Lizzy."

I BREAKFASTED WITH FANNY DELAHOUSSAYE, ARRAYED THIS morning in a dove-grey gown and lace collar that gave the barest nod to the conventions of mourning, but appeared to decided effect against her blond curls and blue eyes. My own brown muslin looked as dull as clodded earth by comparison, and made me feel just as heavy. I sought refuge in silence and Mrs. Hodges's excellent chocolate, but peace was not a quality Miss Delahoussaye prized, and so I was soon forced to all the tedium of an early morning *tête-à-tête*. For Fanny was up early, impatient for her return to London, and possessed of complete equanimity as to its cause.

"For," said she, turning a gold bracelet idly upon her wrist, "I cannot abide the *ennui* of a country existence. One's circle is so fixed, so little varied, that one might complete the sentences of one's neighbour with very little thought or effort. When I am married, I shall suffer myself to spend as little time as possible at my husband's country seat."

"Then perhaps we should wish you the wife of·a man who has none," I replied, with perhaps more of acid in my tongue than I intended.

"How you do tease, Miss Austen!" Fanny cried. "What is a man, without an estate of his own? A poor sort of gentleman, I declare."

"Perhaps—but he *is* very often a soldier, you know; for though it is the profession you prefer above all others, it is generally the province of *second sons*."

"Oh, piffle," Miss Fanny said, returned to her good humour. "What is country life in any case, but shooting and billiards and the coarseness of country neighbours? An establishment in Town, such as an officer possessed of a truly good commission might claim, is far to be preferred. I long to be returned to Hyde Park, and the shops of Bond Street, and the theatre, and a hundred delightful schemes, even if London *will* be rather thin—until Easter at least."

My patience for such a rattle was at an end. "I think it likely that we shall be so engaged, when in London, by matters of a sober and troubling nature," I said stiffly, "that we shall have very little time for diversion."

"One cannot be *always* going about with a long face," said Fanny, intent upon adjusting her bodice. "It behooves us to meet adversity with a certain style. I intend to find Madame Henri—she is quite the most fashionable *modiste,* my dear Miss Austen—as soon as ever I arrive, and order a proper gown for the gallery at the House of Lords. It must be of black, of course, as we are in mourning for the Earl; a pity, for it was never a colour suited to my complexion." Impervious to my disdain, she pursued her delightful fancies with clasped hands and uplifted eyes.

"Only think whom one might meet there!" Fanny cried. "The entire peerage of England assembled in one place! And certain to be moved to tender pity by the interesting circumstances in which we find ourselves. I could not *devise* a scheme more delicious. You *must* come along with me to Madame Henri's, my dear Miss Austen. You cannot afford to look less than your best, at your age."

Madame Henri, indeed! It should never occur to Miss Delahoussaye that I lacked the funds for such an establishment—nor that my mantua-maker of choice was my dear sister Cassandra, and I hers. The price of fine muslin is too dear to make added expense of its fashioning; I should rather spend my shillings on a bit of braid, the better to trim my bodice. But Miss Fanny could know as little of economy as she might of tact.

Somewhat nettled, I spoke with asperity. "And so you have abandoned completely Lord Scargrave as your object, and would now seek a husband among the broader ranks of the great?"

"It was never *my* object to secure Fitzroy," Fanny replied with a careless shrug; "such a cold fellow as he is, all erudition and puff! And in any case, I do not intend to injure my prospects by appearing allied to a man under such a cloud." She dropped her eyes in the way of modest misses, and coloured prettily. "No, Miss Austen, I have long given my heart to another; I am sure you cannot mistake whom I mean. If things *should* fall out badly—if Fitzroy is to hang and Isobel with him—why, then, my choice will be proved aright! For in that case, it is certain that George Hearst should inherit the earldom."

"The Payne family being possessed of no other direct heirs?" I enquired, with a stirring of interest.

"Unless the late Earl has got himself a bastard hidden away," Miss Delahoussaye said, shrugging, "and between you and I, Miss Austen, that is hardly likely—he was an awfully respectable old stick. Did he get a son on the wrong side of the blanket, all the world should know it, and the boy be yet at Eton. No, Miss Austen, the Hearsts are at present the Earl's closest male relations—and who should have a greater claim to Scargrave than Mr. Hearst, who has lived all his life here, and his mother before him?"

"But can he inherit through the female line?"

"I understood from Tom that there is just such a provision in the conferment of the title. George has but to exchange the name of Hearst for Payne, and all shall be settled happily. You will have heard of such things before, I am sure."

And so Tom Hearst has been calculating his brother's prospects— aloud, and to one so lacking in discretion as Miss Fanny—a very little time after Fitzroy Payne was charged with murder. Or was the deadly charge the Hearsts' objective all along, with the seizure of an earldom their primary purpose? Murder has been done, and the innocent made to suffer, for far less.

Fanny was humming a little tune, lost in delightful fancies; I deemed it best to learn as much of the matter from her as possible, and thus turned the subject to her dearest concern.

"And so you would have Mr. Hearst?" I said, with conscious stupidity.

"Miss Austen!" she cried, with a new asperity in her eye. "I will not answer when you tease—for I see that you would sport with me. *Mr.* Hearst, indeed! You *are* a sly creature."

I perfectly understood her meaning, and wondered at Fanny's ability to grasp *some* facts, while remaining ignorant of so many others. Should Fitzroy Payne be condemned, his cousin George Hearst would accede to an earldom, and the Lieutenant's prospects might very well improve. Tom Hearst should find a convenient ear for all his troubles, and perhaps an open hand to make his fortune—although, from knowing a little of Mr. Hearst's poor opinion of the Lieutenant, I would hesitate to consider his purse entirely his brother's to command. But the direction of Miss Fanny's thoughts should brook no disappointment; it was her fondest hope that with George Hearst's good fortune and high estate to add to his honourable commission, Tom Hearst should merit all the felicity that Fanny Delahoussaye's thirty thousand pounds could bring.

Both brothers, I mused as I buttered my toast, had reason enough to want their uncle dead, and their cousin judged guilty of his murder.

But I had no time for such dreadful thoughts, much less for Fanny's idle chatter. I left her calculating the proper length of sleeve for a murder trial among the peerage, and turned my attentions to poor Isobel, a prisoner in her very home.

"JANE," THE COUNTESS GREETED ME BRISKLY, AS I BRAVED the guardsman at her lintel and slipped through the door, "you are just in time. But was ever a friend so faithful in her attendance? Another should have been long returned to the bosom of her family, unhappy Scargrave forgotten." The Countess sat at her writing desk, head bent over paper and pen, her breakfast tray untouched.

"None could forget, Isobel, though well they might

flee. But I am neither so timid, nor so indifferent to your goodness."

"Dear Jane!" she cried, and reached a cold, pale hand to my own. She looked remarkably ill this morning, her haggard countenance hardly improved by the rusty black of her gown; I judged her to have endured a sleepless night, and felt numb at the terrors she must yet face. "Would you perform one last office on your friend's behalf, before we must part?"

"Anything, Isobel, that you would command."

"Place your signature at the foot of this page," she told me, her voice low and trembling. "It represents my final wish in this world."

I looked all my amazement, but Isobel pushed her pen towards me with resolution. "I beg of you, sign."

I could not speak, nor read the provisions of her dreadful will, but affixed the name of Austen to the deed. I saw with sadness Daisy Hodges's awkward scrawl—she who was the Countess's young maid—in the place of second witness.

"Thank you, my dear," Isobel said when I had finished, and folding the heavy sheet, she placed it in my hands. "It is yours, now, for safekeeping. Do you take it to my solicitor, Mr. Hezekiah Mayhew of Bond Street, at the first opportunity."

"My darling girl," I said, deeply affected, "it cannot yet be time for such despair! Much may occur before this paper is wanted."

"It is best to prepare for the worst, Jane, since the worst is all that is left to me. Unhappy Isobel! God be praised that Frederick's eyes are closed! The horror, did he see me so reduced to infamy—and by one that he had loved," she cried, her hands clutching at her hair in distraction. "Faithless Fitzroy! Blackest of men, who can wear such a noble face!"

"Isobel." I reached for her tearing fingers and held them firmly in my own. "How can you speak so? The Earl's fate is as desperate as yours, and he suffers it with like innocence. Surely you do not believe otherwise?"

"I saw the note myself, Jane," my friend said contemptuously. "I saw what he had written, I saw it was in his hand. You found it yourself on poor Marguerite's mangled body. Do not you see what he has done? The maid was right all the while. *Fitzroy* is my husband's murderer. *Fitzroy* was discovered by Marguerite, who endeavoured to make his treachery known. And *Fitzroy* ensured that the maid should speak no more."

"Do not believe it, Isobel," I cried.

"Are you mad, Jane?" The Countess rose restlessly from her desk and commenced pacing before the fire. "What else would you have me believe? That I am guilty of their deaths myself? You need not assay the longer. Know that I feel as guilty as though my very hands extinguished their lives. It was my blind partiality for Fitzroy—my vanity, my desire for admiration, my weakness in the face of passion—that encouraged him in evil. He saw my fatuous trust, and he used it to his ends. *I* was the one intended for blame in Frederick's death, while *he* took all my husband's wealth. But Marguerite confounded Lord Scargrave's plans, by keeping his deadly letter on her person."

The Countess halted before her late husband's portrait and gazed upward in contrition. "I betrayed you, Frederick, if only in my heart; but in my heart, I have already died for it."

I felt behind me for some support, overcome by the breadth of her apprehensions, and found it in her bedpost. I leaned against it with relief. "I fear that you are sadly mistaken, my dear, and will regret these words with time. Bite them back, I beseech you—recall them if you can—before they lodge too bitterly in your heart."

Isobel gazed at me with feverish eyes. "Tell me, Jane! Tell me why you place your trust in Fitzroy, when your friend's is all blasted. Has he worked his charms upon *you*, while Isobel mourned for Frederick?"

"You know it to be impossible!" I exclaimed. "As impossible for one of his honour, as the murder of which you would now accuse him! Isobel, Isobel—were Fitzroy

Payne capable of planning such a deed, he should never have left his note on the maid's person. He should be a fool to incriminate himself so publicly. The maid's true murderer would have us think otherwise; but I feel certain of the note's falseness."

Isobel brushed by me with a strangled laugh. "I know his hand, Jane. Too often have I received it, in words of love as false as Fitzroy's character. No, my friend," the Countess said, calmer now, "I will not share your foolish hopes. For where I am going, hope itself is more foolish still."

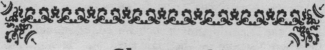

Chapter 14

A Question of a Locket

28 December 1802, cont.

~

I LEFT ISOBEL ALONE, THOUGH I FELT A SICK HORROR AT her despair; and tried to ease my unhappy spirits in preparation for our London journey. In the midst of directing Martha about the packing, I was surprised by a gentle knock upon the chamber door. It opened to reveal Mrs. Hodges, an expression of anxiety on her features; and from her next words, I judged it to be the fear of committing an unwonted impropriety.

"I'm that sorry to disturb you, Miss Austen, and if you've not time for Jenny Barlow, I'll be pleased to tell her so. I cannot think what she can be about, seeking a lady at the kitchen garden door, and not to be put off by the news as you were leaving, but stubborn as a mule about having her say. I've left her in the butler's pantry, but will send her about her business at the least word."

"Indeed, do not, Mrs. Hodges!" I cried. "You did right in seeking me out. Have her come to the little sitting-room directly, and I shall wait upon her there."

The good woman did as she was told, though not without surprise; and giving some last direction to Martha, I hastened below.

Jenny Barlow looked less at ease, though frankly more suited, in the grandeur of even the little sitting-room, than she had appeared in her own smoke-filled hut; her golden hair looked well against the gilt of the picture frames, her eyes picked out the cornflower of the carpet, and, indeed, she might have posed forever, the very soul of a Dresden shepherdess, had I not disturbed her stillness.

"You're that good, miss, to see me, as I can never properly thank you for," she said.

"Considering that you have undoubtedly defied your husband in coming to me, Mrs. Barlow, it is I who must consider myself the obliged," I replied. I thought of seating myself and her, but foresaw the distress she might feel at adopting ease in such a room; she should perch on the corner of a chair, concerned lest her nankeen gown dirty its silk, and her anguish at being treated as her betters would forestall all conversation. I remained standing.

"Have you something to tell me?" I enquired gently.

"Yes—that is, no, ma'am." She looked her distress and doubt of mind, then drew courage with her breath. "It's a favour as I would ask of you."

"A favour?"

"Not on my own account, really, but on account o' my poor sister Rosie, ma'am. Have you sisters of your own?"

"I have one sister," I replied, "who is dearer to me than any in the world. How may I help you, Mrs. Barlow, that your husband cannot?"

"Ted won't have the knowing of Rosie," she said in a low voice, "on account o' her trouble."

"Her trouble? She is—to have a child, then?"

Jenny Barlow looked at me swiftly, then dropped her eyes to her own condition, which was increasingly apparent. "She's only seventeen, miss. Same as me when I had my first. But Ted stood by me, while Rosie . . . 'tis a terrible misfortune for the girl."

"She is not lodged here?"

Jenny shook her head. "She's gone off to London, as the Earl would have it. I've not heard word of her these many months; she never learned to read nor write, and the postage is that dear I couldn't send by her anyways. But you go to London today, I hear, and might have the seeing of her, did you take the trouble."

"I should be glad to, Mrs. Barlow," I assured her warmly, "and I will send word to you as to your sister's condition at the nearest opportunity. I take it," I said uncertainly, "that you *did* learn your letters?"

She nodded. "Pa would have me do so. But Ma died of the having of Rosie, and he placed the pore mite with a woman here at Scargrave when he went into service elsewhere. She was that neglected in her schooling."

"Let me know then where she is lodged," I said, "and I shall do my best to seek her out."

The young woman gave me the address—a not unrespectable street in South London—and consented to take my hand in farewell.

I know little more about Jenny Barlow's fate than I did at our last meeting by her own hearth, but judged it unwise to press her as to its particulars; she has the natural reticence of a born lady, and in the face of such dignity further enquiry would be in very poor taste. That I might hope to learn more of her history from her sister, is a possibility that did not escape me; and if I harbour such a stratagem, I hope it may not flavour too strongly of deceit towards such an unfortunate girl.

I saw Jenny to the housekeeper's rooms, where she was received with an air of doubt by Mrs. Hodges; and returned swiftly to the resolution of my packing. We were to leave just after the noon hour, and I intended yet to walk into Scargrave Close in search of Lizzy Scratch.

THE DAY WAS FINE AND CRISP WITH A LIGHT LAYER OF NEW-fallen snow whitening the road as I made my way into the village. I should spend the greater part of the afternoon in a carriage bound for London, but my legs at least should not feel cramped; and my heart rose with the exercise. The sound of an approaching horse and gig made me turn, and I espied Sir William Reynolds's equipage bent upon my way. That he had noticed me as readily, I discerned by the gig's slowing to a halt by my side.

"Miss Austen!" he cried. "I should have thought you engaged in packing!"

"I make such a sad muddle of it, that I determined to leave it to the kindness of a housemaid," I replied. "Are you already under way for the Assizes, then?"

"I mean only to stop at the Cock and Bull, and then shall be turned towards the post road," Sir William answered. He eyed my pelisse, which I must confess is very much worn. "I take it you have a similar object. Would you care to ride?"

"Indeed, sir," I said, intent that he should not divine my errand, "I relish the prospect of a walk; and so late in the season, one must seize fine weather when it offers."

"It brings the roses to your cheeks," he said fondly, though with misplaced gallantry; I have ever been possessed of a redness in the face, to my horror as a young girl and my grudging resignation as a woman. But I took the compliment in the spirit it was meant; returned his nod, and watched him on his way.

In exchange for a copper, a village lad directed me to the home of Lizzy Scratch. It was scarcely more than a hovel, with a great iron pot set to boil in back; here, I supposed, she did her washing. A tide of young humanity milled about the lintel, separated in age by a very few months, and united in their squint-eyed resemblance to their mother, and by the blackness of their skins and clothing; presumably Lizzy only laundered when she was *paid* to do so. I enquired whether the good lady was yet abroad, and was directed by several jerked thumbs towards the cauldron in the back;

and there I found her, red-faced and perspiring in the chill air, turning linen in boiling water with a long ash stick.

"Mrs. Scratch," I said.

"And who would you be?" She wiped a broad arm across her forehead and peered at me narrowly. "Washin's three shillings the week, less a shilling if you iron it yourself. Leave it on washday—that's Monday—and you can 'ave the fetchin' of it by Thursday morn."

"I have not come about the washing," I said, "but about Marguerite Dumas."

She stuck her chin forward, the better to make out my face—I fear she is much in need of spectacles—and her expression abruptly turned belligerent.

"Yore from up t'a big house. I saw you in the thick of 'em at the Cock and Bull."

"I am a guest at Scargrave Manor, assuredly," I said, "and it is for that reason I have come. The family is desirous of returning the maid Marguerite's possessions to her family in the Barbadoes, and I am here to fetch them."

"You be wantin' 'er things," the laundress said, in a tone of high hilarity.

"I do."

"For to have the sendin' of 'em?"

"It appears the least that one could do."

Lizzy Scratch threw back her head and laughed uproariously. "Pore Margie," she said, wiping her eyes, "if she'd a knowed folk set such 'igh store by 'er few bits, she'd a took 'em with 'er!"

"Have others enquired after the maid's things?" I asked curiously.

"Let's jist say as yore not the first," she replied. "That magistrate fellow 'us by, after the inquest, with Mr. Bott alongside o' him; right put out they was, to find as 'er things was gone. Made as if to say I'd stolen 'em, they did, which they'd no right to, no right a'tall. Margie put 'er bit in the pot while she 'us 'ere, she did, and I'll not be robbin' 'er after she's cold in the ground."

"But who could have taken them?" I asked, bewildered.

"Fellah from up t'a big house."

"A gentleman?"

"Not 'im as did the murdering of 'er, if that's what yore askin'," she said shrewdly. " 'Twas the servin' man of that soldier as lives betimes at t'a cottage."

"I had not known Lieutenant Hearst considered the welfare of the maid," I said, "but, of course, it is properly the duty of a gentleman of the household." That it was more properly Isobel's concern, I did not feel it right to impart to the laundress; but I wondered at the Lieutenant's swiftness of action. "When did his man call for the things, did you say?"

"I didn't," Lizzy retorted, "but I don't mind sayin'. 'Twas the day Margie met 'er Maker, that it was; and if I'd a knowed who killed 'er then, I'd never 'ave sent 'er things back to that place."

"Thank you, Mrs. Scratch," I said; "you have been more than helpful, and in the midst of your duties as well." I reached into my purse and retrieved a shilling, which she quickly palmed, eyeing the remaining coins hungrily. My purse is ever slim, and my finances scrupulous—but in such a cause, I felt an added expense well worth my trouble. I drew out another shilling, and held it with an idle air.

"I wonder, Mrs. Scratch, if you recall a pendant locket among the items turned over to the servant."

"Margie's locket? What you want with that?"

"I understood she prized it highly, and so should especially wish her family to have it. In the jumble of handing her things to the Lieutenant's man, such a small treasure might easily be lost." I reached for Lizzy's palm and dropped the coin in her hand; in the blink of an eye her fleshy fingers closed over it, and she shrugged.

" 'Tweren't worth much, far as I could see," she said.

"If'n 'twere, I'd probably a kept it. But since she'd 'ad it of a man in the 'ousehold, I figured 'twas wise to send it back. He might've come lookin' for it, and the questions 'ave turned nasty."

"Assuredly," I replied, though scarcely recovered from this added revelation. "You knew, then, the identity of the giver?"

"I didn't say *that*." Lizzy Scratch's eyes narrowed. "Any more than I reckin you do, miss. Margie was very close about her man. Always thought he was an upper servant, I did—that Mr. Danson, as valets the new Earl maybe, or one of the head footmen. But I'm thinkin' now as it's the new Earl himself, 'im that was the death of 'er. It makes good sense, don't it?"

MAKING MY WAY BACK TO SCARGRAVE MANOR, I HESITATED before the gate of the cottage in the lane, searching for some sign that the occupants were abroad. I should not wish to meet *either* Mr. Hearst or his brother; but it was very likely that the one was out walking the lanes, moodily surveying the abyss of human nature, while the other was schooling his hunter over the nearest hedge. Summoning my courage, therefore, I opened the gate and walked purposefully up the path.

Scargrave Cottage was intended as a dower house,[1] but the late Earl having no use for such a place, his mother having long since departed this life when he achieved his title, Frederick Payne turned it over to his sister, Lady Julia, as a refuge from the faithless Mr.

1. The dower house traditionally became the home of a widowed lady when her son acceded to his father's title, and took possession of his ancestral seat. The son's *wife* would then accede to his *mother's* title. For example, had Frederick Payne's mother still lived when he became the Earl, she would have been addressed as the Dowager Countess of Scargrave, while Isobel was addressed as Countess.—*Editor's note.*

Hearst. The Hearst boys had grown up under its Tudor eaves; and the Lieutenant spoke with the greatest affection of boyhood rambles among the cottage's blackberry vines. Neatly whitewashed and half-timbered, the place was no doubt picturesque in spring, for a rosebush clung to its lintel, and a fragrant boxwood hedge flourished beneath its leaded panes. In the depths of December, however, the garden looked unloved and forlorn.

The housemaid, one Joan by name, bobbed me a curtsey, and informed me that Mr. George Hearst was within. I immediately regretted my impropriety—a woman alone, calling upon a single male acquaintance—but there could be no turning back, and I suffered myself to be led into the cottage's parlour. It bore all the signs of a bachelor's abode—books lining the walls and prints of grouse hanging above the mantel. A distinct smell, part pipe tobacco and part wet dog, hung in the air, despite the crackling fire. Mr. Hearst had been comfortably ensconced over a book, and rose with an air of consternation I fear my own features mirrored.

"Miss Austen!" he cried. "I did not think to see you until the coach should bear us all hence. Has some further calamity befallen the Manor, that you have hastened here in search of aid?"

"Pray calm yourself, Mr. Hearst," I replied. "I have nothing of an alarming nature to report."

"Then may I ask you to sit down, and take some tea?" He gestured vaguely about the room, as though to indicate any number of chairs.

I surveyed them hastily. Though of a decidedly comfortable appearance, the Hearsts' furnishings were of a sort in which a lady should quickly lose herself. I shook my head in the negative. "I merely wished to have a word with Lieutenant Hearst."

"My brother is not within. But perhaps I may be of service?"

"I fear not," I said abruptly.

Mr. Hearst hesitated, and studied my countenance

with anxious penetration. "I hope to God he has not so far forgot himself—" he began, and then broke off, biting his lip.

"Mr. Hearst," I said quickly, "do not give way unduly to fearful speculation. I know my coming here, in this manner, cannot but seem strange; but you must rest easy in the knowledge that no impropriety on the part of your brother has occasioned it." On a sudden inspiration, I added, "I come on behalf of the Countess, with a message for the Lieutenant, that is all. You know that she is barred from coming herself. Perhaps I ought to speak to the Lieutenant's batman?"

"Certainly. Certainly. I should have thought of it myself." The ecclesiastic's brow cleared. "I shall have him for you presently." He threw down his volume and crossed to the parlour door, but I could not suffer him to leave unmolested.

"Mr. Hearst," I called after him, "I understand that congratulations are due. The Lieutenant tells me that you are to have a living after all. And so it but remains to take Holy Orders."

He appeared first thunderstruck and then uneasy, his eyes dropping to the floor. "I would that it were so simple, Miss Austen," he said. "But not all those who are called are worthy to serve."

And so he left me. As the Lieutenant observed, Mr. Hearst parts only grudgingly with his grievances. Or perhaps my awareness of a matter he has chosen to keep dark, has stirred a guilty conscience. But why? I was not allowed to ponder the matter long, however, for a jocular Cockney voice soon rang out from the doorway.

"So you're the cheeky bit as 'as turned my master's 'ead."

I looked over my shoulder in astonishment, to find a dapper fellow in his shirtsleeves still applying a rag to one of Lieutenant Hearst's boots. "Never done talkin' about you, he is. Miss Austen this, and Miss Austen that! If I didn't know the gent's way with the ladies, I'd swear he was a goner. What'll it be, love?"

I swallowed and maintained my composure with difficulty; *never* had I been addressed in such intimate terms by one of his station. "You are Lieutenant Hearst's batman, I take it?"

"Jack Lewis's the name, and war's the game," he rejoined, scraping an affable low bow, "but I 'aven't got all day, and that's a fact. The old sod'll be 'ell-bent for leather, soon's he gets back from ridin' that nag, and I'll be jumpin' two steps ahead o' his lash all the way to Londontown."

"Lewis!" A curly head peered around the sitting-room door, eyebrows drawn down and scowling. "Don't stand here nattering with Joan, for God's sake—get my damn bags packed."

"As you like, guv," the batman tossed over his shoulder imperturbably. He turned back to me with a wink. "Doesn't like me movin' in on 'is territory." For one fearful instant I thought the fellow might actually seize my hand for a kiss, but he satisfied himself with a grin and a broad nod, encompassing me in some scheme of which I knew nothing, but greatly misgave the outcome. "I leave you to it, *sir.*"

"Miss Austen!" Lieutenant Hearst exclaimed, upon entering the room, all consternation and discomfiture; "I had no idea you were within. Pray, let me call for some tea and make you comfortable! I fear Private Lewis has incommoded you dreadfully." This last, with a scowl for his batman, and a gesture of the head towards the door. Jack Lewis heaved a sigh, ran his insolent eyes the length of my figure, and turned upon his heel; but his air of disgruntlement was entirely for his own amusement, I judged, since he was whistling as he moved down the corridor.

"What an extraordinary man," I said, in a tone of wonderment, uncertain as yet if I had imagined him. "His impertinence is beyond belief, Lieutenant."

"I fear you are right," Tom Hearst replied, gesturing to the one straight-backed chair in the room, and standing until I had seated myself. "I should have dismissed the rascal long ago, but for the obligation I owe him."

"And what can *you* possibly owe such a man?"

He hesitated, and then shrugged. "My life, Miss Austen."

Whatever I had expected, it was hardly this; I felt myself overcome by a surprising humility, and looked to my clasped hands.

"But you did not come to Scargrave Cottage to discuss Private Lewis, however *extraordinary* you may find him." Tom Hearst threw himself into an armchair by the fire. "To what do I owe this honour, Miss Austen, and in the midst of all our packing?"

"In truth, Lieutenant, it is because of your batman that I *am* come. I understand him to be in possession of the belongings of the late Marguerite Dumas, which you so thoughtfully sent him to retrieve of the washer-woman, Lizzy Scratch." I spoke the words as though they were nothing out of the ordinary way, but narrowly observed his response.

"How came you to think of this?" he said, his handsome aspect puzzled.

"Isobel has charged me with returning the maid's things to her family in the Barbadoes," I said. That this was, in fact, an untruth, I forced myself to put from my mind.

"But she has—" he began, and then stopped, as if considering. "It was my very same thought, and had the trip to London not put it out of my mind, the girl's few belongings should already be on their way."

"I must say that I wondered at your thinking of it."

The Lieutenant forced a smile. "I am accustomed, from years of army service, to disposing of the belongings of the men in my company when they happen to be killed," he told me. "It is as second nature to me, to consider the family left behind, and their solicitude for the fate of their loved ones. Often the belongings are precious to them, however little value they might have for us."

"But—forgive me, Lieutenant—the maid was not of *your company*, exactly. She was rather of Isobel's. How did you come to know where her things were to be found? For surely none of the household knew that she had sought shelter from Lizzy Scratch."

He coloured at this, and was silent a moment. "I might ask the same of you, Miss Austen," he said, "for assuredly you know more of my movements than I should have thought usual for a young lady of discretion. But it is of no matter—my greater knowledge of the maid is due only to a greater tendency to dissipation." At this, he grinned ruefully. "When I can abide my brother's silences no longer, I hie me to the Cock and Bull; and at the Cock and Bull, Marguerite's new lodgings were commonly known."

I looked my surprise. "Yet you told Isobel nothing of this?"

"You must recollect that I had no reason to do so," he protested. "When the maid first disappeared from the Manor, Isobel said nothing that suggested she should be found; and I thought Marguerite's departure nothing more than a falling-out between herself and her mistress. Of the letters, and the threats they contained, I learned only with the rest of the household; and by that time, the poor girl was dead."

The story was plausible enough. "But you have not sent the things to the Barbadoes?"

"I had only to request the address of Isobel, and the deed was done; but events have intervened. It was well for me that I did not, for Sir William Reynolds would view the maid's belongings after the inquest yesterday, and came to me much as you have done. But he learned nothing of use to him, by all appearances, and bade me send them on to the girl's family." Tom Hearst paused, and studied me closely. "It is exceedingly good of the

Countess to consider the affairs of her maid when her own are in such a state."

Particularly when the maid has been the cause of her own ruin. The thought, though unspoken, hung in the air between us.

"That is ever Isobel's way," I said lamely, "and perhaps concerning herself with such small matters relieves her of her cares."

"Perhaps." The Lieutenant attempted to resurrect his usual good humour. "I shall have Joan fetch the things directly."

I HAVE MUCH TIME TO CONSIDER LIEUTENANT HEARST'S words as the Scargrave carriage rattles on to London, and have drawn out my journal in an effort to *write* my way towards a better understanding of what they may mean. The journey will last several hours, unrelieved of the tedium of conversing with Fanny Delahoussaye and her mother; Isobel and Fitzroy Payne are conveyed separately, under armed guard, in a discomfort and shame I shudder to contemplate. That this is only the beginning of the indignities they shall endure, I fully understand, and quail at the responsibility with which Isobel has charged me.

The Scargrave tangle becomes more tenebrous with the passing hours, and were I a creature prone to violent emotion, I should despair of ever making sense of it. That the lives of Isobel and the Earl hang in the balance only heightens my impatience with my own understanding. Where I seek for intelligence, in hopes of throwing light upon the puzzle, I find only greater obscurity; and my visit to the Hearst brothers' cottage is no exception.

For though Lizzy Scratch avowed that she had placed the maid's locket in the batman's keeping, it was not among Marguerite's possessions when Tom Hearst turned them over to me. In the cloth bag I received from the cottage housemaid were a few items of worn clothing; a packet of letters in French from Marguerite's relations in the Indies; and a miniature of a woman who might have been her mother. That was all—no books, no trinkets, no keepsakes of any kind; a melancholy collection for the summing up of a life.

And so a hard choice is before me. As plausible as his story might be, Lieutenant Hearst neglected to apprise me of one fact—did *he* remove the gold locket from among Marguerite's possessions, or did his batman, Private Lewis, see fit to do so? And what heavy burden of guilt lay on master or servant, to move either to such an act?

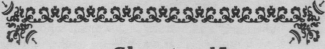

Chapter 15

The Enchanting Eliza

31 December 1802
Scargrave House, Portman Square
~

NEW YEAR'S EVE, AND THE REVELS IN THE STREET BELOW
have raised such a tumult that sleep is banished. I am sitting up by the light of my taper in the rich room I have
been given at Scargrave House. A greater contrast to the
Manor's genteel shabbiness cannot be imagined—here,
all is done up in the latest fashion, with vines and vases
plastered on pale blue walls. It is clear that the late Earl
was a man whose spirits took flight in London rather
than in the country, and that *this* was to be his principal
residence; everything possible has been done to make it a
comfortable home for his new bride, whose apartments
tonight—never before visited by her—are shuttered and
dark, with drop cloths against the dust. The special session of the Assizes having remanded their case to the
House of Lords, Isobel and Fitzroy Payne are banished to
the horrors of Newgate prison, there to live as best they
might until their arraignment; though their stay shall be
short—the trial is to be scheduled early in the next session, some ten days hence—it cannot hope to be marked
by comfort or cheer. Sir William shall be special prosecu-

tor for the Crown, Mr. Perceval being indisposed;[1] and a Mr. Cranley, a barrister of good repute and rising in his profession, shall serve for the defence, though the duties of such are so circumscribed,[2] I wonder he bothers to take the case at all. Mr. Cranley must see an advantage in notoriety—for it is rare that a peer is brought to trial in the House of Lords—and hopes it shall improve his prospects—

(Here the handwriting trails off.)

—a great boom, as though a cannon had gone off near the house—I rush into the hallway in my shift, taper held aloft and pulse quickened, like Banquo ready to cry, Murder! murder! And find that all is quiet in a moonlit slumber, and I am alone with the fancies of midnight and a sharp sense of my own silliness.

Not quite alone, however; as I turn back to my room, I see the quiet form of Lieutenant Hearst, leaning against his doorway, but two removed from mine. He should have sought his own lodgings at St. James, but was pressed by his brother and Fanny Delahoussaye to stay to dinner; and so here he is, bedded down too near me, and watching in the dark.

"You are shivering, Miss Austen," he said, and thrust himself away from the door frame. He walked towards

1. Spencer Perceval (later Prime Minister of England, assassinated in the House of Commons, 1812) was Attorney-General in 1803, and thus should have argued the case for the Crown. His "indisposition" may, in fact, have been overwork—he was engrossed at this time in preparing the prosecution of a Colonel Despard, who had recently plotted the assassination of George III and the overthrow of the government.—*Editor's note.*
2. As noted elsewhere, a defense lawyer in 1802 could do very little for his client—being barred from questioning or cross-examining the prosecution's witnesses or allowing the defendant to testify on his or her own behalf. His role was limited to arguing points of law as presented in the prosecution's case.—*Editor's note.*

me, his blue eyes glittering in my candle flame, the swathe of moonlight dappling the shoulder of his silken dressing gown; altogether an apparition torn from one of my dreams, scented with a whiff of danger.

"I heard an explosion, and feared for the house," I replied, lowering the candle; and I should have turned to go, but something about him fascinated me—the gliding movement of his form, completely graceful in the darkened hall, and with the trick of moonlight, as weightless as an apparition. I thought of the ghostly First Earl, and felt as though turned to stone.

"It is the gunpowder, set off in Southwark at midnight to welcome the New Year," the Lieutenant said. "Pay it no mind." He stopped a bare foot from me, and held my eyes steadily with a sort of wonder, as though he, too, felt himself in a dream.

"What extraordinary hair," he murmured, "all tumbled like that about your face; it's a sight I could not have imagined, and so beautiful in the moonlight. Do you realise what a crime it is, that a woman's husband is the only man ever to see her hair like this? To deny the world such beauty is pure folly. And you have no husband, Jane."

At his use of my Christian name, I became too aware of the impropriety of my position—of how it should appear, should anyone encounter us; and, indeed, of how intimate a scene I had allowed myself to play. My colour rose, my breath quickened, and I made a small movement as if to go. But the Lieutenant raised a finger and laid it against my lips. "Don't," he whispered, "I've caught you in the witching hour, and I must exact my price."

And with that, he bent swiftly and kissed me full upon the mouth, until I tore from his grasp in mortification, rushed headlong into my room, and slammed the door in his face. An echo of derisive laughter was my reward, and the sound of his retreat; and a little later, sharp in the regained quiet, a small click, as of a door being closed. That it came from the room to my right—Fanny Delahoussaye's room—and not from the Lieutenant's, I

had not the smallest doubt. I shall have her wrath to con-
tend with, on the morrow, for it is certain she overheard
us—a scene so little to my advantage, either in its initial
passivity or ultimate flight.

My cheeks are burning with shame and remembered
mortification; never have I been subjected to such a liberty at the hands of a man. Yet worse is the feeling of
sweet elixir that courses through my veins. I am dizzy
with wonder and a want I cannot admit, even to myself;
and so I admit it here, on the pages of my journal. That
he should kiss *me* is beyond belief—and entirely without
sense or purpose. Tom Hearst cannot be in love with me;
for I have never possessed a fortune and am beginning to
lose my beauty, and both are what a man of his straitened
means and handsome looks would think his due. It is in
every way incredible; and so I must ascribe his kiss to the
power of moonlight, and the effect of wanton hair.

I touch a stray lock now, and must declare it nothing
out of the ordinary way, however transformed by moonlight. But I feel a small thrill of gratification nonetheless,
rare for a woman whose wits have always been celebrated before her person. We all of us have our failings;
and mine is vanity. It shall be my last flag flying on the
Day of Judgment.

How to face Tom Hearst, on the morrow? I shall die
of consciousness.

And so the old year is done to death.

1 January 1803

~

I WAS SPARED THE NECESSITY OF FACING THE LIEUTENANT
at breakfast; he and his batman, Jack Lewis, had arisen
early and returned to the Horse Guards at St. James. Not
a word has been let fall regarding the affair of the duel,
or its outcome; I begin to believe it a figment of Miss
Delahoussaye's overheated imagination. The breakfast
room being quite deserted, I was afforded the leisure of

weighing the heavy charge Isobel had placed upon my shoulders, and determining my course of action.

If Isobel and Fitzroy Payne were innocent of the murders, as I certainly believed Isobel to be, then someone had gone to great pains to convince us of their guilt. Firstly, the Earl had died as a result of sweetmeats eaten in the presence of his wife and her maid. Marguerite's dreadful death suggested to Sir William that she had been silenced for having observed Isobel place the Barbadoes nuts in the Earl's dish; but I considered it equally plausible that the maid had been convinced by another to put the poisonous seeds there herself. She had then been deployed in accusing her mistress through plaintive letters, and, her purpose fulfilled, was chiefly of use in being murdered—in order to incriminate Fitzroy Payne.

That Marguerite had formed a relationship of some trust with the murderer was implied by her readiness to await her killer in the isolated hay-shed at dawn. But which of the intimates of Scargrave might that be? If my theory were correct, the maid's partner must be one who gained material advantage by the removal of both the Earl's wife and his heir. George Hearst, who won a living under his uncle's will and stood to inherit the estate if Fitzroy were to die, should gain the most; and he had argued with the Earl the evening of his death, stating aloud that "I know how it is that I must act." Mr. Hearst's character was morose and brooding enough to suggest him capable of violence; and he had fled the house by horseback in some haste and perturbation the very morning of the maid's murder. But was money alone the cause of such anger as I had overheard?

I must needs find Rosie Ketch.

Another who gained from Isobel's misfortune was Lord Harold Trowbridge. But *he* had vacated Scargrave a week before the maid's death. That he might have done this expressly to distance himself from that event, seemed entirely of a piece with his cunning. Having wooed the maid—perhaps in London, when he first attempted to purchase Crosswinds, prior to Isobel's marriage—had

Trowbridge convinced her to dispatch the Earl with the poison native to her country, then left once his object—Crosswinds—was secured? It was as nothing for such a man to send the maid a few words torn from a business letter written to him by Fitzroy Payne, then return by cover of darkness to Scargrave Close, walk to the field at dawn, drop Isobel's handkerchief, slit the maid's throat, and hie back to London with no one the wiser.

—Unless he were avowedly elsewhere, in the company of others, at the self-same moment. I must discover his movements on the day of Marguerite's death. And that meant a visit to his brother the Duke of Wilborough's London residence. How to effect it? For that august family was unknown to this one, a fact Madame Delahoussaye underlined to me more than once when it appeared Lord Harold would remain at Scargrave through Christmas. She found it passing strange that he had deserted his brother the Duke for Isobel Payne in such a season, but knowing little of either Trowbridge or Wilborough, had assumed their relations were not close. But Lord Harold clearly acted from expediency, in forcing the acquaintance; and in more extreme circumstances, I should not be encumbered with greater delicacy. To Wilborough House on any pretext, therefore, I must go, the better to discover his whereabouts on the day of Marguerite's murder.

And what of the others? Madame Delahoussaye I ruled out, as unlikely to benefit in any way from the murder of the Earl, the hanging of her niece, or the similar execution of the peer she had hoped would marry her daughter. But of *Fanny*—could such silliness as possessed the girl hide a malevolent purpose? I could not forget her early morning walk to the paddock, she who did not ride; nor her furtive entry into the shed, nor the bag of coins she had left there. Anonymous philanthropy, I felt, was not in Fanny's nature; if she parted with her pence, it was only under duress. Someone had *blackmailed* Miss Delahoussaye, for reasons I could not divine; and that it might as well be the maid, was urged by the choice of the shed for her deposit-box. Had Fanny grown tired of demands for money, and ended the affair with Marguerite's life?

Why, then, go to such lengths to throw guilt upon her cousin and the newly-titled Earl? Avarice and ambition might counsel it. *Someone* should be guilty of the murder; and that it should not be herself or someone she loved—Lieutenant Hearst—but rather the man she *did not* want to marry, made perfect sense. With Fitzroy out of the way, George Hearst might inherit, and with the proper persuasion, could turn his brother into a titled man of wealth. Fanny intimated as much, only a few days ago; such calculation is natural in one so ruled by self-interest.

But why drop Isobel's handkerchief at the spot? For the satisfaction of having no rival at Scargrave? I should leave that question for later.

Two people yet remained to me—Lieutenant Tom Hearst and his batman, Jack Lewis. That I thought the Lieutenant's lighter character the least likely to be bent to darker purpose, I will not deny; and that a sensibility on my part influenced my views, I may as well admit. But I forced myself to construct an unflattering portrait of the Lieutenant, with all the force of possibility and motive.

In seducing the maid to kill the Earl, and casting suspicion upon Fitzroy once Marguerite was forever silenced, Tom Hearst might hope to win the former Viscount's title and fortune, at the hand of his brother George. This seemed an elaborate sort of plot for a man more likely to act upon impulse, or in the heat of temper; but I could imagine how it was done. The Lieutenant had declared himself resident in London during the period of Isobel's brief courtship by his uncle, for it was then he had met Fanny Delahoussaye. He might have formed a liaison with Marguerite at the same time.

I considered how Tom Hearst's gliding step in the moonlit hall the previous midnight had reminded me of the spectral First Earl. Had the Lieutenant donned fancy dress and tip-toed past my door, all those nights ago at Scargrave Manor, the better to hide the Barbadoes nuts in Fitzroy Payne's gun case? Were he observed entering his cousin's room at that unlikely hour, the fact should be remembered when the nuts' presence was discovered; but no one was likely to suggest that a *ghost* had incriminated the eighth Earl. And Tom Hearst had been at pains the next morning to reinforce my midnight impressions, by declaring that he had witnessed a similar visitation prior to his mother's death.

I reflected uneasily upon the Lieutenant's character. He was playful enough—and so unprincipled, I feared—as to regard the effect of fancy dress as a devilish good joke. I had no proof that he was the spectral impostor, however, and determined to halt the progress of my thoughts, in turning from the Lieutenant to his batman. Certainly one of the two had removed the maid's locket from her things, possibly because it contained his likeness. But which?

The batman, Jack Lewis, was of a station far closer to the maid's own. I considered that smart Cockney fellow, of the glad eye and shameless insolence, and decided he was the most likely to take a Creole girl strolling in Covent Garden. He was more likely than the Lieutenant, as well, to buy her a locket—and commit the indiscretion of placing his miniature inside.

And then a thought occurred to me. Jack Lewis need not have been the murderer of the Earl (who can hardly have been known to him), to be the thief of the pendant. Sorrowing at her death, the batman might readily have retrieved the girl's things from Lizzy Scratch, and then grown fearful at the sight of the bauble containing his likeness. Were it discovered, he was as good as hanged—or so he might have feared. And thus he secreted it somewhere about his person, and said nothing of its existence.

I must endeavour to find out whether I am right or no, at the nearest opportunity.

Which task to undertake first? Lord Harold Trowbridge, Rosie Ketch, or the batman, Jack Lewis?

206 - STEPHANIE BARRON

Since I should prefer the murderer to be Isobel's despicable foe before all others, it seemed best to assault his defences first; but I should need a greater weapon than our slight acquaintance if I were to breast the ramparts of Wilborough House. I bethought myself of Eliza, rose of a sudden from the breakfast table, and sought my bonnet and cloak.

ELIZA, COMTESSE DE FEUILLIDE, IS MY BROTHER HENRY'S wife. She is also my cousin, being my father's sister's child, although reputedly *not* the daughter of my aunt's husband.[3] All that is to say that Eliza was conceived in adulterous love, and my cousin has made it her *métier* from the day of her birth—being an accomplished flirt, a charming adventuress, one of the chief ornaments of Versailles before the fall of Marie Antoinette, and a cheat of the guillotine where her first husband, the Comte de Feuillide, was not. That sad gentleman's demise before the public executioner in 1794 left my bright Eliza returned to England and free to marry Henry some three years later. Though she is nearly ten years older than my favourite brother, and his union with her has been the subject of much unease in the family, I think them not unsuited. I rejoice, in fact, that my cousin is

3. Austen scholars believe that Eliza de Feuillide is the probable model for Jane Austen's most outrageous heroine, Lady Susan, of the eponymous novel. Eliza was probably the natural child of Warren Hastings (Governor-General of Bengal from the 1760s to the mid-1780s), and Jane Austen's aunt, Philadelphia Austen Hancock. Hastings stood god-father to the infant Eliza, and provided a £10,000 trust fund for her support; she later named her only son, who was to die in his youth, Hastings de Feuillide. Warren Hastings is most famous for a spectacular impeachment trial in the House of Commons from 1787–1795, where he was eventually cleared of charges of murder, bribery, and mismanagement.—*Editor's note.*

sobered somewhat by her Austen ties; and that Henry possesses in his wife so lively a wit to challenge his own.

And she is undoubtedly useful, in knowing everyone, and being welcome everywhere.

I arrived at No. 24 Upper Berkeley Street—but a few steps from Scargrave House's door—with a spirit for adventure and a desire to encompass Eliza in my schemes. Fortune was with me—my brother was out and Eliza at liberty. Her maid Manon showed me to the sitting-room, where the petite *comtesse* was tucked up before a brisk fire, her writing things at hand, and her little dog, Pug, established in her lap.

"My dearest Jane!" my cousin cried, thrusting the dog to the floor and standing in haste. "I had not an idea you were in London! Have you eloped with some dashing young man, and come to me for protection?"

"Having heard of the affair of Harris Bigg-Wither, you cannot believe it possible," I said, smiling. "I am sworn off men for a twelvemonth at least, having failed to attract the men I like, and behaved infamously to the ones I abhor."

"You should have been wasted upon such a poor pup," Eliza rejoined dismissively; "and had you asked my advice, I should certainly have counseled you the same. But I suppose your family is mortified? They always are," she finished cheerfully, "when women think for themselves. Well! How are we to celebrate such a meeting?"

"I was hoping to prevail upon you, Eliza," I said, "to accompany me on a matter of some delicacy."

"Delicate affairs being my chief occupation," she observed, her eyes sparkling with interest.

"It concerns the Duke of Wilborough," I continued, "or rather, his brother."

"Trowbridge? Good Lord, you haven't set your cap at *that* fellow, my dear? I'm as fond as the next of dangerous rogues; I was quite susceptible to them, at one time. But Lord Harold is too much of the real thing."

"I think him quite the most evil man I have ever met."

"And with reason." Eliza fluttered her many-ringed fingers in my direction. "There are those who say he was the financial ruin of Sir Hugh Carmichael, *and* that he seduced his wife; in any case, she was sent away to family in Wales until the child was born, and poor Sir Hugh shot himself in the middle of Pall Mall not two months ago. A scandalous business. But how do *you* come to know Lord Harold Trowbridge?"

"I shall tell you in the carriage," I said, "for time is of the essence."

"But, my dear Jane—I must think what to wear. For this old thing cannot do for the Duke of Wilborough's residence. No, indeed." Dismayed, she surveyed her short-sleeved gown, of pumpkin-coloured silk overlaid with bronze braid, and cut as always in the latest fashion. At forty-one, cousin Eliza has not cast off her youth, and to judge from her effect on most gentlemen, her care is well rewarded. She cast a swift glance in the mirror and hurried towards the door, Pug at her heels. "I shall not be a moment, Jane. Manon!"

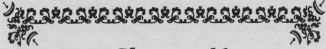

Chapter 16

The Barrister Seeks Counsel

1 January 1803, cont.

WILBOROUGH HOUSE SITS IN ST. JAMES SQUARE, IN ALL the glory of grey stone and the lustre of its ancient name.[1] That Eliza was acquainted with the Duchess of Wilborough, I had long known—it was my chief purpose in her recruitment, for her card, which bore still her French title of Comtesse de Feuillide, should readily gain acceptance where my own poor Miss Austen should languish in the entry-hall bowl. It was as I predicted—the austere fellows guarding either side of the door in livery and white wigs surveyed the grandeur of Eliza's emerald-green gown, tasselled turban, and ermine stole; bowed with a certain contained respect, and returned promptly to inform us that the Duchess was at home.

No one could resist Eliza. She was possessed, always, of the latest intelligence regarding one's acquaintance.

---

1. Wilborough House has since been torn down.—*Editor's note.*

We were ushered up a broad stair and through lofty rooms done up in the fashion of Europe. Painted murals of fat cupids and slender nymphs adorned the ceilings, the walls were sheathed in boiserie, and precious Sèvres vases filled every corner.

"Frightfully stuffy, my dear, like the Duchess's mind," Eliza confided, and I expelled my breath in relief. She, at least, was not overawed.

Through enfiladed drawing-rooms, past set after set of tall doors that opened noiselessly at our approach—a score of footmen alone must be required for the delivery of the Duchess's callers; what she demands for a small dinner party, I cannot imagine. At last we were shown into an intimate lady's parlour, all gilt and white and silk-strewn chairs of the uncomfortable sort deemed necessary for the preservation of one's posture, and faced the Duchess of Wilborough herself. A little woman, of pinched and imperious countenance, who smiled creakily at the sight of Eliza.

"My dear," the Duchess said, extending a limp hand, "so good of you to cheer a friend in her solitude."

"Are you quite alone, then, Duchess?" Eliza enquired, her voice all concern, and bent to clasp the beringed fingers she was offered. "I have brought you my favourite sister,[2] Miss Austen of Bath, only recently arrived in Town. She has been intimate these past weeks at Scargrave Manor, where I believe your dear brother recently visited as well."

"Harry?" the Duchess said with some asperity; "I cannot pretend to know whose houses or whose beds Harry has visited last. But I am obliged to make your acquaintance, Miss Austen, and to see you none the worse for your recent encounter with my brother."

---

2. Though Jane is clearly Eliza's sister-in-law, it was the custom in Austen's time to refer to one's relations by marriage as though they were of birth.—*Editor's note.*

All amazement at her vulgarity, I murmured something in reply, and took the seat the Duchess offered.

"Now," she said, settling her hands comfortably, "you must tell me all you know of the scandal."

"The scandal?" I said, affecting ignorance.

"Regarding Scargrave's death," she returned impatiently. "Is it true the young rogue who was his heir has been enjoying the favours of the Countess?"

It was plain that the Duchess felt complete frankness to be her reward for admitting me to the elevated circle of her acquaintance; and my discomfort must have shown on my face. I knew not what to say. Matters of such a delicate nature should not be tossed about for amusement; and yet, I had come for just this sort of information myself. Eliza rescued me.

"My dear cousin is an intimate friend of the lady," she murmured, leaning forward to offer the full force of her charm; "and Your Grace cannot expect her to betray a confidence of so serious a nature. But *I* am under no such compunction; and I may relate that the Countess and the present Earl are even now locked away in Newgate prison. They were brought before the Assizes soon after Christmas, and remanded to the House of Lords for trial."

"No!" the Duchess said, slapping her hands on her lap; "and Bertie" (by this I took her to mean her husband, the Duke) "will have to hear it in the Lords. How extraordinary! We must send for Bertie at once. For I am certain the trial shall not be long postponed."

"Indeed, it is to be scheduled among the first items of the new session's business," I ventured. "His Grace is not in residence?"

"Lord, no," she replied. "He and Trowbridge have been over in Paris nearly a fortnight, about some wretched business with the West Indies trade. I begged off at the last moment—can't abide Buonaparte, you know, nor that slattern he calls his wife. Intelligence is *not* her strong suit, and her taste in clothes—"

"How adventurous of His Grace," Eliza broke in.

"Very few of his countrymen should risk a trip to France, when hostilities have been suspended so little time."[3]

"I am of your opinion, and told the Duke the same. 'If that upstart invades while you are away, my dear,' I said to Bertie, 'you shall be thrown in prison, and I shall retire to the country.' Of what worth is a concession to trade with the French Indies, when the word of the dictator cannot be trusted? They should content themselves with trading among good English subjects alone. Buonaparte has tried to strangle the flow of British goods, but he shall not prevail while we hold our colonies in the Caribbean."

"How refreshing to hear politics discussed by a lady," Eliza murmured, with an ecstatic look; "and how I envy your husband's chance to visit once more that unhappy country! It will live forever in my memory as the most poignant, and beloved, epoch of my past." She looked down at her gloves, and managed a tear; the Duchess was instantly all sympathy.

"How could I be so cruel as to remind you of such horrors! Forgive me, my dear—and you, too, Miss Austen."

"And so Lord Harold went directly from Scargrave to Paris," I said. "He cannot, then, have learned of the Countess's recent misfortune."

"Indeed, not," the Duchess said, "but I shall write to Bertie directly. Neither he nor Trowbridge would wish to miss the event, of such importance to the peerage."

"I fear, Duchess, that we must leave you now," Eliza said tearfully, as though overcome by bitter memories of the past; "but we have so enjoyed our little visit." She rose in a manner that suffered no protest, extended her exquisitely gloved hand, and turned for the door, myself in her wake.

Behind us, the Duchess rang a bell, and at the door's silent opening, we were pleased to find a footman wait-

3. Britain's roughly twenty years of war with France—from about 1795 to 1815—had a brief hiatus from 1801 to 1803, though the entire island lived in fear of Napoleonic invasion.—*Editor's note.*

ing to conduct us to the street. Without a guide, I am sure that even Eliza should have wandered lost about the corridors, surveyed by Wilborough ancestors scowling from their frames.

Once freed of the oppressive rooms, with their weight of conscious elegance, my cousin breathed a sigh of relief. "Poor Honoria *is* an unfortunate old frump," Eliza said, mounting the carriage step in a swirl of green silk, "but she told us what we desired to learn."

"And in exchange, we may expect her to trample Isobel's name in all the best houses," I rejoined. "I must suppose it impossible that Lord Harold murdered the maid, however, as he was clearly abroad at the time; and so must look to others for the Countess's relief."

"It is not beyond belief, you know, that Trowbridge dispatched a cutthroat in his employ," Eliza mused, smoothing her shawl as the coachman shut the carriage door behind us. "A man of his power and means could do so from anywhere in the realm, at any moment."

"Possible, but unlikely," I said thoughtfully. "He should then have to trust to the man's secrecy until his own return from Paris, and trust is a quality quite foreign to Lord Harold's nature. I think I must consider others as more likely." I turned to her with renewed concern. "Eliza, does the memory of France pain you so much?"

"I shall never cease thanking Fate for throwing France my way," she said, as the carriage wheels began to roll. "By going to the guillotine, the Comte did more for my future than he can possibly have appreciated. He has saved me from many a bore in recent years, and so his death was not *entirely* without purpose."

I RETURNED TO SCARGRAVE HOUSE TO FIND FANNY DELAhoussaye and her mother entertaining a young gentleman by the name of Cranley—a barrister, no less, but suffered to pollute Fanny's presence in deference to his new duties, they being the defence of Isobel and Fitzroy Payne. He rose with alacrity at my appearance, and bowed low

214 - STEPHANIE BARRON

over my hand; a fellow possessed of a cheerful and open countenance, and the aspect of a gentleman.

"I understand you are intimate these many years with my honoured opponent," he said to me.

"Sir William Reynolds? He has long been a friend to the Austen family."

"And an enemy to every hapless criminal before the Bar," Cranley rejoined with spirit. "Though Miss Delahoussaye offers it as her opinion that he is, perhaps, now past his best efforts."

I saw with impatience the sheep-like look of admiration he cast Fanny's way; she had wasted no time in enslaving the poor man to her charms. She was dressed this afternoon in a gown I confess I coveted—black and white striped silk, with braided frogs. When I had expressed my admiration, however, she had declared it to be hopelessly out of fashion and suitable only for wearing before the family. I did not dare *think* what her opinion of my own attire might be, and forbore to praise her finery the more.

"I should never underestimate Sir William," I told the barrister, as Fanny coloured and looked conscious; "even at less than his best, he is decidedly very good. But that is not what you would hear, Mr. Cranley, and I should speak more to the purpose. Tell me what you would know."

"Does Sir William believe himself secure in her ladyship's guilt?"

I settled myself in a chair by the hearth—the carriage ride from Wilborough House had been quite cold—and removed my gloves and bonnet, handing them to the maid who waited by my side. "As secure as he need be," I told the barrister. "You know that he must only prove a case in the minds of the assembled peerage, to see the Countess hang."

"Indeed," he replied, commencing to pace before the fire; a well-made young man, with the quickness of his wits readily upon his face. "Her ladyship is damned by the evidence. Only the maid might have saved her—by admitting guilt, or throwing it upon another—and the maid is dead."

"This would seem to be Sir William's happiest point," I observed. "For he would have it that the Countess dispatched Fitzroy Payne to slit Marguerite's throat, precisely *because* she could incriminate her mistress."

"I have been to see the Countess in her cell," Cranley told me.

Fanny shuddered audibly, and her mother cast her an anxious look.

"Mr. Cranley," Madame said reprovingly, "should not you conduct your business with a *gentleman* of the family? Such words are not for the ears of young ladies gently bred."

The barrister immediately looked his remorse, and allowed as it was true; but I intervened with decided purpose.

"Being both less gently bred, and less youthful, than Miss Delahoussaye," I said, "I should dearly love to discuss the Countess's case." Madame looked her outrage, and summoned her daughter with a gesture; and so the ladies departed, and left me in command of the room.

"How was she?" I asked Cranley, when the doors had closed upon them.

"As might be expected," he replied, with becoming solicitude. "Her ladyship is in the lowest of spirits and possessed of little hope; and nearly driven mad by the disreputable conditions in which she is lodged. The Earl bears it somewhat better; but he is a gentleman in any case, and would face any misfortune with as much equanimity as he might the greatest blessing."

"A more accurate description of Fitzroy Payne I should not have managed myself. You have captured his essence."

The young barrister regarded me sombrely. "You are convinced of his good faith in denying these charges?"

"I am."

"I would that the Countess were equally sanguine."

"I know that she doubts the Earl," I began, in a faltering accent.

" 'Doubt' is hardly the word to describe her feelings. I should say the Countess is convinced of his lordship's guilt."

"That is Trowbridge's doing," I replied, with discomposure. "He has worked to divide them at the moment they most require support, for the mere pleasure of seeing their ruin."

"Trowbridge? *Lord* Harold Trowbridge?" Cranley was all amazement. "How can he be involved in this?"

"Wherever evil is done, he appears like a sort of mascot."

"But how has he worked upon the Countess?"

I began to tick off the scoundrel's methods upon my fingers for Cranley's edification. "He has informed the Countess of the new Earl's insolvency, and of his dissipation—in ways that to her have been convincing. Fitzroy Payne is in want of money, and she *now* sees his indebtedness as a motive for murder; worse still, she believes him to have deliberately incriminated *herself* in both the killings. She had hoped the Earl would use the power of his considerable fortune to defend her Barbadoes estates against the predatory intent of Trowbridge himself—but in this she has been bitterly disappointed. Fitzroy Payne has no fortune to lend. And finally, Mr. Cranley, Lord Harold has revealed to her the existence of Payne's mistress."

Cranley's countenance was puzzled. "And why should such a woman concern the Countess?"

I hesitated. "My dear sir," I said, "as an intimate to all our affairs, you cannot be kept in the dark. And you shall hear it soon enough in London's drawing-rooms, I fear. The Countess believed herself the beloved of Fitzroy Payne, while still her husband's wife; and though she assures me that no impropriety of action occurred between them, the impropriety of such *sensibility* shall convince the public of it in very little time."

"This is a bad business," Cranley groaned, his hands

on the mantel and his head hung towards the fire; "as bad as ever it could be. Neither of them has a witness to their actions at the time of the maid's death; the Countess was alone in her rooms, while the Earl was walking about the Park, as he freely said. Neither can explain how the handkerchief came to be near the body or the scrap of paper on it. And now Lady Scargrave is so mistrustful as to cast suspicion on every one of the present Earl's actions."

"My poor Isobel," I said slowly; "all her faith is blasted."

"Certainly not her faith in you," the barrister replied, brightening somewhat. "She charged me to share my counsel with Miss Austen, in the belief that I should benefit from the same."

"I wonder at her confidence," I replied. "But for me—had I destroyed the note and secreted the handkerchief—the Countess and Fitzroy Payne might yet be at liberty. She has every reason to hate me."

"I doubt she should have escaped suspicion in any case," he rejoined, "when Sir William is so fiercely opposed to her cause."

Indeed, Isobel's life seemed destined for misery. "What do you intend to do?" I asked Mr. Cranley.

"I hope to find the murderer before the day of the trial," he answered with determination, "and present the case for his guilt as my charges' best defence. For you know I shall have no opportunity to attack the edifice Sir William shall build. He shall do his best to make the walls of guilt seem thick and high."

"I shall bend my best efforts in a similar vein," I assured him, "and share with you any discoveries I might make. But if I might offer a word—"

"Anything, Miss Austen." He drew a chair forward, the better to attend to my words.

"Sir William is sure to urge the notion that Fitzroy Payne was desperate for funds, and that his circumstances left no recourse but the murder of his uncle. Can not you find some facts to the contrary? Others in the family must have had equally pressing motivation; and yet they did not fall under suspicion. And then there is the matter of Lord Harold Trowbridge." I told him briefly how that man had benefited by Isobel's misfortune.

At that, the dinner bell rang; time had flown, and I had not even dressed.

"God bless you, Mr. Cranley," I said, rising and extending my hand. "I shall do everything in my power to aid you. But I would ask of you a favour."

"You have but to name it, Miss Austen."

"Convey me tomorrow to the Countess's cell. I would know better, by my own eyes, how she fares; and Fitzroy Payne as well."

"Newgate is no place for a lady," the barrister said, his doubt in his voice.

"Fiddlesticks!" I cried. "You know very well, Mr. Cranley, that visiting the condemned has become a sport for the best society. If Newgate is fit enough to lodge a Countess, it is fit enough for me to call. I shall expect you after breakfast."

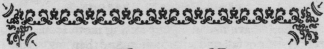

Chapter 17

The Hothouse Flower

2 January 1803

~

LONDON'S AFTERNOON FOG CURLS NOW BEYOND SCAR-grave House's many windows, blotting out the forms of carriage and horse as they pass in the street below. There is a like obscurity in my soul, a darkness bred of too much sadness; I have spent the better part of the morning enshrouded in perpetual night, in the depths of Newgate prison. That I rejoice in my deliverance from that place, I need hardly add, but for my heart-ache at leaving Isobel a prisoner within its walls. But I carry something of Newgate with me still, in the grime and odour of its interior, which sits heavily upon my person.

I have ordered a hot bath, the better to rid myself of the unwholesome stench. Part refuse, part excrement, part human despair, it is noisome, indeed; and I was driven so wild by the foetidness during my return in Mr. Cranley's coach, that I barely stopped at Scargrave House's door to shed my pelisse and bonnet before hastening upstairs to my room. That the Earl's smart Town butler, Simmons—as unlike poor Cobblestone in his youth and vigour as Scargrave House is to the Manor—detected a certain ripeness in my scent, I little doubt, from the curling of his nostrils as I entered; he held my outer garments with the tips of his exquisitely ·gloved fingers, and hastened to pass them to a housemaid, with a frosty injunction that they should be "brushed." Brushed, indeed! A se'nnight's immersion in hot lye and ashes would be unlikely to rid them of Newgate's pollution. But I had dressed in my oldest things, foreseeing how it should be; and could hardly lament the loss of so small a part of my wardrobe in such a cause.

And now the maids have come, with steaming coppers held high, and pronounced the water as yet too hot for my liking. So I have drawn out my journal, and put pen to paper, in the hope of fixing indelibly my impression of that hellish place in which I spent but a few hours. The horror shall pass from my mind with time; but I would retain something of it here, to harden my resolve when despair at Isobel's fate threatens to overcome me. I know her to be innocent, and will not suffer her to spend a minute more than she must in so terrible a hole.

Mr. Cranley was as good as his word, and arrived not long after the breakfast hour—half-past eight, by the great clock that relentlessly chimes the quarters in Scargrave House's entry. His face wore a dubious aspect, and he would have dissuaded me from my visit; but that firmness of purpose, where I know myself to be right, overruled all objection.

I wore my most serviceable gown, a warm wool worsted of dark blue, and my stoutest boots, as though intending a walk over country stiles; and of these I read the barrister's approval as he surveyed my form.

"A clergyman's daughter, you say?" He smiled despite the sombre nature of our errand. "I should almost have thought your father a Colonel, Miss Austen, and yourself well hardened to the privations of campaign."

"Parish work may be as arduous, and its contests as bitter, as the mounting of a siege," I replied, pulling on my gloves. "Have you never been forced, Mr. Cranley, to parcel out the parts in a Christmas pageant, and suffer calumny and abuse for the neglect of some worthy's darling child? But enough. The Countess awaits us."

"Her ladyship cannot do much else," he replied grimly, assisting me into his carriage, "more's the pity. Had she occupation for her thoughts, she might bear her circumstances better."

I stopped, half in the carriage, half out, and stared at him in consternation. "You mean she has nothing of an amusing nature by her?"

"Amusing? I should think not."

I turned abruptly and stepped down, my feet as swift as my thoughts. "Do you wait a moment, Mr. Cranley," I declared. "I know the very article to cheer her."

WE WERE NOT LONG ON OUR WAY TO NEWGATE, IT BEing situated to the east of Portman Square, near the old walls of the City. In a different time, the Earl and the Countess might have been conveyed to the Tower, there to be lodged in chilly dignity appropriate to their station, though offering no more comfort than the prison thrown up in its shadow. As we approached Newgate, I quailed to think of the scaffold that might be erected before its doors, should Isobel be condemned to die. A public execution, with all the humiliation and popular carousing that habitually attends a Hanging Day, was too horrible to contemplate. I turned to Mr. Cranley. "Is it likely, my good sir—if it be that we fail in our efforts to prove the Countess's innocence—must she certainly hang?"

For the space of several heartbeats, the barrister offered no answer, his eyes upon the gloomy walls of the approaching prison. At last he turned to me with sober mien. "The courts are loath to impose such a sentence upon a woman," he replied, "but the deliberate murder of one's husband—particularly a gentleman of the Earl's station—is not a clergyable offence.[1] I fear, Miss Austen, that we have no alternative but to prove the Countess's innocence. And the Earl's as well."

The carriage halted before Newgate's stone gate, and Mr. Cranley jumped out, with a hand for me as I descended. We stopped an instant in silence before those dreadful walls, overlaid with writhing gargoyles and hung with chains; and then a wicket was slid back in the massive oak itself. We were treated to a beefy visage, with a patch over one eye, and a mouth possessed of very few teeth.

"Do you wait a moment, Miss Austen, while I speak to the porter," Mr. Cranley told me, and approached the prison gate. His conversation was swiftly conducted—through the passage of coin from his hand to the other's—and the heavy gate swung open. We were led within the courtyard, cobbled and streaming from the residue of London's fogs; I suffered to think of Isobel's arrival here, a lonely object of contempt, without much of hope to sustain her. It was but another moment before we gained admittance from a trusty at the prison door, and were inside.

How to relate the scene that greeted us?

A narrow, windowless, low-ceilinged place, lit only by torchlight, the better to obscure years of grime and a scurrying at our feet—undoubtedly from rats. An air so thick with smoke and odour as to be suffocating. A repeated clanging about the ears, from bolts drawn back or driven home—or, worse yet, from manacles shaken

---

1. Clergyable offenses were those that might be sentenced "with benefit of clergy," meaning, with a dispensation against the death penalty. Manslaughter, for example, was a clergyable offense, with transportation rather than death the usual sentence. This legal provision arose from the tradition of trying ordained clergy in ecclesiastical courts, but spread to the population at large. —Editor's note.

in despair. I looked about me furtively, not wishing to appear shocked, but Mr. Cranley divined my emotion.

"There is time yet to go back," he said gently. "I would not think less of you, Miss Austen, did you call for my carriage."

"Nonsense," I replied, and affected an air of greater strength than I assuredly felt.

We were placed in the safekeeping of a man Mr. Cranley addressed as Crow, a peculiar person of stunted appearance, with an enormous nose and a heavy growth of dark hair, much matted. He wore on his person an astonishing number of garments, of varying stuffs and sizes—a veritable rag-picker's fortune, to my untrained eye. I learned later from Mr. Cranley that it was Crow's custom to buy the clothes of condemned men, piece by piece, in the days before their execution; the poor souls being desperate for some last sustenance, they were willing to barter all that they owned for the promise of good ale and maggotless bread. I am relieved I knew nothing of the origin of our guide's motley wardrobe, while still in his presence; for I fear I could not have repressed my disgust.

Crow conducted us through a passage so dark and narrow, it barely permitted the span of Mr. Cranley's shoulders, and as the walls were damp with mould, I feared for the barrister's good wool coat. Our guide's taper cast flickering shadows as he progressed before us, as comfortable with his lot as one of the Duchess of Wilborough's footmen. We mounted stairs, and followed still more endless corridors, and glimpsed leering faces from occasional barred doors; a fearful babble assailed our ears, part moan, part feverish talk, part muttered curse.

Our guide stopped short before a door, the taper making a grotesquerie of his bulbous nose and thatch of greasy hair. He fumbled at the waists of his many pairs of breeches, and came up with a large key; which, fitted into the lock, succeeded in turning the bolt. I peered timidly about me. Could Isobel really be lodged within?

She was.

Crow threw wide the heavy door and preceded us into the chamber, his face set in a lascivious grin; and upon following Mr. Cranley across the threshold, I quickly perceived the reason.

All manner of strumpet and pickpocket and gypsy beggar were housed within the room—women blowsy and ragged, tall and short, comely and fearsome to look upon. Some seven were confined together in a space perhaps fifteen feet square; they huddled upon the ground in attitudes of dejection, or stood brazenly in groups, conversing with as much ease as though walking the Strand of a Saturday afternoon. One of these last, a snaggle-toothed hag, sallied up to Crow and ran her fingers through his dirty locks, with a leer to match his own.

"Eh, luv," she cackled, "whattuv you brought us tidday? Summat nice?"

"Leave off, Nance," the gaoler said, thrusting her backwards with a cuff to the head; "I've business with the lady."

"The *lady*, is it? Ho ho." Nance ran her eyes the length of my gown, with remarkable impertinence for one of her station, and spat upon the ground. "*That's* for ladies, that is."

Mr. Cranley offered the protection of his arm, and led me to a door in the far wall opening into another chamber. There, in a darkened corner, I discovered the Countess. Isobel sat upon the ground, her arms hugging her breast, as though that pitiful gesture might offer some protection from the nightmare of her circumstance; she raised a face suffused with dumb suffering at our approach, and her brown eyes widened with horror.

"Jane!" she whispered hoarsely. "How come you to be here? And witnessing my shame!" She looked wildly about, and struggled to her feet, as if to fly from our sight.

"My dear girl," I said affectionately, taking both her hands in mine, "I see no shame, only great forbearance in the midst of so much misfortune. Your courage is a credit to your name, Isobel—your friends can only honour you."

"One friend, at least, I have," she cried, and gripped me in a fierce embrace. Mr. Cranley shut the door of Isobel's cell upon Nance and her confederates, then hovered on the periphery, his eyes averted, until recalled to attention by the Countess's hand.

"And you, Mr. Cranley," she said, in a softened tone; "most excellent of barristers, and a true gentleman. I am fortunate, indeed, in *your* friendship. But you seem distressed, good sir."

"I am only outraged, my lady," Mr. Cranley said, "in witnessing your continued degradation. I had ordered Snatch to obtain more suitable lodgings for you, and the man has expressly violated the terms of our agreement."

Isobel looked away, and raised a hand to her eyes; then faced us with better composure. "I believe the man Crow is incapable of honour, Mr. Cranley. You are well advised to bargain with his superiors, if you wish to waste your coin. But do not concern yourself with me. I care little for *which* room in hell I may call my own; none is likely to offer comfort."

I surveyed the Countess with profound emotion, unwilling to imagine the trials she had already undergone. Her simple dress of black wool was soiled and torn; whose hands had offended her person I could readily guess, having viewed the gauntlet of her cellmates. Her hair was tangled and dirty, and a fearful smell emanated from the folds of her clothes. She was sunk indeed from the wealth and consequence that had been hers but a few weeks before. I embraced her again, overcome with pity.

"I fear we cannot remain much longer, Miss Austen," Mr. Cranley said gently.

"Isobel," I said, "we will have you out of this fearsome place, with your innocence proved and your good name restored. Never doubt that all our benevolence is active on your behalf. Let hope sustain you in this, your darkest hour; we shall see you freed, and Fitzroy Payne with you."

226 ~ STEPHANIE BARRON

"Do not speak his name, Jane. I wish never to hear it again."

I gazed at her averted face and bitter eyes, profoundly disturbed. What fury is love that believes itself betrayed!

"I shall be very much surprised, Isobel, to discover him anything but as innocent as yourself; and in time, you may find in that as much hope as for your own cause."

She bit her lip, and turned to me with emotion. At a nod from Mr. Cranley, I reluctantly released her; but remembered to press upon my friend the book I had fetched at the very carriage door. It was my most treasured novel—*Cecilia*, by Miss Fanny Burney—as certain a mental diversion as one could find, in so terrible a place. But Isobel refused it, with an eye to the women beyond her door, and the treacherous Crow.

"Do you keep it safe, dear Jane," she told me softly. "I shall hope to enjoy its delights in a better time."

"MR. CRANLEY," I SAID THOUGHTFULLY, WHEN CROW HAD led us to the street, "we must endeavour to find a reason for the Countess to hope."

"I agree, Miss Austen. But whence that hope might spring, I cannot say."

"A renewed faith in the Earl might engender it. Did the Countess think his soul less black, she might suffer less despair."

Mr. Cranley helped me into his carriage, and stood by the door; and I understood then he would not accompany me on my return to Scargrave House.

"You must descend once more into that hell?" I enquired, in some distress.

"I must meet with the Earl, Miss Austen; and no lady may be permitted in a cell such as his," the barrister replied grimly. "I fear I have some business with the prison's governor as well, if I can but persuade him to hear me. The Countess and the Earl must be moved to more decent rooms, though a fortune be spent to achieve it."

"You are goodness itself."

"I only do what is required—what any gentleman of feeling would do."

"Most *gentlemen of feeling* would hardly think a month's ablutions enough to rid them of Newgate's stains," I replied dryly. "I remain convinced of your worth, my dear sir."

He inclined his head, somewhat embarrassed, and I moved on with energy to my more important purpose. "Mr. Cranley," I said, "when you speak with Fitzroy Payne, do you enquire as to his methods of correspondence."

"His methods?"

"Indeed—what records of letters sent and received he may retain; whether he logs his postage; and particularly enquire if he makes copies of those missives he writes."

Comprehension dawned upon the barrister's face. "You think of the scrap found in the maid's bodice."

I nodded. "Could we but show that paper to have been taken from some part of the Earl's correspondence, his guilt in having written it might seem less heavy. For any might have sent the note to Marguerite. It cannot be proved that the Earl did so. What indicts him is his hand; the writing is surely his. We must endeavour to show that it was intended for another, and appeared upon the maid only by misadventure."

The light in Mr. Cranley's eyes was enough to satisfy me; that we should soon know all we must about Fitzroy Payne's business, I little doubted, and rejoiced in the excellent understanding of Isobel's defender.

Later that day
~

I WAS TREATED AFTER DINNER TO AN EXTRAORDINARY IN-terview with Miss Fanny Delahoussaye, and am so far from understanding what it may mean, that I write down the essence of it, in the hopes that by so doing, I may better comprehend it.

I had retired to the pianoforte, in an effort to improve my mastery of Mr. Haydn's airs, and reflect upon all that has occurred, when I was surprised by Miss Delahoussaye's appearance at my side. A band of jet beads was drawn across her brow, with a plume behind, and she was resplendent in a dinner gown of black sarcenet. I knew that she looked forward eagerly to her visit on the morrow to Madame Henri's, that breathlessly fashionable *modiste* of Bond Street, and assumed that she wished to bend my ear, the better to glory in her good fortune.

"Miss Austen," said she, in a far warmer accent than has distinguished our acquaintance thus far, "may I persuade you to take a turn about the Orangerie? I do not believe you have yet viewed its delights. In such a season as this, when the streets are impassable, a greenhouse must be preferred above all other amusement. I am sure you should like it of all things."

I saw no reason to hold myself aloof, and gladly consented. The Orangerie was a folly of the sixth Earl, the late Lord Scargrave's father, whose wife was French; he is said to have drawn the structure from the likeness of one on the grounds of Versailles, before that noble palace's destruction at the hands of the French rabble. A quantity and variety of plants are grown in its hothouse atmosphere, such as are rarely met with. The late Earl shared in his father's interest, botany being yet another of his passions; no plant was too costly or too rare for his procuring.

"Mr. Cranley seems a respectable sort of fellow, for a barrister," Fanny began, as we strolled the moist aisles, smelling of green; "you might almost set your cap at him, had you sufficient time, Miss Austen. His profession is not abhorrent to *you*, and his prospects must be declared quite good—at least, for one of your—that is, quite good, indeed."

"I think Mr. Cranley would prefer that *you* secure him, Miss Delahoussaye. He was all admiration while you retained the room."

"You are a sly creature, Miss Austen! But *do* call me Fanny," she said, slipping her arm through mine. I had not the slightest inclination to proceed to further intimacy in such a manner, and so did not offer her my Christian name. "I have been longing for the chance to walk with you alone, for I am in a sad turmoil of mind, and the wisdom of such an one as yourself—so much my senior in age and experience—must be a source of comfort."

So *much* her senior, indeed! The eight years' difference in our ages is hardly the stuff of a generation; but I could not expect Miss Delahoussaye to refrain from malice, when an opportunity for abuse presented itself.

"Such advice as I can give, I will gladly offer; although I must consider our acquaintance as so slight, as to recommend some other party to your interest."

"Our acquaintance slight! I declare! It was not five minutes after your arrival at Scargrave that I felt assured you would be the salvation of my visit to that dreary place, and perhaps the means of securing that felicity—but I am too precipitate. I impose upon your kindness. I had better explain the nature of my distress."

"To be sure," I said, somewhat bewildered.

"You cannot have been long in the company of Lieutenant Hearst without remarking his extraordinary ability to please," she began, with a sidelong glance. "I am sure you cannot."

"He is a charming fellow." And so this is how she intended to broach my indiscretion of New Year's Eve. I had almost succeeded in forgetting it.

"Charming! He is all that is attentive and engaging. And such modesty! Such diffidence! He never comprehends the effect his openness and amiability have on the ladies of his acquaintance. I know that many an one has been persuaded to think *too much* of his notice, his conversation, his little habits of attention, before this." She stopped to caress a blooming plant with one finger. "I am very much afraid that it has caused many to regret their having hoped for so much, upon discovering he intended *too little*. La, an orchid in January! I declare, an orchid is pleasanter than anything in the world."

And so, I thought, taking the import of her first words, I am warned off. Even a second son of a wastrel is too good for a Miss Austen, without fortune or connexion to recommend her. I could not but think a primary object of Fanny's confidence was to apprise me of my danger in encouraging Lieutenant Hearst's attentions; by suggesting his fickleness, she hoped to wound me, and thus win his attention for herself. Though she lacks the appearance of jealousy, her character suggests she cannot be immune to its bite. But how amusing that she should feel that emotion towards *me*, when I had despaired of my power before one of her beauty and fortune!

"As a woman *so much older* than yourself, I must own I have encountered men as charming as the Lieutenant elsewhere," I said carefully. "Amiable as he may be, I have seen his equal before. Your *more sheltered life* to date must excuse you."

At this, she coloured prettily. "I may express too great a partiality for the Lieutenant," she said. "How else can one who is promised to him be expected to regard him, but as the epitome of all that is good and admirable in a man?" "Promised!" I cried, attempting in vain to recover my wits. "I had not an idea of it! And your mother approves?"

"Oh, Lord! Mamma knows nothing about it," Fanny said composedly. "The match is unlikely to meet with favour from her, any more than it would have won Isobel's consent—and you know, Isobel's father was my guardian, and at his death the charge passed to her, until I should marry or reach the age of twenty-five. My Uncle John Collins had long acted in lieu of my father, and had strongly advised my mother to find me a husband befitting my fortune—I am possessed of no less than thirty thousand pounds. He so far persuaded Mamma of the sum's significance, and warned her so repeatedly against fortune hunters, that she will not have me even *dance* with any man who can claim less than five or ten thousand a year, much less a second son."

"You do not share her scruple?"

"Where love exists, how can fortune matter?"

How, indeed! Fortune, or lack of it, has been the main impediment to every trifling attachment of my life; it was certainly the means of dividing me from my first love, and my truest—Tom Lefroy.[2] Young as we both were, I do not believe we lacked anything conducive to our mutual affection and happiness, *but* fortune. But I forbore to give way to self-pity, and agreed with Miss Delahoussaye that her comfortable means must allow her to bestow her affections where her heart chose.

"And you have been promised to the Lieutenant how long?"

"These three weeks."

Three weeks. His attentions to me must, therefore, have been as nothing; I had been deceived by flattery yet again. It is not to be borne!

"I declare," Miss Delahoussaye said expansively, "but it *is* a change! I have been wild about Tom for ages, but he was ever of a mind to abuse me unmercifully; and there was a time last summer when I almost thought him promised to a Miss King, and gave him up for lost. But apparently that went off, and when he came to us at Scargrave, there was never a man more attentive! I must believe it the effect of my purple silk; it *is* a cunning gown, and might almost make my eyes the same shade."

I made some answer, equal to her speech in its lack of sense, and she continued almost without pause.

"Mamma thought nothing of his presence at the

2. Jane Austen fell in love with the nephew of her good friend Anne Lefroy at the age of twenty, while the young Irishman was visiting the Hampshire town of Steventon, where Jane grew up. Anne Lefroy was opposed to the match because of Jane's lack of fortune, and sent Tom away before any engagement was formed. —*Editor's note.*

house, it being taken up with mourning; and he would look glum as all whenever she appeared, and pretend to dance attendance on you, only to brighten immediately once she was out of sight, and profess himself violently in love! A capital scheme, I declare! Only now there is the trial, and Tom and I must live apart, and barely speak; not a ball are we to have, or any amusement—"

"Miss Delahoussaye," I interrupted, "I fail to see where my advice is wanted."

"But you must tell me what to do!"

"In what manner may I be of assistance?"

"Tom—Lieutenant Hearst—was to go to Isobel the night the Earl died. We had determined that she should be told, whether she should give her consent or no, and that we should be married after Christmas if we must go to Gretna Green to do it." Her words were unusually vehement.

I confess to a quickening of my pulse. "And did Lieutenant Hearst obtain his interview?"

"I cannot make out whether he did, but it cannot signify *now*. Isobel is past all consent, and cannot plague us any longer. But it is Mamma I think of; and I cannot believe she will see reason until the marriage is made."

"I cannot stand in lieu of either, Miss Delahoussaye, if it is consent you seek."

"But here is the point, Miss Austen. Tom *will* have us marry as soon as possible—he is wild to get me, I own. And now we are in mourning, and the trial is soon to happen—I declare I am almost distracted! For how am I to marry when the whole world is set against it?"

I confessed that even my age and experience had failed to teach me ways to circumvent such convention; but I ventured the opinion that a marriage within six weeks of the trial might not be considered ill, if it were conducted quietly and without undue pomp. At this Fanny seemed reassured, and professed her unshakable intent of waiting for Lieutenant Hearst until they could hie away to Gretna Green.

Having had time to absorb this news, along with its

implicit warning against such things as kisses in the moonlight, I was possessed of a new thought.

"The maid Marguerite knew of your plans, did she not?" I enquired.

Miss Fanny started, and all the delicate colour of her soft complexion drained from her face. "She never told you!" she cried in protest.

I adopted an all-encompassing wisdom as my best deceit.

"But of course," I said. "You did not think your secret died with her?"

At this, Fanny's breath quickened and the tears started to her eyes; she sat down upon a stone bench and was quite overcome. I suffered from some perplexity—for I had referred to nothing more than a planned elopement, the fact of which she had just imparted. Such distress could hardly spring from *this*. The secret, then, was of far greater import; and it behooved me to learn it. I sat down at her side and placed an arm about her shoulders.

"You need not pay me to keep your confidence, Fanny," I told her. "*I* do not expect a bag of coins by the hay-shed door."

She lifted her pretty face, tear-stained and miserable, and stared at me wildly. "But you understand, then, why we must be married as soon as ever," she said. "In very little time, my gowns shall hardly fit. Already Marguerite has had to let out the seams; and she tried to ruin me for her knowledge. Now Mamma would have us at the warehouses for our mourning, and I *must* have a gown for the House of Lords, and if I stand before a seamstress, she is sure to know in an instant!"

I perceived, at last, the trouble. "When is the child to be born?" I asked her.

Fanny shrugged helplessly. "How should I know? I have no experience of these things. I only know that my corset does not fit, and that my seams are bursting, and that I have felt decidedly unwell these past few weeks. Marguerite said my time should not come until July at least. But she may have been lying." A pair of drowned blue eyes sought my own. "Deceit and self-interest were ever Marguerite's way, Miss Austen." Fanny's voice held unaccustomed bitterness.

"You met with the Lieutenant while still in London," I mused. "After Isobel's marriage—while she travelled abroad."

"It was better that she be ignorant of our concerns," Fanny replied, her eyes downcast. "She did not approve of my meeting Tom."

And with good reason, I thought, remembering the click of Fanny's door several nights past; had the Lieutenant entered her room, even as he parted from me? His conduct was in every way infamous. And here, assuredly, was a powerful motive for murdering the maid and dropping Isobel's kerchief; by these vile actions, Fanny's blackmailer should be dispatched, and her guardian silenced. But what of the damning note in Fitzroy Payne's hand?

Poor Fanny was in no state to be further interrogated; I patted her shoulder, said a few words, and helped her to her feet. We parted at the Orangerie door, she to trip deceitfully to her Mamma, and I to seek my chamber and my pen with a heavy heart.

I CANNOT CONSIDER THE MATCH WITHOUT SOME LITTLE dismay. It has been long, indeed—despite my capricious words to Fanny Delahoussaye—since I encountered a man of Lieutenant Hearst's easy manners and amiability, however false his intentions; and it seems I am forever to witness such men apportioned to an other. I confess to indulging in a review of my affairs of the heart, and wondering for the thousandth time if I did wrong in refusing Harris Bigg-Wither; to avoid the continued painful recognition of all I have been denied, in finally accepting some *one*, would be relief enough from a lifetime of bitter disappointments.

And I am all wonder at Lieutenant Hearst's behaviour! He has snubbed Fanny, and sought my company over hers, whenever opportunity afforded. Were I his professed love, I should find his conduct reprehensible. Was this merely a shadow play as she described, intended to deceive others and fend off the suspicious in his family circle? If so, I can declare Tom Hearst to have engaged in it too heartily, and feel myself to be a laughing-stock. It would have been enough to speak of Miss Delahoussaye with neutral praise, such as any man might bestow; whereas he never missed an opportunity for raillery. Her infatuation with himself, her false pride, her preoccupation with clothes and self-importance—all have been the subject of his disparagement in the course of our riding lessons together. I cannot comprehend it. I might almost believe him regretting his choice; and if he feels so little respect for a woman whose charms alone may have quickened his interest, I cannot feel sanguine about his prospects for happiness in marriage.

And did the Lieutenant *obtain* his interview with Isobel that e'en? And an opportunity, perhaps, to place the Barbadoes nuts in the Earl's dish?

Isobel is past all consent, Miss Delahoussaye had said; and indeed, my friend is now conveniently incapable of opposing the match, and the bestowing of Miss Delahoussaye's thirty thousand pounds. I wonder she could not be persuaded that the marriage would keep Fanny's fortune in the Scargrave family, and thus be made to look with favour on the union; but perhaps that did not serve Lieutenant Hearst's purpose. Isobel—and Fitzroy Payne—would undoubtedly have tied the money in such legal binds as made it virtually useless to him; and it may be that it is *cash* for which Tom Hearst seeks. And if it be that the gentleman is in desperate need of money, I must consider his appearance of guilt as black, indeed.

Or am I merely comforting myself with the thought that he chooses Miss Delahoussaye for her fortune, rather than any preference over myself? Stupid, stupid Jane! Your vanity rises again, even in the hour of its most thorough defeat.

Can such a man, whose fine appearance and good

humour suggest all that is pleasing, be so infinitely dissembling? I declare his charm, and think him a murderer; I encourage his attentions, and find him promised to another. Were I acquainted with his person a twelvemonth, and had ample scope for observation, I should believe myself still as likely to be deceived. No, I shall not begin to understand it, be Miss Fanny Delahoussaye turned Mrs. Tom Hearst, and her third child on the way.

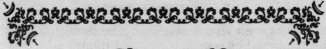

Chapter 18

The Very Mrs. Hammond

3 January 1803

~

I SENT FOR MR. CRANLEY EARLY THIS MORNING, AND WAS
gratified to see that gentleman arrive with alacrity not an
hour later. To stem his apparent disappointment at Fanny
Delahoussaye's absence—she was even then standing before Madame Henri, the Bond Street *modiste*—I bent
myself briskly to business.

"Let us talk, Mr. Cranley, of evidence," I began, closing the study door behind us, the better to guard against
a servant's ears. "The presence near the paddock gate of
Isobel's handkerchief, we may count as nothing. Any person desiring to throw blame upon the Countess, might
readily have obtained her linen, monogrammed as it is,
for the purpose; access to her apartments is not even necessary. I myself have observed Isobel leave her kerchiefs
behind her wherever she goes."

Mr. Cranley nodded. "I had assumed as much."

"And what of Fitzroy Payne? Have you intelligence
of his writing habits?" I perched on the edge of a chair,
and Mr. Cranley did the same, leaning towards me in his
eagerness.

"Your excellent understanding, Miss Austen, is cause for rejoicing," he began.

"Capital!" I cried, clasping my hands together. "You have learned something to their advantage!"

The barrister nodded. "As you are no doubt aware, Fitzroy Payne was engrossed in resolving the business affairs of his uncle at the time of the maid's murder. He remained closeted in the library for days on end, over a quantity of papers, and much correspondence passed between Lord Scargrave and his London solicitors."

"Well I remember it. The solicitors appeared at Scargrave immediately upon the Earl's death, but stayed only a few hours; thereafter all matters were conducted by post. And what a quantity of post! Madame Delahoussaye undertook several times to tidy the Earl's library, and was all agog at the mess."

"According to Lord Scargrave, he never varies from routine in matters of business. In writing a letter, he painstakingly draws up a draft, and then copies it for clarity's sake onto another sheet of paper. It is the final copy which he sends to the recipient."

"He has copies of all his correspondence?"

"He does. I think it possible that the phrase in question was torn from just such a *draft*—left lying about the Earl's library desk, to which everyone might have access—and the rest of the sheet destroyed." The barrister slapped his knees in excitement, and sat back in his chair.

"But how to find the very letter?"

"I am directed to Fitzroy Payne's valet," Mr. Cranley said, looking about him as though the man were hiding in one of the corners, "who retains a list of the Earl's correspondence, as well as his personal papers. If the draft of a letter is missing, we may discover to whom the final copy was sent, and search for the incriminating phrase in its text."

I wished to partake of the barrister's evident satisfaction, but a doubt assailed me. "Do we look among the Manor household as you suggest, Mr. Cranley—where any might have access to the Earl's library and his drafts—or must we consider that the letter's *recipient* might also be the murderer?"

The barrister looked thoughtful at this, and rose restlessly from his chair. "If the maid's murderer received a letter from the Earl containing the incriminating language, he should have no need of a draft; it required only to tear the phrase from the letter itself and send it to the maid. If that is the case, we cannot hope to locate the damaged letter itself." "But we *may* learn the murderer's identity, from finding the phrase of the maid's note in a *draft* of the letter in Danson's possession," I observed.

Mr. Cranley beamed at me in approval. "If, however, the murderer is a member of the household—who searched among the Earl's drafts, and tore the incriminating phrase from the page—then the draft itself should be *absent* from Danson's collection."

"This cannot show the Earl's innocence," I mused, "but it may demonstrate that anyone familiar with the household—and Fitzroy Payne's habits of correspondence—might readily have secured a sample of his handwriting, and without his knowledge."

"We are of one mind, Miss Austen," the barrister said. "Our best hope of securing the Countess's freedom, as well as that of Fitzroy Payne, is to show the guilt of another. There is no avoiding *that*. But until we may locate our murderer, I shall send for Danson."

I rose as Mr. Cranley made for the door. "And do you know where he is to be found?"

"Fitzroy Payne sent him on to his London establishment near his clubs in Pall Mall. Danson awaits his master's trial there in solitude—and, one assumes, some measure of despondency. For if the Earl is condemned, his valet's chances of obtaining a suitable new position must be very slim."

"Danson should be active, then, in assisting us," I replied. "For his future, too, hangs upon it."

MR. CRANLEY BELIEVED THAT HIS ONLY DEFENCE LAY IN attacking Sir William on narrow points of law; but it seemed to me a wiser course to present an equally plausible case for the guilt of another—and though I felt myself to be taking on the crushing role of the Divine Creator, in assaying to mete out punishment or pardon, I felt it incumbent upon me to exert myself to that end. While the barrister was about locating Danson, I determined that *I* should visit Jenny Barlow's sister—and discover why her name had been the cause for such passionate vituperation between the incipient curate, Mr. George Hearst, and his uncle. I suspected it was due to righteous outrage on that gentleman's part at the late Earl's seduction of one of his own servants; but proof was nonetheless necessary.

Did I arrive in the Scargrave carriage, with its arms emblazoned on the doors, I should probably turn Rosie's humble establishment all aflutter; and so I deemed it best to secure a hackney carriage, the better to progress unknown, and thus made my way across Westminster Bridge to South London.

THE ADDRESS JENNY BARLOW HAD GIVEN ME WAS SUCH AS did not disgrace her sister. From the appearance of their exteriors, the homes of many estimable families sit in Gracechurch Street—modest tradesmen, no doubt, and men of profession, whose means have not yet ascended to the West End. I observed many a marble stoop scrubbed clean, and doors pulled wide to the milkman by fresh-faced young maids in starched aprons and mob caps; and felt assured that Rosie Ketch's fortune had been less melancholy than it might.

The hackney pulled up to a well-kept lodging house, with a doorman ready to hand me down; and to him I conveyed my card, and directed that it should be sent to Number 33, in search of Miss Rosie Ketch, and waited for what I might learn. The vestibule of the establishment revealed it to be of modest pretensions and circumstances, as befit the neighbourhood and its inhabitants' means; and I confess myself as ever more puzzled as to how the girl came to be placed there.

Presently a kindly-faced woman of advanced years descended, and made herself known to me as a Mrs. Hammond—a name which must make me start, as having been attached to the woman identified by Harold Trowbridge as Fitzroy Payne's mistress. Observing that she might rather have been his mother, I decided it to be the merest coincidence; and forebore from impertinent questions. She bade me follow her up several flights of stairs, to an apartment of a few rooms and some comfort, though little style.

"And how, Miss Austen, may I be of service?" Mrs. Hammond said, in the manner of a genteel servant, having seated me on a worn settee by the fire and taken her place opposite. "Your card and your name are unknown to me."

"But the name of Rosie Ketch is not?" I enquired.

"I have known a Rosie Ketch," she replied, her kindly eyes nonetheless steely.

"I am come at the behest of Rosie Ketch's sister, Mrs. Barlow, whom I met while a visitor at Scargrave Manor. Mrs. Barlow is in some distress from the fact that she cannot hear from Rosie, and would have news of her by any means; and thus she prevailed upon me to call on her behalf, knowing that I was to be in Town."

"Dear Jenny!" Mrs. Hammond exclaimed, her features softening. "As kind a girl as ever lived. How those two were born of that father, I'll never understand; but Susan Ketch was a lovely woman, and her children take after her, though she died so young in their rearing."

"The girl is within, then?" I said.

"Aye, and she is. Jenny will have told you of her trouble?"

I replied in the affirmative.

"I'll have her out for you in a moment, then, and you can be the judge of her yourself," said Mrs. Hammond; and rising with an energy commendable in one of her advanced years, she disappeared in pursuit of her young charge.

She had no sooner returned, with a slight girl of angelic appearance behind, than there was a knock upon the outer door; and with a curtsey, Mrs. Hammond left me with Rosie Ketch.

That she was far along in her condition was immediately evident; although how frail a girl, and of such apparent youth, could be expected to bear a child, was indeed to be wondered at. She had Jenny Barlow's fair hair and blue eyes, but where her sister's face showed that awareness of the world's harsher cares that maturity brings, Rosie's countenance was altogether innocent. I might readily believe her to have come by her condition, without any understanding of how she had been got that way; and pitied her deeply for the vagary of her fate. That any man could so impose upon such a child, was incredible; but that it should have been the late Earl—as I doubted not from Jenny Barlow's dark looks at his name and George Hearst's accusatory words in his study—must detract from his reputation for goodness.

"You are Rosie Ketch," I said gently.

The girl nodded shyly, her eyes fixed firmly on the floor, and her hands clasped before her.

"I am Miss Austen, Rosie," I told her. "I am come to bring you the love of your sister, who placed it in my charge when last I was at Scargrave. She is all benevolence on your behalf, and her concern has grown with the distance between you, and what I understand to be her husband's injunction of silence. May I assure her of your good health and steady spirits?"

"Tell Jenny as I am well," she said carefully, in a clear, high voice, "though I fear for myself when my time comes, and would have her by me, if Ted can spare her."

"I shall tell her so," I said. "Are there yet many months to wait?"

"I can't say as I know rightly," she said.

"And you have been here how long?"

At that, her eyes glanced to the door, which was even then opening to reveal Mrs. Hammond, ushering her latest visitor within. Imagine my shock upon discovering it to be a gentleman of my acquaintance—none other than Mr. George Hearst!

My surprise must have shown upon my face, or perhaps his own sensibility taught him to expect it; for he looked as confused as I. His intelligence quickly overcame his discomfiture, however, and he impeded my questions with a determined swiftness.

"My dear Miss Austen," he cried, "what *can* have brought you here?"

"Mr. Hearst!" I exclaimed. "I might ask you as much!"

He coloured at that, but said nothing; and recovering himself swiftly, bent over my hand in greeting.

"You are acquainted with Mr. Hearst?" Mrs. Hammond said, looking from himself to me with a shrewd eye, as well she might; for I discerned that she had given him no knowledge of my presence, though knowing me only lately arrived from Scargrave, and more than likely to have encountered him there.

"Indeed," Mr. Hearst said; "it has been my privilege."

"Rosie," Mrs. Hammond said briskly, "you must attend to the washing now; get along, girl. I'll be with you directly."

At her charge's exit, she turned once more to me, and said, not without kindness, "You'll be wanting tea, miss, I expect. I'll fetch it and leave you to yourselves."

As George Hearst clearly awaited my adoption of a seat, I chose the settee once more, and he assumed Mrs. Hammond's position opposite. He regarded me for the space of several seconds, and I, him. I may say that his countenance lacked his customary expression of melancholy; he appeared rather to be freed of some great weight, and at peace with what troubles he may have had.

"I know the confusion my presence in this house must cause you," he began. "I will not pretend to mislead you, Miss Austen. Having found me out, you can expect nothing less than a full recital."

"My own appearance must have similarly astonished you," I rejoined. "*I* am come at the behest of Jenny Barlow, but that she sent you on a similar errand, I must believe unlikely."

"You would be correct," the curate said, nodding. "I am here because of the letter I received of Mrs. Hammond Christmas Eve."

"The day of the maid's murder—the day you made in haste for London."

"I was called hither by Mrs. Hammond, who had only lately heard of the Earl's death," he explained. "She felt certain that Rosie's circumstances should change as a result, and desired me to attend her with any news it might be in my power to convey."

"But why should the lady enquire this of you? Had she not better have asked it of the present Earl?"

"As her grandmother, she is necessarily anxious on Rosie's behalf, and I am the man whose interest must decide the girl's fate."

"Mrs. Hammond, Rosie's grandmother? She did not mention it."

"Rosie's mother was a Hammond, and much beloved by *her* mother, though left behind at Scargrave when Fitzroy established Mrs. Hammond here."

"Then the Earl *is* Mrs. Hammond's patron?" I remembered Harold Trowbridge's look of exultation, as he stood by the library fire talking of Fitzroy Payne's mistress. The grandmotherly woman even now preparing my tea was not at all what I should have expected. "It seems incredible!"

"That such a man should remember the affection of a nursemaid? I suppose it must seem so to you, who can have known him so little; but I assure you, Fitzroy is not without his goodness."

"Nursemaid?" I cried, too late to stifle my astonishment; and at George Hearst's penetrating look, felt the colour enter my unfortunate cheeks.

"You thought her perhaps as having provided a nearer service?" he asked, in a rare moment of amusement; but at my confused dismay, he became sober once more. "No, Miss Austen, Mrs. Hammond is guilty of nothing more than having suckled the eighth Earl at her breast, and that, when he was hardly of an age to place an unpleasant construction upon it."

Certain aspects of the situation readily became clear to me. It was not the *late* Earl, but the present one—Fitzroy Payne—who was responsible for Rosie's condition; she must be the mistress of whom Lord Harold spoke. Payne had sent her to the trustiest woman he knew for safe-keeping, his former nursemaid, her grandmother. That the girl should be having a child was an added blow to Isobel's trust! Though one that Lord Harold, thankfully, had seen fit to keep from her—if, indeed, the rogue knew aught of it.

But what of George Hearst's heated argument over Rosie, the night of the late Earl's death? Perhaps the up-right Mr. Hearst had discovered the matter, and betrayed Fitzroy Payne's confidence to his uncle—who had washed his hands of the girl, to the curate's dismay.

But this was hardly a motive for violent murder on George Hearst's part; and so my efforts to learn something to his disadvantage were all for nought.

"But could Fitzroy Payne be so depraved as to have seduced the granddaughter of his nursemaid," I said aloud, all wonderment, "for whom he clearly felt con-tinued affection, as evidenced by the comfort of such an establishment?"

"The *Earl* seduce Rosie Ketch?" George Hearst said. "Indeed he did not, Miss Austen. For that, I fear, you have to look no farther than myself."

Whatever I had expected, it was hardly this; and I had so little mastery of myself at his disclosure, nor of the revulsion I could not help but feel, at the memory of the poor child's innocence—so ill-bestowed and so completely trodden under—that it was some moments before I could look on him with composure, or deign to offer any words. George Hearst is the very *last* man in whom I should expect to find his passion stronger than his virtue; and amazement warred with disapprobation for the first place in my thoughts.

That he felt all the weight of my contempt, I am certain by his aspect; and that he felt it of himself, and regretted his behaviour, was evident when I was capable of hearing him.

"I shall make no excuses for what I have done," he said, when finally I met his eyes; "it is in every way reprehensible, and a lifetime of devotion to the duties of a clergyman cannot hope to remove the stain of my conduct. It was because of Rosie that I determined to take Holy Orders, Miss Austen, in an effort to repair my ways; and with the goal of winning forgiveness for the manner in which I have injured her, I shall work to my very last breath."

The speech became him, in the force of conviction he threw behind it; but I was all amazement, and would know how it had occurred.

"I can only place the blame on myself," he said, "in that I was ill-suited for the thwarting of my objectives and hopes. I had looked to my uncle for direction, and felt that in my father's absence, the Earl might be prevailed upon to make my fortune; that from him, if not from relations of my own name, I could hope for guidance in some profession. But he would have me manage the workings of his farm—a project for which, Miss Austen, I had little inclination and even less talent. In attempting to oversee the plantings, the harvests, and the tending of the beasts under Scargrave's care, however, I came much in contact with the Barlows; and with Rosie, who lived under their roof at that time in her life, having left the woman who oversaw her rearing some six years past.

"I did not intend to ruin her; I sought merely to find some comfort for the anger and bitterness in which I lived; some recompense, it may be, for all I felt I had been forced to sacrifice; and if my indulgence came at her expense, it was no more than the manner in which my uncle had seen fit to treat me. So I told myself; and so I reasoned, the better to act without remorse, in a sort of blind striking out for vengeance. But that Rosie could be the only person hurt by my conduct—that it should affect my uncle not at all—I saw too late.

"When I learned of her condition, I offered her my hand in marriage, though I knew that little good could come of such a union."

"Rosie would not accept you?" I asked gently.

"My uncle could not accept her," he rejoined, with an expression of grimness, "much to Jenny Barlow's horror and the anger of her husband, Ted. Though they knew me to be so far removed from their sister's station, they had still hoped for the preservation of her respectability, if not the elevation of her place in life. My name only they wished to have, that the child might be known as its father's; for Rosie to live quietly at some remove, supported and free of the world's censure, was their only aim. That I might have sacrificed my hopes to their necessity seemed only to be justice; and so I was prepared to do, but for my uncle."

"You spoke to him of this," I said, understanding coming full upon me, "on the night of his death."

"I did," George Hearst replied, with some astonishment at my perspicacity, "though I thought none could know of it. My uncle was utterly unaware of Rosie's ruin—I had placed her with Mrs. Hammond through my cousin Fitzroy's good offices, the better to keep the Earl in the dark—and when the fact of her condition was made plain, along with my intention to remedy it through the sacrifice of my prospects, my uncle was thrown into a cold rage. The disgrace— the violation of a sacred trust, in the seduction of a Scargrave dependent—and the impropriety, in one who aspired, as I did, to the Church—all were cause for dismay on the Earl's part. He very nearly sent me from the Manor entirely; but it ended instead with his forbidding me to have anything further to do with the girl."

"And with his decision to alter his will," I surmised, "by retracting that promise he had so recently made you, of receiving a living upon his death. How fortunate for you, Mr. Hearst, that he should be taken from this life before he had time to call his solicitors!"

A quick glance from the cleric's hollow eyes, a look eloquent in its anguish. "The denial of the living was as nothing, Miss Austen, when weighed against the denial of Rosie. Only consider that her young life should be blighted in consequence of my sin; that her future should be sacrificed upon the altar of my uncle's pride! I could not bear it. I had determined, when I left him in the library, to go to Rosie at once, and marry her. Scargrave be damned!"

Except that you were saved the trouble, I thought, *your uncle's death having, like Fate, intervened.* The Earl's sudden passage had allowed George Hearst to achieve his dearest aims—the preservation of his beloved's honour, and the awarding of his dearest wish, a clergyman's living. But I kept such thoughts to myself.

"And now tell me, Miss Austen," the gentleman said, "how came you to know all of this? Or did you merely hazard some well-researched guesses?"

I had the grace to blush. "I overheard your conversation in the library that evening—some few words."

George Hearst looked his surprise. "I was not aware of it. I confess that I was distraught, and left the library in great perturbation of mind."

"And now that the Earl is dead," I said, "what is to become of Rosie?"

"When I journeyed to London Christmas Eve, it was with the intent of marrying her; and so I have done," the curate told me. "Rosie is to remain with her grandmother, and the babe to be reared here for some years. Afterwards, it shall be sent away to school, in an anonymous fashion, to receive the education of a gentleman's child."

"Rosie is indeed fortunate," I told him. "She is yet young, and might, with proper care and education, make you a suitable wife, Mr. Hearst. In a living far from Scargrave, where her antecedents are not known, you might yet attain tolerable happiness."

"I have not learned to look that far beyond the present moment," he said thoughtfully. "Much remains to be resolved."

It was then I remembered—if Fitzroy Payne hanged, George Hearst should become the Earl. What a burden this wife should then be felt! For he should be barred from seeking a suitable partner to his new estate, of fortune and standing in the peerage, and must acknowledge Rosie's babe as his heir. I understood, now, his inveterate melancholy; George Hearst's was a fate that seemed ever destined to turn awry.

I RETURNED TO PORTMAN SQUARE IN SOME PERPLEXITY OF thought. I had learned much in recent days of the private lives of Fanny Delahoussaye and George Hearst—had ever a great family been so determined in bastardy?—but nothing that proved useful, on the face of it, to Isobel's cause. The trial was to take place on the ninth of January, making it less than six days that remained to us. More than my circumspect probing was required, if the Countess's innocence was to be shown; and I felt impatience, of a sudden, for the return of Mr. Cranley from Pall Mall, and such assistance as the valet Danson could offer.

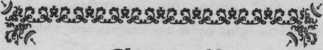

Chapter 19

A Matter for Cashierment

5 January 1803

~

IT WAS NOT MR. CRANLEY I WAS TO SEE IN THE SCARGRAVE House drawing-room the following morning, however, but my dear Eliza—and with her, brother Henry, only recently become a banker after a turn with the Oxfordshire militia.

"Jane, Jane!" he cried, embracing me heartily; "I understand you have run away from brother James and his scolding wife these several weeks, and got yourself into worse scandal than before! A broken engagement, and now a murder trial? What *shall* people say? That Miss Jane Austen is become an Adventuress, and is not to be seen in polite society?"

"Nonsense, Henry," Eliza said briskly; "Jane but seizes her chance for amusement when it is offered, as ever you would do; there is very little to choose between you, but your sex and the freedom it apportions to one and not the other. Were you not both possessed of lively spirits and unconventional tastes, I should have spurned the Austens entirely, and be still resident in France, toying tenderly with one of Buonaparte's generals."

"Indeed, I shall not berate you," Henry said, with a glance for his lively wife from those large grey eyes, so like my own; "I have ever trusted Jane to find her way out of scrapes as readily as she finds her way *in*. But the price of my approval is a full disclosure, my dear," he told me, taking my arm, "for I intend to dine out on the strength of your particulars for a fortnight at least. All London is agog with the Scargrave story, and information is as gold."

And so I told my brother of the murders, and the fate of the Countess and the present Earl—all that Eliza had heard on the way to Wilborough House—and something of Mr. Cranley besides. Of George Hearst and Rosie, or Fanny Delahoussaye's secret, I said nothing. Until such time as disclosure were necessary, I saw no kindness in publicity.

"But, Henry," I concluded, "there is much that you might do to aid the Countess, did you have the inclination."

"Unless you wish me to scale the walls of Newgate with my old militia companions, and spirit her out of the country, I fail to see in what manner I might be of service."

"You are a *banker*, Henry." I looked Eliza's way, and was treated to a rolling of the eyes at her husband's stupidity. "You must be acquainted with certain gentlemen of finance—those entrusted with the concerns of each in this household. I am confident that Sir William Reynolds intends to call Fitzroy Payne's banker to the Bar, in order to show that the new Earl is desperately in need of funds. But others intimate with Scargrave might be equally pressed."

"Almost certainly," my brother said thoughtfully. "Do you but give me their names, Jane, and I shall make discreet enquiries about the Club." He rose, still in thought, and went in search of his greatcoat.

"And now, my dear," Eliza said, when the drawing-room door had closed behind my brother, "Henry is off to business, and you and I are at leisure. What scheme have you devised for our amusement today?" Her long-sleeved velvet dress, of a rich red hue and trimmed in matching bugle beads, was equally suited to a visit to Wilborough House or a turn through Hyde Park in an open carriage, where she might nod to all her acquaintance. I surveyed her gown, and longed to seize the opportunity of my time in London to stroll with my sister Eliza among the shops; but I reminded myself that Isobel was all too deprived of similar delights, and that I must be about the business of her salvation.

"Eliza," I replied, "I should be very much surprised if you were not acquainted with *someone* attached to the Royal Horse Guards."

"The Blues? But of course." She fluttered a hand endowed, this morning, with a shockingly great ruby. "Colonel Buchanan is terribly fond of me, you know—and thought he should have had me, did he not already possess a wife."

"We must renew your acquaintance," I told her, smiling.

Eliza returned my good humour, so much at my brother's expense. "It needs no renewing, I assure you," she confided. "I spoke with the Colonel only last week, at Mrs. Fitzhugh's."

"Then you must call upon him today," I declared, "and carry me with you. He has a person in his regiment of whom I should dearly love to know more."

"LIEUTENANT THOMAS HEARST?" COLONEL BUCHANAN said, turning with the sherry decanter in one hand and my glass in the other, "what possible interest, my dear Comtesse de Feuillide, could you have in such a scapegrace?"

We were established in the cosy sitting-room of the Horse Guards' commander, in the shadow of Buckingham Palace, and surrounded on every side by leather-bound books, sabres in sheaths upon the wall, and some very good oils of horseflesh the Colonel had ridden in battle. He had swiftly set aside some matters pertaining to his men, in order to receive us without delay; and so my faith in Eliza was as ever rewarded.

The cavalryman offered me a glass with a short nod, and turned to fetch Eliza's. Colonel Buchanan was, as his name suggests, a Scot. With his bandy legs and greying red hair, he reminded me for all the world of the old cock at Steventon, who ran crowing about the farmyard with such importance that Cook soon lost patience and put him in the soup kettle. But I feared I should be overcome with mirth, did I pursue the comparison; and so drank my sherry with head demurely bent.

"I have heard such conflicting tales about the Lieutenant," Eliza said, sipping at her glass, her eyes sparkling, "and of late he has been much talked of in connexion with a friend of my dear Miss Austen's. Discretion forbids me from saying more. But when Jane told me of her fears for her friend, I thought immediately of you!" She fluttered her eyelashes in Colonel Buchanan's direction. "For no one should be more forthright—no one be less likely to stand on ceremony in such a delicate matter—than my dear Colonel Buchanan."

The Colonel was not too much of a soldier to dislike a little flattery. He grunted and threw himself into a chair, his booted legs extended before him and one hand thrust into his uniform jacket. With a glance for Eliza, he tossed back the contents of his sherry glass and set it on the table with a decided ring.

"So Tom Hearst has learned to prey upon young ladies of society, has he?" the cavalryman said. "That is no more than I should expect of him."

"My dear Colonel—my dear *William*"—this, with a laying of Eliza's dark lashes against her creamy cheek—"if you *knew* of anything that should counsel against a marriage—if such a union should in your eyes be imprudent—I know you would not hesitate to trust Miss Austen with your full confidence."

The Colonel met my eyes and hesitated, wondering, I

surmised, whether I was myself the lady whose heart Tom Hearst had entangled. Had I been, I should certainly have quailed; for Buchanan's disapproval was written in his hard blue eyes, and his hand rested lightly, out of habit, along the sheathed length of his sabre. A man not to be trifled with—as Eliza was certainly trifling now, did he but know it. I shuddered to consider the duplicity we had employed, here and at Wilborough House, these several days past; but remembered my Isobel, and the judicial proceedings to take place in but four days, and stifled my scruples.

"He is not well thought of among his company, that much is certain," Colonel Buchanan said finally, his eyes still on mine.

"And does this arise from envy, or just cause?" Eliza asked, with some spirit.

"It arises, my dear Countess, from a tendency to wager his fortune too freely and too often, with the result that he leaves debts behind him wherever he goes."

"Bah!" Eliza dismissed the Colonel's words as though he were a callow schoolboy. "That is the story of officers—and never more so than among the fashionable Horse Guards." She was goading the Colonel into fuller information, I knew, and in this aim she readily succeeded.

"I should hope that we are none of us in the straits of Lieutenant Hearst," the cavalryman said stiffly, "or His Majesty must look to others for protection."

"The Lieutenant's outward appearance suggests no such trouble," Eliza said serenely, laying her trap.

"That he has survived this long is a credit to his arrogance," the Colonel burst out, with an eye for me. "But believe, my dear Countess, that Hearst's affairs are in a dreadful state. He had appealed to his cousin—one Viscount Payne, whom I understand is now *imprisoned*—for relief, and been denied. It is everywhere acknowledged that he bears a considerable grudge against that gentleman as a result. But where one relative failed, he soon had hopes of another: he was recently known to have assured his creditors that he should amply satisfy their claims upon the death of his *uncle*, the late Earl of Scargrave, from whom he had expectations of some fortune."

A chill of dread moved up my backbone. "His uncle is recently deceased," I said.

The Colonel turned to assess my countenance shrewdly. "So I had heard, along with all of London. The Lieutenant is known to you, Miss Austen?"

"Some few weeks only. We were lately intimates of Scargrave Manor—where the young lady whom he has entangled, and upon whose behalf we have sought your counsel, was also a guest."

"Scargrave Manor! Another unfortunate mark against the young man. We have all heard what occurred *there*."

"Lieutenant Hearst can hardly be blamed for the coincidence of family, Colonel Buchanan," I said. "It *is* his boyhood home, and he might stay there with impunity, however many of the inmates meet with untimely ends."

"He might, but that coincidence plays too strong a part in that gentleman's fortunes," the Colonel said harshly. "Did not the Crown already hold captive the parties responsible, I might believe him capable even of murder."

I exchanged a glance with Eliza; these were heavy words, indeed.

"My dear Colonel," Eliza murmured, leaning towards him intimately, "your hints are very dark and very vague. Pray tell us plainly what reason you may know against this marriage, and have done."

Colonel Buchanan rose and paced slowly towards the fire, his brow furrowed in thought. The flames caught the gleam of his blue uniform's gold buttons and braid, and threw in sharp relief a scar that bisected his chin. A sabre cut, undoubtedly, and one that had come too close to his neck for comfort.

"It is a highly delicate matter, you understand," he said, turning to face first Eliza and then myself. "No word of it may reach beyond this room, at least until such time as the matter of his cashierment[1] is resolved."

"Cashierment! This is serious, indeed!"

"I would not ruin the character of a man under my command for less," the Colonel said, with a bitter smile. "Tom Hearst is lately accused of such infamous conduct, as cannot rightly be credited to a soldier of His Majesty's Horse Guards."

"And did this involve a young lady?" I enquired, with a terrible presentiment.

"A young lady? Not that I know of," the Colonel replied, with brows drawn down. "No, Miss Austen—it involved cards."

"He is a gamester!" Eliza cried, clapping her hands. "Was ever there a rogue who was not?"

"The Lieutenant is indeed fond of cards, and generally plays for high stakes."

"The only sort of stakes there are," Eliza murmured, remembering, no doubt, something of her late husband at Versailles, where the Comte de Feuillide had won and lost a succession of fortunes to Marie Antoinette's favourites.

Colonel Buchanan commenced to pace about the room, his hands thrust under the tails of his uniform jacket, his black boots gleaming with every step. The direction of our conversation certainly troubled him deeply; and I wondered whether he regretted his frankness. From his next words, however, it appeared otherwise.

---

1. Cashierment was equivalent to a dishonorable discharge. Since officers' commissions were purchased at great expense, particularly in a cavalry company connected to the Royal Household, to be cashiered represented a financial loss. A retiring soldier could sell his commission to another, and profit by his professional investment; while one who was cashiered was dismissed without compensation, and could not sell his position in turn.—*Editor's note.*

"Lieutenant Hearst, my dear Countess and Miss Austen, has always played with the very worst sort of luck. He has been losing steadily throughout the year." The Colonel ceased his pacing abruptly and wheeled about. "Until last month."

"His luck changed?" I said.

"Dramatically," the Colonel rejoined, in a voice heavy with irony. "Some few weeks before his Christmas leave—which was taken at the request of his commanding officer, rather than any desire of his own to seek the bosom of his family—he was all success of a sudden, and won such sums as must astonish."

"Very rash," said Eliza.

"The Countess, as always, has put the matter clearly," Colonel Buchanan rejoined, with a grim smile. "Success at cards, shall we say, went to his head; and the Lieutenant became greedy. He soon made the mistake, however, of challenging a stranger to his corps—one who could thus feel no obligation of affection, of comradeship, of experiences shared. An officer nonetheless, imbued with a sense of honour—and one who had seen this sort of luck before. More sherry, Miss Austen?"

I shook my head, too engrossed in the tale even to sip the wine I already possessed.

"This officer so succeeded in tripping up our friend the Lieutenant, that Tom Hearst was accused of having several cards beyond the usual set secreted in his coat-sleeve."

I could not suppress a small gasp, and won a penetrating look from the Colonel before he continued.

"Lieutenant Hearst vigorously protested the assertion that he had cheated—an offence no gentleman may ever hope to survive—and charged his opponent with trickery. Why such a man—an officer and a stranger—should attempt to secure the Lieutenant's ruin without serious cause, you may well ask yourself." The Colonel regained his chair and stroked his chin with a worn, blunt hand, his eyes on the portrait of a stallion arrayed in full battle harness.

2 5 8 ~ STEPHANIE BARRON

"It is hardly likely," Eliza said. "One surmises that Lieutenant Hearst spoke from guilty rage."

"However it was, others more objective could prove the truth of neither assertion; the Lieutenant and his adversary had been playing long into the night, and had been deserted by their fellows; and no one had seen the cards the other alleged to have been in Lieutenant Hearst's coat-sleeve."

"Was no one prepared to vouch for him before his company?"

"I fear that they had all suffered too much at his hands; and some may have shared the stranger's suspicion," Colonel Buchanan replied shortly. "It ended as all such affairs must and inevitably do end—with Lieutenant Hearst defending his honour in a pistol duel with the gentleman."

With a start, I remembered Fanny Delahoussaye's words at Isobel's ball, an evening that might have been an age ago; the Lieutenant, she said, was arrived from St. James having recently killed a man in a duel. *The affairs of officers are the most romantic,* she had prattled, or some nonsense to that effect.

"They met at dawn, not far from the barracks here in St. James, and Lieutenant Hearst succeeded in dispatching his accuser—which may have satisfied *him,* but only added to his unfortunate reputation. The poor fellow he killed was to have been wed at Christmas."

There was a brief silence as Eliza and I took all this in; but keenly aware of my purpose I shook myself into awareness and sought once more the Colonel's gaze. "And this debacle has ruined the Lieutenant's standing in the cavalry?"

"An affair of honour is a dubious thing," the Colonel told us, with a sharply exhaled breath and another impatient gesture. "The law would call it murder. But among military men, nothing is prized so much as one's honour—it is beyond fortune, beyond birthright; it is become the essence of the man. A duel to the death has long been the established mode of satisfying outrages against one's reputation. Had this been the only blot on the Lieutenant's career, he might have survived it. But taken with his pressing debts, and the fact that others of his fellows have called him cardsharp in the aftermath of the duel, he is now under consideration for cashierment by his superiors."

"Colonel Buchanan," I said, summoning my courage, "forgive me for prying further in such a matter. But were the Lieutenant presently to satisfy his creditors, discharge his debts of honour among the company, and conduct himself in a manner more suited to a gentleman and a member of his corps, could his commission yet be saved?"

"I fear that little might save Lieutenant Hearst," the Colonel replied, his eyes stern, "though women ever believe that love alone shall do it. I dearly hope, Miss Austen, that it is *some other lady* than yourself who has proved so susceptible to the rascal's charms. I should not like to see *you* lost to all reason."

I cursed my ready tendency to blush as I replied. "I assure you, sir, that I am come on another's behalf, and must return with the heaviest of burdens—that of advising one in love to look no further for happiness in the Lieutenant's quarter. It is a burden I have gladly shared with the Countess."

"Indeed," Eliza said quickly, recollecting our supposed purpose for being there, and reaching for her reticule, "I must thank you, dear Colonel, for your readiness to disclose what may only be to the Lieutenant's detriment. Circumstances required that his character be better understood."

"The decision of his superiors should even now have been reached," the Colonel said, "and so you may be saved of your duty. For no young woman should wish to marry a man without fortune, career, or prospects—may he have twenty uncles recently dead."

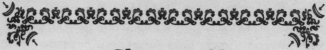

Chapter 20

The Gentleman's Way Out

5 January 1803, cont.

~

BEFORE BIDDING *ADIEU* TO THE HORSE GUARDS, I EN-quired of Colonel Buchanan where the Lieutenant's bat-man, Jack Lewis, might be found, and he had the fellow brought to his rooms—vacating them, in his goodness, when Eliza explained that we were about an errand of my lady's maid. That I had no lady's maid, she did not see fit to advise the Colonel; and so he remained in the dark as to our true purpose, as indeed he had been from the moment of our arrival.

"Miss Austen!" Jack Lewis cried, bouncing in the door with little ceremony; and turning to Eliza, had the grace to bow, though he permitted himself a low whistle. Had I not prepared her for his eccentric behaviour, she should assuredly have been disconcerted; but my cousin only smiled and inclined her head, and the batman looked to me.

"Jack at your service, miss, and 'opin' as you've a kind word for my mate Tom. Perishin' with love, 'e is," he confided to Eliza with a wink.

"I am come to enquire about an errand I believe you

did for the Lieutenant," I told him, "in which I am concerned."

"Ask away, miss," said he merrily.

"It was you who retrieved the maid Marguerite's belongings from Lizzy Scratch, was it not?"

Whatever the batman had expected, it was hardly this. Jack Lewis appeared to have been struck a blow, and stepped back a pace, before recovering.

"I did," he said, his jaw suddenly tight.

"And did you observe among her things a gold pendant locket, such as she might have worn about her neck?"

There was a silence, and Tom Hearst's man shuffled his feet.

"Lizzy Scratch has told me that she gave it to you, Jack, but when I received the maid's things from the Lieutenant for posting to the Barbadoes, the locket was not among them. Is it possible your master took it?"

" 'e'd never do such a thing!" the batman spat out, his expression gone from that of a cheerful monkey to a dangerous cat.

"Then I am left with only one possibility," I said, "and that is that you took the locket yourself."

He threw up his hands in an expression of disgust. "Lizzy Scratch don't know where 'er brats are, of an evening, much less a bit of finery. Since when's 'er word been worth so much?"

"Lizzy Scratch was especially careful in this case," I replied, "because murder had been done. She believed that similar evil might befall her, did she keep any of the maid's things."

He looked in desperation at Eliza, but received only her dazzling smile; and then something in his face changed. "I'll not have you thinking as it was the Lieutenant," he said, "and I only took what was mine in the first place."

"You'd given the locket to the girl?"

"When we was courtin', last summer it was, in London. It was on account of me, and my past with the maid,

262 - STEPHANIE BARRON

that the Lieutenant thought to fetch up 'er things the day she died." For a moment only, Jack Lewis's voice broke; and then again he recovered. "Right afraid, old Tom was, that there'd be somethin' as would lead the magistrate straight to me. My Lieutenant's a loyal man, I'll grant 'im that." He sat down upon one of Colonel Buchanan's chairs and put his head in his hands.

"Had you seen Marguerite since your arrival at Scargrave?" I asked the batman gently.

Jack Lewis raised a sober face and met my eyes unflinchingly. "I used to send a bit o' note by 'er, and we'd visit in the 'ay-shed. But Lord bless me, I never slit 'er throat, miss. I'd never a done that. Margie weren't a bad sort, for all 'er ferrin' ways; just lonely, like, and grateful for a bit'uv a cuddle."

"So you hastened to Lizzy Scratch on the day of the maid's death, and made away with the locket."

Jack Lewis nodded once and averted his gaze. "Could'a knocked me over with a feather when I sees it still among 'er things, and my face clear as a candle inside. Thought they'd haul me up for murder, I did—so's I put it in me pocket, and said no more about it."

"I MUST SAY, JANE, THAT IT LOOKS VERY BAD FOR YOUR POOR Lieutenant," Eliza declared, as Henry's carriage rattled towards Portman Square, "very bad, indeed. I know that look of Colonel Buchanan's too well. He is intent upon making of the man an example, and satisfying his sense of order. The Colonel shall never control gambling, nor yet the duels that often result; but he shall make his officers remember Tom Hearst, and hesitate, perhaps, before they roll the dice."

"I care little for all that," I replied, with some truth. "My mind is sadly tormented with a dangerous possibility. By the time he had arrived at Scargrave, Tom Hearst was surely driven to believe his entire life hung in the balance—his commission, his possible marriage to Fanny, and his *honour*. That beloved possession of every officer. Would he have poisoned his uncle to preserve it? And implicate the Earl's heirs, the better to ensure that his brother George succeeded to a fortune? With Fitzroy gone—and remember, Lieutenant Hearst bore his cousin a grudge, according to the Colonel—he might eventually improve his fortunes, and win Madame Delahoussaye's consent for Fanny and her thirty thousand pounds. With George Hearst the new Earl, Tom should not want for greater means to satisfy his debts. And his corps should hesitate to drum out the brother of a peer, in a manner they should not scruple to cashier the poor relative of a clergyman."

I paused, my eyes upon the rain that had commenced to fall beyond the carriage windows; a lady arrayed in plum sarcenet, with a feathered bonnet to match, raced at a hectic pace along the pavement, her sunshade raised in but poor defence of the weather. I feared the splashing of our carriage wheels should make a fearful business of her handsome boots. "It is in every way horrible, Eliza, and only too plausible."

"But how should Hearst have effected it?"

"Through his batman, Jack Lewis," I replied, turning my gaze to the scenery within the carriage. "He had made the acquaintance of the maid the previous summer, and given her a locket; in visiting Scargrave this winter, it was only too likely that the acquaintance should be renewed. The Lieutenant might have persuaded his man to give the girl the nuts, with the express purpose of placing them in the Earl's tray. He may even have played upon Marguerite—offering her something she valued, in return for betraying her mistress. Certainly she wrote those letters accusing Isobel and Fitzroy Payne with some other aim than blackmail; Sir William could not comprehend why she never asked for money. But her reward was not to come from the Countess, and it was not in the form of silver. Marriage to the batman, perhaps, and safe passage to the Barbadoes?"

"But he killed her instead."

"She knew too much, Eliza. And so he slit her throat while she waited, as she thought, for her lover—Jack Lewis. But it was the Lieutenant who arrived at the hayrick that morning, the Lieutenant who did the deed; and it was Jack who retrieved the maid's things. Tom Hearst knew he could trust to Lewis's silence; you saw how terrified the man was of being tied to the maid's death."

"It is surprising *he* is even yet alive," Eliza said thoughtfully.

"Lieutenant Hearst told me once that he owed the man his life; and even he—with his precious sense of honour—may feel an obligation in such a case. It is in every way convincing, do not you agree?"

"Jane, what shall you do?"

"I shall send for Mr. Cranley at once. Perhaps *he* shall be able to force an admission from the fellow; for in truth, Eliza, we have not a shred of proof."

We were arrived in Portman Square, and Eliza's coachman had pulled up before the doors of Scargrave House. "Will you come in, Eliza, and take some refreshment?" I asked her.

"I confess that I should hate to miss the *dénouement*," she replied excitedly, "if you can bear my company another hour, Jane."

"It shall be my only prop. I move henceforth in enemy territory, my dear."

She bade her carriage wait, and we ascended to the door; only to be greeted upon our entrance to the hall with a loud wailing and such a hullabaloo as may hardly be credited. Maids were everywhere dispatched at a run, and so distracted by the weight of their errands, that they could not stop for explanation; but the sounds of lamentation issued from the drawing-room, and it was thence we hastened.

It was Mr. Cranley I espied first, as I opened the door, standing by the mantel in an attitude of helpless bewilderment; Madame Delahoussaye was seated on the settee before him, her arms around her daughter. Fanny was prostrate with grief. Her blond curls were in disarray about her face, and her eyes were quite ugly with weeping.

"Whatever can be the matter?" I cried, heedless of my duty to Eliza at such a moment.

Madame raised her head, and shook it briefly, an injunction against further enquiry; and with evident relief, Mr. Cranley crossed to the door and escorted us back into the hall.

"I fear I am the agent of Miss Delahoussaye's distress," he told us, "but there was no one else to bring the news, and hear it they must."

"What news?" I enquired, with no little foreboding.

"Of Lieutenant Hearst," the barrister said, and hesitated. "I have only just told his brother. There has been—a tragedy."

"He is not—injured?" I said.

"I am afraid that he is dead."

Eliza's horrified looks mirrored my own. "But *how*?" I cried.

"He shot himself," Mr. Cranley said, "this morning, in the middle of Hyde Park."

MR. CRANLEY, IT APPEARED, HAD BEEN SUMMONED TO A meeting with Lieutenant Hearst by messenger that very morning, and had arrived at the appointed hour and spot to find the gentleman asprawl in a park chair, blood streaming from a great wound in his temple.

"And there is no possibility that he was murdered? You are certain that he ended his own life?" I asked.

"Quite certain," the barrister replied. "A pauper living in the Park had taken shelter under a neighbouring bush, and saw him do the deed."

"And so you were summoned with the sole purpose of making the discovery."

"And of retrieving this," Mr. Cranley said, producing a plain piece of paper sealed with red wax. "It bears your name, Miss Austen."

I took the letter from him, my fingers trembling slightly at the sight of the firm, careless hand that had written my name, and now should write no more. "But whatever can he have to say to me?"

"Perhaps it is a confession," Eliza suggested.

I loosened the wax and unfolded the stiff paper.

St. James, London,
4 January 1803

My dear Miss Austen—

Or rather, my dear Jane—for so I shall always think of you, remembering moments too precious to let slip even in this last midnight of my mortal life. Were I granted one final hour of happiness, I should wish myself back at Scargrave House—leaning in the doorway of my room, waiting for some sight of you in the moonlight, with your hair tumbled about your face. It was so little time ago, and yet a life apart, for all that. I shall never, now, have the opportunity to pursue an acquaintance that might have been profitable to us both—but I forget. You were denied me long before, and by my own cursed conduct.

The men who hold sway over my future are to publish their determination on the morrow. I have learned already from one of their company that the terms are unfavourable to my continued prosperity, the maintenance of my reputation, and, perhaps most important, my claims to honour. With no fortune, and no consideration likely to be granted in future to one with a tarnished name—and furthermore, with Fanny Delahoussaye to consider—I have determined to tread the only honourable path remaining to a gentleman. Were I a rogue, I should book passage on a sure ship, and adventure my fate in a distant land; but I am only a soldier, after all, for whom duty is as a god.

I impose upon you only in this, Miss Austen: to ask that you look after Fanny. She has told me of your knowledge of our sad circumstance. She has her fortune, which, should it escape the clutches of her despicable mother, should preserve her against too great a calumny; but it must be preserved from Madame at all cost. I trust in your goodness.

Farewell, my dear Jane; in your hands, had we met sooner, I might yet have salvaged honour. But we are neither of us to blame for the vagaries of Fate.

I remain, etc.,
Lt. Thomas Hearst

"Damnable coward!" I exclaimed, forgetting myself in my anger, and employing such terms as my sailor brothers might, when similarly pressed; "he has killed himself rather than learn that he is cashiered. A ridiculous waste of a young life—and for what? *Honour.* The concerns of men are past all understanding!" In great perturbation of spirit, I crumpled the letter in my palm and turned away from Eliza and Mr. Cranley, my boots ringing upon the marble of Scargrave's entryway.

"But does he admit to murdering the Earl and the maid?" Eliza persisted.

"The suicide smacks strongly of the presumption," Mr. Cranley said.

I hastened to disabuse him. "The Lieutenant never mentions the murders, or any part he might have played on behalf of another; and with his death, all hope of further elucidation in that quarter must be finished." Of Tom Hearst's tender words for myself, I said nothing; I had not yet learned to comprehend them. "Though we may feel as strongly persuaded as ever of his motives, his opportunity, and his guilt, we shall never have proof."

"We might yet present his end as a part of our defence," Mr. Cranley said, with evident hope.

"It *is* a pity." Eliza's cherry mouth was pursed, and she tapped her lips with an elegant finger. "Since he planned to end his life, the poor man might readily have taken the blame, and allowed the others to go free. There is a certain selfishness about the act, would not you agree, Jane?"

"All suicide is selfish," I said, distractedly, "it is only a question of degree. I fear poor Fanny will feel it most strongly."

"Miss Delahoussaye—was she—" Mr. Cranley began, and then faltered, blushing crimson.

"She was not formally engaged," I said carefully, "but I believe she had reached a certain understanding with the young man."

"From her grief, I had assumed as much," the barrister said, his face crestfallen; "there is no answer to such anguish."

"You may find, Mr. Cranley," I said, not unkindly, "that where Miss Delahoussaye is concerned, time is your friend."

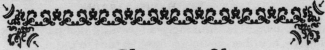
A Position of Trust

WHEN ELIZA HAD MADE HER *ADIEUX*, I BADE MR. CRANLEY
wait for me in the study, and returned with some hesitation to the Delahoussayes. Fanny and Madame were the
centre of a hovering group, encompassed of Simmons,
the butler, and two of the upper housemaids, who held
steaming basins and compresses at the ready. But at my
entrance, poor Fanny raised a streaming face, and breaking from her mother's embrace, extended her hand. "Oh,
Miss Austen!" she cried, as she gripped my fingers in
hers, "is not this dreadful news? No one but you can
know how dreadful!"

"I am sure you excite yourself unnecessarily, Fanny,"
Madame said, with ringing disapproval. "Tom Hearst
is hardly worth such a display, as he has shown in his
manner of departing this life. Did I not fear to upset you
further, I should *rejoice* at this news."

Fanny's only answer was a redoubled expression of
grief, and Madame raised her hands in consternation.

"And from this, Miss Austen, we may learn the value
of *novels*," she said, to my mystification, "for only from

the produce of such cheap pens as the novel-publishers employ, could my daughter have learned to indulge such an unfortunate sensibility. She is all romantic airs, and no sense; but perhaps, now that the Lieutenant's unwholesome influence is removed, we might hope for an improvement in time."

"And did the Lieutenant read *novels,* Madame?" I enquired in exasperation, and bent to bestow my interest on a more worthy subject. Poor Fanny clung pitifully to me, and quite stained my grey wool gown with the force of her tears; her mother snorted in contempt, and rose without another word.

"I can do nothing with her, Miss Austen," she said, forcing a passage through the maids; "perhaps you shall have better luck. I shall be in my room, if Fanny returns to her senses."

I patted the poor creature's back, and spoke such soothing nonsense as succeeds in quieting a child, and instructed the servants and their basins to depart. Presently Fanny's lamentations subsided, with a hiccup and a sniff, and she wiped her plump fingers across her eyes.

"Whatever shall I do?" she said, in a breaking whisper. "I fear, Miss Austen, that with Tom dead, I am truly lost!"

Seeing in her blue eyes that a fresh cloud threatened to burst, I determined to speak briskly, and offer the only help I knew. "We shall make the best of events, Fanny my dear, and hope in Isobel's speedy release. With the Countess restored to freedom, you shall have a support before your mother, and can divulge to her the entirety of your wrongs. Do not scruple to lay them at Tom Hearst's door; he has imposed upon you most disturbingly, and must bear the guilt for his deeds, however dead he might be. But say nothing to Madame at present, and trust in Isobel's excellent understanding, whenever she is returned to us. Something shall be devised for your comfort, and the preservation of your reputation." I assessed the fullness about her stomach. "The interlude at the mantua-maker's you survived without discovery?"

Fanny nodded disconsolately. "I am to have some lovely things, Miss Austen, though they *are* in black." Her eyes welled anew. "And though Tom shall never admire me the more!"

I SAW FANNY SAFELY TO HER ROOM, AND BADE HER TO REST if she might; and then in some distraction, I sought the patient Mr. Cranley below.

"Mr. Cranley!" I cried, as he started from a brown study at my entrance, "was there ever a truer gentleman? And was he ever treated to a house in greater disarray? But share with me your news."

He drew forward a chair without preamble. "I have obtained from Danson the Earl's correspondence. With it should be a list of letters sent on certain dates, with the names of their recipients—for Lord Scargrave is most meticulous in accounting for his postage debts," the barrister added, as an afterthought.[1] "Do I ask too much, Miss Austen, or may I beg your assistance in the task? I should like to have a witness to whatever I may find."

"I shall bend myself to your will, Mr. Cranley," I assured him.

"The Earl's letters are kept locked in this portable desk." Mr. Cranley crossed the room to a small wooden cabinet, whose lid folded back to reveal a writing surface suitable for one's lap. "Danson allowed me to carry it hither."

There were nineteen letters in all, written carefully in

1. Postage was actually an expensive item in the nineteenth century, as letters were billed according to how many miles they traveled. No envelopes were used—the sheet of paper was folded and sealed with wax—and a letter comprised of two sheets of paper was billed double. Most important, the *recipient* paid the postage, not the sender; and so Lord Scargrave's meticulous accounts may be taken as evidence of his scrupulousness in keeping track of his debts. —*Editor's note.*

a strong, even hand, and dating from the day of the ball at Scargrave—a day that might have occurred in a different lifetime. That they were solely letters of business, we readily perceived; and from a hasty comparison of the Earl's list and his extant drafts, we learned immediately that one more letter had been sent than the little desk now contained.

"Capital!" Mr. Cranley cried; "it is as you thought, Miss Austen. A draft was written during one of those difficult days following the late Earl's demise; it was copied, and mailed; and before Lord Scargrave's man had time to file it with the other papers that evening, it was seized and used to form the note found on the maid Marguerite."

"Or the draft may simply have been discarded," I warned, feeling some restraint was necessary; "one may not always conform to habit or rule."

We set to comparing the drafts to the Earl's list, and saw that the missing letter was one of several sent to his solicitors, in Bond Street; it but required a glance from Mr. Cranley to his watch, and a call for a hackney carriage, and we were on our way to their door.

MAYHEW, MAYHEW & CRABB WAS A RESPECTABLE ESTABlishment, as befit men of business who cater to the peerage; the plate secured to the deep green door was of brass, and the marble stoop was well scrubbed. Upon seeing the firm's name so declared, I remembered with a start Isobel's last injunction before leaving the Manor—that I deliver her testament to one Hezekiah Mayhew. I had tarried in doing so, in the hope that all such matters might be deferred some decades, once Isobel's freedom was secured; but now that we stood before the solicitors' door, I bethought me of the document, which I kept safe in my reticule, and placed beneath my pillow at night. I should deliver the deed to Mr. Mayhew immediately, should he be within.

We were ushered to a snug parlour, where a bright fire

cast its glow on several easy chairs; and Mr. Cranley's card had barely been delivered, than Mr. Hezekiah Mayhew appeared to place himself at our service. He was a portly gentleman of some seventy years, quite stooped, with a shining pate that had long since lost its hair, and two bushy white eyebrows that attempted to supply the difference.

"Mr. Cranley," the solicitor said, with a deep bow in the barrister's direction; "it is a pleasure to welcome you to my humble office."

"The honour must be mine," Mr. Cranley rejoined, "as well as my thanks, for having placed the Countess's trouble in my hands."

"This firm has had the management of the Scargrave family's business for eighty years, at least," Mr. Mayhew observed, with an eyebrow cocked for Cranley, "but never have we witnessed so terrible a passage as this. I merely chose the best and most reliable barrister I knew." The grave brown eyes turned upon my face. "And you, Madam, would be—?"

"Miss Jane Austen. I am a friend of the Countess's."

"Miss Austen is ungenerous in her own behalf," Mr. Cranley interrupted smoothly. "She is the greatest friend the Countess could hope to have, and no less energetic in the new Earl's defence."

"That is very well—very well, indeed." Mr. Mayhew's glance was penetrating. "Friends, in my experience, are like ladies' fashions, Miss Austen. They come and go with the seasons, and are rarely of such stout stuff as bears repeated wearing. I am glad to find you formed of better material." With that, he led us to his inner rooms.

Mr. Cranley offered me a chair, and took one of his own before the solicitor's great desk.

"You are here on the Countess's behalf?" Mr. Mayhew enquired, with a glance that encompassed us both.

"Not directly," I replied, "though I am charged with placing *this* in your safekeeping, Mr. Mayhew." I handed him the sealed parchment that contained Isobel's final directions, and felt the lighter for having passed the burden to another. "I would ask that you address the matters it contains when we have presumed upon your time no longer."

"Having other, more pressing matters, to discuss?" the solicitor surmised, his bushy eyebrows lifting.

"We come to you on the Earl's behalf today," Mr. Cranley said.

"Though, indeed, the two can hardly be separated," I broke in. "What may serve to prove the innocence of one, cannot help but assist the other."

"Indeed. Indeed. Pray enlighten me as to your purpose." Mr. Mayhew drew forth a pen and a sheet of paper and set a pair of ancient spectacles upon his nose.

We explained the business of Fitzroy Payne's correspondence, and were gratified to discover that old Mayhew's wits were swift. He seized the importance of our questions directly; a correspondence file was ordered, and the final copies of several letters, whose rougher selves we had previously perused in Danson's desk, were produced for our examination.

And to our great joy, we found that one of them was utterly strange to us. No draft of it had we seen.

Scargrave Manor,
Hertfordshire,
22 December 1802

My dear Mayhew—
I should wish to consult you on a matter pertaining to the Countess's Barbadoes estate, Crosswinds. You will remember that my uncle, the late Earl, was at his death engaged in combating Lord Harold Trowbridge's financial assault upon his wife's plantations. His demise, and the Countess's concern for her material welfare, has caused her to abandon hope of staving off Lord Harold—and she lately signed a document presented by that gentleman which ceded him the property in exchange for a discharge of considerable debt.

I have recently learned from perusing my uncle's papers—which included the Countess's marriage settlement—that there exists a probable legal incumbrance upon her actions. That she was unaware of this when she submitted to Trowbridge's demands, you may fully comprehend, knowing how little women understand of legal matters. In sum, the plantations in question passed to the Countess through her *mother's* line, though managed and overseen by her father, and are to revert to her surviving maternal relatives—in all probability Miss Fanny Delahoussaye—in the event of her death. In fact, the property was placed in the condition of separate estate[2] under the terms of the marriage settlement, with trustees to oversee its security in marriage as they had in the Countess's minority. All such transfer to Lord Harold must, accordingly, be null and void; but he may have bent the law to his purpose in ways that overcome even this obstacle. I should dearly love to hear your sense of the matter.

I intend to be in London the day after Christmas; let us meet in our accustomed place—the library of the Forbearance Club. We shall have luncheon, and talk over these and other matters, and hope to put paid to Lord Harold's schemes.

> I remain respectfully yours,
> Fitzroy, Earl of Scargrave

I glanced up at Mr. Cranley as I finished the letter; *let us meet in our accustomed place* was there, certainly, and crying out for comparison to the fragment found in the

2. Separate estate, or separate property, was a term in the marriage settlement drawn up at a woman's engagement, particularly if she was an heiress. This set certain property—investments or land—in trust, with the income available to the woman, but the property itself beyond the reach of herself, her husband, or his creditors. Such property customarily passed to her female children at her death. —*Editor's note.*

maid's bodice. But it was the content of the letter itself that struck me forcibly—Lord Harold had imposed upon Isobel so entirely, that he had outwitted even himself.

"Are you of the Earl's opinion, Mr. Mayhew?" I asked the solicitor. "Is it so impossible for the Countess to make over her West Indies property?"

The rheumy brown eyes blinked at me shrewdly, and Hezekiah Mayhew cleared his throat. "I have examined the problem narrowly, Miss Austen, and I may say it is indeed a pretty one. A very pretty problem for the Countess and the Earl." He paused, and looked from Mr. Cranley to myself.

"My good sir," Mr. Cranley said urgently, "all these matters may bear upon his lordship's survival; we cannot know until all the information is ours. Pray continue."

"Separate property is, of necessity, comprised of assets," Mr. Mayhew replied. "And as we know, assets may suddenly lose their value, against all expectation. Securities may plummet, banks and their holdings fail; and property—particularly property valued for the crops it produces—lose much of its value. Under the terms of the trust established at the death of the Countess's mother, Amelie Delahoussaye Collins, once Crosswinds is so reduced in value as to bring bankruptcy upon the trust, the trustees may consider the sale of the property itself to satisfy creditors."

The solicitor shifted his considerable girth and reached for a clay pipe. Then eyeing me—it would not do to smoke before a lady—he returned it to its place upon the polished surface of his desk, with a soft sigh and an irritable frown. "And that is very nearly what has happened," he said, for Mr. Cranley's benefit.

"Can the Countess's land be so lacking in value?" the barrister enquired.

"The land is not, but the crops it produces assuredly are," Mr. Mayhew answered bluntly. "In the time of the Countess's father, John Collins, a decision was made to turn from sugar cultivation to coffee." The large white eyebrows came down alarmingly, and Hezekiah Mayhew turned to enlighten me. "Coffee bushes, Miss Austen, take several years to mature; and if they are blighted in their youth—as these unfortunately were—they must be destroyed and replanted. Twice this happened to John Collins; and twice he sought additional capital to supplement his losses. When he finally produced a saleable crop, the world price had dropped due to a rise in production in Brazil; and Collins's beans were hardly worth the blood money he had paid to grow them. The revolts among the slave populations have caused great losses as well—in human capital, and in the destruction of crops and outbuildings by fire; the cost of rebuilding and replanting again required Mr. Collins to seek capital from investors, and at his death, his assets were found to be insufficient to satisfy his creditors. Although the property in trust remained so legally in the Countess's marriage settlement, it is an open question whether her trustees might not be prevailed upon to sell the property itself." He sat back in his chair, which creaked in protest, his hands upon his watch chain.

"But the Countess herself may not do it?" Mr. Cranley pressed.

"She must have the agreement, in writing, of the trustees."

"And who are these men?" I enquired, in an eager accent.

The parched old face creased into a smile. "I fear I misspoke, Miss Austen, from long habit," the solicitor said. "There is only *one* trustee, and she is hardly male—an unusual circumstance, certainly, but reflective of the wishes of the Countess's family. They were originally French bankers, you know, who set up the first bank in Martinique, and they remained a clannish sort of set, never trusting their business to outsiders. As trustees—all family members—died, they could not be replaced; and so only one now remains, a woman and the Countess's aunt, Madame Hortense Delahoussaye."

"And it is solely her permission, Mr. Mayhew, which Lord Harold must secure?"

"It is," the solicitor gravely replied.

I leaned forward in my anxiety. "But he has not yet obtained it?"

Something of interest flickered in Hezekiah Mayhew's shrewd eyes. "Not to my knowledge," he said. "With the Countess's fate hanging yet in the balance, it is probable Madame Delahoussaye will defer any business some little while."

Assuredly she would, if I comprehended the character of Madame Delahoussaye. Her daughter, Fanny, should become the fortunate heir to Isobel's property, however encumbered by debt, in the event of Isobel's hanging for her husband's murder; and if the family pride in property remained as fierce as Mr. Mayhew believed, Madame might throw all the weight of her material resources behind discharging the debt, and restoring the plantations themselves. But why had she not offered Isobel similar support, in the Countess's dire need?

The seed of an idea was taking shape. I stood up in haste. Though the hour was late, every minute was as gold; we lacked but four days until the trial should commence in the House of Lords.

"Forgive me, Mr. Mayhew," I said, with extended hand, "you have been kindness itself, and have greatly assisted our efforts; but Mr. Cranley and I have pressing business elsewhere that cannot wait. I am honoured to have met you, sir—and feel certain that with your penetration exercised on her behalf, the Countess shall escape the clutches of her enemies even still."

"She is unlikely to require my support, Miss Austen," Hezekiah Mayhew said dryly, "when your own is already hers."

Mr. Cranley parted from me at the solicitor's door, having procured a hackney carriage for my return to Scargrave, and hastening himself to his chambers at Lincoln's Inn, the better to prepare his defence of my friends. It was but a few moments to Scargrave House, where

I found Fanny as yet upstairs in a darkened room, and Madame Delahoussaye resting on the settee before the drawing-room fire.

"My dear Miss Austen," Madame said, sitting up briskly at my appearance, "I could not *think* where you had gone—and the house all at sixes and sevens. If you intend to run about by yourself in this manner, it would be well if you were to tell Cook when you expect to return, so that dinner at least is not a matter for conjecture."

"I was not alone, Madame," I rejoined. "I was with Mr. Cranley, in a visit to the Scargrave solicitors."

"With Mr. *Cranley*?" Madame's expression dissolved in contempt, and she ran her eyes the length of my grey wool, as though it were transparent. "I suppose you have set your cap at him. He is not a bad sort of fellow, and quite suitable for one of your position in the world."

I felt myself colour. *Setting my cap at him, indeed.* "That is an expression, Madame Delahoussaye, that I particularly abhor," I cried, perhaps too warmly. "Its tendency is gross and illiberal, and if its construction could ever have been deemed clever, time has long ago destroyed all its ingenuity.[3] I merely accompanied Mr. Cranley on a matter of business."

I turned away, intending to dress for dinner, being unequal to the maintenance of my temper if I retained the room any longer; but Madame called after me.

"Business? What may a *lady* have to do with *business*, pray?"

I revolved slowly and regarded her before answering. "It is Madame who must answer that, and not I."

Something of the sourness in her expression drained

3. Interestingly, Austen's dislike of this phrase resurfaces in her novel *Sense and Sensibility*, in which Marianne Dashwood uses almost identical language to upbraid Sir John Middleton, when he jests that she has "set her cap" at Willoughby. —*Editor's note.*

from her face, and was replaced by obvious caution. "Whatever do you mean, Miss Austen?"

"I had understood that business was a peculiar province of your own, Madame. Particularly the business of your family fortune."

She started at this, and looked somewhat nettled; and seeing that she was for once deprived of speech, I determined to press my advantage.

"Mr. Cranley and I were only now informed of your interest in the Countess's affairs. It seems it is to *you* Isobel must look for financial protection."

"I!" the good lady cried, her composure regained, "she can find no protection from *me*, I assure you."

"That much is evident, from your disinterest in her troubles," I said bitterly. "It is even possible she is past all such protection, in any case."

To these words of reproach, Madame answered me nothing. With glittering eyes, she rose from her place and swept by me, out of the room; and after a moment, I followed in her train. I was greatly fatigued, and looked forward to my dinner, and considered dispensing with the necessity of changing my dress; I should far rather enjoy a tray by my bedchamber fire, than a chilly hour in Madame's company. But I had only gained the comfort of my room a few moments, and undone the quantity of horn buttons that run the length of my gown's back, before the swift passage of footsteps in the corridor demanded my attention. I peered around my door, and observed Madame Delahoussaye disappearing down the stairs, arrayed in a cloak and a very fine hat, indeed. And since she should require the use of *neither* in the Scargrave dining room, I quickly surmised that she had determined to disregard the lateness of the hour, and undertaken to pay a call.

Alone in the doorway, my gown undone, I debated with myself. Madame might do little more than fetch a physick for poor Fanny from the local apothecary; but no—in that case, she should dispatch a servant. Only the greatest need could send Madame forth at such a time—

and I little doubted that it was *my words,* spoken angrily in the drawing-room below, that had done it. I reached for my pelisse and hat, and ran hurriedly for the stairs, clutching at my undone back. I was in time to observe Madame through the drawing-room window, in an attitude of some urgency, as she stepped swiftly into the Scargrave carriage.

SHE LED MY HACKNEY A MERRY CHASE, MADE ALL THE MORE difficult by my injunction to the driver upon engaging him, that he should be at pains not to be observed by our quarry. It is not that the way to Wilborough House was so difficult to find, but that the traffic at this hour, when merchants and gentlemen were bent upon finding their dinners at home or in the exclusive clubs of Pall Mall, should be decidedly snarled. The jostling of carriages and horses, of coachmen and waggoneers shouting invective as hallmarks of their masculinity and claim to place, made any passage a tedious if colourful one; and the anxiety of keeping the Scargrave carriage in sight, without ourselves being seen, was an added fillip of torture.

Madame soon arrived at her destination, however; ordered the coachman to wait; and ascended the august flight of marble steps with alacrity. I recalled that during Lord Harold's Christmas visit to Scargrave Manor she had particularly declared herself a stranger to the Duke and Duchess of Wilborough; and so such a call, at such an hour, was something to amaze. But having observed her flight, I had guessed she would fetch up here; and I had little doubt as to her object in paying homage to those so much above her station. Madame cared nothing for Wilborough, or his lady: it was his brother she sought, her partner in all her crimes.

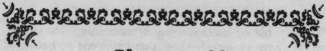

Chapter 22

The Uses of Brothers

7 January 1803

~

WHEN I CHARGED MY BROTHER HENRY TO DISCOVER ALL
that he could of the finances of the Scargrave family,
he set about his work with customary diligence; and so
swiftly achieved results, that he waited upon me this
morning with intelligence of no little import. As but two
days remain before Isobel must appear in the Lords, I was
in a fever of impatience to hear Henry's news.

"My dear Jane," he began, seating himself in an easy
chair in the late Earl's study—the only room in which I
feel completely safe from prying ears, due to its heavy
wood panelling and walls lined floor to ceiling with
bookshelves—"I find that you have taken up lodgings
with a rather rum set."

"You surprise me, Henry," I rejoined. "Is not murder merely one of the country house games a guest may
expect at Christmas?"

"Among our great families, I suppose anything may
be made a game. They have certainly made a charade of
robbing one another," my brother replied gravely.

"A fate to be considered worse than death."

"Or capable of precipitating it, assuredly." Henry's large grey eyes twinkled; he was enjoying his new-won role in the Scargrave drama.

"Begin at the beginning, pray," I commanded him, with some asperity.

"Let us start with Fitzroy Payne."

"I am all attention."

"His circumstances are by no means as easy as he might wish, nor yet as distressed as you have been told."

"Sir William will not have it thus, you may depend."

"Sir William may have no choice. The facts are these: the new Earl is possessed of a considerable estate in the West Indies, acquired by his father and managed by a man who has done little to merit the trust placed in him by the Payne family. In short, the plantations are in reduced circumstances—"

"As I understand many such holdings are, at the present time."

"Indeed. It is not the year to be in sugar production."

"Or coffee, so I understand."

"Jane! Are you become a shareholder in some venture I should know of? Are we to expect you to take a London journal upon your return to Bath, and make cryptic references to the 'Change[1] over breakfast?"

I smiled at his banter and bade him go on.

"The holdings remain, nonetheless, of substantial worth, and may require only an infusion of capital and a change in managers to make them a going concern. That

---

1. Henry Austen refers here to the London Stock Exchange, founded in Change Alley in 1698. Before the mid-nineteenth-century dismantling of restrictive legislation on joint-stock companies (the result of the South Sea Bubble crisis and its resultant 1720 Act forbidding the formation of companies except by royal charter, or Act of Parliament), the Exchange was concerned primarily with public funds: government stock, East India bonds, canal-company shares, and later utilities and dock-company stocks.

the Earl hopes to use a part of his uncle's estate for just this purpose, is a fact Sir William must underline before the House of Lords."

"And his personal debts?"

"Fitzroy Payne lives on the interest from his father's Derbyshire estate, to the tune of three thousand pounds a year—a respectable income, assuredly, but not of the level to cut a certain dash among the glittering set in which he is owned a confederate." Henry hesitated, and eyed me dubiously. "Payne has habits of considerable expense, sister."

That he thought of the rumoured mistress, I readily discerned, and hastened to set him at his ease.

"You may except the illustrious Mrs. Hammond," I assured him. "I have met the lady."

My brother threw up his hands. "I am all amazement. I shall endeavour not to tell our mother of the company you now keep."

"Mrs. Hammond was his nursemaid," I protested. "Lord Scargrave but cares for the woman in retirement."

"Dashed again! I had hoped for something more engaging from the scrupulous Earl. But no matter. His carriages, his horse, his rooms in Town, and the upkeep of the Derbyshire establishment, have strained his funds to the limit—and past it, I fear. I could not find out, however, that there were debts of honour, due to gaming; but I learned that he had discharged such on behalf of another, some few months back."

"Lieutenant Hearst?" I said, with a sudden, sharp pang.

"The gentleman who most succeeded in robbing the family," Henry returned, nodding. "That man's affairs would make an amusing trial, but damme, he has deprived us of the pleasure. The Lieutenant exhausted what little his brother retained of their father's estate—and did the poor Mr. George Hearst wish to buy a living somewhere, it must be impossible for one of his reduced resources. I hope he has come in for a Scargrave living under the late Earl's will."

"I believe he has," I replied, "but that circumstances might forbid his taking it." To show his wife about Scargrave would be a form of purgatory on earth, given the acid tongues and long memories of the local people. But that was George Hearst's affair. "Have you anything further regarding Lord Scargrave?"

"He is everywhere recorded as a man of taste and decency, though adjudged somewhat proud and cold; though people respect him, they do not necessarily warm to him, and that may go against him in public opinion, however this trial turns out. There were once many hopes entertained of his heart, among the mothers and daughters of London's select; but I gather he is now become an object of fearful suspicion, and his value has dropped on the marriage market. You might pick him up on the cheap, by the by, now you have vetted him, Jane; I give you my consent in lieu of Father's, since you have made your brother your confidant."

"I fear, Henry, that the Earl's affections are apportioned to another," I told him, "and that all of society shall know of it in a very little while."

"Worse luck for you, Jane," my brother replied; "did he make a go of the plantations, as his wife you might come in for quite a pretty amount of pin money—and Eliza will have it that there is nothing like being a Countess." As always, the mention of his vivacious wife's name brought a smile to Henry's lips. He had borne with Eliza's retention of her title with good grace.

"Now tell me of Madame Delahoussaye," I urged, with a keener interest.

Henry steepled his fingers before his nose, for all the world like our father, did he but know it. "Though her daughter possesses thirty thousand pounds in trust, the good Creole lady hasn't a farthing in her purse, nor one she can borrow," he said comfortably, little comprehending the effect his words should have. "She depends entirely upon the household of her niece, one reason she is so faithful a companion, and stands to lose much by the reversal in Isobel's fortunes."

"But how can this be?" I cried. "I understood Madame to be a woman of easy circumstances."

"I fear that we may only speak of wealth in the past tense, Jane. In fact, her banker—old Robeson, of the London concern—is most desirous of investigating Madame Delahoussaye's accounts more thoroughly, in what I may only term an audit. Robeson suspects some irregularities in the disposition of some trust income Madame oversees, but would say no more, in deference to the lady's privacy, no matter how much I plied him with Port."

I THANKED HENRY PROFUSELY FOR HIS BENEVOLENCE ON my behalf, and vowed I should never do him recompense for such goodness; and he left me with much to consider. I do not begin to understand the motives for Madame Delahoussaye's behaviour; they are all of a tangle, between her own need and her daughter's prospects of fortune; from Henry's words, Madame should only lose by placing Isobel in a noose—and yet, and yet! That she is concealing something of import, I am utterly convinced.

I believe Lord Harold to be a party to Madame's intrigue, and that neither is a friend to Isobel, or concerned with her fate. But how to force the matter? I am overcome with the proximity of the trial, which is to open the day after tomorrow; and must suffer Fanny Delahoussaye's tirades over the state of her costume. She has emerged from mourning the gallant Lieutenant long enough to harry a bevy of shopkeepers, and my sole consolation in the trial's fast approaching, is that it shall witness an end to such frippery—and to my tenure, for good or ill, among the intimates of Scargrave. I fear that I shall be returning to Bath with a heavy heart, and the knowledge that I have mortally failed a true and innocent friend.

Journal entry, that same day

~

SIR WILLIAM REYNOLDS HAS BEEN AND GONE—A BRIEF VISIT, with the sole purpose of informing me that I am to be called before the Bar as a witness for the prosecution. The magistrate intends me to testify to the finding of the maid's body and all that ensued thereafter, however little I may relish the office. That my old friend suffers for me, and my divided loyalties, I read in his eyes; but Sir William is a man of iron where he believes himself to be right, and my feeble efforts at prevarication availed me nothing.

"I shall be struck dumb by the grandeur of the room, and the assemblage," I protested. "Can not you present my experiences on my behalf?"

Sir William's kind brown eyes could not meet my own. "It is impossible, my dear. You alone discovered the handkerchief and Marguerite, and the scrap of paper within her bodice." A brief smile played over his grave countenance. "Had you been less curious, my dear, or sent your active wits to sleep, we might not have you in this pickle."

And so I shall enter the House of Lords, and seat myself in the ranks reserved for witnesses, below those marked out for peeresses in the gallery—and I must speak before all assembled, without disgrace. Though it is no more than I expected, I am sick at heart; to face Isobel and Lord Scargrave in the box, and pronounce what must be damning to their cause, is a hideous fate. And yet, what choice have I? I shall be sworn, and must speak the truth as I recall it, though friendship—nay, human decency—would argue otherwise.

Sir William departed not long after, having business of a pressing nature. As I waved him down the marble steps to his carriage, he shook his head over the Payne family seal, swathed in black and mounted on the façade of the house over each of the long windows. Thus Scargrave

House proclaims Tom Hearst's death—but another in an increasing cause for mourning.

No further ceremony shall mark the Lieutenant's passing, however; as a suicide, he is to be buried tomorrow at a crossroads some distance west of the city, with a stake driven through his heart. I shudder to think it; for such a man—riven with faults as he may have been—to end in the most indifferent of earth, without benefit of clergy or memorial marker, is in every way horrible. His brother is to accompany the body. The poor batman Jack Lewis—quite downcast and morose—goes along as well, and the good Mr. Cranley; a singular mark of that barrister's devotion to the family's concerns that I must believe is intended to comfort silly Fanny Delahoussaye.

Mr. Cranley looks increasingly worried whenever he calls; and from his few words, I have learned that his defence is to rely solely on the notion that Fitzroy Payne's letter was stolen and Isobel's handkerchief purloined. For, in truth, he has no other suspects— and though I would dearly love Lord Harold Trowbridge to be arraigned, I cannot say upon what charge. There is no evidence to tie any but the Earl and the Countess to these murders; and so I toss and turn in bed of nights, and wonder greatly at what may be the purpose in collusion between Madame Delahoussaye and *that man*. But today, I bethought myself of Frank.

My brother Francis is a post captain in the Royal Navy these two years past, and is presently stationed at Ramsgate, about the coastal defences. I cannot think with Frank to prevent it, that the French under Buonaparte are likely to invade our little island; and in the meanwhile, as he assembles his Sea Fencibles[2] about Pegwell Bay, my dear brother might just as readily occupy himself in determining the use of a private deep-water port in the Barbadoes. That Lord Harold has recently visited

2. This was a corps of fishermen and coastal villagers equipped with boats—a sort of seaside militia—placed on alert in the event of invasion. —*Editor's note.*

France, and is bent upon acquiring such a port in the Indies, must give one pause; there is intrigue here, and Frank is sure to parse out the meaning. I wrote to him this morning, and am impatient for his reply.

And now I must see to my wardrobe, for assuredly I possess nothing grand enough for the witness-bar of the Royal Gallery. And what am I to say? *Only the truth*, Sir William told me this morning, as he stepped into his carriage—but what he believes to be true, and what I *know* to be false, are one and the same.

Chapter 23

A Deadly Contest of Wills

9 January 1803

~

HOWEVER UNFORTUNATE THE CIRCUMSTANCES, I MAY justly say that the display of British might that is the House of Lords, fully assembled for trial—a thing that happens not above once in a generation—has not its equal for solemnity and grandeur. The youngest barons proceeded first, and the august file closed with the most ancient of dukes, all shepherded by heralds and the Garter at Arms—two hundred–odd men, arrayed in robes that signified their ranks in the peerage, filing two by two into benches ranged on either side of the Royal Gallery's Bar. On the high dais sat a chair meant for the Lord High Steward.

Below it were the seats reserved for peeresses; here should Isobel have sat, had fortune been kinder. These gave way to Mr. Cranley and Sir William's place, and then to the witnesses' seats, in one of which I found myself. Lizzy Scratch was to my right, looking well-scrubbed and defiantly in her element, despite the incongruity of her position; I feared her spirits should take a theatrical turn, once called before the Bar. Dr. Philip

Pettigrew sat to my left, and beside him the cherubic scholar of Cambridge, Dr. Percival Grant.

Madame Delahoussaye and her daughter were lodged above, in the spectators' gallery; the briefest of glances revealed their seats to my indifferent eye. Miss Fanny had adopted the dubious mystery of a quantity of black silk veiling about her blond curls; it was sheer enough to disclose a flash of blue eyes and white teeth, while enshrouding her in all the discretion her interesting circumstances demanded. I knew her to be wishing for a greater part in the drama—or a wider stage, at least, for the parading of her costume; and would gladly have exchanged my place for hers.

A solemn bell tolled the hour; all rose; and a Proclamation of Silence was issued by the Serjeant at Arms. The Clerk of the Crown then knelt to present the Commission under the Great Seal to the Lord High Steward, who returned it to him; at which point the Clerk read its substance aloud, at interminable length, and we were treated to a declaration of "God Save the King!"

We must then endure the Certiorari and Return, a summary of the House of Lords' authority to preside over the case, with each and every peer a judge of fact and of law; much precedent was stated for their office, and many mouldy precepts of common law dredged before the assembly; but at last, when I had almost despaired of my sanity, we were informed of the decision of the Assizes to try Fitzroy Payne and the Countess for murder.

"The Jurors for our Lord the King upon their oaths present that the most noble lady Isobel Amelie Collins Payne, Countess of Scargrave, a peeress of the realm, on the twelfth day of December in the year of our Lord one thousand eight hundred and two, in the Parish of Scargrave, did kill and murder Frederick William Payne, seventh Earl of Scargrave. We further find that the most noble Fitzroy Gerald Payne, Viscount Payne, Earl of Scargrave, a peer of the realm, on the twenty-fourth day of December in the year of our Lord one thousand eight hundred and two, in the Parish of Scargrave, did kill and murder one Marguerite Dumas, maidservant, native of the Barbadoes."

At that point, following the proclamation by the Serjeant at Arms, the Gentleman Usher of the Black Rod brought in first the Countess, and then the Earl, and escorted them severally to the Bar, where they knelt until the Lord High Steward allowed them to rise.

Isobel's face was pale, and her once-lovely eyes had lost their lustre; some of the dirt and stench of Newgate had been washed from her person, but the freshness of her twenty-two years was yet overlaid with a haggardness that bespoke great turmoil of mind. The marks of her ordeal could not disguise her beauty, though they added something of romantic interest to her aspect. I had learned, upon my arrival that day, that her conveyance from Newgate was stoned by a mob, and that she was jeered as murderess and whore; the public had passed swift sentence upon my friend, without benefit of a hearing.

Lord Scargrave retained his accustomed command of countenance, evidencing only a deeper gravity in the tightness of his jaw and the unwavering aspect of his gaze. He was led with Isobel to stools placed within the Bar, where the pair should be confined for the duration of the proceedings, and the charges against them were read. The Clerk of the Parliaments then arraigned them, and asked whether they were Guilty or Not Guilty, to which they severally replied, Not Guilty—Isobel in the merest whisper, her hand to her throat, while Fitzroy Payne's voice rang through the chamber. His glance was haughty, his silver head held high; and though, from knowing him a little, I judged this the result of a struggle for composure, I well knew how it should be judged. *Proud and cold,* he would be proclaimed; and his very effort at self-control play against him.

Sir William Reynolds now rose, and the weight of my duty fell full upon me at the sight of his benign old face. *He* was a friend, and *she* was a friend; and between them they had made a mockery of my better feeling.

The magistrate looked very fine, indeed, in a dark grey tail coat of excellent wool, arrayed with a double row of gold buttons; and at his neck, the highest of white cravats I had ever seen—the collar tips reaching nearly to his ears. Thrown over all was a black silk robe; the awful weight of the Law he bore upon his aged countenance; and his bewigged head might almost be that of Jehovah, come to divide the guilty from the innocent. I quailed when his hard brown eyes fell upon myself, though I fancied they softened at the sight of my pale face; and understood of a sudden why the name *Sir William Reynolds* was everywhere greeted with trepidation and respect, among his adversaries at the Bar.

Sir William was prohibited from calling Isobel as a witness; and the only other persons capable of asserting that she had been alone with her husband on the evening of his death were themselves dead. On this point, the magistrate could merely expostulate to the assembled lords, having permission to read the relevant testimony from the written record of the inquest. That only the Countess had survived the night, he said, should make his case. He then called Dr. Pettigrew.

The poor young man was sworn; stated his true name and place of birth, and was duly noted to be a physician who had attended the seventh Earl some three years, and at his death bed. Dr. Pettigrew gave his evidence much as he had at the inquest, and was allowed to stand down; at which point he was followed by Dr. Percival Grant, who testified that the seeds shown to the assembled peers by Sir William were indeed Barbadoes nuts, a toxic poison commonly used as a physick and purgative by the natives of Isobel's birthplace. It was then that I was called.

My legs were as water, and the trembling of my hands so severe, that I fear I appeared to wave to the assembly as I held my left palm high and swore to tell the truth, so help me God. Whenever I am forced to speak or perform in public—at the pianoforte, in particular—my cheeks and throat are overcome with a brilliant rash; I had worn my high-necked gown of deep brown wool on purpose, but must declare it to have failed in its office. Sir William, when he spoke, meant to be kind; I could hear it in the tone of his voice, and cursed him mentally. From his careful speech, the lords who should pass judgement upon Isobel and Fitzroy Payne would surely think me a ninny—and dismiss the worth of any evidence I might give to Mr. Cranley on the morrow.

I stated my name and that I was a spinster of Bath.

"You are a great friend to the Countess, are you not?"

"As I am to you, sir," I replied.

"And you arrived at Scargrave Manor on the very eve of the Earl's death."

"I did."

"For what purpose, pray?" Sir William's eyebrows were drawn down to his nose, as though all such visits to Scargrave must be suspect.

"I was to attend a ball in honour of the Countess's marriage, and stay some weeks," I said, with an effort to throw my voice the length of the chamber. From the number of white hairs and befuddled looks among the assembled peerage, however, I doubted that even the clangour of the Final Judgment should disturb their peace.

"And how did her ladyship's spirits appear on the evening in question?"

I hesitated, and looked to Isobel. Her hands gripped the railing of the accused's box painfully, and her face was studiously averted from Fitzroy Payne's. A greater picture of dignity I could not find in the room, nor one to so tear at the heart. But my friend was deathly pale; and I feared she might faint.

"The Countess was very animated," I told Sir William, "as any young bride might be—opening the dance with her husband, partaking of the food he brought for her, and circulating among her guests to receive their best wishes. I had never seen her ladyship in better health, nor more beautiful"—I hesitated an instant, summoning my courage, and stared Sir William full in the face—"until, that is, Lord Harold Trowbridge appeared, and cast a cloud over her enjoyment."

Sir William started, and narrowed his eyes. "Please keep to the question, Miss Austen," he said.

"So I have done, sir," I protested. "You enquired as to her ladyship's spirits; and one cannot properly mark the decline in them upon meeting Lord Harold—so severe a decline, indeed, that she was forced to quit the room a few moments—unless one comprehends how elevated they were at the evening's commencement."

A short, ruby-faced gentleman sporting a silk robe with four bars of ermine on his shoulder—the robe of a Duke—shot up from the peers' bench with a choleric splutter. "Damme, Reynolds, find out what the woman would say! I'll not have Harry maligned before the entire Gallery!"

The very Duke of Wilborough, poor Bertie by name. My words at least had affected Trowbridge's brother. I shifted my eyes along the ranks of the spectators' gallery and found the one I sought; Trowbridge himself, his dark, narrow face utterly composed, and his unreadable eyes intent upon mine. I quailed, and looked away, appalled at what I might have done. But Isobel's life was in the balance; and if I must cause a riot in the House of Lords to free her, I should do so with equanimity.

The Lord High Steward called for order, with a look of dudgeon and a scowl in my direction; he then ordered Sir William to question me further regarding Lord Harold Trowbridge.

A brief smile twitched at the corners of Sir William's mouth; for an instant, it seemed, he applauded my bravery.

"Miss Austen, were you present at the encounter between Lord Harold and Lady Scargrave?"

"I was."

"And what did you observe?"

"Lord Harold pressed the Countess closely regarding a matter of business, and ignored her request that he should better wait until the morrow. He then being called to the Earl's library, she was freed of him; but the episode cost her dearly in composure."

"And after Lord Harold's departure, did her ladyship remark upon the scene?"

"She did. She said that Lord Harold had hounded her to the ends of the earth, and that she should never be free of him." Another splutter from the peers' bench, which I ignored. "Following the Earl's death, in great despondency, the Countess laid the entire matter before me—for without the Earl, she should be ever more prey to Lord Harold, and her husband's loss was accordingly a severe blow."

"Miss Austen," Sir William said warningly, "pray confine yourself to facts, and leave judgment for the assembly."

"Yes, Sir William."

My old friend turned towards the Lord High Steward. "I would request a recess, my lord, in order to call Lord Harold Trowbridge, and present him as a witness at the Bar. It is best to have *his* story regarding matters between himself and the Countess, rather than Miss Austen's."

"So it shall be," the Lord High Steward pronounced, letting fall his gavel; and I was allowed to step down—Sir William having failed to reach any of the matters for which my testimony was required—that of the finding of Isobel's handkerchief, or the maid's body, or indeed the scrap of foolscap overwritten by Fitzroy Payne's hand.

"YOU HAVE TAKEN A GREAT RISK, MISS AUSTEN," MR. Cranley said gravely, as he handed me a cup of tea in the witnesses' anteroom; "for we cannot know what Lord Harold Trowbridge shall say at the Bar, and we are powerless to counter it. Nor can we show that any collusion existed between him and the maid—as we must, if we are to suggest he is responsible for the Earl's death."

"I offer my apologies, Mr. Cranley," I said humbly, sipping at the restorative liquid; "I confess I did not think that far beyond the moment. I merely wished to divert the assembly from consideration of Isobel's guilt. *You* know that Sir William is not obliged to present evidence that does not support his case; and I was determined to make it known that Isobel depended upon her husband's fortune, and was thus unlikely to have killed him, when at his death it must pass to his heir. But I was unable to say that much."

"Sir William may as readily suggest that the heir's fortune should be Isobel's," the barrister pointed out, "can he but introduce the notion that they were lovers."

"And how should he do that? The maid alone knew; and the maid is dead."

"All of London suspects it; I have heard it myself, in three separate places, during the course of the past week. But all *that* is hearsay. Our greatest danger lies with yourself."

"I shall never pronounce such a thing in public, even did I know it to be true!" I cried stoutly.

"Sir William might demand it of you, Miss Austen, when you are next at the Bar; and you *are* under oath."

I saw then that I had a great deal to learn of the law, and wished heartily that one of my brothers was an adept at the profession; and vowed to be more careful in future. But I had little time to consider how virtuous that future should be—a bell was rung announcing that the proceedings should recommence, and we were obliged to find our seats once more within the House. I observed that Mr. Cranley settled himself in his with a worried frown; and regretted my unfettered tongue.

I soon put aside all thoughts of self, however, for the tall form of Lord Harold Trowbridge strode through the assembly's ranks, under escort of the Court. He moved with his usual athletic grace, an ease that never deserted him; and kept his face to the front of the room. Upon arriving at the witness box, however, he found my eyes, and held my gaze with an expression of amusement. He seemed to feel only delight in my efforts to heighten his notoriety.

The Lord High Steward called us both to attention.

Sir William cleared his throat, and glanced at his notes. I knew he bore Harold Trowbridge little affection, and wondered how my old friend felt, turning to such a man from need. "Did you, Lord Harold, speak with the Countess of Scargrave in the presence of her friend Miss Austen, on the night of the Earl's death?"

"I did."

"Would you describe the nature of the interview?"

"It was a business matter," Trowbridge said dismissively.

Sir William frowned. "A matter for the Countess, and not her husband?"

"As the property I sought to purchase was entirely the Countess's, it was solely her consent that was necessary."

"And how did her ladyship respond?"

"She very nearly showed me the door," Trowbridge said, with a thin smile.

"The Countess was not amenable to your proposals?"

"The Countess has long been opposed to them."

I felt my spirits begin to lift with hope. Perhaps even Lord Harold would speak the truth, when under oath. I glanced at Isobel, and saw that her eyes were fixed upon her enemy as if in a trance; Fitzroy Payne stared at nothing, his thoughts apparently elsewhere.

"And why is that, Lord Harold?" Sir William said.

"Because she does not wish to turn over her property."

"And what property is that?"

"The property I wished to purchase."

He is relishing this fool's errand, I thought, gazing at Trowbridge's heavy-lidded eyes; he says no more nor less than he must, and will drive Sir William mad before he lets slip anything that is damaging to himself. But my old friend the magistrate leaned forward keenly, his eyes fixed on the witness's face, as he posed the next question.

"Lord Harold, was the *Earl* equally opposed to your aims for his wife's property?"

"He was not," Trowbridge said.

I started in my seat, all amazement. A deliberate falsehood! I looked for Isobel, and saw her sway where she sat.

"His lordship wished to complete the sale?"

"The Earl's object was in every way aligned with my own," the rogue calmly replied; and at that, I heard Isobel gasp. As I watched, she slipped from her stool in a dead faint; it was as I thought—the strain had been too great to bear.

A murmur arose from the assembly, and Sir William halted before Lord Harold, his questions suspended. Fitzroy Payne leapt to his feet, all solicitude for the Countess's distress; and this, too, should be noted by the assembled peers. He was restrained by the Clerk, and Isobel righted; her wrists were chafed, and smelling salts administered, and she very shortly opened her eyes; but so ill was her appearance, that the Lord High Steward ordered her conveyed from the room, and the proceedings adjourned for the day.

"WHAT CAN BE HIS GAME?" I QUERIED MR. CRANLEY—NOT for the first time, as I turned back and forth before the drawing-room fire at Scargrave House. We were alone, and wasting away the hours remaining until dinner with little appetite. Fanny Delahoussaye seemed much fatigued from her parade before the House of Lords, and had gone above to rest, to Mr. Cranley's disappointment. Madame had no reason to seek my company—if anything, she avoided it, since our contretemps of a few days before. But I had no time to spare for the sensibilities of Delahoussayes.

"Trowbridge has deliberately lied before the Bar," I declared to the barrister, "and should be cited for perjury!" My tone betrayed my indignation, which was considerable. That I felt responsible for the rogue's appearance at all, I need not underline; and my guilt and remorse only heightened my desire to shake Trowbridge's grin from his insolent face.

"But how are we to prove perjury?" Mr. Cranley asked reasonably. "We have only the word of the Countess that her husband was bent upon fighting Lord Harold. Trowbridge knows as much, and feels secure in his deceit. He may say anything he likes, while the Countess but looks on and faints."

"There is not a man more despicable," I retorted bitterly, and threw myself into a chair with less than my usual grace. "Having dispatched Isobel's husband—her sole defender—Trowbridge would send her to the gallows, the better to win the property he cannot gain by any other means!"

"There is still Madame's consent," Mr. Cranley pointed out. "But perhaps Trowbridge shall kill her as well."

"That is hardly necessary—at Isobel's death, the property shall pass to Fanny, and as the sole trustee, Madame may turn it over to Lord Harold as she wishes. She shall free herself of an incumbrance, and think no more of Crosswinds."

"But she must know that the late Earl's intentions were not as Trowbridge would suggest," Mr. Cranley mused. "Perhaps I shall call her to the Bar when I have my day in Court, and make her declare the Earl opposed to Trowbridge's schemes."

"And now *you* would expose us to risk," I told him. "We cannot know whether Madame has fallen in with Lord Harold or not. For assuredly she has visited Wilborough House. Her consent may already have been won; and fearing to alienate her business partner, she may publicly deny all knowledge of the late Earl's views."

"I fear you are right," Mr. Cranley said, as he rose with a heavy sigh; "and now, Miss Austen, I must bid you *adieu*. Tomorrow comes early, and we have a difficult day before us; I must prepare late into the night, in the event that I am called upon to present the defence." The barrister's face was very weary; and in his countenance I read a little of my own despair.

"Have we any hope?" I said, faltering.

He hesitated, his eyes upon my face. "There is always hope. Did I not believe that, I should have quit the Bar altogether, and long before this."

"Do not coddle me, Mr. Cranley; I am not a child."

"Very well," he rejoined. "There is very little hope, Miss Austen. But even that is reason to persevere."

IT WAS A POOR SORT OF EVENING IN PORTMAN SQUARE; I dined with Mr. George Hearst—who is sunk in more than his usual melancholy in the wake of his brother's suicide—and the Delahoussayes. All were silent but for Fanny, who had heard herself admired at her seat in the Gallery, and could not contain herself; for the author of the compliment was a marquess, and the silly girl valued the opinion in a fashion commensurate with his rank. Did she earn the glances of a duke or two on the morrow, I should be forced to take my meals in my room.

When we had left Mr. Hearst to his solitary Port and his lonely cigar, and repaired, as ladies must, to take tea in the sitting-room, Fanny declared herself a trifle indisposed—as well she might be, with the burden I knew she carried—and tripped gaily to her room, visions of peers in ermine-trimmed robes no doubt lighting her way to bed. I seated myself over some needlework, the better to marshal my thoughts; for I had formed a dangerous resolution at dinner, and should never have a better opportunity to act upon it.

"Madame," I said.

She looked up from her book with a coldness that must give one pause. "Yes, Miss Austen?"

"Have you any views as to today's events?"

Madame Delahoussaye's lips compressed and she returned to her book. "I do not think too little can be said upon the subject."

"That is indeed unfortunate," I rejoined, "for I had hoped you might shed some light on Lord Harold's extraordinary behaviour."

"What can I know of Lord Harold that you do not? From your surprising display upon the witness stand, I should have thought you the man's intimate these several months at least."

"What *can* you mean, Madame?"

The covers of her volume came together with a snap. "That you had no business embroiling such a man in this affair," Madame Delahoussaye declared, "and that your impudence is far beyond your station, my girl." She rose with alacrity, as though to depart.

"But Lord Harold is embroiled in it of himself," I said, feigning bewilderment.

"So *you* would have it." Madame crossed to the sitting-room door and laid her hand upon the knob.

I sat back in my chair and surveyed such haste with amusement. "I wonder at your defending a man of whom you profess to know nothing, Madame."

She turned her head as rapidly as an adder. "It is not Lord Harold I would defend, Miss Austen, but my dear Isobel; and I fear her friends are become her worst enemies."

I snorted my contempt. "I rejoice to hear that protecting the Countess is now become your aim."

"It is the dearest consideration of my heart," she rejoined stonily, and took up again the doorknob.

I drew my needle swiftly through my canvas. "It was on *her* behalf, then, that you visited Lord Harold at Wilborough House but a few days ago?"

Her fingers dropped from the doorknob as though suddenly made nerveless. "I did no such thing. What use have I for such a man?"

"I wondered at it myself. You have always professed yourself his enemy. And so when my sister Eliza remarked upon your having met with him—she is, as you know, an intimate of the Duchess's—I could not satisfy my curiosity. But as you say you did not visit, she must have been mistaken. I dare say it was the card of *some other* Madame Delahoussaye she saw."

Madame did not honour me with a reply, but drew a shuddering breath, and for an instant I thought she might cross to where I sat and seize my throat in her two hands. But her self-mastery was admirable; she merely nodded frigidly, and swept from the room.

I liked her too little to care for her good opinion; I

wished only to frighten her into some exposure, and was very well pleased with the effect of my questions.

I HAD NOT HAD A MOMENT'S REST ALL DAY—HAD NOT EVEN sought my room to change before dinner, the interval between Mr. Cranley's departure and the bell having been too short. So I mounted the steps now in Madame Delahoussaye's wake with a sense of crushing weariness, fearful of the morrow and my own place in it—and found that, to my glad joy, a letter from my brother Frank awaited my eager eyes.

8 January 1803
Ramsgate

My dearest Jane—

Your letter arrived by this morning's post, and I was made so happy by its receipt, I little cared that it proved brief and barely legible upon first reading. When I divined, however, that your sole concern was the nature of deep-water ports in the colonies—no word of your gaieties or writing, and not a question spared as to the health and happiness of your brother—I felt certain you must be taken ill. I had nearly resolved to apply for leave, and hasten to London and your deathbed, when I read the letter again. Whatever the cause of your request, it has a certain urgency that will not be denied; and so I shall leave off raillery and offer a straight reply.

You believe that Lord Harold Trowbridge wishes to purchase the port for some nefarious purpose, and that the woman in whose power it remains desires only to discharge the estate's debt, without questioning the reason for his interest in its acquisition. That Trowbridge has journeyed to France is of singular interest, for it has come to my knowledge—and this must remain our secret, Jane—that a naval engagement may shortly arise in the very waters of which you write, should Buonaparte's forces sail from Martinique, and our own fleet from ports in the Barbadoes. If Trowbridge is aware of this, as well—and with his access to the higher circles, it is entirely possible—he may be plotting some effort on behalf of His Majesty's government, in which event the woman's port should prove essential. More than this, I cannot say; but you know, dear Jane, that the truce between Buonaparte and our King was nothing more than a pause to draw breath. The blow shall come, and on several fronts, I fear; the Corsican would test our Navy's right to rule the seas, and we must not fail.

Write to me again when you have something else in your head besides military strategy; but know that you have, as always, the love of your dearest brother—

Frank

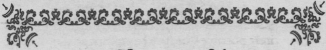

Chapter 24

The Sun King Deposed

9 January 1803, cont.

~

I HAVE A MIND AMAZED AT ITS OWN DISCOMPOSURE—FOR I know, now, why Lord Scargrave had to be killed—why Isobel and Fitzroy must be sacrificed; and it is so that high treason might be done. It is impossible that Lord Harold should act on behalf of His Majesty; he is too much of a charlatan, too readily the property of the highest bidder. No, Trowbridge must be in the employ of Buonaparte himself, and means to betray the Barbadoes—and England's Navy—with Madame Delahoussaye's willing assistance.

Frank had said that the French might well sail from Martinique, the island from which Buonaparte's consort, Josephine, sprang. The Delahoussayes themselves had been a powerful family in that French colony, and I doubted little that Madame's sentiments still veered towards France, however English her frivolous daughter had become. Madame had conspired to wrest Crosswinds from Isobel, burdening the property with heavy debt, diverting the income from the estate to her own pockets, and finally—when Isobel's marriage promised fair to save her from financial ruin—with murder. The maid Marguerite was herself a Creole of French extraction—and had come to Isobel from Madame's household, to serve as spy in her niece's camp. That she owed Madame more loyalty than her mistress, need not even be stated; and for her services to the former she had, no doubt, been well-paid. Marguerite proved useful when it came time to place poison in the Earl's dish; and then had dutifully kept her rendez-vous with death.

I remembered Madame's alacrity in assuming the duties of chatelaine at Scargrave Manor—how she had banished Mrs. Hodges and even Danson from the Earl's library, and insisted upon tidying its wealth of papers herself. She had certainly seen the new Earl's letter to Hezekiah Mayhew, informing the solicitor of Lord Harold's triumph over Isobel. Fearing exposure, Madame had taken the paper away, not perceiving, perhaps, in her eagerness to hide her duplicity, that it was but a copy, and the final draft already posted.

Later, Madame had seized her opportunity to dispatch the meddlesome Fitzroy by placing a fragment of his letter in the maid's bodice after she was dead, and removing the note Madame herself had written to arrange the fatal meeting. For good measure she had dropped Isobel's handkerchief by the paddock gate.

It had not been necessary for Lord Harold to remain at Scargrave, or even in the country; his confederate should manage quite well in his absence. Better that he inform Buonaparte that the port was in his grasp; and receive from him the payment for such betrayal.

I cast about me for pen and paper, and scribbled a note to Mr. Cranley; then I pulled on my dressing gown, hastened down the stairs, and dispatched a footman as messenger to the barrister's lodgings.

I had only, now, to wait.

I SHOULD NOT HAVE SLEPT EASILY IN ANY CASE, BUT TO-night the noises of the ancient house seemed magnified by the reverberation of my heartbeat, the quickened sound of my breath; I hesitated even to move, curled up in my elegant bed, lest the rustling proclaim my certainty of Madame's heinous guilt. Could I have drunk a potion, and become invisible, I should have swallowed it down in a single draught; but I was consigned to feel instead the complete exposure of those who know too much.

Utter darkness, wrapped round by heavy silk draperies, I could not abide, however; and so I pulled back the bed hangings and lit my single candle, ears straining for the sound of a carriage in the dark.

The bells of Westminster rang out in the stillness twelve times; I had come to the witching hour.

And it was then that I heard it—the muffled drag of a high-heeled step, pacing slowly down the corridor. Every nerve in my body froze as completely as though the January wind had swept through my chamber, and I was powerless to move. I knew this sound of old. Could ghosts, then, exchange houses? Had the First Earl as much right to haunt Town as he did country? Or was Tom Hearst returned from his unmarked grave, despite the stake which pierced his heart, to demand another moonlit kiss?

The candle flame wavered twice before my eyes; and beyond it, in the gloom, I made out the handle of my door slowly turning. It must be thrust open by a spectral hand in a moment, and I should have screamed; but my throat was utterly constricted with fear, and only a breathy gasp escaped. A crack of darkness against the jamb, widening inexorably as the door swung inwards with a groan—and the spectral First Earl stood before me, in all the splendour of the Sun King, his glorious clothes grimed with dust and tarnished with years, the cobwebs hanging from his curls and the tips of his beringed fingers.

But the cobwebs were made of grey thread, and the Earl was neither man nor ghost; I remembered the spectre's visitation to Fitzroy Payne's room at the Manor, so many weeks ago, and knew of a sudden who had placed the damning Barbadoes nuts in his gun case.

"Madame," I whispered, seeing the glitter of her eyes in the candle flame; and she returned a hideous grin. Swift as a cat she sprang to my bedside, the door thrust closed behind her, and wrapped a silken scarf twice around my neck. Though my fingers clung to the fabric, and strained against her force, she was made stronger still by violent rage; she would squeeze the life from me, and I must resist. Bursting flowers of light flooded my eyes even as darkness overcame them; my desperate fingers scrabbled at hers, drawing sharp nicks of blood; but we were both of us almost silent, save for my laboured breathing and her animal grunts of exertion—a deadly intensity robbed us of pleas and triumphs altogether.

I began to sway where I sat, too cushioned by the feathered mattress when I most needed hard purchase, and she profited from my weakness to thrust me down on my back, her knee drawn up and braced cruelly against my chest. I could not move her; and the advantage of her position should finish me in a very little time. I prayed as I have never prayed before—a single refrain only, *dear God dear God dear God*—even as I felt my strength begin to ebb. As from a great distance, I saw her grotesque fancy dress thrown by the candle in shadows upon my wall, and felt an absurd desire to laugh; but what emerged was nothing more than a pitiful sob.

With a harshness magnified by the silent absorption of our deadly contest, the door burst open, and a man's form was abruptly outlined against the darkened hall. *Mr. Cranley*, I thought, with rising hope—and then saw that all hope was lost. For it was Harold Trowbridge who stood there, with his evil profile and hooded eye; and that he came to finish what Madame had begun, I felt with all the certainty of despair. The room whirled; I gasped for air; and gave way to a pounding darkness that would not be gainsaid.

* * *

"MISS AUSTEN," A GENTLE VOICE REPEATED IN MY EAR; "Miss Austen!"

As my eyelids fluttered open, I found the earnest gaze of Mr. Cranley bent upon my own. I sat up suddenly, consciousness regained; saw Madame Delahoussaye bound to a chair and staring at me malevolently; and would have started from the bedclothes in my wildness to be free of her presence, did not the barrister restrain me.

"Do not try to speak," Mr. Cranley said; "I fear your throat is badly bruised."

"You came," I croaked, turning my eyes with relief to his.

"Try to give her some brandy," said a voice suffused with concern; and I knew with gladness that it belonged to Sir William Reynolds. Mr. Cranley raised me on one arm, and turned to receive the flask from an outstretched hand—which was attached to none other than Lord Harold Trowbridge.

I thrust the brandy away and reeled backwards, choking and spluttering. "Murderer!" I cried. "That man would have killed me! He is in league with Madame!"

"Lord Harold was your salvation, Jane," Sir William said gently, as he hastened to my side. "He overpowered that woman with not a moment to spare. For I fear *we* should have arrived too late."

"Trowbridge was closeted in my chambers, divulging much that you should know, when I received your note," Mr. Cranley added. "He understood your danger immediately, and flew to your side while I went for Sir William. We deemed it best that a man of the King's Bench be present to receive Madame's confession—did we arrive in time to catch her in another act of murder."

"I do not understand," I said, in my strange new voice; "if Lord Harold is become a friend, why has he endeavoured so long to send the Countess to the gallows? Why *lie*, as he so clearly did, before the Royal Gallery Bar?"

Mr. Cranley gazed across my head at Sir William, and Sir William at Lord Harold. "She shall have to be told, my lord," the magistrate said. And so the man I had thought a rogue pulled a chair close to my bedside.

"My dear Miss Austen," Harold Trowbridge began, "I told you once that I was a dark angel, and you a light one. But I should better have said that we both used our wits to similar ends—only I bend mine to deceive, and you to illuminate."

I raised myself to my elbows in protest. "You claim now to have no interest in the Countess's property? Or in the fortuitous death of her husband?"

"In her property, I remain as desperately interested as ever," he replied, with amusement in the heavily-lidded eyes, "but for reasons that shall soon be made plain; and as for the late Earl, it has been many years since I have thought of Frederick as anything but a friend. I did not kill Lord Scargrave, Miss Austen; indeed, I should more easily have killed myself. For it was the Earl who directed my every movement."

I confess to a confusion of the senses at this revelation. "You must speak more plainly, Lord Harold."

He sighed deeply, betraying for the first time some emotion other than languor, and fixed his eyes upon my own. "A second son—even the second son of a duke—must have a profession, Miss Austen; and I have made mine what the French call *espionage*."

"You are a spy," I breathed.

"If you will. I work only for those whose sacred reputations forbid all mention of their names; I serve the Crown from time to time; and always I go where the law may not—or *will* not." Trowbridge paused a moment for reflection, as if choosing his words to suit his audience.

"These many months past—for almost a year, indeed—I have been in the Earl's employ," he resumed, "for the purpose of divining the true nature of his wife's financial difficulties. Frederick, Lord Scargrave, had long been a friend of her father, John Collins; and at that gentleman's death, he received a sealed letter from his solicitors, begging him to look after John Collins's only child. Isobel came to the Earl at her arrival in England; he was immediately enchanted with her beauty; and his duty to a late friend soon became the necessity of a man in love.

"In very little time he learned of Isobel's financial difficulties; and in her innocence of business, she told him much that caused suspicion in him. Frederick believed her to be the victim of duplicity within her own family, but could not determine how it was done; and I may plainly state that he also feared for her life, and thought to protect her most by offering marriage and himself as a champion for her cause. The late Earl would not see that he alone should prove the greatest threat to her enemies, though I made the point on several occasions; Frederick was possessed of much strength and resolve, and foolishly could not believe himself likely to fall victim to anyone.

"At the Earl's direction and with his funds, I purchased Crosswinds' debt, then held in various hands about the Continent, and approached the Countess in the guise of her chief creditor, pressuring her to make over the property in my name in order to cancel her heavy obligation. It was the Earl's hope that my appearance should force her true enemies into the clear, and expose their purpose; and to my great chagrin, he was correct. I was summoned by him to Scargrave on the night of the ball; I made an obvious advance upon the Countess, in the hearing of her family and friends—and that night, her main protector was foully murdered."

"Can it be possible?" I said, turning to Sir William.

My old friend answered me with a single look. "It can, and is," he said grimly. "Lord Harold has papers in his possession signed by the Earl, vouchsafing his purpose and the means placed at his disposal; and furthermore, he has all the notes representing the Barbadoes debt—from which the Countess is now, happily, freed."

"It was these matters, among others, that we discussed in my chambers tonight," Mr. Cranley said.

"I only returned from France a few days ago, and thus was incapable of halting the proceedings in the Royal Gallery," said Lord Harold. "But I felt it necessary to explain my elliptical speech at the Bar this afternoon. I could not—even under oath—betray the delicate progress of snaring Madame Delahoussaye in a noose of her own making; nor could I unjustly consign the Countess and Lord Scargrave to the gallows." The thin mouth creased in an unwonted smile. "You placed me in a devilish position, Miss Austen; but it is no less than I have come to expect from you. You are indeed a worthy adversary."

I had not quite forgiven such a man. "I should have preferred us to work in concert, my lord," I said tartly, fingering my bruised throat. "Was that so impossible?"

"Not without exposing you to extreme danger, such as you have only just escaped," he returned, glancing at Madame. The lady could only appear ridiculous at this point, despite her murderous hands; her costume was torn, her wig discarded, and a quantity of false cobwebs fluttered about her face. In her eyes, however, I read still her talent for evil.

Even Harold Trowbridge was sobered by a look in Madame's direction. He turned back to his tale with obvious relief. "I remained at Scargrave long enough to ascertain that it was Madame Delahoussaye who harboured the chief interest in Crosswinds—and as its trustee, this was not altogether remarkable. I lacked proof of her malevolence, however, until the day before I left—having pressured the Countess into signing a worthless paper, as a final nasty flourish with which to make my exit. For my true purpose had been satisfied the previous evening, when Madame had approached me with a provocative proposition."

There was the sound of a throat clearing in the corner, and with a profound venom, the bound woman spat. A pustule of phlegm landed on the floor just short of Lord

Harold; with infinite grace and irony, he smeared it to nothing with his boot.

"She told me that however much I preyed upon the Countess, I should never obtain the property I sought without her own consent—and a handsome fee. From her elliptical questions regarding my motives, I perceived that Madame believed that it was the *port* I wanted—until that moment, I had not known the port was so valuable—for reasons of my own; but I little understood then that she, too, had designs upon the port, of a far more destructive nature, and on behalf of a far deadlier client. I knew nothing of the true nature of her schemes, and thought only that she wished to extort a princely sum for her consent to the sale. Having considered her demands—which were enormously high—I was to wait upon her in London after the holiday.

"I left Scargrave the next day, and consulted my brother—who, despite his fatuous appearance, is a man of probity and sense much valued at the Ministry of War—and it was Bertie's view that I should accompany him on a mission he had only then received, of parlaying with his French counterpart regarding the disposition of the French Navy. While in the country, I should endeavour to learn what I could about deep-water ports in the West Indies; and so I agreed.

"I had not been long abroad when it became clear to me why Madame had fenced with me so guardedly—why, indeed, a *port* attached to the property should be so valuable. She had nothing less in train than the betrayal of the British Navy—and she intended to be paid for it twice. Having bartered the port to *me*, she should as readily offer it to Buonaparte—and trust that the French Navy should discourage any thought I might have of pressing my claim. I returned in haste to England, intending to play her like a fish until she should betray enough to incriminate herself; and she very soon waited upon me at Wilborough House, to learn my decision. She had a new impatience about her that I judged to arise from fear; though what had caused her to become anxious—when the trial of her niece was so nearly achieved, and my own suspicions so closely guarded—I could not comprehend. But I have since learned from Mr. Cranley that *you*, Miss Austen, precipitated her unease."

"Though I fixed upon her too late, and lacked any proofs," I admitted.

"And but for her attack upon you, we should still lack them," Sir William told me.

There was a rustle from the corner, and all our eyes turned to the murderess. She struggled with her bonds, her glittering eyes fixed upon me. "Meddlesome girl!" she cried. "But for you I should have prevailed! But I assure you, Miss Austen, I regret nothing I have done, except my failure to dispatch you earlier." Her eyes shifted to Sir William and she smiled cruelly. "You think yourself very clever, old man, in catching me; but we both know who the clever one has been. It was *I* who charged the maid with poisoning the Earl, and then slit her throat to ensure her silence; and you were susceptible to my diversions—the handkerchief, the note in Payne's handwriting—and charged others with my crimes." Madame let forth a piercing laugh. "How I rejoiced, alone in my room at night! You were fools, all of you. My discovery came about by the merest accident. That I failed at the last makes not a whit of difference—in affairs of great moment, one wins or loses by the cast of a die."

"As your patron Buonaparte undoubtedly taught you," Sir William said dryly, "knowing that in the end, it was you, Madame, who should hang; and he who should survive to play at dice another day." He turned to me and patted my hand, his aged brown eyes gaining something in their warmth. "Lord Harold's words might have brought a charge of treason against this lady, my dear Jane, but they should not have solved for us the unpleasantness at Scargrave Manor. For that, we needed you. I only regret that you endured such peril to achieve your Countess's freedom."

I knew not what to say, and so took refuge in my

dearest concern. "Isobel shall go free?" I enquired, looking from one man to another.

"On the very morrow," Sir William assured me, "and Fitzroy Payne with her."

A feeling of exquisite joy overwhelmed me, and I closed my eyes a moment; but of a sudden, I looked for Mr. Cranley. "Poor fellow!" I cried. "To be denied your day before the House of Lords!"

"It might well have been the ruin of my career," that worthy said wryly, "for I certainly had no defence to offer."

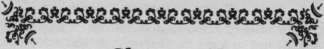

Chapter 25

Jane's Afterword

20 March 1803
No. 4 Sydney Place, Bath

~

I HAVE HAD NEWS TODAY FROM SIR WILLIAM REYNOLDS, OF
Madame Delahoussaye's trial before the Assizes only a
few days past; the proceedings were brief, as expected,
and she has been sent to her Maker this very day. I should
feel a depth of pity for her, had she not stood by with
complete equanimity while Isobel faced a similar fate;
and there is the image of foolish Marguerite Dumas, gri-
macing horribly in her unlooked-for death, that will not
depart from memory. The snow is falling today, late in
season, and I am cast back afresh to the dusky shed in
the paddock, and the dark blood pooled in the straw;
and though I think Madame well departed from this life,
I offer a prayer for her eternal soul.

I have recovered fully from my own misadventure;
the marks on my throat have faded; and I have determined to avoid all proposals of marriage in future, in the
fear that my refusal should precipitate another spate of
killing at some country house or other. The rest of the
Scargrave party are not so sanguine; and like every novel
of manners written by my contemporaries, this story has

ended in marriages all around. Poor Fanny Delahoussaye was the first to assay that happy state—she ran off to Gretna Green with Mr. Cranley while her mother still sat in Newgate prison, and now publishes the news of her expectant condition with hardly a blush. That she had vowed never to marry a barrister, is happily banished from her mind.

Mr. George Hearst received a handsome Scargrave living under the terms of the late Earl's will, which he has effectively traded for one in Newcastle. He has repaired to the north with his Rosie, who bids fair to make an excellent curate's wife with a bit of schooling and gentle attention.

Though Fitzroy Payne is restored to Isobel's good opinion—and in so decided a manner as must make her blush with contrition and shame—he and the Countess are not yet joined in matrimony. The wounds of their past experience remain too raw. There is the weight of public opinion to be braved as well; for though they are saved from the noose, and all the indignities suffered in the weeks before their trial, they remain the object of much speculation. Isobel has retreated from society altogether, while the Earl devotes his attention to securing a suitable overseer for his estates in the West Indies. He has embarked on a plan of visitation to that region in May, and urges Isobel to accompany him; and my friend has not yet told him nay.

Isobel remains in her late husband's London house, the bitter memories of Hertfordshire and Scargrave Manor being as yet too strong. She is freed of her debt, as Lord Harold said, having received from that gentleman a large package of cancelled notes a few days after her liberation. The knowledge of her aunt's betrayal, against the extent of Frederick's goodness, has made my friend sober and sad; but she is young, and possessed of wealth and beauty, and cannot forego living for very long. With time, and forgetfulness, I believe Isobel shall find happiness again in the parity of Fitzroy Payne's mind and youth.

And Lord Harold Trowbridge? A curious man. To

have held his high esteem—as I clearly did—is an honour I only understood when our acquaintance was at its close. He is everywhere misunderstood, mistrusted, and disliked, except by those who need his services; but he commands a fearful respect. I have said in the past that I should rather spend an hour with the notorious than two minutes with the dull; and my taste is proved again to be unerring.

I have here a letter penned in Trowbridge's hand—*To the light angel*—that contains a single phrase only. *My dear Miss Austen*, it says, *we may take this as a lesson: It required a woman to divine what a woman had wrought.*

THE END

About the Author

Stephanie Barron, a lifelong admirer of
Jane Austen's work, is the author of five
previous Jane Austen mysteries. She lives
in Colorado, where she is at work on the
seventh Jane Austen mystery, *Jane and
the Ghosts of Netley*. As Francine Mathews,
she is the author of *The Cutout* and *The
Secret Agent*. Learn more about both
Stephanie Barron and Francine Mathews
at www.francinemathews.com.

If you enjoyed Stephanie Barron's *Jane and the Prisoner of Wool House*, you won't want to miss any of the wonderful mysteries in this superb series. Look for them at your favorite bookseller's.

And turn the page for an exciting preview of *Jane and the Ghosts of Netley*, coming soon in hardcover from Bantam Books.

JANE

AND THE

GHOSTS OF NETLEY

-Being the Seventh Jane Austen Mystery-

by Stephanie Barron

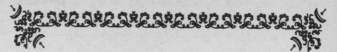

Chapter 1

Bare Ruined Choirs

*Castle Square,
Southampton
Tuesday, 25 October 1808*

~

THERE ARE FEW PROSPECTS SO REPLETE WITH ROMANTIC possibility—so entirely suited to a soul trembling in morbid awe—as the ruins of an English abbey. Picture, if you will, the tumbled stones where once a tonsured friar muttered matins; the echoing coruscation of the cloister, now opened to the sky; the soaring architraves of Gothick stone that oppress one's soul as with the weight of tombs. Vanished incense curling at the nostril—the haunting memory of chanted prayer, sonorous and unintelligible to an ear untrained in Latin—the ghostly tolling of a bell whose clapper is muted now forever! Oh, to walk in such a place under the chill of moonlight, of a summer evening, when the air off the Solent might stir the dead to speak! In such an hour I could imagine myself a heroine straight from Mrs. Radcliffe's pen: the white train of my gown sweeping over the ancient stones, my shadow but a wraith before me, and all the world suspended in silence between the storied past and prosaic present.

Engaging as such visions must be, I have never ventured to Netley Abbey—for it is of Netley I would speak, it being the closest object to a romantic ruin we possess in Southampton—in anything but the broadest day. I am far too sensible a lady to linger in such a deserted place, with the darkling wood at my back and the sea to the fore, when the comfort of a home fire beckons. Thus we find the abyss that falls between the fancies of horrid novels, and the habits of those who read them.

"Aunt Jane!"

"Yes, George?" I glanced towards the bow, where my two nephews, George and Edward, surveyed the massive face of Netley Castle as it rose on the port side of the small skiff.

"Why do they call that place a castle, Aunt? It looks nothing like."

" 'Tis a Solent fort, you young nubbins," grunted Mr. Hawkins, our seafaring guide. "Built in King Henry's time, when the Abbey lands were taken. In a prime position for defending the Water, it is; they ought never to have spiked those guns."

"But we have Portsmouth at the Solent mouth, Mr. Hawkins," Edward observed, "and must trust to the entire force of the Navy to preserve us against the threat from France." The elder of the two boys—fourteen to George's thirteen—Edward prided himself on his cool intelligence. As my brother's heir, he was wont to assume the attitudes of a young man of fortune.

My nephews had come to me lately from Steventon, after a brief visit to my brother James—a visit that I am certain will live forever in their youthful memories as the most mournful of their experience. I say this without intending a slight upon the benevolence of my eldest brother, nor of his insipid and cheeseparing wife; for the tragedy that overtook our Edward and George was entirely due to Providence.

Nearly a fortnight has passed since a messenger out of Kent conveyed the dreadful intelligence: how Elizabeth Austen, the boys' mother and mistress of my brother Edward's fine estate at Godmersham, had retired after dinner only to fall dead of a sudden fit. Elizabeth! So elegant and charming, despite her numerous progeny; Elizabeth, unbowed as it seemed by the birth of her eleventh child in the last days of September. The surgeon could make nothing of the case; he declared it to be improbable; but dead our Lizzy was, despite the surgeon's protestations, and buried she has been a week since, in the small Norman church of St. Lawrence's where I attended her so often to Sunday service.

I suspect that too much breeding is at the heart of the trouble—but too much breeding is the lot of all women who marry young, particularly when they are so fortunate as to make a love-match. Elizabeth Bridges, third daughter of a baronet, was but eighteen when she wed, and only five-and-thirty when she passed from this life. With her strength of character, she ought to have lived to be eighty.

It remains, now, for the rest of us to comfort her bereaved family as best we may. My sister Cassandra, who went into Kent for Elizabeth's lying-in, shall remain at Godmersham throughout the winter. Dear Neddie bears the affliction with a mixture of Christian resignation and wild despair. My niece Fanny, who at fifteen is grown so much in form and substance as to seem almost another sister, must shoulder the burden of managing the younger children, for the household is without a governess. There is some talk of sending the little girls away to school, that they might not brood upon the loss of their mamma—but I cannot like the scheme, having nearly died when banished as a child to a young ladies' seminary. The elder boys, Edward and George, endured their visit to brother James at Steventon and appeared—chilled to the bone with riding next to Mr. Wise, the coachman—on Saturday. They are bound for their school in Winchester on the morrow.

Their happiness has been entirely in my keeping during this short sojourn in Southampton. I have embraced the duty with a will, for they are such taking lads, and the blight of grief sits heavily upon them. They forget their cares for a time in playing at spillikins, or fashioning paper boats to bombard with horse chestnuts. The evening hours, when dark descends and memory returns, are harder to sustain. George has proved a restless sleeper, crying aloud in a manner more suited to a child half his age. He will be roundly abused for weakness upon his return to school, if he does not take care.

My mother, I own, finds the boys' spirits to have a shattering effect upon her nerves, which invariably fail her in moments of family crisis. No matter how diligently Edward might twist himself about in our reading chairs, engrossed in *The Lake of Killarney*, or George lose a morning in attempting to sketch a ship of the line, their exuberance will drive my mother to her bedchamber well before the dinner hour, to take her evening meal upon a tray.

Yesterday, I carried the boys up the River Itchen in Mr. Hawkins's skiff, and stopped to examine a seventy-four that is presently building in the dockyard there.[1] The place was a bustle of activity—scaffolding and labourers vied for place in a chaos of scrap wood and iron tools—and left to myself, I should not have dreamt of disturbing them. But under the chaperonage of Mr. Hawkins, a notorious tar known to all in Southampton as the Bosun's Mate, we received a ready welcome from the shipwright. Mr. Dixon is a hearty fellow of mature years and bright blue eyes who takes great pride in his work.

"Miss Austen, d'ye say?" he enquired sharply over our introduction. "Not any relation to Captain Francis Austen?"

"I am his sister, sir."

"Excellent fellow! A true fighting captain, or I miss my mark! And no blubberhead neither. You won't find Frank Austen playing cat-and-mouse with Boney; goes straight at 'em, in the manner of dear old Nelson."

"That is certainly my brother's philosophy. You are acquainted with him, I collect?"

"Supplied the Cap'n with carronades last summer, as he could not secure them in Portsmouth," Mr. Dixon replied. "He should certainly have need of them, once the *St. Alban's* reached the Peninsula. A great hand for gunnery, your brother. Now! What shall we find to engage the interest of these young scrubs, eh?"

He scrutinized my nephews' faces, well aware that nothing more was required to command their full attention than the spectacle of the seventy-four.

1. A third-rate ship carrying 74 guns, this was the most common line-of-battle vessel and a considerable number were built during the Napoleonic Wars; by 1816, the royal navy possessed 137 of them. They weighed about 1,700 tons and required 57 acres of oak forest to build.—*Editor's note.*

The great third-rate towered above our heads, her keel a massive construction of elm to which great ribs of oak were fixed. She was nearly complete, the decks having been laid and the hull partitioned into bulkheads, powder magazines, storerooms, and cabins, with ladders running up and down. The Itchen yard is ideally suited for such a ship, for the river water flows in through a lock, and the finished vessel may float down to Southampton Water in time.

"Jupiter!" Edward exclaimed. "Isn't she a beauty, though! How long have you been a-building?"

The shipwright gazed at his work with ill-concealed affection. "Nearly three years she's been under our hands, and you shall not find a sweeter ship in all the Kingdom. No rot in her timbers, no crank in her design; and we shan't hear of this lady falling to pieces in a storm!"

"Are such things so common?" I murmured to Mr. Hawkins.

The Bosun's Mate glowered. "Have ye not heard of the Forty Thieves, ma'am? All ships o' the line, built in rotten yards? Floating coffins, they were—though I served in no less than five of 'em."

"Good Lord."

"When is she to sail, Mr. Dixon?" George enquired.

"We expect to launch her at Spithead in the spring. Perhaps your naval uncle will have the command of her! Should you like to look in?"

"*Should* we!" the boy replied. "Above all things!"

"Jeremiah!" Dixon called. "Yo, there—Jeremiah! Now, where is that Lascar?"

A dark-skinned, lanky fellow with jet-black hair ran up and salaamed, in the manner of the East Indies. A

Lascar! The boys, I am certain, had never encountered a true exotic of the naval world—one of the renowned sailors of the Seven Seas. I smiled to see Edward's expression of interest, and George's of apprehension.

"Jeremiah at your service," he said, with another low bow. "You wish to see the boat, yes?"

Mr. Dixon slapped my nephews on the back so firmly George winced. "Get along with ye, now. The Lascar won't bite. Refuses even to touch good English beef, if you'll credit it; but he's a dab hand with a plane and a saw."

Nearly an hour later we bid Mr. Dixon goodbye, and Mr. Hawkins turned his skiff towards home. Yesterday's water party proved so delightful, however—so exactly suited to my nephews' temperaments and interests—that on this morning, their last day of liberty, I was determined to get them once more out-of-doors.

THE ABBEY RUINS, AND THE SCATTERED HABITATION that surrounds them, lie southeast of Southampton proper, just beyond the River Itchen. In fine weather, of a summer's afternoon, one might walk the three miles without fatigue; but with two boys on my hands, and the weather uncertain, I had thought it wiser to make a naval expedition of our scheme. As the diminutive craft bobbed and swayed under the boys' restless weight, I feared I had chosen with better hope than wisdom.

"Sit ye down, young master, and have a care, or ye'll pitch us all over t'a gunnels!" Mr. Hawkins growled at George. Mr. Hawkins is not unkind, but exacting in matters nautical. I grasped the seat of George's pantaloons firmly; they were his second-best, a dark grey intended for school in Winchester, and not the fresh black set of mourning he had received of our seamstress.

The Bosun's Mate maneuvered the skiff into a small channel that knifed through the strand, and sent the vessel skimming towards shore. Above us rose Netley Cliff, and the path that climbed towards the abbey.

"That'll be Netley Lodge." Hawkins thrust a gnarled thumb over his shoulder as he rowed, in the direction of a well-tended, comfortable affair of stone that hugged the cliff's edge. "Grand place in the old days, so they say, but nobody's lived there for years."

"And yet," I countered as the boat came to rest on the shingle, "there is a thread of smoke from two of the four chimneys."

The Bosun's Mate whistled under his breath. "Right you are, Miss! Somebody has opened up the great house—but who?"

"Perhaps a wandering ruffian has taken up residence," George suggested hopefully.

Mr. Hawkins shipped his oars. "Beyond is the village of Hound—nobbut a few cottages thrown up, and scarce of folk at that, what with the war. They'll know in Hound who've lit the fires at t'a Lodge."

A freshening wind lifted Edward's hat from his head, and tossed it into the shallows; he scrambled from the boat in outraged pursuit.

The Bosun's Mate sniffed the salt air.

"Weather's changing. 'Twon't do to linger long, Miss Austen, among those bits o' rubble. I'll bide with a friend in Hound while ye amuse yerselves at t'Abbey." He tossed a silver whistle—the emblem of his life's ambition—into George's ready hands. "Just ye blow on that, young master, when ye've a mind to head home. Jeb Hawkins'll be waiting."

THEY RAN AHEAD OF ME, STRAIGHT UP THE PATH, IN A game of hunt and chase that involved a good deal of shrieking. I very nearly called after them to conduct themselves as gentlemen—my mother, I am sure, would have done so—but I reflected that the path was deserted enough, and the boys in want of exercise. In such a season the visitors to Netley must be fewer than in the summer months, when all of Hampshire finds a reason to sail down the Water in search of amusement. The summer months! Even so! I had visited Netley last June in the company of the vanished Elizabeth—charming as ever in a gown of sprigged muslin, with a matching parasol. Elizabeth, who would never again walk with her arm through mine—

I breasted the hill, and caught my breath at the sight of the Abbey ruins: the church standing open-roofed under the sky; the slender shafts of the chancel house and the broken ribs of the clerestories; the grass-choked pavement of the north transept; and the cloister court, where wandering travellers once knocked at the wicket gate. A tree grows now in place of an altar. Ivy twines thick and green about the arched windows, as though to knit once more what the ages have unravelled. A futile hope: for all that time destroys, cannot be made new again, as my poor George and Edward have early discovered.

The boys plunged into the ruined church, and continued their game of pursuit; I proceeded at a more measured pace. I have come to Netley often enough during my residence in Southampton, but familiarity cannot breed contempt. This place was built by the good monks of Beaulieu in 1239, and throve for more than three hundred years as only the Cistercian abbeys could: wealthy in timber, and in the fat of the land; a center of learning and of prayer. There are those who will assert that by the reign of King Henry the Eighth, prayer was much in abeyance; that but a single volume was found in the library at the Abbey's dissolution; and that the monks were more eager to ride to hounds— hence the name of the neighbouring hamlet—than to offer masses for their benefactors. King Henry dissolved the monasteries of England in 1537, and with them, Netley; and the yearly income from all the property thus seized was in excess of a million pounds. Henry used his booty to political effect, rewarding his supporters with rich grants of land; and Netley Abbey was turned a nobleman's manor.

There is an ancient legend in these parts that one wellborn lady, forced into the veil, was walled up alive in the Abbey walls; but though many have searched for the lady's tomb, no one has ever found it. There are stories, too, of scavengers among the Abbey's stones, struck dumb and blind in attempting to lift what was not theirs. Whether haunted or no, the manor did not prosper, and ended, with time, as a blasted testament to King Henry's ambition.

I have long been partial to the Roman Catholic faith, as the object of devotion of no less a family than the Stuarts: maligned, neglected, and betrayed by all who knew them. I must admit, even still, that Henry's seizure of monastic property, and its eventual decay, has proved an invaluable contribution to the beauties of the English landscape.[2]

2. The opinion given here is a rough paraphrase of sentiments Jane first expressed at the age of sixteen in her *History of En-*

Do spirits walk among the fallen timbers of this house? Do they mourn and whisper in the moonlight? I have an idea of a shade, poised upon the turret stair, her white habit trailing.

Absurd, to feel such a prickling at the neck in the middle of the day—to pace insouciantly down what had once been a sacred aisle, as though under the gaze of a multitude; to listen attentively to birdsong, aware that the slightest alteration of sound might herald an unwelcome intruder. Ladies have often called upon the ghosts of Netley—there is nothing strange in this. . . .

In the distance, I heard young Edward's shout of triumph and George's, of despair. The birds continued to sing; a shaft of sunlight pierced the ruined window frame, and a breath of wind stirred the ivy. I traversed the south transept and turned for the turret stair, which winds upwards into the sky—the turret itself having crumbled—and gives out onto the Abbey's walls. Here one may walk the perimeter of the ruin, with a fine view of the surrounding landscape. My head into the wind, I paced a while and allowed myself to consider of Elizabeth.

I am not the sort to indulge in grief; I have known it too often and too well. The older I become—and I shall be three-and-thirty this December—the more I take Death in my stride. I have not yet learned, however, to accept the caprice of its whims—nay, the absurdity of its choice, that would seize a young woman of health, beauty, prospects, and fortune, a young woman beloved by all who knew her—and yet leave *Jane:* who am possessed of neither fortune nor beauty nor a hopeful family. I live as but a charge upon my relations.

Would I, in a spirit of sacrifice, exchange my ardent pulse for Lizzy's silent tomb? If a bargain could be made with God—a bargain for the sake of young Edward and George, or the little girls so soon to be shut up at school—a bargain for dear Neddie, crushed in the ruin of his hopes—would I have the courage to strike it?

I cast my eyes upon the flat grey sheen of Southampton Water—on the smoking chimneys of Hound, tumbling towards the sea; on the distant roofs of Southampton town, glinting within its walls. Dear to my sight, who am selfish in my grasp at life. *Forgive me, Lizzy. Though I loved you well, I cannot wish our lots exchanged.*

The boys' voices had grown faint. Thunder pealed afar off, from the easterly direction; the unsteady day had dimmed. I descended the turret stair, grasping with my gloved hands at outcrops of broken stone, and sought my charges in the ruined refectory.

This was a groined chamber seventy feet long, lit by windows on the eastern side. For nearly three hundred years the Cistercians had dined here in silence, with their abbot at their head. The remains of a fresco adorned one wall, but the fragile pigments had worn to nothing, and the saints stared sightless, their palms outstretched. The refectory was empty.

Or was it?

Just beyond the range of vision, a shadow moved. Light as air and bodiless it seemed, like a wood dove fluttering. My heart in my mouth, I swiftly turned: and saw nothing where a shade had been.

The sound of a footfall behind me—did a weightless spirit mark its passage in the dust?

"Have I the honour of addressing Miss Austen?"

I whirled, my heart throbbing. And saw—

Not a ghost or envoy of the grave; no monk concealed by ghoulish cowl. A man, rather: diminutive of frame, lithe of limb, with a look of merriment on his face. A sprite, indeed, in his bottle-green cloak; a very wood elf conjured from the trees at the Abbey's back, and bowing to the floor as he surveyed me.

"Good God, sir! From whence did you spring?"

"The stones at your feet, ma'am. You *are* Miss Austen? Miss *Jane* Austen?"

"You have the advantage of me."

"That must be preferable to the alternative. I am charged with a commission I dare not ignore, but must require certain proofs—*bona fide's,* as the Latin would say—before I may fulfill it."

"Are you mad?"

He grinned. "I am often asked that question. Would you be so kind as to reveal the date of your honoured father's death?"

Surprise loosed my tongue. "The twenty-first of January, 1805. Pray explain your impudence."

"Assuredly, ma'am—but first I crave the intimate name of Lady Harriot Cavendish."

"If you would mean Hary-O, I imagine half the fashionable world is acquainted with it. Are you quite satisfied?

"I should be happy to accept a lady's word." He bowed again. "But my superiors demand absolute surety. Could you impart the title of the novel you sold to Messrs. Crosby & Co., of Stationers Hall Court, London, in the spring of 1803?"

I stared at him, astonished. "How come you to be so well-acquainted with my private affairs?"

"The title, madam."

"—Is *Susan*. The book is not yet published."[3]

"Just so." He reached into his coat and withdrew a letter, sealed with a great splotch of black wax. "I hope you will forgive me when you have read *that*."

I turned over the parchment and studied the seal. It was nondescript, of a sort one might discover in a common inn's writing desk. No direction was inscribed on the envelope. I glanced at the sprite, but his raffish looks betrayed nothing more than a mild amusement.

"I have answered your questions," I said slowly. "Now answer mine. What is your name?"

"I am called Orlando, ma'am."

A name for heroes of ancient verse, or lovers doomed to wander the greenwood. Either meaning might serve.

"And will you divulge the identity of these . . . *superiors* . . . for whom you act?"

"There is but one. He is everywhere known as the Gentleman Rogue."

Lord Harold Trowbridge. Suddenly light-headed, I broke the letter's seal. There was no date, no salutation—indeed, no hint of either sender's or recipient's name—but I should never mistake this hand for any other's on earth.

From the curious presentation of this missive, you will apprehend that my man has been in-

---

3. Austen wrote the manuscript entitled *Susan* in 1798 and sold it to Crosby & Co. for ten pounds in the spring of 1803. The firm never published it, and Austen was forced to buy back the manuscript in 1816. It was eventually published posthumously in 1818 as *Northanger Abbey.—Editor's note.*

structed to preserve discretion at the expense of dignity. I write to you under the gravest spur, and need not underline that I should not presume to solicit your interest were other means open to me. Pray attend to the bearer, and if your amiable nature will consent to undertake the duty with which he is charged, know that you shall be the object of my gratitude.

God bless you.

I lifted my gaze to meet Orlando's. "Your master is sorely pressed."

"When is he not? Come, let us mount the walls."

Without another word, he led me back to the turret stair, and up into the heights.

"There," he said, his arm flung out towards Southampton Water. "A storm gathers, and a small ship beats hard up the Solent."

I narrowed my weak eyes, followed the line of his hand, and discovered the trim brig as it came about into the wind.

"Captain Strong commands His Majesty's brig *Windlass*. My master is below decks. He asks that you wait upon him in his cabin. He has not much time; but if we summon your bosun and the two young gentlemen, and make haste with the skiff, we may meet his lordship even as the *Windlass* sets anchor."

"You know a great deal more of my movements, Orlando, than I should like."

"That is my office, ma'am. He who would serve as valet to Lord Harold Trowbridge, must also undertake the duties of dogsbody, defender—and spy." He threw me a twisted smile; bitter truth underlay the flippant words.

"His lordship does not disembark in Southampton?"

"He is bound for Gravesend, and London, with the tide. You will have read of the family's loss?"

I reflected an instant. "The Dowager Duchess?"

Lord Harold's mother, Eugenie de la Falaise, formerly of the Paris stage and wife to the late Duke of Wilborough, had passed from this life but a few days ago. I had admired Her Grace; I mourned her passing; but I could not have read the *Morning Gazette's* black-bordered death notice without thinking of her second son. It had been more than two years since I had last enjoyed the pleasure of Lord Harold's notice; and though I detected his presence from time to time in the publicity of the newspapers, I have known little of his course since parting from him in Derbyshire.

"Had the dowager's death not intervened, his lordship should have come in search of you himself. But Fate—"

"Fate has determined that instead of Lord Harold, I am treated to an interview with his man," I concluded. "Pray tell me, Orlando, what it is that I must do."

ELIZABETH GEORGE

A GREAT DELIVERANCE
_____ 27802-9 $6.99/$8.99 in Canada

Winner of the 1988 Anthony and Agatha Awards for Best First Novel
"Spellbinding . . . A truly fascinating story that is part psychological suspense
and part detective story."—*Chicago Sun-Times*

PAYMENT IN BLOOD
_____ 28436-3 $6.99/$8.99

"Satisfying indeed. George has another hit on her hands."—*The Washington Post*

WELL-SCHOOLED IN MURDER
_____ 28734-6 $6.99/$8.99

"[This book] puts the author in the running with the genre's masters."—*People*

A SUITABLE VENGEANCE
_____ 29560-8 $6.99/$8.99

"Both unusual and extremely satisfying."—*The Toronto Sun*

FOR THE SAKE OF ELENA
_____ 56127-8 $6.99/$8.99

"George is . . . a born storyteller who spins a web of enchantment that captures
the reader and will not let him go."—*The San Diego Union*

MISSING JOSEPH
_____ 56604-0 $6.99/$8.99

"A totally satisfying mystery experience."—*The Denver Post*

PLAYING FOR THE ASHES
_____ 57251-2 $6.99/$8.99

"Compelling . . . infinitely engrossing."—*People*

IN THE PRESENCE OF THE ENEMY
_____ 57608-9 $6.99/$8.99

"Combining the eloquence of P.D. James with a story John Grisham would envy,
George serves up a splendid, unsettling novel."—*People*

Ask for these books at your local bookstore or use this page to order.

Please send me the books I have checked above. I am enclosing $_____ (add $2.50 to
cover postage and handling). Send check or money order, no cash or C.O.D.'s, please.

Name _____

Address _____

City/State/Zip _____

Send order to: Bantam Books, Dept. EG, 2451 S. Wolf Rd., Des Plaines, IL 60018
Allow four to six weeks for delivery.
Prices and availability subject to change without notice.   EG 3/97